The Queen's Player

The Lost Years of William Shakespeare, Book 2

Anthony R. Wildman

The Queen's Player

Plutus Publishing Australia

ISBN 978-0-6489454-4-4

To Robert

Also by Anthony R. Wildman:

What News on the Rialto?

The Lost Years of William Shakespeare, Book 1

The Diplomat of Florence

A Novel of Machiavelli and the Borgias

Two Gents in Italy

A Journey through Italian History and Culture

Chapter 1

The archbishop waited, fingers twitching at his robes as he tried to disguise his impatience while Henry of England, newly crowned as the fifth king to bear that name, sent packing some importunate friends from his younger days who had come to court in expectation of preferment. *Remember that he is but a youth*, a little voice in his head kept telling him, *though he may seem older than his years.* Listening with half his mind as the king berated his former friends, he remembered what the old king, bent and worn with the cares of his crown, had said of his son: 'a rude youth, which with grief will end his father's days'. Yet upon the assumption of his royal state, that rude youth had acquired the stamp of majesty, and the archbishop knew he might need to tread carefully. Still, he was an experienced counsellor of state, and must appear so in this, his first appearance before the new king.

'Look no more for favour at my hands than at any other man's.' Having thus disposed of old loyalties, the king turned at last to his archbishop. 'Now, my good lord Archbishop of Canterbury, what say you to our embassage into France? Can we, with right, make claim to her throne?'

The archbishop inclined his head, shook out his sleeves, and extracted a large piece of parchment from within the voluminous folds of his robes, the appearance of which caused the king's face to crease in alarm. Though the churchman knew its contents by heart, he also knew he had to appear to be a serious and thoughtful scholar, and so he made a show of unrolling the parchment and examining it, as if he had never seen it before. Then, after a guttural clearing of his throat, he began to declaim in a loud, ringing voice, 'Your right to the crown of France came by your great-grandmother Isabel, wife to King Edward the third and sister to Charles, the French king.'

The king nodded, satisfied by this brief answer, and opened his mouth to speak, only to be cut off—to his own astonishment and that of the rest of the court—by his archbishop. 'And yet, my lord, I might say more. There is no bar to your claim except this: "*In terram Salicam mulieres ne succedent*". That is to say, "No woman shall succeed in Salic lands", which the French claim to be the realm of France.' He let that sink in. 'Yet their own authors affirm that the land Salic is in Germany, where Charlemagne, having subdued the Saxons, left behind and settled some French. Who, holding in disdain the German women, established this law—to wit, no female shall inherit in Salic land. Which Salic land is, as I said, in Germany.'

'I thank you, my good lord archbishop.' Henry now had a perplexed frown on his face, as though unsure what all this might mean. The frown deepened even more when his prelate, instead of bowing and withdrawing as expected, began speaking again, his voice distant and dreamy, as though in a trance.

'Besides, their King Pepin, who deposed Childeric, descended from Blothild, the *daughter* of King Clothair, and did by this right make claim to the crown of France. Hugh Capet also, when he usurped the crown from Charles of Lorraine, conveyed himself as heir to the daughter of Charlemagne. So it's as clear as is the summer's sun. King Pepin's title and Hugh Capet's claim both appear to hold in right and title of the *female*. And since the kings of France from these two do descend, so it may be said that unto this day they also hold their title in the female line.'

A loud guffaw came from somewhere beyond the circle of courtiers surrounding the king. Had he gone too far? Yes he had, and the expression on the king's face, now openly annoyed with his prolix churchman, confirmed it

'May I, archbishop, make this claim by right upon France?' King Henry, biting off each word, clearly brooked no more dissimulation.

The archbishop knew it was time to bring the scene to an end, but he remembered that he had one last thing that he must say. 'Yes, my lord, you may go easily into France. And if the French king denies your claim, as likely enough he will, then must you take your sword in hand and conquer. Let the usurped Frenchman know, although your predecessors have let it pass, that you will not. For your countrymen are willing with purse and men to aid you. And this is all I can say, my good lord.'

'That's a relief,' the king muttered in a tone audible only to the circle of men around him. Then he raised his voice. 'We thank you, my lord of Canterbury. What say you, my good lord of Oxford?'

The Earl of Oxford sent a contemptuous glance at the priest before turning, all smiles, to offer his own counsel to his king. Leaving them to it, the archbishop bowed several times as he backed his way through the curtained door. Once out of sight of the royal court of England, he proceeded to remove his mitre and robe, transforming himself in the process from a wordy and too-knowledgeable prelate into plain William Shakespeare, company book-holder, general factotum and occasional actor with the troupe known as Queen Elizabeth's Men.

The royal palace from whence he had just withdrawn was in fact no more than a temporary wooden platform erected at one end of the yard of the Bel Savage Inn, whose muddy floor accommodated an audience of apprentices and labourers, tradesmen and their goodwives, and whose galleries (which ordinarily gave access to the inn's rooms) provided a vantage point for the finer sort, the gentry and wealthier merchants. And this narrow space behind the painted cloth backdrop served as their tiring-house, where the actors donned and discarded costumes, and prepared for their entrances.

His outer robes discarded and carefully placed on their rack, Will turned to behold the impish face of Richard Tarlton, done up in his costume as Derrick the Tailor, huge pins inserted into his sleeves and hat. 'Ready for a blast from Billy when he comes off, Will? You tried his patience this time, I'll warrant.'

Will grinned back; Tarlton had taken a liking to him that first day four months ago when he had joined the company, and good-natured badinage was the language of their growing friendship. 'I'm not worried, Dick. Billy is never angry for very long. Not with me, anyway. And besides, I think my little addition improved things, don't you?'

'It could do with improving, that's true enough.' Tarlton shared Will's own opinion that *The Famous Victories of Henry V* was pretty poor stuff, though it played well with the audiences, who loved its knockabout humour and the story of England's great triumph against the perfidious French. 'Where on earth did you get all that nonsense about, what was it, "the Law Salic"?'

'I read it somewhere—in Holinshed, I think,' Will said with an airy wave of his hand. 'It must have stuck in my mind and just came out again as I was about to do the speech.'

Smiling at the look of astonishment on Tarlton's face, he turned to peek through the curtains and watched the play proceed. The French ambassador delivered a contemptuous gift of tennis balls from the dauphin, the king made a loud proclamation for war and appointed the lord chief justice to be his deputy in England for the time being, while he went off to invade poor France. Scene concluded, the actors retreated towards him, coming into the makeshift tiring house as Tarlton, John Laneham, another of the company's senior actors, and Adam Arkwright, one of the company's young squeakers who was costumed as a goodwife for this scene, passed them on the way out.

William Knell removed his crown, tossed it onto the pile of discarded costumes at the back of the little space, and ran a hand across his brow where the

4

crown had left its mark. 'Good God, Will, what was that little piece of mischief all about?' he said in a low voice. 'You threw me quite off my stride.'

'It didn't take you long to get back into it, Billy.' Will slapped the actor on the back. 'I just thought the good archbishop's character needed a bit more life, that's all.'

'You wanted to show off, you mean.' This came from John Towne, the darkly handsome young actor who had, until a few moments ago, been inhabiting the character of the Earl of Oxford. 'The script is there for you to follow, Shakespeare, not amend whenever it suits you during a performance.'

Predictably, Towne's sneering condemnation sent Knell straight to the opposite corner of the barnyard.

'Will's improvisations usually improve the script, John, so don't be too harsh on him,' he pronounced, daring Towne with his eyes to argue to the contrary. 'Anyway, I rather like it, all that stuff about the Salic Law. It sounds like the kind of nonsense an archbishop would say. Why don't you write it into the script and we'll see how it plays out in the country? Now, where are the Duttons? Their scene is next; they should be here.'

'I'll go and look for them,' Will said, only too happy to escape from the middle of this little tiff, and he ducked out through the door at the back of the tiring house. Skipping across a filthy puddle of water that had pooled in the cobblestoned gutter, he went through another door into the low-roofed taproom, full of acrid smoke from half a dozen tobacco pipes and buzzing with the noise of those afternoon drinkers who had no interest in the theatrics going on in the yard behind the building. Pushing his way to a bow window whose shutters had been opened to let some air into the fetid space, he stood looking down at the tousled heads of two young men seated in chairs facing out towards the street, watching a party of travellers disembarking from a coach.

'And what, pray, are the king of France and his son the dauphin doing here?' Will enquired pleasantly, causing one of the two, who had been in the process of putting a tankard to his lips, to choke and splutter on his ale.

'Oh, God, it's you, Will.' Lawrence Dutton was the elder of the pair, redheaded brothers who were almost identical, save that the younger brother, John, was shorter and possessed a prominent mole on his left cheek. 'We just slipped out for a quick drink. Surely we cannot be due back on stage just yet?'

'Imminently. Come on, get yourselves up and into the tiring house. You know there will be hell to pay from Billy if you miss your cue.'

Sheepishly, they downed the last of their ale and followed Will back through the crowd and out to the tiring house, where they were given a withering look of contempt by Knell. They had barely finished donning their costumes when Tarlton and the others pushed through the curtain, the laughter of the crowd attesting to the fact that Dick Tarlton had once again been giving his comic genius free rein.

The play went on through another half-dozen scenes during which Will was kept busy with all his usual off-stage duties during any scene in which he did not himself have a part: providing sound effects such as trumpet blasts and drum-rolls, imitating thunder by rolling a cannon ball along the gallery above the stage, making sure that each performer entered on cue, occasionally hissing the words when any of his colleagues seemed to be suffering a momentary lapse of memory, and helping with costume changes for the actors who were playing multiple parts.

Then at last the play was done and they were all on stage doing the final jig, a comical dance that always ended their performances. Tarlton was their leader in this, his round face with its squashed nose and wispy moustache contorting into wild grimaces, his wiry body leaping and twirling with a vigour that would have done credit to a man of half his fifty years, all the while singing, banging the drum that was strapped to his waist and blowing great blasts on his pipe. His energy was infectious, and by the time they had finished and were taking their bows, every member of the company was drenched in sweat.

As the last of the crowd made their way laughing and singing out of the inn-yard and into busy Fleet Street, the players were left alone in the middle of the stage, letting the excitement of the performance drain away.

'That was quite a box to the ears you gave me, Billy. They are still ringing.' John Laneham rubbed the affected organ with comical exaggeration. The blow to which he referred had been landed way back in scene five, in which the young prince Henry, not yet king, strikes the lord chief justice for refusing to release one of his roistering comrades from custody in the Fleet prison.

'I'm sorry, Jack. I must confess to having been carried away in the moment. Come on, I doubt not that an ale or two will repair any damage.'

'Now that sounds like a sovereign plan,' Tarlton agreed. 'Come on, lads, let us to the taproom and see what's to be had. I don't know about you, but I am famished.'

That sounded tempting to Will; he had missed the usual midday meal, having been busy supervising the stagehands. Supper wasn't usually served at the Bel Savage until five, which felt like an age away to a young man who was fond of his food. But duty still called, and he hung back as the others made their way in the direction of the taproom.

Only Knell noticed that Will wasn't following. 'Not coming, Will?'

'No, Billy. I have to make sure the properties are looked after and stowed away. And the books must be done. You go on; I'll be there shortly.'

'Can't you leave the properties to Jem and Luke? They are reliable enough.' Knell shrugged when he saw the look on Will's face. 'All right, I can see you are determined. Your devotion to the cause is admirable, young man. But I would hate to see you starve, so I'll make sure we keep something aside for you. Don't be too long.'

Will smiled his thanks and turned away to watch the two stagehands who had begun the task of collecting the props and moving them into the storage room that the inn had allocated for the purpose. Knell was quite right, of course—Jem and Luke needed little supervision from him, for they had been with the company for many years. But the truth was that he still felt that he was something of an outsider in the Queen's Men, and an outright imposter when it came to joining in the backslapping camaraderie that usually followed performances.

He had joined the company only in February, on the same day that the town criers had gone through London announcing the death of the Scottish Queen Mary. It seemed as if every church bell in the city had been rung at once that day, a great, joyous cacophony that rolled over the rooftops and invited the populace to abandon their work and come out into the streets dancing and laughing at the news, signifying as it did the removal of at least one threat to the ever-precarious stability of the English state. Will had been caught up in the general happiness, the cheering and shouts of 'God save our Queen!' as he'd made his way along Cheapside to his lodgings. But he'd also had his own private cause for joy, for he had, that very morning, been contracted to Her Majesty's own company of actors, the Queen's Men.

Well before he'd met with Tarlton and Knell in a private parlour at this very inn, Will had known that the dice were loaded in his favour, for his candidacy had been pressed upon them by no less a personage than Sir Francis Walsingham, the Queen's principal secretary. So they could hardly refuse to see him, however curious they might have been as to why Sir Francis should have taken such a sudden interest in the affairs of the company, let alone intervene on behalf of an unknown young man from Warwickshire with neither acting experience nor any other discernible talents beyond a fair hand and a good memory.

What they could not know—and Will could not tell them—was that he had recently returned from an extensive mission in Italy undertaken at Walsingham's behest. Ostensibly travelling as a tutor-companion to the Secretary's young ward, his task had simply been to deliver a letter to one of Walsingham's many agents. But matters had become more complicated when he discovered that his contact was dead, and he ended up uncovering information that was of great importance to the future of England. In return, Walsingham had undertaken to help Will make his start in the career to which he had been drawn two years before, when he had stood in the yard of James Burbage's new playhouse and been enthralled by a performance of Thomas Kydd's *The Spanish Tragedy*. Will felt it only fair that Walsingham, having plucked him from the streets of London and sent him off to foreign parts, should now help him to resume his course.

He had tried his best to satisfy their curiosity, saying that Sir Francis had been prevailed upon to promote his cause as a favour to Burbage, with whose son Richard he was friends. There was a little grain of truth in this—he and Richard were indeed friends, and Burbage senior was known to be in the famously puritanical secretary's favour, having recently performed some small services for him. It had been enough to deflect their curiosity for the moment, though he sensed that both men were shrewd enough to work out that they weren't being told the whole story.

In the end, they had decided to test his skills by handing him a pile of new plays, precious master copies that had been licensed for performance by the Master of the Revels, from which he'd had to write out all the individual parts for each actor, marking them up with entrance and exit cues and other annotations to ensure a smooth and seamless presentation. No doubt they had expected this would keep him occupied for several weeks. Tarlton had been astonished when Will turned up with the completed players' parts just two days later.

'Well, lad, you're quick, I'll give you that,' the actor had said, thumbing through the various sheets carefully written out in the neatest script that

9

Shakespeare could manage. 'And accurate, too. Just as well, we don't want to be in trouble with that old stickler Tilney, do we?' Edmund Tilney was the Master of the Revels and all-powerful in London's theatre world, for it was he who determined what plays could and could not be performed, and his office approved the text of every script; any deviation from the authorised version could result in the company's license being revoked.

Will's quick and accurate work seemed to break down whatever reservations Tarlton might have had about this cuckoo who had been thrust so unceremoniously into their nest, and he soon communicated his approval to the rest of the troupe. Whom Tarlton approved, the company must perforce accept, and so that morning in February 1587, his appointment as book-holder and overseer of the company had been formally ratified, with a pay of five shillings a week—an amount that would no doubt gratify his wife when he reported the fact to her in his next letter

After stammering his thanks, it occurred to him that he had not the slightest idea what a company book-holder was actually supposed to do. 'Why, everything,' Tarlton had laughed when Will timidly put the question to him. 'Everything except the acting, that is.'

Which, it turned out, was the literal truth. To start with, he was the custodian of the precious master copy of whatever play they were performing, and in the mornings, when they were rehearsing, he helped the actors con their lines, time their entrances and exits, and generally make sure that the performance was seamless. Then, while the actors had a break for lunch, he got the stage ready, making sure the stagehands placed the props in the right positions, and that costumes were on hand for the actors to don ready for the performance. Once all was in readiness, he sounded the trumpet to announce that the play was about to begin.

And when the day's performance was done, it was his job to make sure that properties were dismantled and stored, precious costumes put away in their chests, and the even more precious playscripts put back under lock and key until they were needed again. Then there was the book-keeping. The little clay cash boxes into which the playgoers had deposited their pennies had to be broken open, the day's takings totted up, and the relevant amounts entered into the ledger.

The bustle and excitement of the day over, after a hurried evening meal he would take a bundle of playscripts home and settle down to copy out the parts, mark them up with basic stage directions, and prepare the prompt-board for the next day's performance. This was the part of his routine that he most enjoyed. Even though it was mundane work, something that any well-trained scrivener could do, he somehow felt as though he was participating in the process of creating the play, taking it from the page to the stage. And his sponge-like mind was learning, understanding how the play worked, the rhythms of its language and the structure of the drama.

Such was the life of a company's book-holder. If he felt a twinge of frustration that he was not yet an actor, he consoled himself with the thought that he was at least getting an invaluable education in inner workings of the theatre, which he would one day put to good use. And then six weeks ago Tarlton had announced that Will was to join them on their forthcoming tour of the countryside, and that he would be on the stage well before then.

'I don't think anyone would deny that young Will here has learned the ropes of our odd craft in record time,' Tarlton had told the assembled troupe, an amused glint in his eye. 'We will need him on the tour, and besides, it would be a handy opportunity to get him up on the stage; having a spare actor would be a boon.'

Tarlton's announcement had so taken Will by surprise that all he could do was look modestly down at his boots in an effort to disguise his satisfaction, uncomfortably aware of the raised eyebrows and pursed lips of some members of the company.

He would remember until his last day on earth the moment when he'd first stepped out onto the stage. It was just a little part in *The Seven Deadly Sins*, but even so, he had been terrified before walking through the curtains, trying to calm his nerves by telling himself that it was no different from his school days back in Stratford, acting out scenes from Plautus or Ovid before his schoolfellows. But once he'd got out on the broad wooden platform and saw all the upturned expectant faces surrounding it, a curious calm had come over him, and instead, he had felt a sort of suppressed elation that had banished his nervousness entirely. He had delivered his half-dozen lines flawlessly, made his exit without tripping over anything or otherwise making a fool of himself, and grinned in self-satisfaction at an equally pleased Tarlton, waiting for him behind the curtain. Since then he had been on the stage almost every day, always in small roles, and his confidence had grown bit by bit.

Grown so much, in fact, that in their performances over the last week he had started to make little improvisations, small changes at first, in-jokes and word plays inserted out of a sense of mischief, though he had never been quite so bold as his made-up speech today. Such interventions were not always welcome, and he had soon learned to be careful who was opposite him when he went off on one of his flights of fancy. Tarlton and Knell always took it in good part, often responding with their own extemporisations as a humorous way of putting him in his place. The Dutton brothers were simply confused, and Laneham could barely control his giggles when confronted with one of Will's little sallies. John Towne, on the other hand, though always professional on stage, usually vented his disapproval the minute he was off it—as he had today.

'We're finished, Mister Shakespeare, and by your leave we'll go off now and get some vittles. Unless you need anything else?'

Jem's voice broke into Will's thoughts as he finished counting the day's takings—a respectable five pounds—and he held one hand up while with the other he carefully noted the amount in the ledger.

'The costumes are locked away? The properties stored?' He asked the questions purely for form's sake, as an assertion of his own authority, and he didn't wait for an answer before waving the two stagehands on their way.

Putting the cash in a little leather bag, he locked it away in a small iron-bound chest, and took it upstairs to Billy Knell's chamber, which doubled as a temporary company office while the Queen's Men were performing at the Bel Savage. The room was empty, with barely a sign that it was occupied, for Knell was fastidiously tidy. Turning to leave, he caught his own reflection in the large mirror that was propped on the room's only table. He was not ordinarily a vain man, but something made him stop and peer more closely at the glass.

The image whose soft brown eyes stared back at him was well-favoured in a solid sort of way, clean-shaven, free of blemishes, and with a mass of reddish-brown hair that was beginning to recede above a broad forehead. He was twenty-four years old, and this was undeniably the face of an adult, a man who had seen something of the world and learned from it. Yet the last bloom of youth had not yet faded entirely: he saw a boyish sense of mischief lurking there behind the mask of seriousness, and his lips twitched into the knowing half smile that could, as he knew from experience, both charm and infuriate.

Was this the face of an actor? He thought of his colleagues: Knell's bearded, dignified visage exuded authority, but Tarlton had a squashed-up face that made you want to smile the instant you laid eyes on him. John Towne had saturnine looks that made him seem mysterious and distant, even menacing, while Laneham had a craggy face that was seamed with creases and lines that made him look worn and earthy—he might as easily have been a farmer than an actor.

So perhaps the face that God had given him wasn't important, as long as it wasn't seriously disfigured (and even then, he remembered once seeing an actor who possessed a long and jagged scar down one cheek, which didn't seem to inhibit his performance at all). What you did with it was more important, it seemed to him. No-one laughed when Dick Tarlton played a serious role, even though he had done nothing more than judiciously apply some paint to his face. It was all a mystery, into whose secrets he, a novice, was yet to be fully inducted. With a shrug and a sigh, he turned away and made his way back down the stairs to the inn's main hall.

The big, smoky room was crowded with noisy drinkers, and it took him a moment to spot his colleagues, standing in a knot in a corner by one of the windows that overlooked the street. The sound of their raised voices carried across the room, and as he came closer, it appeared that they were in the middle of a spirited argument. With a jolt, he realised that he himself was the subject of debate, and he stopped short on the edge of the group, trying not to advertise his presence.

'I for one have had enough of Shakespeare's antics,' John Towne was saying, his voice low but carrying. 'It's hard enough to remember your own lines without having him insert new ones whenever he feels like it!'

'*I* don't have any difficulty keeping up with him.' John Laneham emphasised the pronoun ever so slightly. 'Though he does make me want to laugh at all the wrong moments.'

One of the Duttons—Will couldn't tell which one from his position behind them—chuckled at that comment, earning him a furious look from Towne.

'You won't be giggling, Lawrence, if the Master of the Revels strips us of our license for meddling with an approved text.'

'What nonsense you talk, John,' Knell replied, making clear his contempt for his fellow actor. 'It was a trifling piece of improvisation, and anyway, Tilney will never hear of it.'

'Don't you believe it; there are informers everywhere. I'm surprised you can't see it, Billy. Your brains have gone soft, I reckon. Comes from marrying a child.' Towne's mirthless smile taunted Knell, who had married fifteen-year-old Rebecca Edwards the year before and was sensitive about the twenty-year age gap between them. The others exchanged swift glances and found renewed interest in the contents of their ale mugs.

'Enough, John. That wasn't called for.' Tarlton's voice was hard as he placed a restraining hand on a visibly furious Knell's forearm. 'Billy is right; we are safe enough. And anyway, we are the Queen's Men, are we not? Tilney would think twice before he oppresses us. Even so, Mister Shakespeare, perhaps you could give us at least a little warning before you make any more changes to the playscripts, eh? For the benefit of those members of the company who might struggle to rise to the occasion.'

A startled Will realised that Tarlton must have known he was standing there all along. He could do nothing other than raise his shoulders and spread his hands in a gesture of contrition, embarrassed as the other members of the company registered his presence and shuffled aside to make room.

'I am sorry, Dick, truly. I meant no offence, and the last thing I wish to be is the cause of dissension within the company.'

'Don't distress yourself, Will. You can't be responsible for other men's quarrels.' That was accompanied by a sharp look in Towne's direction. 'Now, I suggest we have a last round, and then call it a day. We all have an early start tomorrow.' That was met with groans. The company was to begin its tour to the country in the morning, which meant a start before dawn to get the wagons loaded up before they got on the road.

When the last round of ale arrived, Will found himself standing next to an uncharacteristically glum William Knell. 'Cheer up, Billy. I know what it's like when your marriage makes people's eyebrows go up,' he said. 'My Anne is ten years older than me, and that set tongues wagging in Stratford, I can tell you. You just have to make a joke of it and show you don't care.'

'I know, I know.' Knell sighed, lifting his tankard to acknowledge Will's advice. 'I should ignore fools like Towne. But he works hard to get under my skin and sometimes I can't help myself.'

'He is a good actor, and I wonder that he should take such exception to my foolish little games.'

'He's not as good as he thinks he is.' Knell glanced across to the other side of the room, and when Will followed his gaze, he realised that John Towne was watching them, a speculative look on his face. 'But don't let him stop you from exercising your talents on our behalf, Will. You have a rare skill with words, that is obvious, and we can do with some fresh thinking.'

It was true; the company's audiences had been in sad decline for some years for reasons that no one seemed able to identify. 'Well, it's time for me to take my leave. I have a lot to do before we get on the road tomorrow.'

'It will be good to get out of the city, that's certain. Just a pity that serpent is coming with us.'

Walking home later that evening, Will wondered at the rancour in Knell's last words. John Towne was, to be sure, a difficult, prickly personality, but there seemed to be something between him and the otherwise genial Billy Knell that went deeper than mere professional jealousy. He hoped that whatever it was would not get in the way of the success that the company needed from the tour. With a mental shrug, he cast off any such worries—it was going to be a grand adventure, and he was going to make the best of every opportunity that came his way.

Chapter 2

Their departure the next morning might have been early, but it wasn't too early to attract a crowd of young urchins and idlers who congregated around the gateway of the Bel Savage, looking for a bit of excitement to enliven their otherwise dull existence.

Not that the members of Queen Elizabeth's Men were trying to avoid scrutiny. On the contrary, it was traditional to embark on a tour with as much fanfare as they could muster, to which end the company's two servants were instructed to give a regular blast of the trumpets, while the actors—dressed as custom required in the royal livery, their tunics emblazoned with the red and white Tudor rose front and back—exchanged shouted witticisms with those passers-by who stopped to watch and give them a wave.

For this tour, which was to be quite a long one, they were equipped with two open wagons, pulled by big horses fitted out with fine leather harnesses, gold medallions, and silver bells that tinkled and chimed with every step they took. From tall poles mounted on each corner of the drays, long, brightly coloured pennons snapped in the fresh breeze, adding to the general air of gaiety.

Behind the drivers, each cart was piled high with everything needed to put on a play. From the components carefully packed into the wagons, Jem and Luke could, in the space of a few hours, transform guildhall or innyard, or for that matter, the candle-lit great hall in the house of a local grandee, into a makeshift theatre.

'You'll see. The country folk will lap it up,' an enthusiastic Laneham had told a dubious Shakespeare. 'A painted cloth backdrop, a tent for a tiring house, and a few props—a column or two for ancient Rome, some newly cut branches to make a forest, banners on poles to suggest a battlefield—and it will all work a treat.'

There were twelve members of the touring company all told, including the two stagehands. In deference to their seniority, Dick Tarlton had a seat in relative comfort next to Jem, who was driving the leading cart, and William Knell sat next to Luke in the other. But there wasn't enough room to afford them all to have seats, so they took it in turns, four actors finding perches among the costumes and props, and the other four walking ahead so as to avoid the dust and mud thrown up by the horses' hooves. Will elected to walk for the first leg through the city, accompanied by the Dutton brothers, who were in high spirits, laughing and joking with the passers-by, and a dour Robert Wilson, a veteran actor who had only joined them that morning, having missed the previous week's performances at the Bel Savage with a stomach illness.

Behind him, he could hear Tarlton entertaining the company's two boy-actors, Adam Arkwright and Ned Bentley, with improbable tales of life on the road. Adam, the younger of the two, was a gangly, hesitant fifteen-year-old, but showed promise as an actor. Boyish, blonde-haired Ned was eighteen and the company's leading player of female roles, in which he excelled, having a fine, high voice, an excellent memory and alluring good looks that required but a little application of powder and rouge to produce a counterfeit of young womanhood that was most convincing. Now, though, he was giggling uncontrollably at Tarlton's witticisms. Even John Towne seemed to have caught the spirit of the morning, back in the second cart with Laneham and Knell, and every now and then Will would hear his high, carrying voice shouting a laughing insult with somebody in the street.

In this mood of high good humour, the little procession made its way along Fleet Street, through the Ludgate and across the stinking Fleet ditch. By the time they reached the church of St Clement Danes, the houses began to thin out and the little crowd of well-wishers had long ago abandoned them. Leaving behind the straggle of buildings that followed the river down to Westminster, they turned north-west along a muddy, rutted road enclosed on each side by low stone walls, beyond which stretched open farmland.

By the time they stopped at the old monastic church of Saint Giles-in-the-fields for a hasty meal of ale and pasties, they had well and truly left the noise and smoke and stink of London behind them. For Will, it felt like a release of sorts, almost as if they were going on a holiday, though he knew he would be working as hard as ever over the next few weeks. Nevertheless, his heart sang in tune with the birds as they went deeper into the English countryside.

***

Three days later, he and Knell were crossing the stone bridge across the Thames into the market town of Abingdon, having ridden ahead on hired horses to find accommodation and make sure that all was in readiness for their performances in the town's guildhall.

They were expected, letters having long since been sent to the town's mayor, Thomas Reade, who greeted them on the steps of the hall. 'Welcome to Abingdon, Master Knell. It does my heart good to see you again.'

'And mine to see you, Mayor. Allow me to introduce our new book holder and general factotum, William Shakespeare.' Will politely returned the mayor's nod as Knell continued, his eyes glancing across the street to where a group of prosperous-looking goodwives stood exchanging gossip. 'How do things fare in Abingdon since our last visit, Thomas? The town does well, I hope?'

'The barge-trade is quieter than usual, but the tanners and brewers are busier than ever. And two new printers have set up since you were here last, so you can get your playbills printed right here in the town.'

Will's glover-trained nostrils had detected the stink of the tanneries as they'd crossed the bridge; tanners and brewers could usually be found wherever there was a good supply of fresh water. Abingdon did indeed seem like a comfortable place, its local trades complemented by its status as a crossing place for the Thames, which brought travellers to stay in its many inns. Will had counted five of them just between the bridge and the guildhall.

'And has the council approved our programme?' For a company as illustrious as the Queen's Men, the approval of the local town council ought by rights to be nothing more than a formality, but some councils could be touchy about their prerogatives, and Will detected a tiny note of anxiety in Knell's question.

'Oh, there were the usual demurs; we have one or two Puritans who object in principle to anything that might give the people joy, and there were mutterings about the peace being disturbed by the brewers' apprentices and the like, but in the end they saw sense.' Will suspected that this piece of understatement disguised some powerful political arm-wrestling by the amiable but clearly tough-minded mayor.

'We can always rely on your powers of persuasion, Thomas.' The bottom half of Knell's face, half-hidden behind its square beard, twitched into a grin to match the humorous sparkle in his blue eyes. 'The rest of the company should be here this afternoon. Perhaps you could direct Will to some local inn where we may be accommodated?'

'That is taken care of. Widow Hawley has agreed to put you all up at her place, just down the street from the guildhall, under the sign of the crossed keys. Take care with her, Mister Shakespeare, she might seem jolly, but she is sharp as a knife when it comes to the price of her rooms.'

Will nodded to acknowledge the advice. 'And after I have concluded negotiations with Mistress Hawley, perhaps I should have a look at the hall to make sure all is ready for our stagehands when they arrive?'

'Of course, though I am sure everything will be in order. The lads have been sweeping the floors and cleaning out the storage room at the back all morning, all the windows have been cleaned, and new candles have been ordered—best wax, as Master Knell specified.'

'I would expect no less,' Knell said. 'Abingdon has always been most welcoming to the Queen's players, Will, and I am sure you will find all is in order. Now, why don't you get about your business and I will meet you at the inn in an hour or so, shall we say?'

Thus dismissed, Will nodded his farewells to the mayor and turned to make his way down the street in the direction of the inn. No doubt the company's leading player would spend the next hour in a tavern somewhere, collecting gossip from the mayor, who was evidently a good friend, over a tankard or two. Billy Knell was, Will had noticed, avid for local news at every place they stopped, interrogating innkeepers and merchants with a kind of genial efficiency to extract every last morsel of fact and rumour.

The Crossed Keys Inn, when he found it in a back lane just off the main street of Abingdon, was a simple affair of two stories with what looked like a newly tiled roof, half a dozen windows whose shutters had been thrown open to admit the morning sunshine, and a neatly painted sign bearing the inn's badge. At one end of the building, a gateway led beneath the rooms above into a small yard, where a young boy was pulling water from the well.

Enquiring as to the whereabouts of Mistress Hawley, the boy gave him a curt nod of his head in the direction of a door, beyond which he found himself in the central hall of the inn, a dimly lit space even with the windows open. Above, he just could make out the rafters of the roof in the gloom. A small gallery ran around the first floor to give access to the upstairs rooms, and a fireplace stood under the chimney opposite the windows, at present unlit though there was a lingering smell of woodsmoke that suggested it had only recently been dowsed. Half a dozen tables and benches filled most of the space at ground level, and there were jugs and tankards placed on each, as if in readiness for business, although at that moment, the hall was deserted.

Will was about to call out when a door next to the chimney opened and a small, rotund grey-haired woman came bustling in, her arms filled with linen, above which a pink-cheeked round face peered at him through suspicious grey eyes.

'Well, lad, don't just stand there, lend a hand! These sheets won't find their own way up to the bedchambers.'

A bemused Shakespeare accepted the pile of cloths that the little woman thrust into his arms. 'And where, Mistress Hawley, would you like me to put them? I fear I am not familiar with your establishment.'

'Upstairs, you fool, where else? Bedlinens are meant to go on beds. That much should be obvious even to an idiot like you.'

Will just stood there, a confused look on his face, causing the little woman's eyes to narrow even further. 'Who are you, sirrah?'

'Master William Shakespeare, company factotum of the Queen's players. Here to arrange rooms for myself and my colleagues.'

'Sakes, boy, why didn't you say so? The mayor told me you was all arriving this afternoon and I thought you were the man what old man Jennings, him that owns the Nag's Head, was sending to help me prepare the rooms.' If she felt any contrition at the mistake in identity, Mistress Hawley was not about to say so. 'Well, since you are here and have your hands full of my linens, you might as well take them upstairs for me.'

Access to the upstairs gallery was by way of stairs set in one corner of the hall, up which the innkeeper trotted energetically, leaving Will to keep up as best he could, trying not to trip as he peered over the pile of sheets. Depositing his burden on one of the beds in the first chamber they came to, he attempted to regain control of the situation.

'You were not entirely misled, Mistress Hawley; the rest of the company are indeed expected later this afternoon. But I am here early to make arrangements for their lodging and victuals. How many beds do you have, exactly?'

'Well now, let me see. Upstairs there's ten good beds, two more down in the parlour, and another two over the stables. Three penny a night, Mayor Reade told me.' Her bright blue eyes regarded him steadily, but with a look of amusement, as if she fully expected him to challenge this outrageous demand.

'Obviously, Mayor Reade has not been to London recently. A room like this one would command no more than a penny a night.' Not strictly true, but he felt he should match her for brazenness.

'Aye, well, that's as may be, but you won't find any other inns in Abingdon that can accommodate you all in one place.'

'You have the advantage of me there, Mistress, since I cannot spare the time to search out every innkeeper in the town. But contrary to what you or the mayor might hear, the Queen's Men are not swimming in gold. I can offer you tuppence per night, and a penny for the beds over the stable, no more.'

Her swift nod of agreement confirmed his guess that this was the rate that she'd really been after. They engaged in a few minutes more of spirited negotiation over the details—the quality of bedding to be provided, the price of victuals to go into the meals her cook was to prepare each day, the cost of stabling their horses—and then, satisfied, she offered her hand in conclusion of the bargain. That done, her demeanour underwent a complete change from calculating woman of business to obsequious hostess, and by the time William Knell arrived, they were chatting amiably in the small parlour off the main hall.

'Here, Billy, have some of Mistress Hawley's excellent cheese. It goes wonderfully well with the local ale.'

While the innkeeper took herself off to the buttery to refill her ale-jug, Will brought his colleague up to date with his negotiations, for which the company chief gave him an absent-minded grunt of approval.

'What did the mayor have to say?' Will asked. 'Is all well for our performances here? You seem to be a little distracted.'

'Yes, yes, everything is fine. In fact, he is pleased that we are here to divert the population a little.'

'Do they need diversion? From what?'

'There are new reports that a huge Spanish fleet is about to set sail, carrying a great invasion force to throw the Queen off her throne and bring England back to the Catholic church. Reade says the rumours have greatly unsettled the local people here.'

The words penetrated Will's mind with the force of a Jovian thunderbolt. He knew more than most about the Spanish plans for the invasion of England—certainly more than either the mayor or his own actor colleagues—having played a part in collecting information about them for Sir Francis Walsingham while he was in Italy. Indeed, it was to that service that he owed his position with the Queen's Men. But since then he had all but pushed what he knew out of his conscious mind, having been sworn to secrecy.

He wrenched his attention back to Knell, hoping that he had managed to disguise his moment of startled comprehension. 'But surely, we are deep in Oxfordshire and far from the coasts? Why would the people here be unsettled?'

'Abingdon is but sixty-five miles from Bristol, so if the Spanish come up the Severn it could be threatened. Though I grant you that possibility is remote.

25

Thomas did tell me that all the southern counties have been instructed to prepare for a possible invasion, though there is great confusion as to exactly what should be done and by whom. So it does seem to be rather more than mere market-place gossip.'

'Well then, we must do our part by distracting the sweating masses and make them laugh and sing, must we not?' Will drained the last of his ale and got to his feet. 'Speaking of which, I should go and have a look at the guildhall and make sure all is in readiness there.'

'Your zeal is to be commended, but they have oft hosted us in Abingdon, and I am sure all will be in order.'

As indeed it was. A temporary stage had already been erected at one end of the hall, beneath a musicians' gallery that projected from the wall above. Reached by a hidden flight of stairs, the gallery would serve admirably as an upper stage from which to blow trumpet blasts, and painted cloths hung from its underside would give them a backdrop and a space behind that would serve as a tiring-room. The whole space had been swept, and a couple of servants were busily trimming and installing new candles in the sconces that lined the walls.

The rest of the company arrived in the early afternoon, tired from the morning's travel but otherwise in exuberant spirits. While the actors settled themselves into Mistress Hawley's inn, squabbling amiably over who got which room, Will occupied himself with directing the efforts of their two stagehands, though in truth they needed little supervision from him and accepted his occasional directions with the patient deference of professional for newcomer.

That night, the ale flowed freely at the Crossed Keys, much to the delight of Mistress Hawley. For the company, this tour was almost a holiday, for they were only performing old plays with which every actor was familiar. In London, where the crowds had a seemingly unquenchable thirst for novelty and a noisy intolerance of repetition, their daily routine was like a treadmill—learning lines and rehearsing productions for which the ink had barely dried on the page, to be performed the same afternoon. But in the provinces they could relax a little since the audiences were less demanding and as amused by the familiar as much as by novelty.

Dick Tarlton, though, was not about to allow things to get out of hand on their first night of proper touring, and he called a firm halt to proceedings well before midnight, by which time even Mistress Hawley's fiscally induced abundance of goodwill towards her guests had begun to wear thin, and her two harried serving-girls were looking decidedly worse for wear.

And so Will found himself climbing the stairs to the little room above the parlour he was to share with John Towne for the next two nights. As he entered, the other man had already discarded his doublet and breeches in preparation for bed, the neatly folded clothes placed on the top of a small travelling chest he had positioned at the foot of the narrow bed which he had already claimed as his own. That meant Will was relegated to a truckle bed that one of the maids had placed on the other side of the room under a narrow window that looked out onto the street below.

Towne's smile of greeting was brief and suddenly extinguished, merely going through the motions of civility. Turning away, he picked up a small comb and ran it through black hair that was beginning to thin across the crown, though it was thick enough elsewhere. Examining his appearance in a small mirror, he gave the ends of his long, rather luxuriant moustache a tweak, ran the comb through the neat beard that decorated his chin, gave a grunt of satisfaction and then slid beneath the thin sheet on his bed, from which position he regarded his companion with barely disguised impatience.

'I hope you are not going to sit up all night working on those damned playscripts, Shakespeare.'

Will glanced at the clutch of pages he was holding in his hand, the scripts for the play they were to present the following morning. He had indeed intended to spend an hour marking them up, but given Towne's evident hostility to any such idea, he abandoned that plan and put the pages down on the table.

'They can wait for the morning, I'm sure,' he said equably, and began preparing himself for bed.

He was about to blow out the candle when an alarmingly loud groan came from the other side of the room. 'John? Are you all right?'

The other man swore softly. 'It's nothing, just a toothache. It has been plaguing me all day.'

Will picked up the tallow candle and by its wavering light, rummaged in his bag for a small vial. 'Perhaps this will help. Give me your handkerchief.'

'What is it?' Towne was suspicious, though he handed over the small linen square he had been clutching to his cheek in a vain attempt to stem the pain.

'Just oil of cloves.' He poured a little of the oil onto the handkerchief and handed it back to Towne. 'Hold it against the gums, near the pain.'

After a few moments, the frown disappeared from the narrow face, and Will was rewarded with a small smile of gratitude. 'That is miraculous,' Towne said, the words a little indistinct as he continued to clutch the cloth to his gum. 'Where on earth did you learn that little trick?'

'I travelled a little in Italy before I joined the company and I learned of it while there. Before we left London, I found an apothecary and bought a small supply. I thought it might be useful.'

'You are a surprising young man, Shakespeare, I will say that. And I did not know that you are a travelled man. How did you come to be in Italy?'

'I was engaged as a companion-tutor to a young nobleman, who was to study at the university in Padua, though we travelled to Venice first.' His voice trailed away as the invocation of those fabled places transported him back in time and across the continent, and he saw again that shimmering city on the water, with its towers and domes and fine squares.

To Will's surprise, Towne's usually unreadable face was softened by a smile. 'To journey beyond the confines of village, town, or even one's country of birth enlarges us, and does not leave the traveller untouched in heart or mind.'

'Is that the voice of experience? Have you ever travelled abroad?' Will asked, curious to see where this unlooked-for unbending would go.

'A little, though not so far afield as your journeys. I went to France for a time. Studying also.' The smile broadened to something resembling a grin. 'Though if my memory is a reliable guide, I spent more time drinking and fighting than studying.'

'Is that where you got the scar?' Will hazarded; he had always been a little curious about the scar, old and faded almost to invisibility, that ran diagonally down one cheek.

The smile disappeared and the closed look came back as if a shutter had slammed shut across a window. 'Aye. In a duel. The other man paid with his life for this cut.' He shrugged as if to dispose of the matter. 'Anyway, it was long ago, and I left France shortly after.'

'You learned swordsmanship in France?' Everyone in the company knew how to handle a sword, since their audiences, well-versed in street violence, expected the actors' feigned combat to seem real, but John Towne was regarded by all as their most skilful fencer.

'Oh, I knew how to handle a blade before ever I went to France.' That was sardonic; hinting at a brawling youth, perhaps. 'But the fencing masters there honed my skill, it is true. You are fairly handy with a sword yourself, I noticed. Where did you learn?'

Will laughed, remembering. 'On the deck of a ship after I had made such a fool of myself trying to fight off some barbary pirates that I determined to remedy the deficiency lest I lose my life in the next such encounter. My young lordling taught me.'

'And did you ever have another bout with them—the pirates, I mean?'

'No. In fact, I have never had occasion to draw my weapon in anger since. Only for our pretend fights on the stage.'

'Well, at least we will know who to turn to for training when the Lawrence brothers get into a tangle with their swords again,' Towne said, chuckling as he blew out the candle, sending wisps of evil-smelling smoke into the darkness.

***

Drawing in a deep breath, Will put his lips to the long tube of the trumpet and transmitted all the air in his lungs into a long, powerful blast of sound that instantly stilled the noise coming from the crowd on the other side of the tiring-house curtain. In the anticipation-filled silence, he counted silently to ten, and then pulled the cloth aside to allow William Knell to march onto the stage, raise his arms, and declaim the opening lines of the play:

> *'Thus to our grief, the obsequies performed*
> *Of our—too late—deceased and dearest queen,*
> *Whose soul, I hope, possessed of heavenly joys,*
> *Doth ride in triumph amongst the cherubim.*
> *Let us request your grave advice, my lords,*
> *For the disposing of our princely daughters,*
> *For whom our care is specially employed,*
> *As nature binds, to advance their states*

In royal marriage with some princely mates…'

This, the first performance of their tour, was one of the company's standards: *The True Chronicle History of King Leir and his Three Daughters*, author, according to Tarlton, one George Peele. Will remembered reading the story upon which the play was based in his salt-stained and battered copy of Holinshed's *Chronicles*, about an ancient king of Britain who resigns his power and tries to divide his kingdom between his three daughters. Foolishly, he attempts to extract protestations of their devotion to him as a condition of inheritance. Two of them play along, cynically flattering the old man, but the third daughter, Cordella, does not, simply observing that she loves her father as a daughter should. Enraged, the king banishes her from his court and divides the kingdom in two between the other daughters, Goneril and Ragan. Marrying the powerful kings of neighbouring Cumbria and Cornwall, the two false and flattering daughters first reduce their sire to penury, and then begin to compass his death. Cordella, meanwhile, has fled to France where she has met, fallen in love with and married the King of Gallia, travelling incognito with his companion, named as Mumford in the play (a most unlikely name for a Frenchman, Will thought).

He had nothing else to do during the first part of the play except to stand by with the master copy of the playscript, ready to assist should any of his colleagues suffer a momentary lapse of memory, so he positioned himself at one side of the tiring-room, where he could peek through the curtains and see both performers and audience. The latter, quieter and more respectful than their noisy London counterparts, were a mixture of persons high and low all mingled together in a way that would be unheard of in the capital. There, the wealthier sort sat in the galleries on benches, some with the additional luxury of cushions, separated from the poor people, the tradesmen and their apprentices, the doxies and the goodwives, who stood on the muddy floor surrounding the stage.

But in Abingdon's Guild Hall, only Mayor Reade and his colleagues were honoured with seats, placed on a raised platform to one side of the stage. Dressed in their formal gowns, they looked with benign authority upon the townspeople, for they were there to be seen as much as to observe the performance. As for the people themselves, they were clad in their Sunday best—the men in black and wearing their tall hats, the women in plain sober gowns and simple white bonnets, very different from the finery usual in London. Will felt a shiver of familiarity. This was how people dressed for church in his hometown, Stratford-upon-Avon, in nearby Warwickshire.

They all seemed enthralled by the story of King Leir and his wayward daughters, closely following the action with barely a murmur except when some moment of comedy prompted a sharp burst of laughter. His eyes roamed across the crowd, fixing on a face here and there: a fat and jolly-looking grand-dame whose mouth hung open in fascination and whose face turned red as she laughed at every jest; a youthful apprentice, cap perched precariously on an unruly thatch of hair, frowning in concentration as he tried to follow a poetical version of English with an ear that was more tuned to his local dialect; a man who might perhaps be a schoolteacher, dressed all in black and stooped a little with advancing age, eyes sparkling with an appreciation of the subtle meaning in the same words that so bamboozled the apprentice.

It was, Will thought, a rather heavy-handed play that laid out its blunt moral arguments with little subtlety, though it was leavened with some fine comedy to provide an occasional lightening of the otherwise sombrely serious atmosphere. That wasn't the only challenge that this particular play had offered. The three women's parts were substantial, and though Ned Bentley handled his part with ease, Adam was as yet inexperienced and needed a lot of coaching and prompting to remember his lines. Furthermore, because it wasn't possible to double the women's roles, John Laneham had been drafted to play Gonorill, the oldest of the three sisters.

'I am a bit old to be playing women's parts, don't you think?' Laneham had said, rather doubtfully, when Knell suggested it in the morning's rehearsal.

'True, you're no competition for either Ned or Adam, but Gonorill is the evillest of the play's characters, and you can play her as a crone.'

Now, watching the play unfold on stage, Will thought it was a touch of genius. Slathered in powder and stalking about using a harsh crow-like voice, Laneham was evil itself. He was matched by the other senior actors. As the aged king, his beard powdered white and lines of age painted on his forehead, Knell raged about the stage, counterfeiting royalty as though he had been born to it. And John Towne, his toothache now seemingly gone, was craftiness personified as the murderer sent by Goneril to kill Leir.

As for Will, he had a small part as an ambassador that took him onto the stage just twice, brief scenes which he played as straight as possible, resisting the urge to improvise. Back in the tiring house, his listened to laughter floating in through the curtains as the Dutton brothers and young Adam Arkwright played through a comic scene full of sharp double-meanings, the three of them tumbling through the curtains barely able to contain their mirth. The play reached its climax when Cordella was reconciled to her father and Gallia announced that he would invade Britain to restore his father-in-law's rights. That involved some strenuous trumpet-blowing for Will and some energetic mock swordplay on the stage for the rest of the company, impersonating the clashing armies.

Then at last the evil sisters and their husbands were vanquished, the final moralising speeches were delivered, and Tarlton led them all out onto the stage for the usual light-hearted jig. As the audience left, chattering and laughing, Mayor Reade rose from his chair and walked across the stage to join the assembled actors. 'Well done, well done indeed. Never have I seen so fine a play, nor so skilfully enacted. You have done Abingdon proud, my friends.'

If that was the finest play the mayor has ever seen, he clearly has not travelled far, was Will's secret thought as he joined the others in having his hands grasped and wrung by various members of the council. He noted that some of those gentlemen, the most austerely dressed of them, refrained from joining in their colleagues' enthusiasm and stood a little to one side, their faces fixed in masks of barely disguised displeasure. Puritans, he thought. Nothing the company did, short of an old-fashioned morality play, would ever please those gentlemen. But eventually, the town council finally departed, leaving the actors alone on the stage.

'What was the take, Will?' Knell asked, as the two stagehands, who had spent most of the performance standing rigidly on either side of the stage dressed as guards, began the task of collecting together the props and removing them for safekeeping.

'I don't know, Billy, for I haven't counted the bags yet, but I'll wager it will be four or five shillings.'

Tarlton laughed and rubbed his hands together. 'If it is as much as five, and we take the same again tomorrow, it will be a profitable stop indeed, and a good omen for the rest of the tour. Come lads, let us to the Crossed Keys and see what Mistress Hawley can find for us by way of food and drink. We've all earned a feast this evening.'

Mistress Hawley and her kitchen-girls must have been hard at work all afternoon, for what awaited them was a feast indeed—pies and pasties, boiled eggs, salmon swimming in a vinegary sauce, and a pile of roast capons weighed down the table in the main hall, while the serving girls were ready with tankards of ale and jugs of wine, all compliments of Mayor Reade. Before long the atmosphere at the Crossed Keys was one of cheerful conviviality as the actors mixed with the regular patrons of the inn.

From somewhere in his pockets, Dick Tarlton extracted a short clay pipe and a pouch containing tobacco leaves, which he proceeded to push and prod into the pipe's bowl. Once satisfied that the leaves were packed in satisfactorily, he lit the object from a taper, breathed in and then exhaled a great stream of acrid smoke, the smile on his face expressing both physical pleasure and a certain smugness.

'He smokes the damned stuff just to be fashionable, you know,' Knell said to no one in particular.

'Well, that was true when I first took it up, but I have quite come to depend upon its calming effects since.' Tarlton paused to hold his pipe at arm's length, admiring it for a moment before clamping it once more between his teeth. 'But not everyone thought it was exactly fashionable even then. Once, I was sitting in a tavern between two very drunk men. Seeing the smoke come out of my nose as I exhaled, one of them cried "Fire! Fire!" and threw a cup of wine at my face to quench what, in his drunkenness, he took to be a conflagration. "Make no more stir, my friend," said I, "for the fire is quenched."'

Knell, who had doubtless heard the tale many times before, let out an exaggerated groan. But the others were all mightily amused and, knowing that it would take little to encourage him, begged Tarlton to tell some more stories from his life as a travelling player. With a smile, he launched into a long and improbable story involving a horse, a haughty steward, and a bowling-green that soon had them all clutching their sides with mirth. Of course in such company Tarlton could not be allowed to have the stage all to himself, and first Knell, then Laneham offered their own comical tales, more pipes were lit, and the inn's hall became a loud boisterous fug of smoke and rosy faces.

Thus did afternoon become evening, and evening full night, before they all finally stumbled off to their respective beds, close to midnight.

The following morning's rehearsal for the afternoon's play—a comedy, *The Friar of Nottingham*—went well enough, despite the company having sore heads

35

all round, and Tarlton, who seemed to have a constitution of which an ox would be proud, gave an inspired performance, in his element as a lecherous friar in love with a shepherd girl who turns out, after many convolutions of the plot, to be a boy. Their closing jig was particularly spirited, and the crowd departed in high spirits, which were matched by the company when Will announced that their takings for the day were a full seven shillings.

'You're bringing us good luck, lad,' Billy Knell said, patting him on the back as he was locking the day's takings away in their little travelling strongbox. 'If this keeps up we'll all be able to retire at the end of the tour!'

Knell exaggerated, of course. As sharers in the company, he and Tarlton and several of the others would keep the lion's share of the profits. Jobbing actors like Will and John Towne and the two boys, Adam and Ned, would receive their six shillings a week, and if they happened to have a poor run would be expected to go without entirely. But such was the lot of actors, and it was a bargain he had accepted the day he'd joined the company. Still, he was happy enough, and he went to bed imagining the look on Anne's face when she saw the bolt of fine wool he would send her from London to make into a new dress, paid for with his pay from this tour.

Chapter 3

The next day they were on the hot and dusty road again, following the river towards the town of Oxford, a mere three hours distant. Wanting to make an impression, they had that morning donned their royal livery and decked out the cart with ribbons and flags. As the spires and towers of Oxford came into view, Will and Ned Bentley took turns blowing great blasts from the trumpet. By the time they rumbled across the bridge into the town, the noise had attracted a small crowd of students, apprentices, goodwives and labourers.

The black-gowned students were the noisiest of the lot, taking great delight in exercising their wit by exchanging quips with the actors. One, recognising Dick Tarlton, went so far as to break into verse:

> *'Tarlton, I am one of your friends and none of your foes.*
> *Then I pray you tell me how thou came by your flat nose?'*

The little gaggle of companions around him hooted at this cheeky reference to Tarlton's broken and misshapen nose, but the bold youth waved them to silence and went on:

> *'Had I been present at the time on those banks,*
> *I would have laid my sword over his shanks!'*

Tarlton, not at all put out, gave a huge laugh and stood up. Defying the antics of the swaying cart, his hands on his hips, he shouted back a retort:

> *'Friend or foe, if you must needs know,*
> *Mark me well:*
> *With parting dogs and bears by the ears,*

This chance fell:
But though my nose be flat,
My credit to save,
Yet very well can I by the smell,
Scent an honest man from a knave!'

'You have quite overmastered me, Master Tarlton,' the student managed to shout between thumps on the back from various members of the crowd.

Thus entertained, the company was in high spirits when they finally arrived in the centre of Oxford. It was a town that Shakespeare knew well, as it was a regular stopping place on the road between Stratford and London. In fact, they were to be lodged at a large and rambling tavern on Cornmarket Street where he had often stayed, universally known as Davenant's Inn, after its owner John Davenant, a large, round-bellied and red-faced man in his middle years, whose unfailing good humour had defied the tragedy of losing his first wife and only child to the plague some years back, and had won him a new wife, a small but energetic woman who ruled her husband with an iron rod in all matters to do with the running of the inn.

They were to have a long stay in Oxford, a full five days, so, while Tarlton and Knell hurried off to the town hall to register the company's arrival in the town with the city's officials, Will had his hands full negotiating an appropriate tariff, arranging victuals, and sorting out the details of their accommodation. Easygoing Davenant might have been inclined to be generous, but his wife was having none of it, though she extracted her concessions with a good-humoured chaffer that Will found hard to resist. Still, in the end, he was satisfied with the arrangements and was enjoying an ale and a gossip with her husband when the company's two principals returned from the town hall.

Though Oxford was a growing city, it did not possess a hall of suitable size to present plays. There were several such halls in the university, but the dons, fearing the effect of such frivolity upon the disposition of their students, had long forbidden their use by touring theatrical companies, a ban that even the Queen's Men could not defy. So they were to perform at another inn called the Crown and Sceptre, just up the street.

Their program for Oxford was almost entirely a diet of serious history plays— their old familiar *Henry V*, *King Leir* again, and *The Troublesome Reign of King John* with just *The Three Ladies of London*, an allegorical comedy about the evils of usury, to offset all the seriousness. Late that afternoon, while they waited for the carpenters to nail in place the last few planks on the stage, Will queried Knell on this point. The actor stroked his beard, put his head on one side, and answered question with question. 'You know how the company was formed, do you not?'

Will nodded; he had heard the tale in London. Sir Francis Walsingham had been deputed by the Queen to raid the acting troupes of two of her courtiers, the earls of Oxford and Leicester, from whose ranks a new company would be formed under her patronage. It was said that she'd done so to curtail the rivalry between the two men, who had been using their companies to curry favour with her.

'Well, Walsingham might have been solving a political problem for the Queen, but he saw an opportunity to further another aim. He made it clear from the start that the Queen's Men were also to be an arm of the state. We were to present plays that uplifted public morals, encouraged Protestant observance, damned all Catholics, and above all, supported and extolled the virtues of peace and prosperity under Her Majesty's rule.'

That sounded like Walsingham, a man whose cunning would do Machiavelli proud. It also explained their choice of plays in Oxford. *Henry V* looked back to a golden age under the leadership of a great Lancastrian king, from whose line the Queen herself had sprung, *King John* exemplified the perils of weak kingship, while *Leir* warned against the dangers of disunity and moralised on the rewards of doing one's plain duty.

'More's the pity then that they aren't better plays.'

'Oh? You think you could do better, lad?' Knell chuckled.

Will evaded the question. 'They do lumber along, don't you think? And they make their ever-so-worthy points with all the subtlety of a wild boar thrashing through the undergrowth.'

'Yet the people like them. You are an educated man, Will, I know that, and you have an ear for what works in the theatre. Your little additions and adjustments to our playscripts prove that. But never forget that our audiences, particularly those outside London, are made up of common men and women, on whom subtlety, as you term it, would be lost.'

'Perhaps. But I've watched them from behind the tiring-house curtains, and I tell you, the groundlings follow what we do on stage with as much attention as the gents and ladies up in the galleries. They might not be poets themselves, but they love what poets create for them.'

'You *do* think you could do better, don't you?' Knell said. 'Well, mayhap we will be able to give you a chance to try when we are back in London. God knows we need new plays there if we are to compete against the Admiral's Men and all the others.'

That was a startling prospect, and though it was at best a half-promise, Will was reduced to silence at the thought that he might soon be writing plays for the Queen's actors.

'Now that is a rarity—Will Shakespeare lost for words!' Knell smiled. 'It looks as though the carpenters are done at last. Let's have a look at their handiwork and then get back to Davenant's for supper.'

Their first performance in Oxford did not go well. *The Troublesome Reign of King John* was usually a crowd-pleaser—a patriotic concoction in which the hapless king battles the pope, the King of France, and his own fickle barons, attempts to dispose of his own nephew and claimant to his throne, and ends up dying of poison administered by monks. But that day, everything seemed to have conspired to create theatrical mayhem.

There had been no premonition of trouble when they had arrived that morning. Everyone had been in high spirits as they had inspected the inn's yard, a large rectangular space surrounded on all four sides by a gallery, perfect for seating the gentry. Spectators entered through a low arch at one end, and a five-foot-high wooden stage had been erected at the other. Painted canvas curtains hung from beneath the section of the gallery that ran above the rear of the stage, creating the space that would be their tiring-house, and at each side of the stage, tall flagpoles soared up above the line of the inn's roof, at whose peaks long pennons snapped and cracked in the breeze to signify that a play would be performed that day.

Their rehearsal had gone without difficulty, though Will had noticed that young Ned Bentley, their Queen Constance in the afternoon's performance, was looking a little pale. The boy's handsome features had attracted the attention of one of the barmaids at Davenant's Inn, who had plied him with copious quantities of wine the night before. But he had delivered his lines well enough, and Will didn't think any more of it until the play was about to start, at the second hour after noon. That was when he realised that Bentley, whose task it was to utter the opening lines of the play, was nowhere to be seen.

A furious Dick Tarlton despatched Will in search of the youngster, who he found back at Davenant's, his head in a bucket near the privy, attended by the young lass who had been fluttering her eyelids at him since the day they had arrived.

'I don't know what's wrong, sir,' she said. 'We were talking an hour ago, happy as you please, and then he starts emptying the contents of his stomach all over the place.'

A white-faced Bentley hauled himself upright and swayed slightly as he faced Will. 'I'm sorry, Mister Shakespeare, truly I am. I must have eaten something that disagreed with me.'

More likely his constitution had surrendered to the assaults of too much unwatered wine. But there was no use in upbraiding the boy now; no doubt he would feel the sharp side of Dick Tarlton's tongue before the day was out, and Will had no wish to add to his misery. Instead, he left him in the care of his would-be sweetheart and hurried back to the Crown and Sceptre. As he clambered up the steps behind the temporary stage, he could hear the noise of a restive crowd coming from beyond the tiring-room curtains.

'God's blood, Will, where is he?' Billy Knell hissed. 'We are near half an hour late going on, and the audience will be in a lynching mood if we delay much longer.'

As if to emphasise his words, the tiring-room curtains rippled as they were subjected to an assault of apple cores that were being hurled by the impatient folk gathered below the stage.

'Come on, get on with it!' someone out there shouted. 'We'll be here until midnight if you don't get started soon.'

'Right, Will, I am afraid you will have to take Bentley's part,' Tarlton commanded, once Will had explained in a quick breathless sentence what had happened. 'Meanwhile, I'll go out and tame the wild beasts.'

With which he thrust the curtains aside and, a huge grin on his misshapen face, marched confidently out across the stage. Hands planted firmly on his waist, he proceeded to amuse the crowd with a long story about a late-night encounter

42

with the London town watch. The alchemy of the comic's genius soon transmuted the crowd's sour annoyance into happy laughter.

Will, meanwhile, struggled into a dress much too small for him, having been designed for the youngsters, who possessed much slimmer frames than his own broader build. He hid his hair beneath the coif and veil of Queen Constance as John Laneham helped apply some powder to his cheeks and colour to his lips; it was just as well that he had shaved that morning.

At last, the play got under way, its first few scenes passing in a blur. He knew his lines well enough, for as the company book-holder he was probably the only one among them who knew every line in the play. But he was still new to the acting craft, and it took all his hard-won skills to deliver the lines with conviction, particularly playing a woman, something he had rarely done in his short theatrical career. Yet, as always when he was on the stage, he was transported into a kind of half-ecstatic state, every fibre of his being responding to the challenges of the performance, his mind taken over by the persona of the long-dead Queen Constance.

But the fates that govern players had not, it seemed, quite done with them yet. *King John* had only one comic scene, in which the king's bastard nephew, seeking to extract some bullion hidden in a monkish storage chest, opens it to discover instead a woman (Adam Arkwright, coyly dressed as a nun), who he supposes to be the monk's mistress. This required a small piece of stagecraft. The chest, placed unobtrusively at the back of the stage, only had three sides, allowing Adam to sneak into the open fourth side and curl himself up in readiness for when John Towne, acting the part of the Bastard, commanded that the lid be opened. It was a simple trick, and one that would have gone perfectly had the two stagehands remembered to put the chest on the stage in the first place.

Instead, Towne was forced to extemporise a line or two—something he hated doing—commanding in a loud voice that the chest be brought onto the stage. Jem and Luke at least had wit enough to realise what had gone wrong, and abandoning their positions pretending to be men-at-arms, went off to collect the strongbox, sweating and grunting as they carried it on with Adam already concealed inside. Fortunately, the audience didn't seem to notice that anything was amiss, judging from their laughter and applause when a somewhat flushed Arkwright emerged, all girlish innocence as he played out the scene.

As if these mishaps had conjured some mischievous theatrical sprite, they were followed by a series of other small accidents. At one point Knell came on stage having forgotten to don King John's crown. Then, in one of the battle scenes, Towne's normally deft swordsmanship seemed to desert him, resulting in Robert Wilson giving out a loud yelp as he received a passing cut on the arm.

Irritating though these little incidents were, the audience seemed untroubled, and by the time Adam Arkwright, now dressed in more manly garb as the boy-king Henry III, delivered the play's rousing final lines—*If England's peers and people join in one/Nor Pope, nor France, nor Spain can do them wrong*—the playgoers in the yard and galleries above were happily cheering and clapping with approval.

Nevertheless, it was a disgruntled company that gathered back at Davenant's Inn, thoroughly out of sorts, though Dick Tarlton tried to cheer everybody up. 'Never mind, lads. It wasn't the worst performance I've ever been in.' With which he launched into a long and rambling reminiscence of a theatrical disaster from his past.

Like his colleagues, Will was relieved that their chief took it all in his stride, though he noticed that Knell listened with mere politeness to a story he must have heard dozens of times over the years, and Towne had a glowering look of impatience as though he could not wait for Tarlton to finish his tale.

'That's all very well, Dick,' he said coldly, killing stillborn any laughter from the rest, 'but you are too easy-going. That boy should be thrashed for making us a full half-hour late on stage. And Shakespeare deserves a reprimand for not ensuring the damned monk's chest was in the right place when needed. We need to have some discipline, not stories from your distant history that make everyone laugh but do nothing to improve the professionalism of the company.'

Tarlton's face flushed and his hands bunched into fists, but an explosion was forestalled by Knell, whose turn it was to put a restraining hand on his old friend's arm. 'Ned may warrant being given some counsel, but not a thrashing. He is a member of our company, not a servant. As for Will, we would have been in even deeper trouble had he not stepped in and performed so splendidly. And you handled the difficulty with the chest well enough, John.'

'Don't think you can deflect me with a bit of flattery, Knell!' Towne's savage rebuff caused Knell to visibly recoil. 'And as for Shakespeare, he did well enough, but had he been minding his duty last night he would have been making sure that stupid impressionable boy did not take too much drink in the first place.'

That, Will thought, *is very unfair*. As company factotum he had, it was true, many unspecified duties, but playing the nursemaid to the younger members of the company was not one of them.

His instinct to reply with a hot retort was silenced by a quick shake of the head from Tarlton, who, having recovered his composure, intervened to use his authority to bring the argument to an end. 'Enough, John. You have made your point, but no good purpose is served by these recriminations. I will talk to Ned and remind him of his duty, but otherwise let us leave all to lie and think instead upon the morrow. And Will, though I know you have proven yourself most competent in your duties, perhaps a little extra attention to the staging tomorrow, eh?' The slight, almost imperceptible rise of Tarlton's eyebrows took the sting out of any rebuke implied in these last words, and Will played along with a shrug and a nod.

Their dinner that night began in a subdued key. A fully recovered Ned Bentley joined them, sheepishly making profuse apologies for his absence and the trouble it had caused. Towne just sniffed and looked away, but the others welcomed their errant colleague to the table with a few crude jests and a thump or two on the back.

After a while, the hum of conversation rose and by the time they had finished their collective good humour had been restored. Even so, there was little enthusiasm this evening for extended carousing, and one by one they said their goodnights and made their way off to their rooms. In the end, only Dick Tarlton and Will were left alone in the big central hall of the inn, a jug of wine and the remains of a block of cheese on the table between them.

'You did well today, Will,' Tarlton said for what must have been the fourth or fifth time that night; he was a little drunk. 'I don't know how you managed to remember all of those lines and deliver them at a moment's notice, but I am damned glad that you did.'

'I don't really understand it either, Dick. It's just something I have been able to do since I was a boy at the grammar school in Stratford. It used to irritate the schoolmasters, I think.'

'I should imagine it would.' Tarlton grinned, pouring wine into his goblet, offering to do the same for Will, who declined with a shake of his head.

'Enough for me. If I am to meet John's standard of perfection tomorrow, I need a clear head.' He could not quite keep the resentment out of his voice.

'Don't let him bother you. Knell and I decide what's what in this company, not John Towne, who is after all just a jobbing actor.'

Will decided to ask a question that had been on his mind all evening. 'Why do he and Billy strike such furious sparks off each other? Sometimes it seems as if they can hardly bear to be in the same room together.'

Tarlton fixed his attention on his wine glass, swirling the thin yellow liquid around in contemplation. 'They were rivals in love. You know that Billy married Rebecca Edwards two years ago?'

'Yes, of course. The whole company knows it.'

'Well, Rebecca is young—she was just fifteen when they married—but she is a strong-minded lass. Beautiful, too, and she was being wooed by half of London. Her father's a mercer, and canny as you might expect any member of the merchant breed to be, so he wasn't going to let her marry unwisely.'

'And John Towne was one of her suitors?'

'Aye, and if she had been given her own way in the matter, she would have married John, not Billy. She was smitten with him. Though you might not think it, he possesses a silver tongue when he chooses to use it, and he is a good-looking, well-set-up fellow. And though they always observed the proprieties, it seemed obvious to me at least that they were in love, at least for a time.'

'So why didn't they marry?'

'Her father. He took against John for some reason and would not give his consent. And then Billy threw his hat into the ring, and from her father's point of view, he was a much more suitable match. He is an established actor, well set-up, with a share in the company, and connections at court.'

'And all this while both men were working together on the stage?'

Tarlton breathed out a regretful sigh. 'I counselled Billy against going after the Edwards girl, for the good of the company, but he would have none of it, so besotted was he. It is the only time he and I have ever had a serious quarrel.'

Will sympathised with both men—Towne for his obvious disappointment, Knell for having to endure the whispers of the foolish as the price for being in love with a lass so much younger. He had suffered something of the same himself

47

in small-town Stratford, though his case was the reverse, having married a considerably older woman at a young age. This circumstance had prompted all sorts of rumours about their marriage ceremony being conducted at the end of the pitchforks of her farmer relatives, because he had supposedly gotten Anne with child. That none of it was true did not make it sting any the less.

'There's something else,' Tarlton went on, evidently now in a mood to unburden himself. 'John has been agitating ever since to be allowed to buy a share in the company, but Billy has refused to countenance any such thing. Towne says he has the money, though from where I cannot say, and he is a competent enough actor, so ordinarily we would not hesitate to accept him. The others were mostly in favour, but Billy just kept saying no. And that was that.'

'Why? Surely he would want to mend fences now that he has won Rebecca's hand? After all, he and John must work together.'

'I know not why he is so adamant. When I pressed him, he just said that we didn't know everything about John, but that he was unfit to be a sharer. He wouldn't say anything more than that.'

'And so we must all work to keep the peace between the two of them.'

'Aye, that we must.' Tarlton's face creased into a crooked grin. 'Never mind, lad. Have one last glass with me before bed. All will be well, and things will sort themselves out one way or another. I've lived long enough to know that is the case more often than not!'

It was impossible to be downcast for more than a moment or two in the presence of Dick Tarlton, and Will was himself of an optimistic disposition by nature, so he returned the grin and accepted the proffered wine jug. Then they rose from the table and made their way up the stairs.

Halfway up, Tarlton stopped and laid a hand on his younger colleague's shoulder. 'We rely upon you, Will, you do know that? You are the best book-holder we have ever had, you have a gift for the stage and a way with words. One day, I prophesy, you will be offered a sharer's part in this or some other company, and you will make a name for yourself in London. And I will watch with pride from my retirement.'

Will did not know what to say to that, though his smile and the slow flush that coloured his cheeks seemed eloquent enough for Tarlton, who gave him one more slap on the back and made his way to his room, chuckling to himself and leaving the bemused younger man to make his thoughtful way to bed.

Will collapsed on the rough truckle bed, oblivious to the snores of the Dutton brothers who occupied the big double bed on the other side of the room and lay for a while playing through scenes in his mind of a glorious future as a sharer in the Queen's Men, acting and writing plays that would win the name of Shakespeare eternal fame, until at last, he fell into an exhausted sleep.

Chapter 4

It was market day in the town of Thame, and the market square was a bobbing sea of people. From their booths, the traders shouted the prices and attributes of their wares and haggled good-naturedly with their customers, folk who had come to Thame from all over the county. Fat chickens, hung up by their feet for inspection by critical matrons, struggled and squawked in protest at the indignity of their treatment. Pigs squealed and grunted on Hog Row. Farmers piled up their eggs, butter and cheese on long trestle tables, and the drapers pinched cloths between their fingers to demonstrate its quality to doubtful dressmakers and tailors. Beneath the feet of the swirling crowds, dogs darted with all the optimism of their nature in the hope they might pick up a scrap of food falling from the hands of citizens breakfasting on newly roasted meat. Shouts and laughter as friend greeted friend rose above the general hum of conversation, and a pair of tumblers entertained a circle of wide-eyed children while their mothers exchanged news and gossip.

Though it was still early, the day was already hot and humid, unusually so for mid-June, and the flags and banners hung limply from the moot-hall that stood at one end of the marketplace, where Will Shakespeare and Ned Bentley stood handing out bills to advertise the performance that was to begin after the market closed at noon. They were both dressed in their stage clothes—full court costume, complete with thick padded doublet and starched ruff. Under his breath, Will cursed the heat that caused trickles of sweat to run down his neck from beneath the high black hat perched on his head. It would make the afternoon's presentation of their old familiar *Henry V* an uncomfortable affair in the close confines of the yard of the White Hound Inn.

Handing the last of his bills to a severe-looking matron with a cheery exhortation to 'come along and see the greatest tale of English glory enacted by the finest actors in the kingdom', he grasped the youth by the elbow and steered them through the throng in the general direction of the inn, down at the far end of the marketplace.

'Another minute in this ruff and I swear I will melt into the ground,' he said, twisting adroitly to one side as an oafish apprentice, his eyes already glazed with drink, stumbled past in the opposite direction. 'Have you got your lines down pat, young fellow? They must trip off your tongue if you want to avoid another rebuke from Mister Towne.'

Since his disgrace in Oxford, poor Bentley had been all meek subservience towards the other actors, doing his best to rehabilitate himself with them. They had all been forgiving, for Ned was a likeable young man, all except John Towne, who had continued to carp and criticise at every small error the boy made, on stage or off. That had made Will all the more determined to protect the youngster and help him to do better on the stage.

'I think so, Will,' Bentley said, a little timidly, as they entered the yard of the White Hound, where the two stagehands were busy dragging a table across the stage to its rightful position for the opening scene of the play. 'But sometimes the words just disappear, and it takes me a moment to find them again. Does that ever happen to you?'

'It happens to everyone,' he said, untruthfully. It didn't happen to him, ever. But Will knew that his peculiarly retentive memory was a gift that few of his fellow-actors possessed. Knell had it and could con a new script and memorise it in moments, but the others, even Tarlton, often had to work hard to keep all the words in their heads, so Bentley was hardly unique in his occasional failure to remember his lines on stage. 'That is why we try and help each other on stage when our memories fail, and why I am always nearby with the playscript, ready to prompt you.'

'Everyone *is* kind,' Bentley conceded, with a winning smile that instantly turned down into a grimace. 'Except Mister Towne. I don't ever seem to be able to please him.'

There was nothing Will could say to that, so he just patted the boy on the back. 'You are a fine actor, Ned, you know that. Just try not to let John get under your skin. Now, run along and get yourself ready for the rehearsal.' He smiled as he watched Ned make his way across the yard, exchanging cheery waves with Jem and Luke.

Though this was its first outing on this tour, *The Famous Victories of Henry V* required little in the way of rehearsal, so familiar was it for most of the company, and by midday, they had completed a quick run-through to everyone's satisfaction. An hour later the innyard was full of people good-humouredly jostling each other for a place close to the stage, cracking the walnuts and hazelnuts that they had purchased at the market to provide them with sustenance through the afternoon's proceedings, laughing and making ribald jokes about the shortcomings and foibles of local personages. Above in the galleries, the better-off, having paid their extra penny for the privilege, settled themselves on benches and stools, fanning themselves against the heat which had steadily worsened since the morning.

Behind the tiring-house curtain, Will looked around at his fellow company members to check that everyone was in place and ready, jerked a commanding nod and put the trumpet to his lips. The blast of sound instantly stilled the audience. After a heartbeat's wait, William Knell thrust the curtain open and strode onto the stage, followed by John Laneham and Robert Wilson, and their play was launched.

It was a near-flawless performance. Apart from one or two minor lapses, everyone remembered their lines, all the stage effects worked without difficulty, and the audience was surprisingly well-behaved considering the quantity of ale that had flowed that morning in the marketplace, something that always risked rowdiness among the apprentices. At the end, sweat pouring from their brows after the exertions of their jig, they were given some rousing cheers and left the stage feeling well-pleased with themselves.

It was only after the performance had ended and they had gathered in the White Hound's taproom for well-deserved refreshments that trouble started. It began, as strife often does, with an innocent question. Robert Wilson had been entertaining them with a long story about a stage-play that had gone terribly wrong: actors had forgotten their lines, props were missing, and at one stage the tiring-house curtain had completely fallen down, revealing actors in half-dress and costumes piled up on stools ready to be worn. All this was told with a hilarity that was completely unexpected coming from an actor whose chief characteristic offstage was dourness.

Will had always found Wilson an almost unapproachably chilly man but was emboldened by this apparent relaxation of his mask to wonder out loud how he had come to be in the acting trade in the first place.

'That is another tale, for which I require more ale.' Someone duly obliged, passing him a full tankard. 'When I was a youth, I lived in Canterbury, where my father is a schoolmaster. There was a girl, a maid who was no maid, if you know what I mean, with whom I was accustomed to tumble from time to time. She was an orphan, both parents having died in the plague, and lived with her two uncles on a farm just outside the town.

'One day she came to me, told me that she was with child and that I was the father. For some reason, she had formed the notion that I was rich and demanded that I either married her or paid her money to keep silent and pretend that the child was someone else's by-blow, which it probably was in any case, for it was well-known she made her favours available all over the town. Naturally, I refused her demands, but she had managed to convince her uncles that I was the culprit, and they came after me with pitchforks, demanding that I marry the lass.

'So I packed up my things and fled to London, and, to make the long short, I found work holding the gentry's horses at The Curtain. It was boring work, and I began to amuse myself and passers-by with various comical routines, mimicking the actors they had just seen on stage. Eventually, one of those actors, amused by my impersonation of him, decided I had the makings of a proper performer, and took me under his wing. And so, many years later, here I am.'

Having delivered himself of this story, Wilson seemed almost embarrassed at having spoken at such length and lapsed into a silence that was instantly filled by the booming voice of Dick Tarlton. 'You should have been more inventive with your Kentish lass, Rob. I once was in a similar predicament when I was wrongfully accused of getting a gentleman's maid with child. I was brought before a justice, a pompous old man, who said, "It is a marvel, Mister Tarlton, that you, being a gentleman of good quality, and one of her majesty's servants to boot, would venture thus to get a maid with child." "Nay," I replied, "rather it would be a true marvel if the maid had gotten *me* with child!" Which so amused the old justice that he immediately dismissed the charge.'

Most of the company chuckled dutifully, all except John Towne, whose face creased into a grimace. 'Fah! All that these stories tell me is that women can never be trusted. They are fickle, flighty, will promise to be faithful and obedient but change their minds when it suits them, hoist their skirts for every passing youth who catches their fancy, and will trap the unwary for their own advantage without scruple.'

Lawrence Dutton laughed. 'Oh, ho! Do I hear the voice of a man thwarted in love?'

54

Will caught the quick exchange of glances between Dick Tarlton and William Knell to which Dutton seemed oblivious, and decided this might be dangerous ground, best avoided. 'Ah, the fair sex; how they do confuse and confound us poor men with their wiles,' he said, bestowing his broadest smile on them all. 'Yet as those of us who are married can attest, our lives would be the poorer without them. Men might strut about the world as though it were a stage, attracting all eyes with their finery, but it is women who, though compelled to a proper silence in the outer world, are the masters-at-arms, nay, the very generals of the household. They feed and clothe our children, chastise the servants, ensure there is food on the table and ale in the tankard on those rare occasions when we are home, with all the efficiency of a quartermaster. And of course they keep their bed warm for us.'

That little homily was greeted with smiles, but Will's attempt to divert the conversation into more agreeable waters did not deter Towne, who seemed to have an axe in need of grinding. 'Are you so sure, Shakespeare, that your wife is always keeping the bed warm only for you?' Towne's sneer was venomous and his glare an open provocation.

Will visibly struggled to keep his features benevolent. 'I am sure, John. I would stake my life on her fidelity.'

'Well, no doubt.' Towne raised his hands, palms outwards, in an apparent show of contrition which he instantly undermined. 'She is perhaps no longer of an age to attract the attentions of young gallants, always supposing that such creatures exist in rural Warwickshire. Men who have married younger wives, however...'

'What,' William Knell growled, 'is that supposed to mean?'

'Marry, I mean nothing except what I say, which is that young women, in matrimony or without, are ever sirens to youth.'

'Don't play the mealy-mouthed lawyer with me, Towne. It is my Rebecca of whom you speak, upon whose character you smear the excrement of calumny with your insinuations!'

'Did I say her name?' Towne was demure, infuriating Knell even further. The rest of them could do nothing except watch in a little pool of appalled silence.

'You didn't have to. Come, you blackguard, out with it—what do you mean?'

'Well, since it seems you wish to be told that which half of London knows but has contrived to keep from you these past months, your wife, sir, has been straying from the hearth while you travel the country.'

For a moment Knell seemed unable to say anything, his mouth opening then snapping shut to set in a look of fury. 'You lie, you dog! You repeat idle gossip as though it were God's gospelled truth.'

'I do not lie, Knell. Your beloved Rebecca has a paramour, the son of a grocer, no less. They have been seen on the streets together.'

'Which means nothing.' Knell's voice faltered a little. 'No doubt she was properly chaperoned, in any event.'

'She was not.' One of Towne's eyebrows creased upwards, taunting the other actor.

'You make a serious accusation, Mister Towne,' Tarlton said. 'No gentleman would do so if he had no proof. *Do* you have proof? If so, you had better produce it.'

If Tarlton had hoped to call Towne's bluff, he was mistaken. With another of his provocative smiles, he reached into his doublet and pulled out a square of white linen, a handkerchief, which he unfolded and held up dramatically for everyone to see. 'This was found beside your wife's bed. Unless she has changed her name in your absence, this little piece of linen damns her.'

56

He spread the handkerchief on his palm so that the monogram—the letters 'JH'—was clearly visible in one corner.

'No! I will not believe it.' The pain on Knell's face was distressing, even as he attempted a rally. 'Anyway, this means nothing. Just initials on a kerchief that could belong to anyone.'

Towne's face twisted into a sneer. 'The grocer boy's name is John Heminges. No doubt he dropped it in his haste to dress after a night of fornication.'

'You are lying, and you have fabricated this… this so-called evidence!'

'Am I? Have I?' Towne's voice was soft in contrast to the hysterical tone of his antagonist, almost purring. 'You cannot be surprised at her infidelity. She never loved you; it was her father who insisted upon the marriage.'

This was finally too much for Knell. 'You will pay for that slander, you cur!' With a rasp, the sword that hung at his hip was out of its scabbard and sweeping dangerously through the air, causing the others to take a frightened and hasty step backwards.

Every member of the company except the two boys and the two stagehands owned a sword, and wearing them was habitual in London, where the possibility of unexpected violence lay around every corner. But in the peaceful countryside, the habit had for the most part been in abeyance. Will wondered what mischievous god had prompted both Towne and Knell to strap them on today.

Unexpectedly, Towne left his sword in its scabbard and just gave Knell a contemptuous smile. 'Come on old man, you can kill me if you can catch me.'

Having cast that final provocative dart, he ran for the door, closely followed by Knell, who seemed grimly determined not to allow his tormentor to escape. The other members of the company watched them disappear in open-mouthed confusion. Will, driven by some instinct acquired in the shadowy back streets of

Verona, hesitated only for a moment before rushing after the two actors. Outside, the sullen heat and brightness of the sun checked him momentarily. By the time he had recovered his wits, he realised that Knell and Towne were already some distance down the street. Without waiting to see if the others were following, he set off in pursuit.

The slight form of John Towne disappeared into a narrow lane, Knell in hot pursuit. Following, Will puffed his way past half a dozen silent and shuttered houses before emerging into the open fields beyond. There, a small grassy knoll, perhaps five or six feet high, rose from the stubbled farmland, up which Towne raced and then turned to face his pursuer. Emerging from the lane just behind Knell, Will fleetingly wondered why Towne had chosen this particular lane. Had he known that it led to an eminence from which he might wring some advantage against his bulkier adversary?

Only then did Towne finally draw his sword and drop into a defensive posture, legs apart and slightly bent at the knees, sword arm raised and the other arm hanging loose for balance. *Of course*, Will thought, *he has fought duels before.*

There was little time to process that thought before the clang of iron on iron signalled that the fight had begun. Knell's first furious thrust was expertly parried, his sword turned aside by a deft flick of Towne's weapon. He retreated a step, deflecting in his turn a sweeping cut that missed his nose by the tiniest of fractions. Sensing his opponent was off-balance, he grunted and thrust his sword directly at the other man's face. Far from showing any fear, Towne's narrow visage creased into a tiny smile of triumph as he dodged the clumsy blow and took a few steps backward up the mound. Following, Knell stumbled over an exposed tree root, and at that moment Towne's sword flashed out with the speed of a viper's strike.

Knell gave a small animal cry of pain. His sword dropped onto the turf and he collapsed slowly to his knees, hands clutching at his throat. Will was just in time to catch the wounded actor as he fell back into his arms. He pulled a kerchief from his doublet and pressed it over the wound to stem the flow of gore that was oozing out of the wound in his neck and was already soaking Knell's doublet and shirt. The cut was only an inch or so wide, as far as Will could see, but must have been quite deep, to judge from the volume of blood.

Towne, seemingly unconcerned with his colleague's fate, stood atop the mound, leaning on his sword. 'You saw, Shakespeare. It was self-defence. I did not draw my sword until I had no choice.'

'Right at this moment, John, I care not one whit either way. The coroner can decide that. In the meantime, we need a physician, and quickly.'

Towne nodded and went off back down the lane, though at a leisurely pace that seemed almost insolent. Clearly, whatever justification he was ultimately going to advance for his actions, he cared little whether his victim lived or died.

Left alone, Will's attention returned to his injured colleague, whose face had gone pale beneath the black beard and whose eyes were flickering behind closed lids as he began to drift into unconsciousness.

'Stay awake, Billy. Help is on its way.'

Knell's eyes snapped open at the sound of Will's voice, and his mouth began to move in speech, so soft that Will had to bend over to hear.

'Towne... not what he seems... have proof.' The words were slurred, indistinct, and Will wasn't sure what he was hearing. Knell grasped his sleeve and seemed determined to be understood. 'You must stop him!'

Stop him from what? And what proof did Knell have about... well, about what?

'Never mind that now, Billy. Help is on its way, and we will get you back on your feet in no time.' He said the words with more optimism than he felt, and in any event, they didn't reassure the other man, who just increased his grip and struggled again to speak, this time more lucidly. 'No. I am done for. Look out for Rebecca for me, Will. Promise me!'

There was nothing he could say in the face of his friend's certainty of his imminent death, except to nod dumbly, though quite how he was going to look after a young widow in London he had no idea.

The sound of feet pounding up the lane heralded the very welcome appearance of Dick Tarlton, closely followed by the Dutton brothers and Robert Wilson.

'Towne told us what happened, and he's gone with Laneham to find a physician,' Tarlton said breathlessly as he knelt and peered into Knell's ashen and now unconscious face. 'Will he last, do you think?'

Will shook his head wordlessly. 'He might live if the doctor gets here soon, but I fear the cut has severed something vital in his neck. Someone should go and find the constable.'

Tarlton nodded and barked an instruction to Lawrence Dutton to go in search of the local authorities. The others, Tarlton, John Dutton and Will, could do little except crouch in uneasy silence beside the unconscious Knell and wait for the doctor to arrive. The wounded actor's breath now was coming in ragged gasps, and his face was as white as if it had been painted for the stage, and Will, holding the blood-soaked kerchief in place, could almost feel the life-force ebbing away.

That impression was confirmed when the physician, a fussy little bespectacled man, took one look and shook his head. 'There is little we can do except try to make him comfortable.'

So they lifted the limp body and carried it back to the White Hound, where the shocked innkeeper gave them the use of a small parlour on the ground floor where they laid the injured man on a table, pillows propped behind his head and several blankets laid over his lower body. The doctor had tied thick bandages around his neck, and though they had helped to stop the bleeding, it was obvious that Knell was fading quickly into oblivion. Sure enough, an hour later, William Knell, one of the most perfect actors on the London stage, was dead.

Chapter 5

Exhausted and mud-spattered, Will urged his equally tired horse into a canter across the fourteen arches of Clopton Bridge and into the familiar streets of Stratford-upon-Avon. It was close to dusk, and the citizenry was out and about enjoying the long evening light, forcing him to slow to a walk as he made his way up Henley Street to his family's house, a fine two-storey gable-roofed building little different from its neighbours save for the sign hanging from a projecting pole at its eastern end advertising the services of John Shakespeare, maker of fine gloves for gentlemen and ladies. The window below the sign was closed and shuttered, but during the day it would be open so that customers could come and converse with Will's father in his workshop, place their orders and collect their goods, or just stop by for a gossip.

Dismounting and tethering his horse to the hitching rail outside the front door of the house, he ignored the curious stares of the neighbours and pushed open the door, following the sound of voices through to the building's central hall. There he stood unnoticed for a few moments, a mute observer of a cosy family scene. A long trestle table was set before the fireplace, laden with the half-consumed remains of the evening's supper—loaves of bread, cheese, apples, a pot of honey, a chicken stripped of most of its meat, and several jugs of ale. At the table's head, his father sat in his big chair, a cushion at his back, while the rest of the family were ranged along benches on either side, all engaged in loud and argumentative chatter.

It was his mother who noticed him first, as she rose from her stool and turned to look for something on the sideboard. With an uncharacteristically flustered squeal, she shouted his name and grasped him in a warm embrace, then held him at arm's length, regarding him critically. 'You look exhausted. And you've lost weight. Is anything wrong?'

How like my mother, Will thought, *always anticipating the worst*. He reassured her with a grin. 'No, Mother, all is well, I have just had a hard ride from Banbury, that's all.'

The rest of the family crowded excitedly around him. His brother Gilbert pumped his hand with unfeigned delight, a broad smile on a face that was almost a mirror of Will's own. Apprenticed to a local haberdasher three years ago, he had grown into a broad-shouldered and amiable young man. Next to demand his attention was Richard, at thirteen, excited and voluble. Only when the two males had exercised their rights did his shy but lissom and startlingly pretty sister Joan press her claim with a soft kiss on the cheek. Meanwhile, seven-year-old Edmund clung shyly to his mother's skirts, appearing somewhat overawed by this apparition from far-off London.

Throughout, John Shakespeare watched with a fond smile on his rosy-cheeked face. Will, released from his siblings' embrace, turned to make a more formal greeting. He sensed something weary about his father, as if the flash and fire that had always driven him had been reduced steadily to embers. Yet the welcoming grin was the same as it had always been, gap-toothed and jolly, communicating an invitation to mischief. They embraced briefly, and his father held him at arm's length for a moment, inspecting him. 'Don't listen to your mother. I swear you look broader and stronger every time I see you. It must agree with you, this theatrical life.'

Releasing his son, he fished around in his doublet pocket, from which he extracted a small clay pipe and a small packet of tobacco leaves that he proceeded to stuff into the bowl.

'Must you, John? It will stink the house out,' Will's mother said.

'A house in which I am still master, Mary, despite your attempts at usurpation.'

That earned him a weary sigh. This was clearly a battle often fought and she always lost. The pipe was duly lit from a spill caught from the fire, and after a little preliminary coughing, his father settled back in his chair and regarded his son. 'It's always a joy to see you son, but I must say it is a little unexpected. We had thought you still in London. What brings you home so suddenly?'

'That is a long tale, Father, that I will be happy to relate, but first, where is Anne? And the children?' He felt a tiny pang of anxiety at their obvious absence from the family's supper.

'They're next door. Little Hamnet has a fever,' his mother said, then went hastily on when she saw the expression on Will's face. 'Do not worry, it is nothing serious. Anne just thought it better to eat apart from the rest of us until he is better.'

'Go and see her, Will,' his father said. 'I am sure we can all wait to hear your news.'

Will gave them all a grateful smile and made his way to the other end of the house and through the connecting door that led to the two-roomed cottage next door where his wife and three children lived. There, he found Anne feeding their son barley soup from a bowl which she almost dropped with surprise at the sight of her husband. 'William Shakespeare! Don't you ever affright me like that again, I'm like to scald both myself and the boy.'

Sheepishly, Will threw his hands in the air. 'I am sorry. There was no time to send ahead to tell you I was coming, and I expected to see you next door with the rest of the family. How fares the lad?'

'Oh, he will do well enough. It is nothing, a small fever from which he is already half-mended. Susanna and Judith are upstairs asleep. Go and look in on them while I get Hamnet settled, and then we can talk.'

With a meekness that might have surprised his friends in London, he did as he was told without demur and climbed the stairs to look at the sleeping faces of his two daughters, the one his first-born and the other twin to the sick boy down below. They had been tossing about in their sleep and the bedclothes were disordered. Doing his best not to waken them, he rearranged the blankets and went back downstairs.

'So why *are* you here?' Anne echoed his father's question. That was sharp, as if she was a little annoyed that he had appeared from nowhere to disturb her settled, domestic life.

'Can we leave Hamnet for a half hour or so? I may as well tell the story once to everyone.'

They left the child sleeping in his cot next to the fire and returned next door to the main part of the house. By then Joan and the younger children had been sent off upstairs to bed, and only Gilbert remained downstairs with his parents.

Gratefully accepting a tankard of ale, Will settled down to relate the story of the tragic events in Thame.

'But you are going on with your tour, you say?' his father said. 'I know nothing of the theatre, but it seems to me that losing an actor might make things difficult.'

'Not one, but two, since John Towne is now in custody until the coroner should return his verdict. Yes, it does make it very hard to stage some of our plays, but it is not impossible.'

In fact, the company had debated for hours whether they should abandon the tour entirely, but Dick Tarlton had been adamant that they should go on. 'Will can take on a full acting load,' he had said, ignoring Shakespeare's surprised look at this pronouncement, 'and he can edit the playscripts a little so that we can double roles. It will require hard work and a lot of improvisation, but we can do it. Are we not the Queen's Men? The finest acting troupe in the country?'

And so, after a brief pause to arrange a hasty burial for their late colleague, they had left a surprisingly unperturbed John Towne in the hands of the local constables and made their way to Banbury, where, after two hectic days of performing, he had prevailed upon Tarlton to allow him to make this fast visit to his home to spend a day or two with his family, promising to re-join the company at its next stop in Leicester in three days' time. In the circumstances, it was a lot to ask, but Tarlton in the end saw that he had little choice but to agree if he was to keep Will's services.

'Anyway,' he told his family, 'though it will be very hard work, it is a great opportunity for me to prove myself as an actor. They have only given me small roles before now, but with the company two actors short there will be little choice but to give me the greater parts to play.'

'That is all very well, husband, but are they paying you any more money?' Anne said, eyebrows arched in a query that would brook no evasion.

Fortunately, he had an answer that would satisfy her. 'Dick has promised me a sharer's portion of the takings for the rest of the tour, which is generous of him. And he says that if I prove myself, in time, there is no reason why I should not be allowed to buy a sharer's part in the company.'

'That is something at least.' His wife's approval was grudging. She had always been dubious about his theatrical ambitions but had long ago realised she would never prise him away from the path he had been determined to pursue ever since his return from Italy.

66

'Was he a good man, this actor who died?' his mother asked.

'Billy? Aye, I think he was. He was generous to me at least, looked after the younger members of the company, and took his craft seriously. The others always called him their perfect actor, and he was like a brother to Dick Tarlton.' Will refrained from saying that he had a fierce temper, could be very touchy and did not suffer fools gladly. Let the man's weaknesses be buried with his body and let his reputation, the only thing that would live after him, be burnished with praise.

'Then I will say a prayer for his soul on Sunday,' his pious mother said. 'And for his wife and children.'

'He had no children, just a young wife in London,' Will said automatically, frowning as he recalled that injunction the dying man had laid on him to look after Rebecca. He had mentioned it to no one, not even Tarlton, and had no idea how he might ever discharge the obligation, if obligation it really was.

'London! What is it like there, Will? I so long to see it!' The wistful look on Gilbert's face made Will smile, taking him back two years to when he had been the same age as his brother was now. So must he have looked—restless and impatient with the confines of Stratford, curious about the wider world.

'I am sure Will can tell you all about London on the morrow, Gil,' his father said firmly, forestalling his elder son. 'But your brother has had a long day and a hard ride, and he deserves a good night's sleep.'

The look of disappointment on Gilbert's face made him feel guilty, but in truth, he was grateful for his father's intervention. 'Tomorrow, Gil, I promise,' he said, throwing an arm across his brother's shoulders. 'But father has the right of it—I need my bed.'

'Poor Gilbert,' Anne said when they were back next door in the cottage. 'He worships you, you know, and desperately wants to come down to London. But Father is determined he should stay here and stick to his trade.'

'Selling buttons and ribbons? I am hardly surprised he wants to escape that.'

'You would rather he followed in your footsteps, Mister Shakespeare? Wandering the globe looking for adventure? Nay, your father is right; one vagrant in the family is enough.'

'I am hardly a vagrant,' Will protested, laughing. 'I am a principal actor in the Queen's own company. Just think, I might be performing before Her Majesty when we get back to London.'

'And I am sure she will be as excited by that prospect as you are.' Anne's sarcasm just made Will laugh harder, recognising that his pomposity deserved to be punctured.

'Come, lass, let's to bed. I want to see if I can remember how to make love without waking small children.'

'I thought you were tired.'

'Oh, I am sure the fire can be stoked easily enough with a little encouragement. I'm not an old man yet...'

Later, drowsily happy after a bout of delirious if hushed love-making, his thoughts for some reason turned to Rebecca Knell and, feeling the need to unburden himself, he whispered to Anne the promise that her husband had extracted from him as he lay dying.

'But what, really, did he ask of you?' As usual, Anne went to the heart of the question. 'Not much more, surely, than to keep an eye out for her wellbeing. Though how you can do that if you are travelling halfway across England before you get back to London, I know not. Did he have any money, this actor?'

The question took him by surprise. 'He owns a share of the company, of course, though whether that can be turned into ready cash I don't know. And he was our most successful player and a prudent man, so I expect he saved some money.'

'And his wife will be his sole inheritor, will she not? She may well be a wealthy young woman once probate has been granted.'

'Aye, you're right enough,' Will said, blowing out the candle and wrapping his arms around his wife's body. 'But I will go and see her when we are back in London, for the sake of my conscience.'

'A pretty girl, is she?'

'I know not, never having met her.' Will knew his wife well enough to know where this innocent question was going. 'But you need not worry about my virtue, my girl. There is but one woman in my life.'

Anne sniffed. 'Men can resist anything except temptation when it comes to women.'

'Sadly true,' Will said ruefully, and put an end to any further speculation, covering her mouth in a kiss.

***

Will spent the following day enjoying the pleasures of domestic life: talking nonsense to the twins, Hamnet having recovered sufficiently from whatever had ailed him to burble happily on his father's knee; encouraging a shy Susanna to tell her father a little about her daily doings; exchanging gossip with the neighbours and friends who, having heard that the prodigal son had returned, decided that they must drop by John Shakespeare's house; and gorging himself on his mother's excellent cookery.

After dinner, he and Anne retired early to the privacy of the little cottage next door, where they talked over a glass of sweet wine and one of his mother's blackberry tarts.

'Your father is spending again,' Anne said, with no other preamble, after they had settled themselves into their chairs. She did not need to elaborate—Will knew that his father had an alarming tendency to extravagance, something his mother had never been able to curb. It had led to all sorts of troubles in the past as he had tried to make ends meet by engaging in various forms of financial shenanigans, not all of them on the right side of the law.

'I did notice the new chairs and the wall-hangings upstairs. But he says that business has been good…'

'He is being somewhat less than honest.' Anne was purse-lipped tart. 'The workshop has been busy, yes, but not so busy as to pay for his extravagances. It's not just the new furniture—he is spending money entertaining the town's councillors and the mayor, in hopes of returning to the council. And he is trading in wool again.'

That made Will sit up straight. Why his father had ceased attending council meetings was something of a mystery, but it had led to him losing his place the year before. No doubt he was anxious to win his way back into favour by spending up large, but this was a risky way of financing it since wool trading in England was closely regulated and you needed a license to buy and sell. That didn't stop tradesmen like his father from chancing their arm, for there was a lot of profit to be made, but it carried a heavy fine—or worse—if he got caught.

'Should I talk to him?' Even as he asked, Will realised how futile such a conversation would be, for his father, though he had an outwardly amiable disposition, was both proud and stubborn, and would not brook questioning from his son on the subject of his finances.

'Of course not,' Anne said, confirming his thoughts. 'You know what he is like. But I thought you should know. I fear that he will come on hard times again when the bills come due. And you know how dependant we are on him. We live in this house, the children and I, at his favour, and your income, such as it is, won't pay for another roof to go over our heads should he be forced to evict us.'

The challenge in her words was obvious. She had always been dubious about his career in London and did not believe that as an actor he could ever earn enough to ensure his family's financial security.

'Let us hope that it never comes to that,' Will said, summoning as much conviction as he could. 'Anne, I swear to you that I will never see you and the children out on the street, no matter what happens. I know you think my life as an actor is not real, not a sensible way to make my way in the world, but I have seen what success looks like in London. You pointed out yourself that Rebecca Knell will be a wealthy woman on her inheritance from poor Billy; he made himself wealthy just from the proceeds of acting! And I can do so much more than that.'

'You said something of the kind before you went off to Italy, Will Shakespeare. We cannot live on promises alone.'

He sighed. This was an argument he could only win by delivering results. 'You are right.' He threw his hands in the air in surrender and gave her his most winning smile. 'All I can say is that you must trust me when I say that one day I will buy a great house here in Stratford and install you as its lady, and you will be proud to be known as Mistress Shakespeare.'

Something in his earnestness must have broken through, for she just looked at him for a moment and then gave a great, musical laugh. 'I swear, Will, you could charm the very birds out of the trees.'

***

Early the next morning, he slung his saddlebag over the rump of his horse, now recovered after a day's pampering in his father's stable, bade farewell to his family and trotted down the street in the direction of the road to Leicester. The

71

warm and sunny weather of the last few weeks had given way to a damp drizzle that soaked through every gap in his clothing, and by the time he rode beneath the arch of Leicester's south gate in the gathering gloom of the evening, he was tired and uncomfortably wet.

It was not hard to find the inn where the company was being housed. The Blue Boar was a large and imposing establishment that faced onto the High Street in the middle of the town, famous as the place where King Richard III last laid his head to sleep the night before he met his end at the battle of Bosworth, a century ago.

Dropping gratefully from the saddle, he was cheered by the familiar sound of Dick Tarlton's booming voice. 'Now here is a sight for sore eyes! Come in out of the damp, Will; you look like death.'

'Aye, and I feel half-dead too. My backside is not made for sitting on the rump of a horse for days at a time, I fear.'

Leaving his mount in the capable hands of the stable lads, he followed Tarlton into the inn's main hall where the rest of the company was sitting down to supper. After a backslapping welcome and a slice of beef pie to quell the hunger pains from the road, the company's chief beckoned Will aside to a small alcove in the corner of the hall where he poured them each a tankard of beer from a huge earthenware jug.

'I am sure you are in great need of sleep, Will, but I fear I must ask you for one service ere you seek your bed.'

'Let me guess, you need the play rewritten before the morrow.' Will was unsurprised by Tarlton's nod; he had been thinking about exactly that subject to while away the time on his journey north. 'I assume we are still going to perform *The True Tragedy*?'

'What else, in King Richard's last resting place?' Tarlton grinned. The play in question, *The True Tragedy of King Richard III*, was one of the company's history staples, performed regularly both in London and on tours like this one, and it dealt with the grim crimes of the last Lancastrian king, who had died just a few miles from Leicester at Bosworth. 'You know the problem. The play has, what, thirty characters? Difficult enough to stage with ten players, and we are now down to eight.'

'Where are we to perform? And when?'

'In the Guildhall. Have you been to Leicester before?' When Will shook his head, Tarlton went on, 'It is a fine space with a good gallery across one end from which we can hang the backcloth. Your usual stage directions should work without difficulty. We are to begin the performance at two of the clock.'

Which meant that he would have to complete the re-writes and copy out the changes to the players' parts in good time for them to rehearse first thing in the morning. 'I had better get started then.' He hauled himself to his feet. 'Who has drawn the short straw to share a room with me tonight?'

'No one. You have a room to yourself, and Luke has already taken paper and ink upstairs.'

The luxury of having a whole room to himself would be some reward at least for what promised to be a long evening. Yet, despite his physical tiredness, his mind seemed exceptionally agile when he sat down at the table and, by the uncertain light of a couple of rush candles, got to work.

The play was a straightforward telling of the story of King Richard III, who had usurped the throne after the death of his brother King Edward, conspiring to murder the latter's two sons and then proclaiming himself king, only to be himself killed in battle by Queen Elizabeth's grandfather, Henry, Earl of Richmond, the first Tudor monarch. Around this tree trunk was wrapped the sinuous vines of the author's prose, to which Will had now to apply his pruning shears.

Fortunately, having half-anticipated some such request from Tarlton, he had given the matter some thought as he'd bumped and jogged his way northward. Before long, he was deep into the task, working swiftly to excise unnecessary lines and rearrange scenes so that their diminished band of players could appear on stage in two or even three roles with adequate time for costume changes and the like.

As he worked, he wondered who the play's original author might be. There was no indication of its provenance anywhere in the manuscript propped on the table before him, and Dick Tarlton had been vague on the question. Whoever the author, Will suspected that the present Earl of Oxford must at the very least be the writer's patron, judging from the surprising number of lines that he had assigned to the earl's ancestor.

It was sometime after midnight before he was satisfied that he had a workable version of the play. He still needed to copy out the changes into the players' individual parts, but that could be done in the morning. His last wry thought as he fell asleep to the sound of rain drumming on the roof just above his head was that at least he would not have to suffer John Towne's carping criticism of his efforts.

The next morning he woke to find the rain had cleared. Descending to the innyard, he found Tarlton sitting on a bench, yawning and scratching his crotch, a tankard of ale before him. Squinting in the bright sunlight, he greeted Will with a cheery wave, shuffled over to make space on the bench, and hailed the serving girl who had been about to disappear inside. 'Bessie my lass, ale for our master fixer-of-plays here!' Smiling at the girl's mock-curtsey, he turned back to Will. 'So, what do you have for us, my young friend?'

Wordlessly, Will handed over the sheaf of pages and waited while Tarlton scanned them, all the while issuing a stream of muttered comments. 'I see you have got rid of Mistress Shore. Just as well; I never liked that bitch. "My kingdom for a horse!" I like that, much better that the original line. I always thought it was a bit limp. Yes, that works—the Dutton brothers can switch with each other there, very neat.' He looked up. 'But you seem to have written out most of the Earl of Oxford's lines. Can I ask why?'

The question took Will by surprise. 'No real reason. It's just that the playwright seems to give the earl an outsized place in the plot for what is in every other way a minor character.'

A sardonic smile creased Tarlton's homely features. 'It's just as well the earl—the present one, not the man in the play—will never see what you've done to his play.'

'*His* play? The Earl of Oxford wrote this?' Will could not have been more astonished if Tarlton had told him it had been written by an ape. Earls might dabble in poetry, but they didn't write plays.

'Aye, but don't tell anyone. My lord the earl doesn't want the world to know he ever did such a lowly thing as to write for the stage. He did it as a kind of juvenile exercise, many years ago, in one of his attempts to flatter the Queen when he was in need of her patronage. That's why it has all that nonsense at the end, rehearsing Her Majesty's lineage and making sure the audience knows how well off we are with her on the throne. I hope you have left all that in, by the way.'

Will nodded, though he had been tempted to cut it since it seemed to be a rather pompous way to end a play. Tarlton, he remembered, had been a member of the Earl of Oxford's troupe, and had abandoned it when Walsingham plundered the earl's players (and those of the earl of Leicester) to form the Queen's Men. He must have brought the play with him. 'Does the earl know that we still perform it?'

'He does, though he does not come to the theatre.' Tarlton smiled. 'My lord of Oxford is of a somewhat extravagant nature, and not wise in either love or money. The Queen herself had to give him an annuity a couple of years ago just to keep his estate afloat. So when he is not at court, he spends most of his time at his house in Aldgate, amusing himself by scribbling poetry and penning the odd play.'

'So I don't need to put him back into this performance?'

Will was relieved when Tarlton shook his head. 'No, we are safe enough. It will never be seen in London in this form.'

'Still, it seems a pity to waste a night's work. Maybe I will write it anew one day as a completely new play.'

'You do that, Will, you do that.' Tarlton gave him a sharp look, almost as if seeing him for the first time. 'And here's a prophecy—it will be a great play and will put your name on everyone's lips. Which will be a true miracle, since no audience in London gives a fig who wrote the plays we perform.'

Tarlton gave him a cheerful dig in the ribs, chuckling at his own wit, and got to his feet. 'Now, where are those slug-a-beds? It's time to rehearse. Let's get to it!'

Chapter 6

The noise from the crowd in Leicester's Guildhall was deafening, a rolling surf of applause and laughter that hit the players standing on the makeshift stage with a physical force. Will, standing for the first time in his theatrical career in the middle of the line as one of the principal players, was still perspiring with the exertions of performing his several roles—including, ironically, what was left of the part for the Earl of Oxford—as he took his bows.

This particular play was popular among the people of a town so closely associated with the hunchbacked king, but it was gratifying that they seemed to approve of his somewhat cut-down and modified version of it. Still, it all felt like a dream, sweaty and real, yet at the same time, liable at any moment to dissolve into mist.

Once offstage and cleaned of face-paint, the players endured the fulsome compliments of the local mayor, delivered in a pompous speech that seemed to go on forever, before finally being released for a well-deserved supper at the Blue Boar Inn. Over beer and a good wine, the latter an extravagance provided by Tarlton at his own expense, they dissected the afternoon's efforts in their usual manner, at once both self-critical and effusively complimentary, often in the same sentence. But there was one subject upon which everyone agreed—Will had worked a minor miracle in preparing the play so that they could perform it in their short-handed state.

Though he tried to remain modest in the face of their back-slapping approval, he knew his face wore a grin that stretched from one ear to the other, and he could not restrain a soaring sense of pride. Here at last was proof that he, William Shakespeare, son of a regional tradesman, could write and act with the best. For the first time since he had returned from Italy and taken up this new career, he felt confident that he could succeed in it.

'I have some good news for you all,' Tarlton announced, once the company had finally calmed down and settled into the serious task of eating and drinking. 'By the time we get to Cambridge, we will have an extra player. Toby Mills has sent to say that he is riding post from London to meet us there.'

Tankards thudded on the table in approval, for Mills was a popular and likeable member of the company.

'So we will only be one down,' John Laneham said, 'at least until we know John Towne's fate. Have you heard anything more of him, Dick?'

'As far as I know he is still in gaol, awaiting the coroner's verdict. But I doubt he will be joining us before we get back to London, if then.'

'What, you don't think they will hang him, do you?' Lawrence Dutton sounded shocked, as though the thought had only just occurred to him. 'I mean, it was self-defence, wasn't it?'

'So John says.' Tarlton's tone was curiously impartial. 'Will here was the only witness and his deposition agrees, does it not?'

Will nodded, a little uncomfortably. By rights, he too should have been detained in Thame, awaiting the arrival of the coroner, but Tarlton had prevailed upon the constable to accept instead written testimony to be provided to the hearing in due course. In that testimony, Will had described exactly what he'd seen that afternoon.

But what he had not described—could not describe—was the look in Towne's eyes as he'd struck the fatal blow, neither could he give voice to the nagging suspicion that Towne had deliberately provoked the whole episode. He was, after all, an expert swordsman and should have been easily able to ward off Knell's clumsy and rage-fuelled attack without fatal consequences. Yet Will could not discern a motive for such a premeditated act, other than jealousy over Knell's marriage to the girl he evidently loved. Would that motivate a man to murder? In some men, perhaps, but it seemed unlikely in a man as cold as John Towne. It was a puzzle that made him uneasy.

As Tarlton moved the conversation on to other subjects, Will wondered whether the comic also harboured reservations. Billy Knell had been his long-time friend and collaborator, and his death had been a shocking blow. Though he was outwardly as ebullient as ever, to Will's eyes, Tarlton seemed diminished in some way, his energy dimmed and his zest for life watered down. And whenever he spoke of the events in Thame, he adopted an uncharacteristically guarded, cautious tone, as though he did not want to reveal what he was really thinking.

Stumbling his bleary way up the stairs to the blessed peace of his private room, Will's head was filled with thoughts about the play they must perform on the morrow, for which he still had to write out the parts he had amended in order to deliver it with just eight players. Tossing his doublet onto the bed, he opened the windows to let in some air and the last of the evening light. It would be some time before it was fully dark, so at least he would only need one candle by which to work. Turning away, he smiled as the sound of his erstwhile companions breaking into a bawdy drinking song drifted up from the street below.

It was only then that he noticed the small travelling chest that someone had placed on the little table that he used as a desk. It was a plain thing made of some dark wood, about two feet long, a foot wide and about the same high, and unadorned except for the initials 'WK' inlaid into the lid in ivory, and a polished brass lock from which a small key protruded. Whoever had delivered the box had left a folded note next to it which, when he opened it, was in Dick Tarlton's crabbed hand, and addressed to him.

This is Billy's document box, which I have not had the heart to open, since it no doubt contains papers of a personal nature. May I prevail upon you to go through the contents and remove any documents pertaining to the company's affairs and give them to me, and then put the box into a place of safety in one of the carts so that it may be returned to his wife when we return to London.

Frowning, Will stared at the box, a little impatient with his chief. After all, it wasn't as if he didn't have enough to do. He was tempted to put it on the floor and ignore it until the next day, but curiosity got the better of him. Sitting down, he lit a candle and turned the key to open the lock. When he lifted the lid and peered inside, he was relieved to find that it was almost empty, just a dozen or so documents. Hopefully, it wouldn't take long to sort through them.

Several letters were not in Knell's hand and proved upon inspection to be from his wife. These he hastily replaced in the box, having no desire to read them. Then there were copies of the deeds to some properties in London, one or two other legal-looking documents of which he could not make head nor tail, and half a dozen pages of what looked like straightforward notes.

Skimming through the latter, he soon saw that they were quite detailed reports on each of the towns they had passed through on the tour. In short, almost cryptic sentences, Knell repeated the essence of conversations he'd had with merchants and shopkeepers, innkeepers and apothecaries, town officials and local priests. There were reports from Reading and Steventon, towns where they had stayed overnight before their first actual performance stop in Abingdon, and there was a report of the conversation between Knell and Mayor Reade about the unrest in the countryside occasioned by rumours of invasion. Will found himself gaping with some astonishment at the sheer variety and number of people from whom his late colleague had been collecting information.

It was obvious what these notes were: intelligence on the local conditions and the state of mind of the folk living in the countryside and the towns through which they had passed. Had Knell been acting as some kind of informer? There were many such 'watchers', they were generally called, to distinguish them from 'intelligencers' who were entrusted with more complex missions, and they were usually paid a small stipend to report on anything that might be of interest to the government in London. As Will knew from his own brief time working in the centre of Walsingham's spy service in Seething Lane, the government was in constant fear of plots and insurrections.

Tucked beneath this sheaf of papers was another, the sight of which sent a shock of recognition through him, for the bulk of it was written in code—a code that Will instantly recognised as one of those used by Sir Francis Walsingham's band of intelligencers, one of the simple substitution codes such as he had himself used in Italy. Why would Billy Knell have been keeping documents written in code? And one used by the Queen's chief spy, at that?

But the first two paragraphs had been left in plain English.

> *Sir,*
>
> *As instructed, I have taken pains to observe the morale and general condition of the countryside through which Her Majesty's company of players has passed in these last few days, the summary of which is this—the population is fearful of the prospect of England being invaded by a foreign power, and of a return to the persecutions and troubles that her majesty's reign has for so long suppressed.*
>
> *I have enclosed in plain my detailed report on the conversations I have had with sundry merchants and other gentlemen during our progress through the realm so that you may verify for yourself my conclusions.*

After that, the rest of the page was entirely in code. But there was no way that he could translate it without knowing the word that had to be substituted for the first few letters of the alphabet in order to construct a cipher. Walsingham's chief codebreaker, Thomas Phelippes, had used a dozen such keywords routinely, and perhaps he could try one of those, though they were changed regularly and it was now almost two years since Will had worked at Seething Lane and most likely they were obsolete.

Well, he had no time to do anything about it for now. Putting everything back, he locked the box and slipped the key into his pocket. When they left tomorrow, he would find a place to keep it safe somewhere in their cart, and he would tell Tarlton that there was nothing in the casket that was of any importance to the company, which was, strictly speaking, nothing less than the truth. Perhaps when they got to Cambridge and Toby Mills had joined them, he would find some time to decipher the mysterious paper and decide what he was going to do with the rest of the documents. Take them to Seething Lane, he supposed, though he had no enthusiasm for that course of action, for he had no desire to find himself once again in the clutches of Sir Francis Walsingham and Thomas Phelippes. He had served his country well in Italy and he considered his duty to the government discharged.

They had two more days in Leicester, days that were hectically busy for the whole company, rehearsing in the morning and performing as usual in the afternoon. Having safely stowed Knell's strongbox in one of the lockers that lined each side of their cart, usually used for storing the more valuable or delicate of their stage props, and having reported to Tarlton that the box contained nothing of interest to anyone other than Knell's wife, Will tried to forget about it entirely, an endeavour in which he was only partially successful—the thought of the box and its contents seemed determined to stay with him, aching like a bad tooth.

Then at last their long run was over, and in the half-light of a misty dawn, they made their way through the city gates to follow the road beyond through the forested countryside towards their next destination, the university town of Cambridge.

***

The sight of Christopher Marlowe's sardonically grinning face in the crowd just below the stage in the Cambridge Guildhall startled Will into gaping silence just as he was to deliver his opening lines in *King John*, in which he had been entrusted for the first time with the principal role of the king himself.

'A king, I say, that may in rule and virtue both, succeed his brother in his empire!' Ned Bentley repeated the last line of Queen Eleanor's opening speech, a look of panic in his eyes at his colleague's unexpected silence.

Shaking his head, Will gathered his wits. 'Forgive me, gracious mother,' he extemporised, 'my wits are led astray by grief at the death of my royal brother and by the contemplation of my state. Though far unworthy of so high a place, as is the throne of mighty England's king, yet will I sustain the heavy yoke of pressing cares that hang upon a crown...'

The look of relief on the face of poor Ned as he recognised the familiar text almost made Will laugh out loud, which would have been entirely out of character for the grim and harassed King John, and he would no doubt have earned a stern reproof from Dick Tarlton and the other members of the company. Fortunately, he was able to restrain himself, and the rest of the play unfolded as smoothly as the gently flowing waters of the river Cam, though throughout he was aware of the presence of his old friend down there among the crowd. At the end, when the actors had performed their customary dance and Tarlton had told his last joke, he caught Marlowe's eye and raised his eyebrows in a silent query. The response was a swift jerk of the head in the direction of the entrance to the Guildhall, which Will took as an invitation to meet outside.

As the hall emptied, the actors gathered behind the tiring-room curtains and thumped Will's back in approval for this, his first leading role. It felt more than a little churlish to beg off from the usual post-performance celebration back at their lodgings, but they all took it in good part and went off in high spirits, singing a bawdy song that would have brought blushes to a courtesan's cheeks. A few moments later he was outside, peering anxiously up and down the busy street, afraid that he might have misunderstood Marlowe's cryptic signal.

He needn't have worried. There, lounging beneath one of the wooden arches of the town's market arcade, Marlowe stood in his usual sartorial splendour, bright yellow doublet, extravagantly slashed breeches, white silken hose and fine leather shoes, each sporting a brass buckle. Sweeping off his feathered hat in a grinning gesture of welcome, he crossed the busy street and claimed Will in an embrace that was surprising in its strength, coming as it did from a slight though well-muscled frame.

'You cannot imagine what a shock it was to see you in the crowd!' Will laughed. 'I nearly dried up completely.'

'But you recovered soon enough. That's what I like about you, Will, nothing much upsets that composure of yours. Come on, let's go and find somewhere to drink where they won't gossip about us.'

'Gossip about us? Surely not. I am just a travelling player and you are, what, a student? Though no one would guess that from your clothes.'

'A student no more. They have awarded me my master's degree, though that fool Robert Norgate tried to stop it. As for gossip, in a town full of chatterers, it never ceases, and I have annoyed enough people here to become a target for their malicious tongues.'

Having delivered himself of this speech, Marlowe jammed his hat back on his head and took Will firmly by the arm. They wove their way through the market and into the tangle of streets beyond, where they turned right, then left, and then right again down a small lane to a little tavern, just a single room with a few tables and benches scattered about and a kitchen at the rear from whose door the welcoming smell of roasting meats emerged. Marlowe was obviously well known to the owner, a tall and cadaverous man wearing a grimy apron around his waist and a greasy woollen cap on his head, and in moments they were comfortably settled in a corner of the deserted room, tankards of ale in front of them.

Marlowe had hardly changed since the last time Will had laid eyes on him, almost nine months ago, at Sir Francis Walsingham's house in London. The unruly mass of brown hair, the seductive hazel eyes that invited you to join their owner in mischief and laughter, and the small, pouting mouth with its wisp of a moustache, all these were the same, and the flamboyance of his dress had always been his way of showing his disdain for the rules of ordinary society. Will allowed himself an inner smile at the thought of the battles his friend must have had against the university's strictures enforcing the drab black dress code for its students.

Yet something about him suggested to Will that his friend was more than usually care-worn. Two small furrows between his eyes told a tale of too-frequent frowning concentration, and there was a wariness behind the impish demeanour, expressed in occasional furtive glances left and right that hinted at some unknown fears.

'So who is Robert Norgate?' he asked, more to break the small silence that had grown between them than because of any real interest in the subject.

'The master of Corpus Christie College, where I have been enrolled these last years.' Marlowe was sour. 'An upright, priggish, learned man who is also an utter fool. He never liked me, told me to my face that he was going to deny my degree on the grounds that I had been too often absent from the college.'

'And you could hardly tell him that you were absent on the Queen's business.' Having himself had to dissemble in the face of similarly inconvenient questions, Will sympathised with his friend's dilemma.

'Of course not! And to make matters worse, Norgate had heard from God knows where that I intended to go overseas again, which seemed to enrage him even more.'

'Are you? Planning to go away again?'

'Not at all.' Marlowe leaned across the table to speak more confidentially, even though they were entirely alone, even the tavern-keeper having found something to occupy him in the kitchen. 'You may not know this, but there has been a steady trickle of Cambridge scholars who have left the country to go and join the papists at their college in Rheims. In the last year, the trickle has become a flood; more than a dozen have left.'

Will nodded, encouraging Marlowe to continue, intrigued as to where the conversation was going.

'Anyway, Tom Walsingham sent me a letter, asking me to keep an eye on my fellow students at Corpus and report on any who seemed likely to bolt across the Channel. That was not, I can tell you, a welcome request. Spying on known Catholics is one thing; spying on my fellow students is another.'

The flash of misery that showed on Marlowe's face was eloquent. Will remembered Thomas Walsingham, the young, dashing cousin of Sir Francis, with whom Marlowe had always seemed to have a special bond. No doubt refusal of his demand was a thing impossible for Marlowe to contemplate.

'So I went about the college, as discreetly as I could, trying to plumb the minds of those who might be suspect. Somehow, I don't know how, a rumour started that I was intending to bolt myself, and that rumour got to Norgate's ears. You can imagine how much trouble that could cause.'

Will could indeed imagine it. Marlowe would be placed under a cloud from which he could never escape. Except, of course, that he had.

'What did you do?' he asked, knowing that his friend would enjoy telling this part of the tale.

'I wrote to Tom and asked him to deal with it since I was in this trouble on his behalf. So he prevailed on Sir Francis to ask the Privy Council to send a letter to Norgate stating that I had no such intent and directing him to award my degree without any further delay. From the look on his face when he told me, I think the master must have choked on that letter when he first read it.'

Ale slopped onto the table as they clashed their tankards together in laughing celebration of this confounding of petty authority.

'And now you have your degree? What is next for Master Christopher Marlowe? I imagine the clergy is out of the question.' Shakespeare was being playful, for he well knew Marlowe's views on all matters religious, which were, to say the least, dangerous. After all, it had been barely thirty years since men and women had been sent to the stake to be burned to death merely for professing their adherence to the new faith, let alone flirting with outright atheism, as Marlowe did.

'Of course it is; yet another reason Norgate hates me. I made it clear from the beginning of my studies that I wasn't going to waste my education droning on about a mythical afterlife in some obscure parish. No, it's London for me. Robert Greene and Tom Watson have both written to say that they have lodgings that we can share, so I am off as soon as may be.'

Will remembered Greene, a big, redheaded, loud man with the demeanour of a ruffian and the tongue of a poet, if a somewhat waspish one. Thomas Watson, on the other hand, he had never met, though he knew him by reputation as the author of a collection of sonnets in the Italian mode that had made him famous in England's literary world.

'What will you do there? Write poetry, I suppose, though that will not pay your creditors nor buy your supper.'

'The world loves poets, but few are prepared to pay them, that is sure.' Marlowe's laugh was merry. 'No Will, I intend to write for the stage. The playhouses are desperate for new plays, and they will pay handsomely for them. Besides, can plays not also be poetical?'

The boldness of those last few words struck Will like a thunderbolt. Most plays, like the one in which he had performed that very day, were written in a kind of plodding prose that was workmanlike enough, but rarely made the heart soar. A writer who could apply the rhythm and metre of poetry to playscripts would be doing something entirely new. Yet could such a notion work? He was sceptical. The educated gentry in the upper rows might well be enchanted, but the ill-educated masses, the groundlings who crowded around the stage avid for action, blood and gore, would they not be bored by such high-flown language?

Unworthy envy chased hard on the heels of those thoughts. Marlowe, with his new-minted master's degree from one of England's great universities, could afford to entertain radical ideas, for he would surely be welcomed with open arms by the theatrical world in London. Whereas Shakespeare, with his grammar school education, would be seen as a mere provincial, an upstart not to be taken seriously.

'And I suppose you have plays ready for them.' Though he said it with a laugh, he could hear a sour note in his voice, though Marlowe seemed not to notice it.

'Some. A little piece about the passion of Aeneas for Queen Dido—all doomed love, betrayal, suicide—and I have one or two other ideas that have not yet made their creeping journey from head to page. And *Tamburlaine*.'

Will frowned, stretching his memory. 'The play about an oriental king? Weren't you working on it before I went away?'

Marlowe sighed. 'My nemesis. It seems to be in a permanent state of being almost finished. That's why I must go to London—the city herself will be my muse and stir my stupefied brain into action.' Tankards rose and fell again. 'But what about you, Will? You are obviously a good actor, and you have found a place in one of the country's great acting companies. Is that the limit of your ambition?'

The question was posed in a friendly enough tone, but there was an implied challenge in the words that stung a little. 'Anybody with a good memory, a modicum of imagination and a willingness to play the fool can be an actor, and I flatter myself that I have all three in sufficient abundance to succeed on the stage. But no, it is not enough. Just to be an actor, I mean. I love it all and I want to master it all—acting, staging, writing. And since I must provide for my wife and children, I intend to profit from the theatre too.' He shook his head slightly, surprised at himself. This grand vision for his future had been swirling around in his head for some time, but his native caution had always counselled against speaking it out loud, lest he be thought vainglorious and overweening.

Marlowe's hoot of laughter startled the little tavern's patron, who glared at them. 'Then let us go forth, bold conquerors of London's stage. All shall fall upon their knees before us, in awe at our genius!' Each of these statements was accompanied by a loud thump on the table as Marlowe's tankard crashed down, slopping ale everywhere. Will giggled in turn, his earlier envy washed away in the tide of his friend's goodwill.

'But seriously, Will, whatever else you do, you *must* write. Remember when we used to sit around drinking with Greene and Dick Burbage and the others? I used to watch you, inhaling their talk as if it were some exotic oriental perfume. And then there is all that you learned in Italy—Tasso, Petrarch, the art of writing sonnets—that you must not let go to waste. You have something in you, my friend, something that will one day astound the world.'

'Oh, I doubt the world will be so easily astonished,' Will said wryly, a little disconcerted by this surprising declaration, with its echo of Tarlton's words just a few days before. 'But, in truth, finding the time to write anything of substance is my biggest obstacle, with everything I must do for the company. You wouldn't credit just how much work there is to do before a play gets to the stage.'

'Yet you must have written something? That play based on Plautus that you were working on?'

'*The Comedy of Errors*. Lost on the same plain of perpetual incompleteness as your *Tamburlaine*, I fear, for lack of time. But perhaps I will do something with it when we are back in London. Mayhap Tarlton will consider buying it for the company. Though he is for now somewhat distracted, since Billy Knell's death.'

'I'm sure he will. He is known as a shrewd judge of plays. That was a sad business, in Thame. I only saw him upon the stage but once, and he was perfect. The world of the theatre will be poorer without William Knell in it.'

Will nodded. 'Aye. He was a good man and a good friend. And his end was too untimely.'

'An accident, though, was it not?'

'Of that, I am not so sure.' Perhaps it was time to unburden himself of the suspicions that had been haunting his mind since that appalling day. 'His killer was skilled with the use of the sword, an experienced duellist, while Billy was at best a clumsy swordsman. It ought to have been simple for Towne to avoid bloodshed. And it seemed to me at the time that there was something cold-blooded about the way in which he provoked the argument, as if he knew he would eventually enrage Knell to the point where he would attack him.' He

90

stopped, frowning, and remembered the look in John Towne's eyes when he made that final, fatal thrust—contempt, triumph, but not anger.

'But you have no proof of his intent?' Marlowe's quicksilver personality switched from dreamy poet to alert interrogator. 'Without it, he can at worst be charged with manslaughter, and even then it would be difficult to secure a conviction.'

'True. But there is something else. Billy left behind some papers. Detailed reports on the state of the countryside, and another document that was partly in code. I think he was employed as some kind of intelligencer.'

Now Marlowe's interest was well and truly piqued. 'In code, you say? Did you recognise the code?'

'Yes. It was one of Thomas Phelippes', though I could not decipher it, lacking the key.'

'Ah. So most likely he was employed by Seething Lane. But how does that connect to John Towne?'

'It doesn't directly, though perhaps the coded document will tell us, once it has been translated. But Knell muttered something as he was dying, that Towne was not what he seemed, and that he had proof. Perhaps the proof is in the coded paper. And Dick Tarlton told me that Billy had stoutly resisted Towne's application to buy a share in the company on the grounds that he was not of a suitable character to become a sharer.'

'That would be a first,' Marlowe snorted, 'for a theatre troupe to weigh a man's character against the value of his gold. But still, there was clearly something between them.'

'Well, there is the little matter of Knell's wife. Apparently, Towne was in love with her, but she married Billy instead. At her father's insistence, it seems.'

'What a tangled web! 'Tis a tale worthy of the theatre, don't you think?' Marlowe was now positively jolly. 'Anyway, the key must be in that paper. Do you have it with you?'

Will shook his head. 'No, it is safe back at my lodging.'

Outside, the town's churches began to ring their bells to signal the imminence of Vespers and Marlowe's face creased in irritation. 'I may have graduated, but for the moment I am still required to observe the canonical hours of the college, so I must go. But I am intrigued by your story, my friend. Why don't you bring these papers of yours to my rooms tomorrow morning, and let us see if we can make head or tail of them.'

Watching Marlowe make his confident, swaggering way up the street towards Corpus Christi College, Will felt a sense of relief at having shared his suspicions about the affair at Thame with someone adept at the dark arts of intelligencing. If anyone could sort out this puzzle, it would be Christopher Marlowe.

Chapter 7

It was perhaps an hour after dawn the next morning when Will passed through a gate and into the narrow, muddy lane that ran between the church of St Benedict and the northern front of Corpus Christi College, at that hour crowded with churchgoers on their way home after the dawn service. Picking his way between chattering matrons and knots of loudly argumentative students, he found himself at another arched gateway, the entrance to the college itself.

Confronted by a haughty porter, he asked for directions to Marlowe's rooms, expecting to have to explain calling at such an early hour. But at the mention of Marlowe's name, the porter's face split into a wide grin that was accompanied by a twinkle of amusement in his eyes.

'If you're a friend of Master Kit's, you are most welcome, sir. Let me just mark your name down in the register—Shakespeare, did you say?—and I'll send you to him directly. You will find him in the kitchen, I expect, taking tobacco and getting under the cook's feet.'

The image of Marlowe sprawling on a bench, pipe in hand and exchanging gossip with a red-faced cook seemed so far at odds with the perfectly dressed popinjay he knew that he laughed out loud.

'I know, sir.' The porter grinned back. 'Doesn't seem likely, does it? But he's a rare one, is Master Kit, doesn't look down his nose at the serving folk the way some do, and he's always ready with a joke and a story when you need one to cheer you up. Come on, I'll take you to him.'

Beyond the tunnel-like entrance, the porter conducted him across a central cobbled courtyard, all but deserted at that hour save for one or two black-clad students making their leisurely way across the rectangular space. Streams of smoke ascending from the chimneys suggested that the occupants of the various rooms were up and about, though the windows that faced onto the court were still shut tight, their glass panes glittering in the morning sun like so many diamonds.

On the far side of the quadrangle, a plain unadorned door led to a big kitchen bustling with activity. The morning's meal was being prepared ready for the arrival of students, hungry for their breakfast in the main hall, which was just visible through a door on the far side of the kitchen. The cook, far from being the fat and jolly woman he had imagined, was almost the opposite—a thin and narrow-faced woman whose vigilant blue eyes missed nothing and who rapped out commands to her team of half a dozen serving girls and under-cooks with all the assurance of a general on the field of war.

The appearance of the cook might not have conformed to his expectations, but Kit Marlowe was sprawled across a bench exactly as he had imagined, a happy smile on his face as he exhaled a great stream of smoke and genially waved his pipe in Will's direction.

'Welcome to Mistress Quigley's kingdom, Will,' Marlowe said. 'Mind you don't get under her feet, though. She has a tongue on her that would reduce a duke to silence if he got in the way of the smooth operation of her kitchen.'

The cook, looking up from a platter of fruit she had been inspecting, directed a mocking scowl at Marlowe. 'A proposal that will never be put to the test, since the appearance of a duke or even an earl in my kitchen is almost as likely as a scholar refusing a second helping of pudding. Which is to say, most unlikely. Now, Master Kit, if you have finished fouling the air with your tobacco smoke, I need that bench and table so that my girls can have a quick bite before the hungry hordes descend on us.'

Marlowe jumped to his feet, swept his hat off his head and made an elegant bow towards the cook as deep as if he were in front of the Queen herself. 'Your very wish is my command, mistress! Come, Will, let's away upstairs to the library, the last place any self-respecting scholar is likely to be seen at this hour.'

The library, when they reached it by way of a spiral stair cut into the wall, was indeed deserted. It was a fine, high-ceilinged room lined with bookshelves on three sides. On the fourth, there was a range of tall windows through which the morning's light illuminated a jumble of tables and chairs strewn with books and papers. With a proprietorial air, Marlowe shepherded Will to a small table placed just under one of the windows, from where they had a view across the quadrangle. The surface of the table was empty save for a few sheets of blank paper and a pen-stand, from which half a dozen quills fanned out like the tail of a peacock.

'You seem to be popular with the serving-folk, Kit,' Will said as they settled into their chairs.

Marlowe laughed. 'They like me because they know I am one of them at heart. My father is but a shoemaker, after all, something I don't ever forget. Besides, I find their talk restful after listening to the bombast and cant hurled about the halls of the college by the privileged sons of deacons and bishops who inhabit this place. Now, where is this bloody paper you are so exercised about?'

Not for the first time, Will found himself bemused by the unpredictable changes in his friend's manner, from modest everyman to withering critic to practical intelligencer, all in the space of a few sentences. Tipping the contents of his leather satchel onto the table, he waited while Marlowe quickly read the various reports, his lips moving silently as he made out the words.

'This is straightforward enough,' he eventually said when he had turned over the last page of the un-coded portion of the report. 'Quite clearly, your Master Knell was engaged by someone to report on the morale of the people in the country through which the Queen's players were to pass. Now, let's have a look at your coded letter.'

Will passed it across to him. 'As you can see, part of it is in plain and part is in Phelippes' common code, but is indecipherable without the key. I've tried every word that I remember him using, but none of them produce any sense.'

'Not surprising; they are changed every few months. Let me try with the last keyword that I used.'

For the next ten minutes, Marlowe worked in near-silence, first scribbling out the substitution code itself, and then painstakingly decrypting the letter, report or whatever it was, occasionally muttering under his breath as its meaning slowly became clear.

'Well, you were right—Knell was working for Sir Francis.' Marlowe pushed the decoded version across the table for Shakespeare to read.

> *Sir F, I write in cipher because there is a traitor among my fellow actors, by name of John Towne. I have proof he is a secret Catholic and engaged in conspiracy against HM.*
>
> *My proof is that I heard Towne speaking to a man that he met late at night at a house in Abingdon, presuming himself to be in secret and safe from prying eyes.*
>
> *I knew not this man, a tall fellow with a hawk nose who, by his voice, seemed gentle-born. He spoke with T in a low voice and with some urgency. I could not make it all out, being in a place of concealment, but T was being instructed to find himself a place in the household of Lord Strange, there to await further communication from France. The other man then said that when the country was roused to rebellion and a new king proclaimed in place of Her Majesty, T would have a vital part to play. As they parted, the stranger made the sign of the cross over his head.*

This was the essence of what was said, but I have every
word in my memory and I shall repeat all to you when I
return to London.
I will continue to watch T for the duration of our tour and
report if I learn anything new.
WK.

'Lord Strange?' Will said. The name was familiar, but he could not work out how.

'The earl of Derby's heir. Ferdinando Stanley. Strange—or Strang, as some pronounce it—is an old family title.'

Of course. Only days ago he and his fellow actors had performed *The True Tragedy of King Richard III*, at the end of which Thomas Stanley was rewarded with the earldom of Derby after the battle of Bosworth, upon which field he had ensured that Henry Tudor—Stanley's stepson—would prevail by a last-minute change of allegiance. In doing so, he had risked the life of his son, another Lord Strange, who was being held hostage against the father's loyalty by the king. Presumably, the present Lord Strange was a sprig of that same Stanley family tree.

'So why would this supposed Catholic priest direct Towne to join Lord Strange's household?'

'I don't know. Strange is something of a patron of poets and writers and is fond of the theatre, or so Greene tells me, but that is as much as I know about him.'

Will was sceptical. 'It all seems a little hard to credit. The good Lord knows I don't much like John Towne, but I find it hard to believe that he is a traitor. Difficult and touchy, yes, but I have seen nothing else about him to suggest that he is a sympathiser with those Catholics who would like to see the government thrown into turmoil.'

The look Marlowe gave him was mildly amused. 'He would not be much of a spy if he made such sympathies obvious. But in any case, this is not sufficient evidence to draw a conclusion either way. For that, we would need the detail of what Knell saw and heard, and that died with him.'

'And there is the matter of his rivalry with Towne for the hand of Rebecca Edwards. Billy's motives might have been less than pure.'

'True, though trying to implicate a love rival in a plot like this as a means of getting revenge might be a little far-fetched.'

Will felt they had reached an impasse. 'So what shall we do with all this?'

Marlowe shrugged. 'There isn't much we can do except make sure that Knell's report gets into the hands of Sir Francis and his people in Seething Lane. If you like, I can take them with me when I go down to London.'

'Would you? I would take them myself, but I cannot abandon the tour and we won't be back in London until August at least.' Will made no attempt to hide his relief. Grateful though he was for Sir Francis Walsingham's intervention to get him his position with the Queen's Men, he had no desire to find himself entangled again in intelligence work, however peripherally.

Marlowe nodded, sweeping the various papers together into a neat bundle and slipping them into his doublet. 'Consider it done, my friend. Besides, I am in need of some credit at Seething Lane, since I can no longer be of any use to them as an intelligencer.'

Will's mute query, conveyed by way of raised eyebrows, prompted Marlowe to explain. 'In their determination to ensure that the master of the college awarded my degree, their lordships of the Privy Council were a little over-enthusiastic.

Their exact words were "it is not Her Majesty's pleasure that anyone employed in matters touching the benefit of the country should be defamed by those who are ignorant of all such affairs". A pleasing endorsement, to be sure, but if Norgate and the university's council all know that I have been employed in the Queen's business, it will become common knowledge in no time. Which means my chances of further employment by Sir Francis are now almost negligible. And the money he pays therefor.'

Marlowe's downcast look surprised Will. He had not realised how much his friend depended on the regular income he was paid from Walsingham's London headquarters in Seething Lane. He did not know what to say and was relieved when the door at the opposite end of the library opened to admit a tall, cadaverous man dressed in black from head to foot, who peered across the room through spectacles perched precariously on the end of a long, supercilious nose.

'Master Marlowe. I might have known you would be skulking here instead of attending church. You may have acquired your degree, young man, but that does not entitle you to avoid your obligation to worship as Her Majesty has laid down.'

Marlowe seemed entirely immune to this rebuke, offering the smallest of shrugs and a thin smile in response. 'I thank you, Master Norgate, for reminding me of the rules. I had, I confess, entirely forgotten them in my excitement at meeting an old friend and scholar from across the seas.'

Will stifled a laugh; he could see where this was going to go.

The master looked suspiciously at Marlowe and then at Will. 'Well, Marlowe? Who is this?'

'Allow me to present Signor Crollalanza, a scholar of great renown, lately of the university of Padua.'

Will offered a deep and theatrical bow. '*Bongiorno*, Master Or-gate. I am most honoured to make the acquaintance of such a distinguished *professore* as

99

yourself,' he said in a thick Italian accent. 'Signor Marlowe has been telling me much about your fine college. You must forgive me for keeping him from his, how do you say, ecclesiastical duties?'

'Norgate. My name is Norgate.' The master was testy. 'From Padua, you say? You don't look like an Italian.'

'Oh?' Will tried to look offended. 'And how should an Italian look, signor? Perhaps you suppose that we are all as black as any African? That we have rings in our ears and oil in our hair?'

'Signor Crollalanza has come to deliver messages to me from my friends in London,' Marlowe said, his face a picture of innocence. 'My friends in the government.'

Norgate considered this for a moment, his eyes locked on Marlowe's as if deciding whether or not to believe this lie. Then a small sigh signalled his surrender. 'Very well then, Marlowe, I shall leave you and Mister, er, Crollalanza to it. Just try to remember that until you leave here you are still under the rules of the college.'

He turned on his heel and strode across the room, shutting the door firmly behind him. Marlowe placed a finger on his lips to forestall the inevitable outburst of laughter which, if it penetrated beyond the door into the master's hearing, would give the game away entirely. Gesturing, he led Will towards a different door that led to some stairs and thence out into a grassy field, across which they faced the college chapel, where, unable to contain their mirth any longer, they burst into a fit of giggling.

'Crollalanza, indeed!' Will said, wiping tears from his eyes. 'I hope that Master Norgate never connects William Shakespeare of the Queen's Men with the Italian scholar he just met.'

'Oh, he never goes to the theatre.' Marlowe's hand circled in a dismissive wave. 'And I know for a fact that he possesses not a word of Italian, so even if he saw your name on some playbill, he is not likely to understand that Crollalanza is an Italian version of it.'

'No wonder he hates you. I imagine he cannot wait to be rid of you.'

'The feeling is mutual, I assure you. Anyway, enough of all that. I have packing to do if I am to be on the road to London tomorrow morning.'

'And I have rehearsals to attend. Truly, it was good to see you again, Kit. You have relieved my mind on the subject of Knell's papers—they are far safer with you than trundling halfway across the country with me.'

Marlowe nodded and opened his arms to embrace Will. 'Take care, my friend. I will see you in London.'

***

From Cambridge, the Queen's Men made their way east to Bury St Edmunds, where they put on *Famous Victories* and one of their old warhorses, *Sir Clyomon and Sir Clamydes*, a romance involving the sons of two kings, a dragon and a princess. From there, their wagons trundled across the flat open heathland of Suffolk until they reached the coast at the busy port of Ipswich, where they entertained an earthy audience of tradesmen, noisy apprentices, well-dressed merchants and their dowdy wives with a revenge tragedy called *Locrine*, which Will had frantically revised to suit their reduced circumstances the day before the performance. After a scrambled rehearsal in the morning, it went off well enough, though there were some ragged entrances and exits and one or two stumbles over Will's changes to a play that most of the company knew well in its original form.

Dick Tarlton, recognising from experience the signs of a troupe that was reaching the end of its endurance, decreed that they should have a few days' break before proceeding with the rest of their tour, cancelling the performances that had been planned for the next four days. He smoothed over the irritation this caused with the keeper of the inn where they had been performing with the gift of a few pounds and the promise that they would spend up on food and drink.

The short break achieved its end, and it was a refreshed and rejuvenated company that made its way southwards to their next stop, Colchester. After a few hectic days presenting *Leir*, *King John* and *The Seven Deadly Sins*, they had several more days of travelling to cross the Thames using the ferry at Tilbury, a perilous affair during which they almost lost a precious wagon and all of its contents when the skittish horses decided that they did not trust the bobbing conveyance that was to take them across the water. Eventually, the reluctant animals were coaxed aboard, and they made it to the southern bank without incident.

After that, the Kentish leg of their tour took them to Canterbury, Dover, Folkestone and Maidstone, with two and sometimes three performances in each. It was an exhausting schedule for everyone in the company, and especially for Will, now a fully-fledged actor. But by the time they returned to a London sweltering in the early August heat, he felt as though he had acquired years of training in every aspect of the art of making plays, squashed into just a few intense months. He had taken the stage in roles both male and female (the latter being the cause of a good deal of hilarity among his colleagues), he had learned the art of improvisation when one of his colleagues lost his lines, he knew how to make adjustments and repairs to their precious and expensive costumes, he had strummed a lute to accompany songs sung on stage, and of course, he had cut and patched many of their plays to suit their reduced circumstances. As they made their tired way along Fleet Street towards the Ludgate he felt for the first time that he could truly hold up his head and say that he was a man of the theatre.

He remembered that half-joking, half-serious conversation with Marlowe, back in Cambridge, 'I will master it all—acting, staging, writing—and I will profit from it all.' Well, he had made a good start on the first two, and Tarlton had all but promised that the company would welcome a playscript from him when they got back into the swing of things in London. Falling into bed in his tiny room after a quick meal at a nearby ordinary, his last thoughts before sleep were of the plays he would write, his *Comedy of Errors* and a new play about King Richard III, and a cloudy vision of himself standing upon a stage receiving the accolades and applause of all.

Alas, all his aspirations came crashing to the ground but three days later. After a hurried conference with the company's other sharers, Tarlton gathered everyone together in the yard of the Bel Savage Inn.

'I fear that I have news that can please no-one,' he said, after a few opening remarks that did nothing to disguise his obvious dismay at what he had to say next. 'As you all know, our company has always had two parts, so that one troupe may be performing here in London, while the other is touring. But it seems that, while we were away, the London players had a very poor season indeed.'

'No surprise there,' John Laneham muttered to Will out of the side of his mouth. 'London is tired of our old medley style and wants something new.'

Will barely heard him, for he sensed what was coming next.

'So it has been decided—reluctantly, most reluctantly—that the company will be reduced in size for the time being, to just one group of players. And we will be reducing the number of plays we perform here in London.' Tarlton's kindly misshapen face looked genuinely distressed, his eyes miserable. 'I can see that you know what this news means: there will only be enough work for the sharers, and we will have to let every hired man go.'

Which meant that Will, who had gone to bed just two days ago dreaming of a bright future, was now out of work.

'I would that things were different, Will,' a tired and harassed-looking Tarlton said after everyone else had left. 'We have no choice. We might wear the Queen's livery, but she expects us to pay our own way, and for now, the company coffers are in a parlous state. And we must find the capital to pay out poor Billy's share to his widow.'

Tarlton was seized by a bout of coughing that left him red-faced and wheezing. Will felt a little sorry for a man he had come to like and respect, who was clearly unwell. 'I'll not pretend that it is not a blow, Dick, but I blame you not. You will have to release me from any obligation to the company, though. I need money and must needs find other ways to profitably employ my wits.'

'Of course, lad, of course. Do what you must. But we will be back on our feet again in a few months, and we will need plays. Put your pen to work and we will buy.'

With which half-promise they parted. Making his way home, he wandered distractedly through the Ludgate and up past the printers and bookshops of Paternoster Row, contemplating a future that was now darkly uncertain. He had saved some money, to be sure, but he had those three mouths to feed back in Stratford, as well as paying his rent in London, and it would not be long before what funds he had were gone. Despite the brave face he had put on things with Tarlton, the truth was that the bald announcement that afternoon had come as a shock to the hopes for the future his mind had constructed—a future both profitable and glorious in the world that he had come to love over the past eight months.

Yet William Shakespeare possessed a hardy and optimistic soul, and before long he began to look for silver linings on this darkest of clouds. Freed of the demands of a working company of actors he would at least be free to write, and write he would. By the time the Queen's Men returned from their next tour, he would have one, two, even three plays ready for them.

That thought cheered him up and by the time he arrived home, his native sunniness had returned, and he greeted his landlady with a smacking kiss on the cheek and a laugh that left her standing bewildered as he disappeared up the stairs to his attic room.

Chapter 8

Like its neighbours, the house before which Will stood had an unassuming three-floor façade, brick on the ground floor and lath and plaster above pierced by glass-paned windows and topped by a roof of wooden tiles. A wisp of smoke found its way out of a tall brick chimney and climbed into the sky to join the haze created by its myriad fellows, the permanent, acrid fog that hung over London at all seasons. It looked prosperous and comfortable, and might perhaps have been taken for the residence of a London burgher. In fact, it was the home of the late William Knell, and his wife, now widow, Rebecca.

Broad Street belied its own name at this point, narrowing as it squeezed between the houses on its eastern side and the bulk of Austin Friars church to the west—better known these days as the Dutch Church, since half of it had been given over for the use of foreign Protestants resident in the city, the other half being used as a storehouse—and so the cobbled street with its rivulet of filth running down the middle was in shade much of the day. Still, it was a prosperous looking thoroughfare, and more importantly for an actor like William Knell, conveniently close to the Bishop's Gate and the road that led north to the theatres in Shoreditch.

A sudden gust of chilly wind bustled by, rattling shutters and causing Will to shiver and shake him out of his bemused contemplation of his former colleague's apparent prosperity. Squaring his shoulders, he took the last few paces that would bring him to the door and rapped sharply on its wood. Someone—mistress or servant, he could not tell—must have been watching him from behind those opaque windows, for the door was opened with an alacrity so surprising that he almost made an involuntary step back into the street. The serving girl who had achieved this feat seemed entirely unsurprised by his appearance at the door.

'Mister Shakespeare?' Will nodded. 'The mistress is expecting you, sir. Come this way, if you will.'

He did not have far to follow, for the main parlour of the house was close to the street. There, he was left alone for just a few minutes before the door opened once more to admit the owner of the house.

Will's first thought was that like Helen of Troy, Rebecca Knell possessed a face that might seduce men into self-destructive idiocy—a perfect oval with unblemished white cheeks that had just a hint of rosiness about them, ending in a dimpled chin. Lustrous brown hair fell in long tresses from beneath a simple head-dress across shapely shoulders, and her body was slim and neat, with perfect breasts confined tidily by the bodice of her gown. But it was her eyes that were most captivating—blue and sparkling with mischief beneath the two even arcs of her brows. They were eyes that invited Will to join her in some mysterious joke, and which seemed to give a lie to the rest of her features, at present arranged into the solemn expression appropriate to a young woman just three months widowed.

'Mister Shakespeare. Welcome to my home.' Her voice had a lilting musicality to it that was as beguiling as a siren. 'May I offer you some refreshment? We have, I think, some sweet wine and cakes in the pantry.'

'No, no, Mistress Knell, please don't trouble yourself. I have but recently broken my fast.'

She slipped gracefully onto a long settle that ran beneath the room's expensively glazed main window that gave a distorted view through its small square panes of the Dutch church just across the street. Will took a chair opposite.

'You must call me Rebecca, Mister Shakespeare. I may be a widow, but I feel much too young to be carrying the burden of such a matronly title.' This was accompanied by a display of even white teeth in a quick, shy smile. 'I must confess to some surprise when I received your note informing me of your

107

intention to call. I have not had a visit from any others of my late husband's colleagues, except for dear Master Tarlton.'

'Well, I come partly on business, though now you make me ashamed that I have not called before, if only to convey my condolences.'

'That was not my intention, Mister Shakespeare, believe me.' Another disarming smile. 'But you are here on business, you say? Since William died there has been rather a lot of that.'

'It is fairly simple business, so I shall not burden you too much.' Will opened his worn leather satchel and withdrew a stack of documents, all neatly held together by a red ribbon. 'After Billy died, Dick Tarlton asked me to go through his things and extract any papers that might pertain to the affairs of the company. But I kept the documents of a more personal nature, letters and the like, various deeds and promissory notes, intending to return them to you as his heir upon the first opportunity. Regrettably, affairs have detained me, and it has taken longer than I might have wished to bring them to you, for which I am most sorry.'

This last was not quite true. Will could have come to the Knell residence at almost any time in the month since he had returned to London, for it was at most a twenty-minute walk from his own lodgings. Yet something had held him back— the recollection, perhaps, of that awful day in Thame, which he had no desire to relive by recounting its events to what he presumed would be a distraught widow.

But the woman sitting demurely on the settle in front of him seemed far from distraught. She showed little curiosity about the package of letters, setting them aside with the ribbon intact. If she was moved to see her late husband's handwriting on the cover of the topmost letter, she gave no visible sign of it, merely folding her hands into her lap once more and returning her gaze to her visitor with a mildly enquiring expression on her face.

'Do not distress yourself, Mister Shakespeare. I will examine them all later, when I am at leisure.' She frowned, opened and closed her mouth as if she could not decide what she wanted to say next, and when she did speak, she seemed almost reluctant to do so. 'I understand that you were with William when he died?'

'Yes, I was.'

'Tell me what happened. Master Tarlton was vague as to the details.'

Will silently cursed Dick Tarlton. This was the very conversation he did not want to have. 'What exactly did he tell you?'

'That William got into a fight with John Towne and that Towne accidentally stabbed him, in self-defence, he said.' Her voice was flat and toneless; she might as well have been relating some item of gossip heard in the markets, an event of interest but of little importance.

'There is little more to tell. Billy was in a fury, he chased John down a side street that was blocked by a mound of earth and John had no choice but to draw his sword and defend himself against Billy's attack. He maintains that the fatal blow was accidental, though we shall have to await the coroner's verdict on that point.'

'William could be emotional, I know, but Master Tarlton evaded me when I asked what caused such a furious disagreement. He said it was a professional matter, but I am not sure I believe him.' Again, the slight hesitation, this time accompanied by a sigh. 'I assume, Mister Shakespeare, that you know John Towne was a suitor for my hand before I married William. Was that the cause of the quarrel?'

'Not directly. Their former rivalry hung between them, a ghost held at bay only by the requirements of our profession, which demand we collaborate whether or not we are friends. They bickered constantly over everything, and it sometimes seemed that whatever Billy said, John would say the opposite, just to provoke him. But this quarrel was over something more personal. A matter involving, I am unhappy to say, a slur upon your good name.'

Rebecca looked at him for a long moment. 'Tell me all,' she finally said, a flinty tone in her voice. 'And do not, I pray you, try to spare my feelings, for I am no weak-kneed maid to be cosseted and coddled. I have endured a storm of gossip's stones and arrows before this on account of the age difference between myself and William.'

'I well know it; Billy confided as much to me ere he died. Society's cruelties are legion.' Having delivered himself of that platitude, he decided that there was no point in any further prevarication. 'This was no mere matter of gossip. Towne alleged that you were enamoured of another man, had been seen in the streets with him, and he produced evidence of infidelity. It was that which sent Billy into a rage.'

'Proof? What, had he spies in my bedchamber?' One side of her mouth twitched into a hesitant half-smile, as if to say that the whole idea was absurd.

'Not exactly. He produced a kerchief, which he claimed had been found beside your bed, with the initials "JH" embroidered in one corner.'

'Which he no doubt said belonged to John Heminges.' The beautiful face suddenly hardened into anger. 'No, you don't have to say anything, Mister Shakespeare. Your eyes tell me that you believe Towne's words to be true, and thus I stand condemned.'

'I know not whether he spoke truth or falsehood. I simply report what he said to your husband, in front of witnesses.'

'All of them men, no doubt. Men who will condemn me as a whore without a second thought. Such is the lot of women, Mister Shakespeare—condemned to share our lives with men who have been chosen for us by our fathers, regardless of whether we love them or not. We must manage their households, bear their children, put up with their habits, nay, worship at their very altar, as though they were God Almighty himself, and do all without complaint. Our husbands can take mistresses where they choose, but wives cannot even seek male friendship without calumny being poured upon our heads like boiling oil from the walls of a castle.'

Will said nothing. What could he say? She was right. Women were chattels to be bestowed in marriage wherever would bring the greatest advantage to their families, and it was a rare father who would ignore such interests to please an emotional young daughter. Never before had he wondered whether that was just, but Rebecca Knell's vehemence gave him pause. What, he wondered, would he do if in some distant future his own Susannah or her sister Judith, wanted to marry for love against his wishes?

She let out a long, low sigh, as though expelling her anger. 'It is true that Master Heminges was a regular visitor in these last few months while William travelled with the company. He is a sweet man and personable, close to my age. We became friends, exchanged confidences, met to talk and laugh at his silly jokes. And that is all we were—are—just friends. That I swear.'

'And the kerchief? Towne said it was found in your bedchamber.'

'So says John Towne. I have no idea how it might have got there. Heminges may have lent it to me and I merely dropped it by the bed. I don't remember.' She frowned and the angry look came back. 'Zounds, Mister Shakespeare, must I put my maids to the question to prove my innocence?'

Will was startled by the unexpected profanity. 'Forgive me, Rebecca, I meant no offence.'

The moment of fury disappeared as quickly as it had appeared. 'No, I am sure that you did not, and you must forgive me for my intemperance. I am but a weak and foolish woman, ever subject to my emotions.'

'Strong emotion affects all of us, man or woman, and to feel either love or hate is not in any way foolish, though it may make us act like fools.' He smiled, thinking of his own turbulent courtship. 'For certes, love at least has oft made a fool of me.'

She tilted her head a little to one side, with a quizzical look. 'You do not seem like other men, Mister Shakespeare. You do not judge.'

'Who am I to judge anyone? Let us leave that to those who have been set up with tribunal and staff, and meantime take the world as it is and people as they are.'

She considered him for a moment, and Will sensed she was making her mind up about something.

'Let me be truthful with you. I must confess that I was never in love with William. We married at my father's insistence and against my wishes. I soon discovered that marriage was not going to be easy, for my husband had a streak of jealous cruelty that he exercised upon me whenever he was at home.' She shook her head to still Will's instinctive protest. 'You think you knew him, Mister Shakespeare? You did not. Oh, I doubt not that he was a jolly companion upon the road and a wise and skilful player on the stage, but when at home he was froward, suspicious and angry. Nothing I could do or say would please him, and more than once he gave me blows.'

This was a side of Knell that Will had never imagined. That he could be prickly when his honour was impugned, he well knew—it was that very weakness that had led to his death. But he would never have believed that his jealous suspicions should lower him to beat this beautiful young girl who, though clearly high-spirited, seemed innocent of the crimes of which Knell must have imagined she was guilty.

'I see you are shocked. Yet, though his presence when at home was often painful to me, you must not think that I did not care for my husband. There was a great difference in our ages, it is true, but I respected him and still had a certain affection for him, despite all.' A wry smile brightened her face. 'Though in his dying he has given me the greatest gift possible—that of my independence.'

Will laughed. She was right. In England, widows were the only women who could decide for themselves who they would see, how they would spend their time, and how to dispose of their property without the intervention of a male. And presumably, Rebecca Knell was the heir of a not-inconsiderable fortune, if the various deeds that Will had seen in Knell's strongbox were anything to judge by. Not to mention the proceeds of her late husband's share in the Queen's Men, which she would receive once the remaining sharers could be gathered to ratify the transfer.

'Tell me, Mister Shakespeare, do you know when the coroner will return a verdict upon William's death?'

It was unsurprising that she should be concerned with this question, for her inheritance could not proceed until the legal formalities were complete. 'I am afraid I cannot tell,' he said. 'Towne is still in custody, I believe, and these matters move slowly in the country.'

'And what do you think that verdict will be? Do you think it truly was a case of self-defence?'

'There is no evidence that would suggest the contrary,' he said cautiously. 'My own experience of John was that he could be difficult and argumentative, and seemed always to be carrying a grudge against the world, but he did not seem to me to be a murderer.'

'He is a strange man. Unpredictable.' She sighed, and again that look of calculation flashed into her eyes, instantly extinguished. 'I cared for him deeply, you know, before my father forbade me from seeing him and arranged my marriage.'

'And now? If he were to return to London a free and exonerated man, would you welcome him?'

'No, I would not!' Seeing that the violence of her words had startled her visitor, she lifted her hands from her lap, palms outwards, a gesture that seemed to be a plea for understanding. 'I was in love with John, it is true, and—to my shame—I continued to see him in secret after William and I were married, whenever chance would permit. Do not condemn me; I could not bear it, the prospect of never seeing him again, and our meetings, though clandestine, were always chaste.' She sighed. 'But it was impossible, and in the end, we quarrelled.'

'Quarrels can be mended, surely?'

'Not this one. It was over something… fundamental.' A look of revulsion came over her face, as though remembering whatever had caused their argument was too awful to contemplate. 'He is a dangerous man, Mister Shakespeare, capable of great violence. I feared for William's life for as long as John and he were in the same company.'

'And so you wonder if what happened in Thame was deliberate. I don't think so, though he may have seen an opportunity for revenge and taken it, which is not quite the same thing. In any event, it will not be murder unless the coroner pronounces it so.'

'Then we must wait upon his judgement.' She frowned again. 'And if John is released, will he be allowed to re-join the Queen's Men?'

'I don't see why not, though it may be some time before we are back on the stage.'

114

'Well, he will have to find some employment, since he cannot go back north to Lancashire, where he came from.'

'Oh? I did wonder where he was born. I would have guessed either Lancashire or Yorkshire, though he has all but banished the northern accent from his voice.'

'His father died when he was young. His mother remarried and he quarrelled with his stepfather and ran away to London, and there eked out a living doing this and that. He told me that he was employed as a horse-holder at the Curtain Theatre, where he persuaded some actor to take him on as an apprentice.'

'This was before he went away to the continent? He said that he went there to study.'

'I think so, though he always closed up, clam-like, whenever our conversation veered in that direction. I do not know to this day what took him to France, whether to study or for some other reason.'

Will remembered something. 'Did it ever seem to you that he might have papist leanings?'

'What a peculiar question to ask, Mister Shakespeare. If John Towne is a secret Catholic, he keeps it well disguised. But then he is an actor, is he not?' The mischievous look came back. 'Perhaps *you* are a secret and dissembling member of the papist sect, sir.'

He clutched his hands to his heart and laughed. 'A hit, a palpable hit! You have found me out.'

The soft chime of a clock somewhere in the house told him that it was past his time to depart, and he rose, still smiling, and made his farewells.

Making his way home to Silver Street, he thought about John Towne, still under lock and key in Thame. Did he still harbour any feelings for Rebecca? If he did, it seemed unlikely that he would find a welcome in her arms, and given his obviously passionate, not to say violent nature, there was no telling what might come of any such rejection. Will decided that he would do what he could to keep an eye on her and ensure she came to no harm. He felt he owed that much to the shade of William Knell.

As for the doubts about Towne's loyalty that Knell's secret report had raised, nothing Rebecca had told him much illuminated that subject. *Well*, he thought as he walked past the square-towered church of St Alban and into Silver Street, *all of that is no concern of mine*. Sir Francis Walsingham and his gang could deal with it, and he need not be troubled by it any further.

Chapter 9

Will shivered and pulled his cloak more tightly around himself to prevent the water that dripped from the brim of his hat from getting through to his skin. He hurried along muddy, crowded Cheapside towards St Paul's Cathedral, quietly cursing the fickleness of the weather gods who had chosen the moment he left his lodgings to hurl this summer rainstorm at the city of London.

Skipping across puddles and dodging around knots of matrons gathering before the shopfronts, he came to a narrow gatehouse leading through to the churchyard of the cathedral, whose water-washed grey stones glistened in the weak sunlight beginning to peek through the clouds.

He stopped for a moment, awed as always by the sheer size and grandeur of the vast medieval building with its elegant buttresses and flat-topped central tower, which had once been topped by a graceful wooden spire until it was burnt down after being struck by lightning twenty-odd years before. The churchyard, a large cobblestoned space that surrounded the church itself, had originally been enclosed by walls, but with the passage of time and the ever-pressing need in London for housing, it was now lined with three-storey buildings, shops on the ground floor and residences above.

Turning right, Will searched for the familiar sign, a crudely drawn representation of a cannon that hung above the door to Edward White's bookshop. Pushing open the door, he found himself in a small, cosy room devoted entirely to the display and sale of books. Pamphlets of every description were piled on the big table in the middle of the room. The shelves that lined the walls were full of leather-bound tomes, and books were stacked on the floor in tottering piles that looked as though they might collapse at any moment. It was a chaotic yet comfortable scene, and Will felt the usual small flush of pleasure as he breathed in the familiar smell of paper and old leather—a peculiar, indefinable scent that was as sweet to him as the smell of any rose.

'Well now, if it isn't William Shakespeare, back from the country.' The greeting came from a small, red-faced and grey-whiskered man of middle years who sat at a desk occupying a corner of the bookshop, the only space not covered in books. Indeed, in contrast to the disorder everywhere else, the desktop was a picture of neatness, papers carefully stacked, the ink-pot placed just so, and half a dozen new quills laid out ready to be turned into pens by the knife set next to them.

'Good day to you, Mister White. It has been too long since last I graced your doorway. The shop has grown no tidier, I see.'

The bookseller shrugged in a gesture that conveyed hopelessness and helplessness all at once. 'What can I say, Mister Shakespeare? London seems to be awash with books and tracts of one kind or another. Every day the printers send me more stock to sell, and I never seem to be able to find the time to organise everything properly.'

'Too many people with nothing to say busily saying it. London is a talking-shop, no doubt about it.' Will picked up a volume at random, one of a pile of what looked like a new print run that perched on the edge of the big table. He grunted in surprise when he saw the name on the title page. 'Rob Greene has been hard at work while I've been away, I see.'

White rose from his chair and came over to peer at the slim volume through spectacles that emerged from the pocket of his doublet. 'Ah, yes, *Morando: The Tritameron of Love*. Mister Wolfe sent that round from Paternoster Row just this morning. I doubt not that it will sell as well as all of Master Greene's other works.'

Will flicked through the first few pages. It was dedicated to Philip Howard, the thirteenth Earl of Arundel, a Catholic lord who had been released from prison only two years ago. How like Robert Greene to court controversy by dedicating his latest work to a catholic recusant; no doubt the earl had paid for the work to be printed. Within, the cover said, the reader would find 'certain pleasant conceits perfectly discoursed, and three doubtful questions of love most pithily and pleasantly discussed'.

'Well Edward, I think I must have a copy since I am to dine with the author this very afternoon. And you had better tell me what it is about since I won't have time to read it before I see Master Greene.'

'I cannot with certainty tell you what it is about, since I have not read it myself as yet. But the gist, Wolfe tells me, is this—a group of courtly gentlemen and gentlewomen of Italy discuss the nature of love. Or some such thing. That will be sixpence for you, Mister Shakespeare, though my normal price is eight pennies.'

Will smiled as he handed over the coins. The little book that was now his newest possession would no doubt make for lively if high-flown reading. His glance at the dedication page had given him a sense of the style, full of references to Roman emperors, Persian kings and classical literary allusions, all designed to show off the author's university education, of which Robert Greene was exceedingly proud.

Resisting the bookseller's attempts to entice him to part with more pennies from his purse, he made his farewells.

Outside, the rain had stopped and the clouds cleared as suddenly as they had formed, allowing the throng that had been sheltering inside shops and the great church to emerge and resume their daily business. Will's own business that morning took him in the opposite direction, into the church itself, and he hurried across the yard into the cool darkness of the entrance to the north transept. The nave was busy, as always, merchants and lawyers chatting in clusters, exchanging news and speculating on the future.

'Here I am, Will.' The voice of Ned Bentley came from over his shoulder, and he turned to see the young boy-actor grinning at him from between two of the pillars that lined the nave. He was ridiculously good-looking. Hair the colour of summer straw, long blonde lashes over dreamy blue eyes, downy cheeks that as yet had barely made the acquaintance of the razor, and even white teeth enclosed by a wide, rather sensuous mouth. Dressed as a woman, as he usually was when on stage, Ned was a superb counterfeit of the real thing, and even that day, clad in a sober and sensible brown velvet doublet, fashionably slashed breeches and white hose, he was a vision of youthful comeliness.

He was also, for now at least, sharing Will's tiny room at his lodgings just off Cheapside. Losing his six shillings a week while the Queen's Men were in recess was bad enough for Will, but for Ned, it was catastrophic. He had few other immediate prospects and he had no family in London (unlike young Adam Arkwright, whose father, an apothecary, lived in Billingsgate). Taking pity on the boy, Will had offered him the other half of his bed, at least until such time as the company re-formed and they were both once again able to draw a wage.

'You've managed to find your way out from under the covers at least.' Will had left him softly snoring in bed early that morning. 'Come on, let us away to The Mermaid.'

Threading their way through the crowded church, Will smiled at the open-mouthed look of wonder on Ned's face. He remembered when he had first come into London's greatest church and been struck dumb by the sheer size and grace of the cathedral's soaring arches. He had been surprised, too, by another service that the church provided, one not at all religious.

'I never saw a church so dedicated to business.' He laughed as they passed a clutch of tradesmen gathered around a broadsheet pasted up on one of the nave's pillars; one of many such. 'There are more merchants, tradesmen and lawyers passing through here every day than congregate at the Royal Exchange. I never saw a church anywhere in Italy that was so used.'

Ned frowned. 'It does seem, well, sacrilegious, don't you think?'

'Aye, it is that. But it is also very English.'

Out in the churchyard, the heavy grey clouds of earlier had been reduced to tattered shreds and the cobbles were bathed in bright sunlight once again. Taking the north gate, they made their way down Cheapside until they came to the octagonal pile of the Cheapside Cross, where carriages and drays trying to pass each side of the monument found themselves in a whip-cracking, shouting tangle. The two young men navigated their way through with some difficulty before turning right into Bread Street. Two buildings down stood the Mermaid Tavern, a sprawling establishment whose owner had paid some artist to paint a vision of aquatic loveliness on the big sign that hung above the door.

Inside, the inn's main room was filled with chattering people gathered in knots and groups around the fireplace, in the two big bow windows, and seated on benches at long tables. Peering around, Will could not immediately identify anyone he knew, until the familiar visage of Richard Burbage emerged from the crowd, arms wide in greeting and a big grin on his handsome face.

'Will! I wasn't going to make an appearance today, but then Kit told me you were coming, and all my excuses melted into thin air like wraiths before an exorcist. And here you are, in the flesh at last, looking as prosperous as a tax-farmer.'

'Looks deceive. I am as poor as any church-mouse, at least until the company gets back to work. But I do not complain, for life has been kind to me in this last year. How does your father?'

'Well enough, though he is beginning to feel his age. Complains of aches in his back at the mere sight of a hammer and awl, and is becoming more irascible by the day, but otherwise, he is much the same as last you saw him. And who is this comely young man?'

'Richard Burbage, meet Ned Bentley, also of the Queen's Men,' Will said formally. 'Ned was one of our squeakers on the late tour.'

'Pleased to meet you, Master Burbage,' Ned said, blushing a little.

This caused Burbage to laugh. 'Master Burbage is my father. I am plain Richard, or even plainer Dick to my friends, a circle to whose membership you are most welcome. Come on, Greene has arranged a room upstairs with victuals.'

'Rob must be in funds for once,' Will said to Burbage as they climbed the stairs that led up to a gallery and thence to a nondescript door.

Burbage paused with his hand on the latch. 'Not only in funds but in high spirits too, which is apt to be a tiring combination in Rob.'

With that, he flung open the door. In the room beyond, a group of young men crowded around a table, their faces flushed as they looked up in fascinated thrall at another who stood on the table's middle, booted feet planted firmly among the platters of food and jugs of wine and ale. Tall and broad-shouldered, he was endowed with a great thatch of red hair that swept up and back, that, combined with slightly protruding green eyes, gave its owner's face a permanently surprised look. The hair's counterpoint was a long, pointed and equally rufus beard framing a small dainty mouth from which emerged a surprisingly melodious voice, considering that it came from within so big a frame.

'...and the boy, doubting nothing, did as he was told and made his way to some house of ill-repute, whence neither he, the thief, the sugar, spices, or linen were ever heard of again. So, my masters, many have in this manner been deceived. Let this be a warning to beware any such unprofitable guests.'

The big man gave a deep bow, flourishing his hat in an exaggerated sweep of the arm, to general applause and shouts of approval from the assembly. Straightening, his intense emerald gaze landed upon the little group by the open door. 'As I live and breathe! Dick Burbage!'

He leapt from the table, knocking over a half-empty tankard of ale in the process and lurching a little as he landed. Steadying himself with a little help from one of the younger men, he straightened and marched across the room to embrace the slighter frame of Richard Burbage in a bear-like grip.

'Steady, Rob.' He laughed breathlessly. 'I am not like to survive too many such greetings with my ribs intact.'

Releasing Burbage, the big man turned his attention to Will and Ned. 'And Mister... Shake-scene? Shake-shaft?'

'Shake*speare*, as well you know, Robert Greene.' This was an old joke that Greene had delighted in making over and over again when they had first met two years ago. 'Ignore this oaf's ponderous humour, Ned, he is merely jealous that his name is not half as memorable.'

'Young Bentley here is also with the Queen's Men,' Burbage said gently.

'Bentley? Are you related to the late John Bentley?'

'My uncle,' Ned said. 'It was he who arranged for my apprenticing to Master Tarlton before he died.'

'A very small world, that of the theatre, is it not?' Greene was merry. 'Come and meet everyone else and—more important by far—enjoy some food and drink before these heathens consume the lot.'

'Everyone else' turned out to be the 'Tri-Toms' as Greene called them—Thomas Watson, Thomas Lodge, and Thomas Nashe—and a tousle-haired, short-legged man with a squinting eye named George Peele. Will knew none of them except by their reputations, of which that of Watson was the most burnished.

'Watson's latest passion is for the writing of plays, though why a true poet such as he should sully his mind with such things is beyond me.' Greene laughed before moving on to introduce the others. 'The university at Cambridge has in its wisdom just awarded Nashe his bachelor's degree, and they may even be foolish enough to give him his master's if he can stomach their rules for long enough to complete his dissertation. And what to say about Tom Lodge?' Greene stroked his beard and raised an eyebrow in a pretence at consideration. 'His father was a Lord Mayor of London, you know, so he is almost royalty. He scribbles out pamphlets, none of them good, but he will, I prophesy, run away to sea.'

Lodge, a burly, compact man, dismissed this last sally with a shrug. 'Not much of a prophecy, Rob, since I told you but half an hour hence that Captain Clarke has offered me a place in his expedition to the Canary Isles.'

'So you did, and in confidence too. Ah well.' Greene turned to the last member of the little group, the man with the dishevelled hair. 'Now, George here is another of your play-scribblers, and a good one, too.'

'I much admired your *Arraignment of Paris*, sir,' Burbage said. 'As fine a playscript as I have ever read. And my father tells me you will have a new play for him soon?'

Peele nodded. '*Jack Straw*. It is almost complete, though the parts need copying out and the manuscript needs to be fair-written for the master's approval.'

'Will could help with that.' Burbage was enthusiastic. 'He has a fine hand and Dick Tarlton says he has never worked with a quicker man of the pen. No doubt my father will contribute something to pay for his time since he is in much need of new plays.'

Shakespeare was not at all sure he wanted to be yoked into partnership with a man he had only just met, but work was work, after all, so he inclined his head in agreement.

'I would welcome the assistance, Mister Shakespeare. In truth, I am weighed down with work at the moment.'

Introductions and greetings completed, everyone sat and returned to the serious business of talking, eating and drinking. Robert Greene, usually impoverished to the point of penury, must indeed have had a windfall, judging from the amount and quality of victuals that remained on the table. Barely had they sat down before more appeared, delivered by shiny-faced maids who struggled up the stairs laden with trays and jugs. But though the assembled company devoured the chicken and fish, eggs and cheese, and poured the thin red wine down their throats with an enthusiasm its quality did not deserve, it was talk that they were principally there for, and talk they did, most loudly.

What talk it was! In an observing rather than participating mood, Will listened with some amusement to the banter flying back and forth. It was like watching a knightly melee of old, a scrambled combat of honour, each participant trying to outdo all the others, but with words substituting for swords and epigrams for lances. A quip was answered by an apt quotation in verse from some obscure Latin poet, upon which another insisted upon a Greek alternative. Barely had one speaker finished a sentence before another thumped the table or shouted to get everyone's attention. The result was sheer cacophony, deafening and bewildering.

Amid all the noise, Greene acted as the ringmaster. Deftly intervening with that beguiling voice of his whenever the discussion became too heated or was about to approach a dead end, he pricked their pretensions and brought them all back to earth with some tale of London's streets, usually involving the unsuspecting victim of a thief or trickster—'coneys', he called the victims, and 'coney-catchers' their predators, terms that were new to Will—that reduced them all to helpless laughter. Then, like a trickster himself, he launched the whole group off onto another flight of fancy with some learned observation or another.

It was all a performance. Greene despised the stage, but the man would have made a fine actor. He was a curious bag of paradoxes—at once deeply learned and yet outwardly profane in manner of speech and dress. He had attended Cambridge and debated with professors but preferred the company of the thieves and cutpurses who haunted the stews of Southwark. He was a big, powerfully built man who nevertheless spoke softly and rarely lost his temper, though Will thought that if he ever did so it would be a sight to inspire awe. He had liked Greene from the day they had met, though he was more than a little intimidated by him.

'What good fortune has enabled Rob to fund such largesse?' he asked Burbage, talking over the head of Ned Bentley, who, clearly overawed by the company in which he found himself, had taken refuge in devouring as much food as he could.

'His latest pamphlet. It seems that he has prevailed upon old White to pay him in advance, in anticipation of future sales. Quite how he achieved that feat, I know not, but knowing Rob, there must have been some blackmail involved somewhere.'

'Well, I doubt that Mister White will be the loser; Rob's pamphlets are usually popular. In fact, I have myself contributed to his future success.' Will patted his doublet, within which he had stuffed his newly purchased copy of *Morando*.

'What is it about, this pamphlet?' Ned Bentley asked, his appetite sated for the moment.

'It is about love. Of what else do poets write?' Burbage grinned. 'The conceit is this—over three nights, ladies and gentlemen of an Italian court debate three questions: whether loves does much, but money does all; whether or not it is good to *be* in love; and lastly, whether women are more subject to love than men.'

'Is that all? Does nothing else happen? They just sit around and talk?' Ned was incredulous. 'I think I should die of boredom if I had to listen to such stuff.'

'Ah, but it is such beautifully argued nonsense, my young friend,' said a sardonic but familiar voice from behind them.

'Kit! I was beginning to think you would never arrive.' Will scrambled to his feet and turned to embrace his friend, whose arrival had otherwise gone unnoticed in the clamour from the other end of the table, where the poets were busily discoursing on some lofty subject or another that had lost the interest of the three actors.

'I was waylaid by that rogue Henslowe, who seemed to think I owed him money. It took a while and some quantities of good hock to convince him otherwise.'

Burbage was amused. 'If you owe money to Philip Henslowe, I doubt a few glasses of wine will induce anything other than a temporary loss of memory, my friend.'

'True enough, Dick, but I have another currency with him, for I have promised him a play to grace the stage of his new theatre in Southbank.'

'*Tamburlaine*?' Will asked, startled. 'Is it finished?'

'No, but it will be, and before the year is out. The Admiral's Men will do it, I think.' The Admiral's Men, a theatrical troupe who had the patronage of Charles Howard, the Lord High Admiral of England, had taken permanent residence at Henslowe's theatre, the Rose, new-built among the stews and bear-baiting pits of Southwark, on the southern side of the Thames.

'Even so, I would make sure I got payment in advance if I were you,' Burbage said. 'My father says 'tis best to count your fingers three times after any dealings with Philip Henslowe.'

Marlowe raised his hands and wiggled all ten fingers. Then his eye alighted on Ned Bentley. 'And who, might I enquire, are you?'

'Edward Bentley, Master Marlowe, late of the Queen's Men.' Ned couldn't quite suppress a stammer of nerves at meeting yet another of these literary men, with whose conversation he could barely keep up.

'William Shakespeare! Where have you been hiding this vision of comely youth?'

'Ned has been staying at my lodgings since the company got back to London. He has no other friends or family here since his uncle died.'

'Sharing your lodgings and your bed, no doubt. I am jealous.'

Will felt himself colouring. He had never thought that he shared Marlowe's well-known predilection for his own sex, but sometime in the night, he had woken to the sensation of Ned's youthful body pressed against his, one bare arm resting on his chest. No doubt the boy's embrace had been unconscious, but it had succeeded nevertheless in arousing Will's lust, and they had engaged in a brief but energetic bout of lovemaking. Having achieved mutual release, both had fallen back to sleep, a condition in which he had left Ned that morning. Since then, they had not had any opportunity to speak of it, so Kit's joking remarks were untimely, to say the least. Ned, though, seemed untroubled, and just offered a shy smile.

'He's safer in Will's bed than yours, I'll warrant.' Greene's voice floating from the other end of the table saved Will from having to reply. 'There's not a youth in London who is safe from Kit Marlowe.'

'You exaggerate, Greene, as always. It is only the handsome lads like young Ned here who interest me, and there are few of those in this pox-ridden town. Now, tell me about this new pamphlet of yours, *Morando*, is it? *The Tritameron of Love*? You fancy yourself as an English Boccaccio, eh? Though a puny one to be sure. The Italian managed to keep his debates going for ten days, not a mere three.'

And with that, the room exploded into noise, as each of the poet-playwrights competed with each other to heap ever more elaborate insults upon the imperturbable head of Robert Greene, who answered each quip with a joke, a quotation or an oath, depending on the merits of each speaker. It was all very entertaining to Shakespeare and Burbage, though Ned found it a little bewildering. But eventually, the noise subsided and the conversation became general. By then, it was early evening and the light from outside had fled. The serving girls had lit just enough smoky cheap tallow candles to keep the darkness at bay and illuminate the assembly in a soft, wavering glow that cast long and fantastical shadows up the walls.

The appearance of the landlord of the Mermaid bearing a reckoning that ran to several sheets of paper brought proceedings to an end. Greene paid the bill without demur but was clearly not inclined to spend any more of his own money filling his friends' bellies with drink. That, he declared, they could pay for themselves at some other establishment. With much patting of backs and long, hiccoughing speeches of farewell, the group stumbled down the stairs and out into the fresh, cool air of the street, where they stood milling about, waiting for a lead to take them to their next adventure for the night.

It was no surprise when Marlowe took charge. 'Let us to the Boar's Head. The landlord there loves a poet, and in his ecstasy at entertaining no less than five of London's best scribblers, he will no doubt forget his reckoning.'

This announcement was greeted with cheers, and they all began to move off down the street. As they did so, Kit caught Will by the sleeve and drew him aside. 'I delivered your papers to Seething Lane.'

For a moment Will was confused and it took him a few seconds to register that Marlowe was talking about the papers he had found among William Knell's belongings. He had almost completely forgotten about them until this moment. 'What did Sir Francis say? Were they of any importance?'

'He wasn't there, and neither was Phelippes. I gave them to Walter Williams instead.'

Will frowned. It was unfortunate that neither the secretary nor his chief codebreaker had been there, for Will had little confidence in the acuity of Williams, a rather pettifogging junior clerk who lacked judgement and might indeed choose to ignore the whole matter. 'What did Williams say?'

'That he will give the documents to the secretary as soon as may be. Though that may take a while since Walsingham is sick and away resting at Barn Owls.'

'I am sorry to hear that. Though I never wanted to get caught up in his plots, he has been kind to me. Is his sickness mortal, do you think?'

Marlowe shrugged. 'Williams says that he hasn't been the same since Sir Philip Sidney died.'

Sidney had been Walsingham's son-in-law, and his death at just thirty-one years of age in the Netherlands the previous year had occasioned an extraordinary outpouring of grief. The immense funeral had, it was said, almost bankrupted the secretary.

'Well, we have done our duty, and neither you nor I owe anything further to Seething Lane. Come on, we'd better catch up with the others.'

Chapter 10

'No, no, Gabe! Mycetes must be weak, effeminate, in his first appearance. A comic figure, someone the groundlings will laugh at. Then, when he is overthrown, he will seem the more tragic. And Tom—Cosroe's disdain for his brother must drip from your tongue. You despise him and Meander both.'

'What if I stammered a little?' Gabriel Spencer suggested. 'Or a lisp? Would that be too much?'

'No, not a lisp. You are meant to be the king of Persia, not a simpering Spaniard. But a stammer will do well, I think. And make your voice a little higher.'

This was a Kit Marlowe that Will Shakespeare had never encountered— intense, focused and passionate. Gone was his usual insouciance, the ironic demeanour that made a joke of everything. They were rehearsing Marlowe's play *Tamburlaine the Great*, and the playwright was determined to have his say in how it should be presented by the hapless actors to whom his remarks had been directed. In Will's experience, players did not much like being told how they should perform the words written for them by anyone, let alone a jumped-up poet. Yet the actors of the Lord Admiral's Men seemed to be taking Marlowe's interventions in good part, so obvious was it that his only care was for the effective presentation of the drama.

They started again, running through the opening scene of the play, in which Mycetes learns that Tamburlaine, the former shepherd and now leader of the Scythians, is attacking the outer edges of the Persian Empire, and despatches troops to deal with the menace. Will, leaning against one of the newly painted columns of the Rose theatre, smiled as Spencer stammered his way through the

131

speech and leered at his minion and presumed lover, Meander, played with distant dignity by Richard Cowley, another of the Admiral's fine troupe of actors, while Tom Downton followed Marlowe's instructions to the letter, pacing about the stage and hurling his lines with barely concealed contempt for the king and his catamite.

On one side of the stage, Kit settled on a stool, one foot tapping away mindlessly, the finished playscript gripped in his hands. He watched every movement of the actors and listened to every word they uttered with an intensity that they might have found unnerving had they looked his way. As it was, they were too intent on delivering their lines with force and conviction to be much bothered by the presence of the poet-playwright on their stage. It was something Will had come to know well, this ability of actors to disappear into the role they were playing, impervious to all except the necessities of performance.

As the rehearsal settled into its rhythm, Will's attention wandered, and he found himself contemplating this new theatre, which its owner, Philip Henslowe, had called the Rose, after the rose gardens that filled the space between two warehouses just outside the theatre's door. Though now, in late summer, the blooms had begun to turn brown and the paths were littered with petals, the gardens made for a pleasant approach to the theatre's entrance. They were an island of beauty in the middle of the riotous environs of Southwark, a notoriously wild area on the south bank of the Thames famous for its gaming houses and brothels.

But Henslowe and his business partner John Cholmley had built the Rose here for another, entirely prosaic reason—like Shoreditch, where London's other theatres stood, Southwark was outside the boundaries of the city proper. And therefore they were beyond the legal reach of the Puritans who controlled the city council, for whom all theatres were a source of great uneasiness, if not downright evil, and who would have closed them down if they could.

The playhouse was so new that it still smelled of freshly sawn wood and newly applied paint. When he had arrived that morning, plasterers had been applying the final layers to the fourteen sides of the outer wall, and he had dodged a boy perched on the shoulders of his master, trying to hang a big swinging sign over the entrance door—the red and white Tudor Rose, naturally; Henslowe would not miss any opportunity to curry favour with the authorities.

Inside, carpenters were working to finish installing the benches up on the second balcony, oblivious to the rehearsal going on below. Just inside the theatre entrance, bright red cushions were piled up, ready to be rented to those patrons who were prepared to pay an additional penny to ease the pain induced in gentle backsides by the hard wood of the benches. All in all, it was an admirable picture of industry.

Will had first laid his eyes on the finished playscript that was now being brought to boisterous life on the stage in front of him just a few weeks earlier, when a diffident Marlowe had taken it out of his satchel and laid it on the table at the Mermaid.

'It's finished?' Will had said, more than a little surprised. Kit had been working on *Tamburlaine* for so long that it had almost acquired a mythic status, a project whose completion seemed always to be off in the distant future.

'Finished as it will ever be. Anyway, it has to be, since Henslowe is at me day and night to deliver it to the Admiral's Men by the end of the week. Though, in truth, I think he is just anxious to have a new play to open his new theatre.' Marlowe had frowned. 'No other eyes have seen it until now, and though I do not fear the scorn of Henslowe, nor actors, nor any other critic, I confess to some apprehension. Perhaps you could read it through before I give it up to the tender mercies of the actors?'

'Me?' Will had been taken aback by Marlowe's unexpected diffidence. 'Of course I will read it. I am flattered that you should so value my opinion.'

'It is not flattery, my friend. I know of no one else who can understand what I have done, and at the same time know how it will play in the theatre, how it will sound and look to the groundlings and the gentlemen in the galleries alike.'

Will had taken the precious pages back to his lodgings, settling down with a cup of wine to read it through by the light of a candle. What he read had astonished him. He'd thought he knew drama; in his short career in the theatre, he had read and fiddled with many plays both tragic and comic, had acted out scripts that were clever and witty, and in some cases, had struggled through texts that should have been consigned to the fire, not given on the stage. But this was like nothing he had ever encountered, a story of vast sweep and great power, told directly and simply.

In what Shakespeare instantly saw was a stroke of genius, Marlowe had told the tale almost entirely in blank verse, that style of poetry in which there was no formal rhyming pattern, deriving its rhythm instead from the pattern of the syllables that made up each line. By doing so, he had made the words of his play sound like music. It had been strange to his inner ear as he'd read through the script, yet at the same time, the words and phrases conveyed their story at a steady, tripping pace that would keep the groundlings entertained, even if they found some of the poetry harder to understand. It was, in short, a work of brilliance.

Still, he could tell that Kit had never trod the boards of any stage, and Will had seen that he could offer some modest suggestions to his friend that might improve its presentation, but of the playscript itself, he could find nothing to amend and the next day had handed it back to Marlowe saying merely, 'It is perfect. Change not a word.'

Watching now as the first scene ended with Mycetes' brother Cosroe entering upon a plot to dethrone the hapless king, he felt that he had in some obscure way shared in the creation of this new work simply by being its first auditor, and he

134

awaited with some nervousness the next scene, in which Tamburlaine, the shepherd king turned conqueror, made his first appearance.

Tall, handsome and broad-shouldered Edward Alleyn was made for the part. Clad in a vast sheepskin cloak and a tall fur hat, he looked every inch the conqueror, and dominated the stage the instant he strode onto it. Behind him came half a dozen other actors similarly garbed, and Ned Bentley, made up as Zenocrates, the daughter of the Sultan of Egypt, Tamburlaine's recent captive.

'Makes a pretty girl, doesn't he, your Ned?'

Will had not noticed the arrival of Philip Henslowe and was startled by the words, whistled through the gaps in his teeth in a low insinuating undertone. He did not much like the man—an unkempt, wild-haired straggle-bearded fellow whose small shrewd eyes seemed always to be evaluating everything they saw for potential profit. The source of his wealth was not known, though it was rumoured he had inherited by way of his wife, and he had properties in Sussex and there in Southwark. His present business interests were many, including ownership of a brothel that stood just a few feet from this very theatre.

'He's not "my" Ned, Henslowe. Unlike you, I do not have a proprietor's interest in any human beings.'

The theatre owner's hands went up in a mockery of placation. 'My apologies, Mister Shakespeare. I meant it only as a figure of speech. You *are* sleeping with the boy, are you not? Or have I been misinformed?'

'It is none of your business who I am sleeping with. But Ned lodges with me, yes.'

The answer was disingenuous, for in truth he and Ned had become, for want of a better term, lovers. Quite how that had happened, Will could not make out. From that first fumbling grope, their sexual encounters had become a regular nightly event, a friendly, laughter-filled grappling that seemed somehow entirely innocent.

His liking for the boy had grown into a genuine affection. It had troubled him at first, but in the end, he had decided that his love for Ned was quite different from the passionate attachment he felt for his wife. Both emotions could live side-by-side in his heart without doing any violence to his soul. How long his infatuation—for so he characterised it in his mind—would last, he could not tell. But for now, he was as happy as he had ever been in life.

Henslowe, seeing that his cast was not going to hook any fish, shrugged and turned his attention back to the stage, where Tamburlaine was busily wooing Ned/Zenocrate, throwing off his shepherd's cloak to reveal the armour and axe that would communicate to the audience his true character as a soldier and conqueror (Will was pleased with that little device, his own suggestion when he had talked the play through with Kit). Henslowe was right—Ned did indeed make a pretty girl. But he was also a fine young actor, and Will was proud of the boy as he made his way through the courtly steps of being wooed by the all-conquering hero—demure, scornful and outraged by turns.

The play moved on. Showing himself as much ancient Machiavel as skilful general, Tamburlaine defeated his adversaries one by one. First, he suborned the soldiers sent against him to turn their coats, then convinced Mycetes' brother to join him in return for the throne should they succeed in their war against the Persian king, only to renege on that promise. Then he defeated and captured Bajazeth, the foolish and weak emperor of the Turks, imprisoned him and his wife in an iron cage, fed him on scraps, and only let him out so he could suffer the further humiliation of being used as Tamburlaine's footstool. Bajazeth ended his agony by committing suicide, bashing his brains out against the bars of his cage, an act that prompts his wife to do the same. Though there were no groundlings in the theatre to gasp at the sprays of pigs' blood that would accompany this scene when it was performed on the morrow, Will was certain their base instincts would be well satisfied by its horror.

Tamburlaine's will for power was unstoppable, and at last, he confronted the Sultan of Egypt, the greatest of all his adversaries. Besieging Damascus, he captured the Sultan, whose life he spared and returned to power, extracting as his price the hand of his daughter, Zenocrate, with whom he had fallen in love during her earlier captivity at his court.

Alleyn's powerful voice echoed across the empty theatre as he declaimed the closing lines of the play:

> *'And now, my lords and loving followers,*
> *That purchased kingdoms by your martial deeds,*
> *Cast off your armour, put on scarlet robes,*
> *Mount up your royal places of estate,*
> *Environed with troops of noblemen,*
> *And there make laws to rule your provinces.*
> *Hang up your weapons on Alcides' post,*
> *For Tamburlaine takes truce with all the world.*
> *Thy first betrothed love, Arabia,*
> *Shall we with honour, as beseems, entomb*
> *With this great Turk and his fair empress.*
> *Then, after all these solemn exequies,*
> *We will our rites of marriage solemnise.'*

Will joined enthusiastically in the scattered applause from the small group that had been watching the rehearsal from the beginning—stagehands, a few apprentices who had wandered in from the street, and a smattering of actors from other companies, drawn there out of curiosity about this new play. Henslowe, who had disappeared in the middle of the rehearsal, was now moving through the little crowd, thrusting wads of handbills at any who would take them and urging all and sundry to tell their friends about the Admiral's Men and their marvellous new play. 'It will, I prophesy, be the talk of the city by tomorrow night.'

Though Will was inclined to agree with this sentiment, he had no interest in making small talk with the gathered actors, and instead hurried up the small set of stairs on one side of the stage and pushed through the curtains into the tiring-room. It was a familiar scene of joyful pandemonium—costumes jumbled everywhere, half-dressed actors scrubbing the paint off faces flushed with excitement and exertion, harassed stagehands doing their best to make sure that props and even more valuable costumes were put away before they were damaged in the general chaos.

Standing in the middle of the tiring-room, Alleyn struggled to remove the false beard glued to his chin while half-listening to Gabriel Spencer and Richard Cowley chattering away. Will, crossing the room, paused for a moment to add his congratulations on a successful rehearsal, before heading towards the play's author, who was deep in conversation with a still-costumed Ned Bentley. For a moment, Will felt the smallest twinge of jealousy, instantly banished by the dazzling smile that lit up Ned's face as Will approached.

'What do you think? Will it do?' Marlowe asked, smiling.

'Oh, it will do. It will do very well.' Shakespeare matched the other's lightness with his own grin. 'You are a genius, my friend. Even Henslowe thinks so.'

'Henslowe! Wouldn't know a good play from a country dumb-show.'

'But he does know what will separate the hoi-polloi from their pennies, and he thinks *Tamburlaine* will do that most effectively.' Will turned to Ned and cupped the youth's chin in his hand. 'And he thinks you are a very fetching Zenocrate, young man.'

'I *was* good, wasn't I?'

'Oh, ho! The very voice of precocious youth.' Marlowe wagged his finger. 'Yes, you were very good today, but you must be better tomorrow. And if you're not, I shall prevail upon Mister Henslowe to enslave you in his brothel, where your arse can service any dung-breathed bumpkin who can afford your price. What do you think he would fetch, Will? A penny a time?'

'At least.' Will laughed.

Ned stuck his tongue out, simpered, gathered his skirts together, and twirled in a full circle before giving them an elaborate curtsy. 'Since you are being so mean to me, I shall bid you gentlemen, if you can be so called, an amiable farewell. And I shall be good tomorrow. *Very* good!'

Marlowe giggled as the boy flounced off to join the chattering circle around Alleyn. 'I must thank you for bringing Ned to us, Will. He is a fine young actor.'

'The Queen's company is a demanding school, particularly while on tour.'

'Are you in love with him?'

Marlowe's change of subject caught Will by surprise. 'In love? No, I don't think so. But I like him. Very much.'

'Me too.' Seeing the look on Will's face, he hurried on. 'Do not fret, he is safe enough from me. I would not do anything to disturb your contentment, my friend. Now come and help me separate Alleyn from that circle of sycophants, lest his ego grow so monstrous that he forgets his lines on the morrow.'

***

Marlowe need not have worried, for Ned Alleyn did not forget a single syllable of his many lines in the opening performance the following day, nor was he to forget them at any of the many performances he delivered thereafter. Watching from a privileged position among the gentry in the first balcony of the Rose, Will was struck again, as he had been the day before, by the startling match between man and role. Alleyn literally *was* Tamburlaine, his tall and powerful frame draped in its exotic robes eclipsing all others as he strode about the stage delivering Marlowe's brilliant blank verse.

And it was not only Alleyn who gave a performance to be remembered, that sunlit late October afternoon. Every member of the company seemed touched by the divinities of the acting craft, inspired by the originality of Marlowe's text to give even the least line dramatic meaning.

As for the audience, they sensed from the first words of the prologue that they were about to witness something new in the theatre. The usual noisy background provided by the groundlings—the low hum of conversation that was never quite stilled by the action on stage, the hiss of beer bottles being opened, and the crack of nuts being extracted from their shells—soon subsided into an enraptured hush as the grandiose story unfolded. They giggled at Gabe Spencer's lispingly effeminate Mycestes, cheered Alleyn's first appearance on stage as the shepherd-king and gasped as Badajoz and his wife Zabena satisfactorily simulated bashing their brains out against the iron bars of their cage. But between these episodes they listened and watched with an attention that Will found surprising, used as he was to audiences who expressed their pleasure or dissatisfaction in the most raucous fashion.

At the end, the applause was deafening, the crowd's enthusiasm sweeping even the most jaded theatregoers among the gentry up in the first balcony to their feet. No merry jig was needed to send the audience off in a happy mood after this play, and the players seemed destined to spend the rest of their lives on the stage taking bow after bow. In a surprising gesture, the play's author was summoned to the stage by Alleyn, who introduced him as 'our most perfect playwright', bringing forth another wave of cheers and applause. Marlowe acknowledged the adulation with a sweeping bow that would have done a courtier proud, before retreating with the others through the doors at the back of the stage.

Climbing up the stairs beside the stage and going into the tiring-house as the last of the spectators made their way out of the theatre, Will was greeted by a flushed and still costumed Ned Bentley. He listened with amusement and more than a little pride as the young actor chattered on, seeking both admiration and reassurance in the same breath. He duly bestowed both while helping the boy out of his dress and watching him climb back into his somewhat worn hose and shabby doublet.

In the middle of the big stage, Marlowe was deep in conversation with Philip Henslowe. Or, more accurately, the writer was listening with ill-disguised impatience as the oily theatre proprietor talked at him, his face decorated with a smile that was, for those who were used to his habitual gloominess, more than a little disconcerting. Marlowe, catching Will's eye, waved at him. Telling Ned to wait outside, he made his way over and was startled when the playwright grasped his arm and leaned his head close to Will's ear. 'Get me away from here. He's driving me mad!'

The whisper was hardly audible and went unnoticed by Henslowe, who barely stopped for breath and continued talking, ignoring Shakespeare entirely. 'You must write another. But perhaps with less in the way of exotic costumes. They cost a fortune, you know. No, you probably don't know; a gentleman of your quality would not be expected to know such things. But we must have another *Tamburlaine*. There *is* more of his story to tell, is there not? And if not, you can make it up.'

'Leave off, Henslowe,' Shakespeare interjected, earning himself a look of annoyance. 'You will make more than enough from this *Tamburlaine* to cover your costs and make a handsome profit, if I am any judge. Kit, the others told me to say that they are gathering at the Falcon and beg you to come and take an ale with them.'

'Us' in this instance was himself and Ned, but it was enough of an excuse to allow them to make hurried farewells and depart, leaving a disgruntled Henslowe to stump off across the stage.

'He really is the most annoying man,' Marlowe said as they went through the door behind the tiring-room that led out into the street. 'Always talking about money.'

'It is his chief motive for everything, to be sure.' Will was benign. 'But we should be thankful that he sees the opportunity to profit from the theatre enough to build this place.'

'True enough. *Ah, fair Zenocrate!—Divine Zenocrate!—Fair is too foul an epithet for thee!* Even in a boy's costume...'

Ned, turning from where he had been contemplating the high wooden amphitheatre of the bear-baiting pit, over on the other side of the rose gardens, just giggled. 'Art thou my Tamburlaine? Nay, you are too short.'

'Everyone is too short compared with Alleyn. Come on, that skinflint Henslowe has managed to dig deep into his purse to find me some money, so let us treat ourselves to a good dinner. Are the others really at the Falcon?'

'I'm not sure, to be truthful,' Will said, 'but Rob and George were at the play, it is the nearest tavern on bankside, and for certes Greene could not go without a drink before making the journey across the river. So by deduction, it does seem likely they will be there.'

They made their way to the riverbank, where a row of ferry boats was moored awaiting late afternoon customers, the ferrymen whiling away the time playing cards. The Thames was as busy as ever, small boats making their way between the anchored fleet of stately galleons, wherries and barges taking advantage of the ebbing tide to slip downriver. Over to their right, London Bridge spanned the river on its nineteen arches, beneath which the water was churned into a frothing torrent as it forced its way between the piers. On the opposite shore, smoke plumed upwards from innumerable chimneys into a cloudless sky, and Will could hear a constant low hum, the sound of the city's thousands carrying on their lives in the streets and lanes and alleyways of the capital. It was a familiar and unremarkable scene to the three young men who had made London their home.

But that day, they did not need the services of a boatman, instead turning west to walk along the wide rutted road that ran between the riverbank and the buildings, a mix of dilapidated dwellings and equally ramshackle warehouses. Rising behind the moss-grown tiled roofs, Will could see the tops of the rough wooden arenas where the masses were entertained with bear- and bull-baitings, a form of entertainment whose attractions entirely escaped Will, though he realised that they appealed to the same instincts that caused audiences to cheer at the sight of an actor pretending to beat his brains out against the iron bars of his cage. This late in the afternoon they were silent and deserted, the bloody arena floors sanded and swept, and the dogs kennelled until they should be released again to torment bull or bear.

A few minutes' walk brought them to the Paris Garden steps and the Falcon Tavern, an imposing three-story building overlooking a jetty busy with boatmen dropping off and picking up passengers for the trip across the river. Inside, they found Robert Greene ensconced in one corner of a taproom lit by afternoon sunlight streaming through the tall windows that faced onto the river, a pipe in one hand and a vast tankard of ale in the other. His face was wreathed in smoke and smiles as he held court with the others gathered about him—George Peele, with whom Will had been working to finish his play, *Jack Straw*, Tom Watson and, perched nervously on a stool to one side, a thin, nervous-looking man who Will did not recognise.

'Marlowe! And Shake-shaft!' Will grimaced at Greene's boomed greeting. 'Newly come from the place of triumph. You honour us indeed. You have truly created something new in the theatre, Kit, and I take my bonnet off to you.' He matched action to words by sweeping off his hat, a rather crumpled-looking velvet cap, and going down in a deep bow. As always with Greene, there was something of mockery in the gesture, but as he straightened, Will saw genuine respect and affection in his eyes.

'You liked it, then?' Marlowe seemed surprisingly tentative. Will had never known him to care a fig for the opinion of others, but he seemed overwhelmed, as if he could not quite believe that his play had at last made its way to the stage and was a success.

'We have talked of nothing else for the last half hour.' Thomas Watson smiled. 'Even Kyd here thinks it most original. Almost as good as the *Spanish Tragedy*.'

Will looked with renewed interest at the thin man at whom these remarks were directed, the author of one of the most popular plays ever performed on the London stage and the first that Will had seen when he'd come to the capital two years ago. Kyd was in appearance entirely unremarkable. Dressed in a sober brown woollen doublet and dark green breeches with scuffed shoes and a plain, unadorned cap on his thinning brown hair, he might have passed for a junior clerk in some counting-house.

'You quite misrepresent me, Thomas,' Kyd said. 'Greene is right, Kit, you have mastered us all with *Tamburlaine*, and we will all have to go back to school if we are to better it.'

'Or perhaps I will better it myself. Henslowe is already after me for another play, though this one damned near wore me out.'

'A pox on Henslowe and all theatre-owners,' George Peele said vehemently. 'They suck us dry, take all the profits and expect us to produce on cue like some kind of milch-cow.'

'Then you are fools, all of you,' Greene said amiably, 'to enslave yourselves so for the paltry reward of the adulation of sweaty apprentices and addled goodwives. You won't find me writing plays.'

***

'He will, you know,' Marlowe said later as they sat in a bobbing ferry making its way across the river. 'Write plays, I mean. Rob might think that the printers love him for those high-flown tracts of his, with their ancient gods and nymphs, and his musing upon the nature of love, but it is his coney-catching pamphlets that really sell and fill his doublet pockets with money, and who buys those? Sweaty apprentices and addled goodwives.'

Will nodded, a little distracted by Ned, who was looking decidedly pale after an afternoon spent imbibing far too much wine and ale, and from the look of him threatened to throw up everything in his stomach at any minute. 'That's why he dedicated his *Morando* to Lord Arundel, I suppose. He is tilting for patronage, like Watson, or better yet, a secretaryship, like Kyd.' Tom Watson enjoyed the financial support of the Earl of Oxford, and Kyd was personal secretary to the Earl of Pembroke.

'Not much chance he will get a penny from Arundel. He's broke.' Marlowe, as always, seemed to know everything about the aristocracy. 'So Rob will eventually lower himself to writing plays if he wants to earn a living and win the fame for which he hungers.'

They were approaching Paul's Wharf and the boatman skimmed his little skiff between the other watercraft and up to the weedy sodden piles with the skill of long experience. Holding the boat steady against the choppy water, he watched with detached amusement as the two older men helped propel the youth unceremoniously up onto the jetty with a quick shove on the backside before climbing up themselves.

'Need any help to get him home?' Marlowe asked as Ned stood swaying on the slippery wood of the jetty, his eyes glassy and unfocussed, an idiot's smile on his handsome face.

Will slipped an arm around the boy's shoulders to support him. 'We will be all right. It isn't a long walk. Take care of yourself. It's getting dark.'

With which they parted, Kit for his lodgings in nearby Bread Street, and Will and Ned to the little garret room they shared off Cheapside. Ned mumbled incoherently to himself, leaving Will to his own thoughts, which went back to that impassioned lament from George Peele earlier in the day. It was true—a writer of plays, even one as celebrated as Tom Kyd, was paid a fee for his labours, sometimes a quite handsome fee, but thereafter the play became the property of the company that was performing it, and it was the company that took the receipts from every performance thereafter. And since players must have somewhere to play, they had to share those profits with the likes of Henslowe, who could turf them out if he thought they were no longer bringing in the crowds. The only path to true prosperity in the theatre was to have a share in both company *and* playhouse.

And it also came to him, as they finally arrived home and he dumped the by-now almost inert form of Ned Bentley onto their bed, that this would be his future. Though he had not yet written a word except to patch up others' plays and had barely a farthing to his name by way of capital, one day he, William Shakespeare, would be the writer of plays as splendid as Marlowe's *Tamburlaine*, in which he would act, and which would be performed by his company in his own theatre. It was a fine dream, and he fell asleep smiling at the thought of it.

Chapter 11

'Who is that man? He has been loitering there for the last half-hour, at least.'

Pulling a shirt over his head, Will peered over Ned's bare shoulder and out the open window to the street below, where he beheld the lanky form of Walter Williams, his sometime colleague at the London home of Sir Francis Walsingham in Seething Lane. Williams, seeing Shakespeare's face, gave him a gap-toothed smile and blew him a mocking kiss.

'A spectre, come to haunt me from a past life,' Will said, to Ned's mystification. 'I'd better go down and see what he wants. Why don't you get dressed and we can meet at Mistress Mary's around noon?'

'All right. Mister White said he wanted some help with deliveries and the like this morning, anyway.'

With clear reluctance, Ned turned away from the window and began rummaging among the pile of clothes on the floor for shirt and hose, giving Will a moment to admire the youth's willowy nakedness. Legs slipped into hose, points tied and shirt shrugged on, he sat on the edge of the bed and began pulling on boots. Leaving him to it, Will donned his doublet and tied his belt, took his hat from its place on a hatstand in the corner of their little room, and made his way down the two flights of rickety stairs and out the front door onto busy Silver Street.

'Got yourself a catamite, have you?' Williams leered, arms crossed on his skinny chest as he leaned against the wall of the house opposite. 'What would they think in Stratford town, I wonder?'

'You never change, Walter.' Will glared at the other man, doing his best to contain his temper; Walter Williams had always set him on edge. 'Ned but shares my chamber, since I am not so rich that I can afford the luxury of a room all to myself. Now, unless you are taking up some new occupation as a thief or pickpocket—or was that your old trade before Sir Francis took you up? I can never remember what part of London's gutters you climbed up from—I assume you are loitering here upon instruction, with some message for me from your betters. If so, out with it and you can relieve me of your stench.'

Williams seemed unmoved by this little tirade, to Will's disappointment. 'I do not care to bandy words with a bumpkin from the provinces,' he said loftily. 'But yes, I am here on the Queen's business. You are commanded to a meeting.'

'Commanded, am I? A meeting with whom? And where?'

'I am to take you, upon this instant, to the Royal Exchange. As to the "who", you will have to wait until we get there to find an answer to that question. Come, they are waiting.'

Williams started to walk down the street and was almost at the corner before he stopped. He turned, annoyed, and stood with hands on hips. 'God's wounds, Shakespeare! Do you expect me to shout the Queen's business at the top of my voice in the street?'

Will said nothing, just stared.

With a sigh, the other turned and trotted back up the street. 'You were ever a stubborn bastard. It is Thomas who awaits, along with another whose name I was told not to mention.'

'Ah, well, why didn't you say so in the first place? I am always happy to go and see my old friend Tom Phelippes. Though I doubt he did any "commanding", I'll be bound.'

'It was his request, most respectful. Now for the love of God will you come along?'

Will swept off his hat and went down in a mocking bow. 'Your servant, Walter. Lead on.'

It was but a ten-minute walk along busy Cheapside, though it required some dexterity to thread their way through the crowd, for Cheapside was both street and market, lined on each side with shops whose stalls intruded upon what might otherwise have been a broad cobbled thoroughfare, reducing it to a narrow space in which shoppers competed for space with carts, carriages, horses and pedestrians. But this chaos was familiar to both young men, and they negotiated its perils with ease, squeezing themselves against a wall at the Cheapside Cross to allow the passage of a cart filled with carcasses coming into the city from Smithfield, and weaving a path through the laughing, raucous crowd of goodwives gathered at the open-sided pavilion of the Great Conduit, where they gathered each day to draw water for their washing and exchange gossip with their friends. Finally, having achieved their journey in silence, a sort of unspoken truce having been declared between them,

Though Will had never been inside, he had walked past this temple to commerce many times. The fine four-storey brick building was adorned at every point with the grasshopper emblem of the exchange's builder, Sir Thomas Gresham, including one huge, gilded version that Will thought must be at least ten feet long that was perched precariously atop the tall belltower that stood next to the main entrance. Beyond, they entered a big courtyard surrounded by colonnades that sheltered the congregating merchants and traders who went there to exchange news and views about the subjects that have fascinated the merchant kind since time immemorial: what cargoes were coming or leaving the great port of London, and whither they were bound, what prices were being quoted, the rumours of peace and war coming from abroad, the latest changes in tastes and fashions from which they might profit, and the cruel and exorbitant nature of all taxes upon trade. Above, the shops on the long balcony that ran around the first floor were doing a busy trade selling their mousetraps, birdcages, shoeing-horns, lanthorns, patent remedies, books old and new, gold trinkets and fine glass goblets.

'It's like Venice,' Will said, stopping to look around. 'They have a market like this called the Rialto.'

Williams showed his annoyance at this interruption to their progress with a pout and a sniff. 'I've never been there. Shall we go on, if your lordship has had enough of gawking at the sights?'

Will laughed, pleased to have once again succeeded in provoking his escort.

Instead of passing through the gate into the second courtyard that lay beyond the first, Williams led the way up two flights of stairs to a door that opened into a narrow dark corridor. A few feet along, he stopped at another door and gave three discreet taps. A muffled response came from within, and he lifted the latch to push the door open and entered. Following, Will found himself in a big square room whose brightly lit interior was a shock after the gloom of the corridor. The illumination came from big windows, open to admit light and air, and the room itself was sumptuously appointed with wood-panelled walls, green Turkey carpets, chests, settles and a big worktable covered in neatly stacked papers.

'You have come up in the world, Thomas,' Will said to the thin blonde man who, abandoning his contemplation of the street below, turned to greet them.

Phelippes grinned. 'It is grand, isn't it? But sadly it is not mine. I have merely been given the use of the room for a few days by its rightful owner, Sir Horatio Palavicino. You know of him?'

'The Genoese who conjures money out of thin air whenever the Queen runs short of cash? Yes, I know of him, though I did not know he was a knight.'

'New-minted this very year. Anyway, he has allowed me the use of his office for a few hours so that we could have a private talk.'

'Why here and not Seething Lane?' In Will's experience, Tom Phelippes rarely left his lair, so he could only conclude that this was a conversation that he didn't want overheard by anyone, even those trusted servants of Walsingham's who worked at his house near the Tower of London.

Phelippes shrugged. 'A matter of convenience, that is all. Beale will be here shortly for the main business, but I wanted a privy word with you before he gets here.'

Will remembered Robert Beale from his short time working at Seething Lane before he'd gone to Italy. He was a big, burly man with a bluff manner, an occasional diplomat who often acted as Walsingham's deputy. And Beale's impending attendance at this meeting might also explain the choice of venue, for he was rather self-important, and may not have reacted well to a summons to Seething Lane.

'What is this all about, Thomas? I made it plain to Sir Francis that I was done with intelligencing when last we saw each other, and I had thought he had released me from any further obligation to him.'

'And so he did.' Phelippes was unperturbed. 'But you have, however unwittingly, involved yourself in another piece of intelligence work.'

It took Will a moment to think what he could mean. 'Billy Knell's report? Aye, but that was a simple matter of duty, of passing on information that was clearly intended for Sir Francis. I did not expect that I would be further involved.'

'Robert will explain everything when he gets here. Walter, you can go now.'

Williams had been lounging in a chair on the other side of the room, picking at his nails and seemingly disinterested in the conversation, but on hearing his name, his head came up and he opened his mouth in protest. 'But—'

'But me no buts, sirrah.' Phelippes was suddenly stern. 'Your task is done, and I wish to have private speech with Mister Shakespeare. Go back to Seething Lane. I am sure there is a great deal of work awaiting your attention.'

Williams sulkily picked up his hat and made his way to the door, shooting a venomous look at Will as he passed.

'Spare me whatever you are going to say, Will,' Phelippes said, raising a hand. 'You and Marlowe have made poor Walter's life a misery ever since you first laid eyes on him. He is, I grant you, something of an idiot, but he has his uses. Now, before Beale gets here, there is something I wanted to ask you. How is your father?'

'My father?' Will was startled by the question. 'He is well enough. Why do you ask?'

Phelippes picked up a paper from the desk and fished in his doublet for a pair of thick spectacles. 'This is a copy of the minutes of a town council meeting in Stratford held a week ago.' He settled the spectacles on his nose and began to read. 'John Shakespeare, master glove-maker in the town of Stratford-Upon-Avon, has, it is reported, made secret purchase of two bales of wool for the purpose of selling the same, for which he has no license. In light of Mister Shakespeare's past service to the town as a burgess, no action is being taken for now, pending further information.' Phelippes put the paper down. 'Your father has been somewhat foolish, Will.'

'How so? It is an allegation. You know what gossip in country towns is like.' Of course, his defence of his father was hollow. Had Anne not told him that his father was doing exactly this thing when he'd last been at home?

'True, but he has attracted the attention of the local magistrates, and they will be keeping an eye on him.'

'How came you by this report, Thomas? The doings of a provincial town council would hardly seem to be the stuff with which you usually concern yourself.'

Phelippes smiled. 'We look after our own, Will. You did us a great service in Italy and Sir Francis wanted me to do whatever I could to ensure that you and your family came to no harm. So I have taken a greater interest than usual in the goings-on of this particular provincial town.'

Will stared at his former colleague, calculating. It was clear that he was there because Phelippes and Sir Francis wanted some further service of him. They might be sincere in saying that their interest in his foolish father's doings was well-motivated, but their possession of this information also gave them a hold over him should he refuse whatever they were going to ask.

'What should I do?' he asked, deciding there was little point in voicing his suspicions. Thomas might be short-sighted, but he read men as well as anyone Will had ever met.

'Nothing for now. I will arrange for someone to warn your father that he is being watched and that he had best desist from any activity that shades close to the law. You might find occasion to do the same when you are next in Stratford.' Phelippes nodded, seeming satisfied that this piece of business was now concluded. 'By the way, Sir Francis asked me to pass along his greetings. He would have been here himself, but he is unwell.'

'I am sorry to hear it.' Will was genuine; he liked the severe old man who had, after all, engineered his start with the Queen's players. 'Is his illness serious?'

'You know Sir Francis—perpetually complaining of being too hot or too cold, of having aches in his bones and pains in his head. This is a little more serious than most of his complaints, but is, I hope, but a passing fever, sufficient to keep him in his bed and send me in his place.' The blue eyes resumed their usual inquisitorial focus. 'How are you spending your days, Will? I hear you keep interesting company.'

He shrugged, pretending nonchalance, though in truth he had an ever-growing list of worries, the chief of which was, as ever, money. 'Since the Queen's players have been idle, I lack an occupation for the present. Though I am trying to write. As for the company I keep, 'tis just Marlowe and his friends.'

'Ah, Marlowe.' Phelippes frowned. 'Our young Kit is a puzzle for which even I cannot find a cipher. What is the engine that drives him? He flouts convention at every opportunity, places himself at the very edges of the law, yet he is trusted by all. You would not credit the information he was able to extract for us in France when we sent him to spy among the Catholics.'

Will laughed. 'Kit is trusted because every man thinks that what they see is his inner self, whereas his real self is kept hidden from everyone. But he is a genius, that now is undeniable.'

'*Tamburlaine*, you mean? I have not been to the play, but much has been reported to us about it. A singular work, indeed, and it seems popular. Did your play receive as much approval from the clammy masses?'

'My play?' For a moment Will was puzzled. 'Oh, *Jack Straw*. That was George Peele's work. I merely helped him with a few scenes.'

'I am told that you wrote a good deal more than that, and even Peele has been heard to say that he could not have finished it without you.'

This was true, though Will was startled to hear that Peele had said as much. What had started as a mere copying job had turned into a much more extensive collaboration after Shakespeare had gently suggested some modest improvements to the original. Peele, far from resenting Will's suggestions, had enthusiastically adopted them, and they had quickly forged a happy writing partnership.

'George is too kind. It was no *Tamburlaine*, but it did quite well.' Will said, trying to sound modest. 'Truly, I don't know why you bother asking me questions, Thomas, since you seem to know all the answers.'

Phelippes laughed. 'I would not be much of an intelligencer if I did not, now would I?'

Their wry laughter was interrupted when the door swung open to admit a bulky man of middling height, whose greying hair and silver beard made him look older than his forty-five years, though he still moved with the contained energy of one who was in his youth an athlete.

'Hello, Robert,' Phelippes said. 'You remember William Shakespeare, no doubt?'

'I do. They tell me you are an actor these days, with aspirations to poesy. Following in Marlowe's rather unsteady footsteps, I suppose. Bloody silly life.' Having delivered himself of that judgement, he flung himself down on the nearest settle. 'Well, Thomas, we don't have all day. Have you told Shakespeare why he is here?'

'No, Robert,' Phelippes said, patiently. 'We agreed that we would wait until you arrived.'

'So we did.' The big man turned his attention back to Will, whose air of polite enquiry was unlikely to fool Beale, whose black fathomless eyes disguised both intelligence and ruthlessness. 'It's about those papers you found among William Knell's things.'

'So I had assumed,' Will said. 'Kit and I sent them on to Seething Lane because it seemed obvious that they were of some importance, but I fail to see what other connection they have with me.'

'We will get to that. But first, let me ask you a question, and I beg you to answer honestly, how secure do you think our state of England is at this time?'

It was a startling thing to ask; almost any answer could be construed as treasonous. He wondered whether he was being entrapped in some way, but an encouraging glance from Phelippes suggested otherwise.

'I am but an actor, Master Beale, whose purview of such lofty matters must be limited,' he began, hurrying on when a twitch of Beale's fingers dismissed such verbal caution. 'I would say that England is a good deal more secure since the Scots Queen met her end in February.'

'I know. I was there. Though it was not a pretty sight, I praise God daily for our deliverance from the schemes of that woman. Go on, what else?'

'We are told daily that Her Majesty is in good health, for which God be praised. The Scots are quiet, and for once there is no trouble in Ireland. I was told when the players were touring that the coasts have been warned to prepare for an invasion from Spain, but so far no such threat has appeared on the horizon. In short, the country is enjoying the blessings of peace.'

'Yet appearances can deceive. King Philip's invasion, though long foretold, cannot now happen this year, for it grows too late in the season for campaigning. But come it will, most likely next summer, and we must prepare for it, though Lord Howard assures us daily that his mariners will succeed in defeating the Spanish before ever they can link up with Parma's thousands waiting to cross the narrow sea.'

Will was beginning to grow impatient. He was well aware of the Spanish plans for sending a huge fleet—an *armada*, they called it—up the Channel to provide the necessary protection for the armies gathering in the Spanish Netherlands, since that was the essence of the strategy laid out in some detail in the documents that he had brought back from Italy almost a year ago to the day.

'Perhaps the Lord Admiral is right, and all will be well,' Beale went on, 'but Sir Francis and I must consider the possibility that the sailors, however valiant, might fail in their mission. The safety of the realm cannot be entrusted solely to a policy that is so dependent upon the vagaries of wind and storm.'

'If Parma lands, surely he will be met with the stoutest resistance. And I still do not see what all this has to do with me unless you are expecting me to take up pike and sword in the realm's defence.'

'Patience, Shakespeare. We will get to that. But you are right in this respect— we are not afeared that our soldiers and yeomanry cannot defend the country. Rather, it is treachery within that we fear—plots to abduct or murder her majesty and replace her with a Catholic puppet just as the Spanish are landing on our soil. You look surprised. Do you not think such a thing could happen?'

'But with Queen Mary now dead, what pretender is left who could hope to take the throne?'

'There are other potential candidates within our borders, Will,' Phelippes said, 'sprigs of the royal line who may harbour pretensions to the throne and who could be suborned into treason if they thought they might be able to take advantage of the chaos of an invasion.' He stopped and looked at Beale, who nodded his permission for Phelippes to continue. 'One such candidate is Ferdinando Stanley, Lord Strange, Derby's son and heir.'

So *that* was what this was about. Will remembered the name that had so puzzled him when he and Marlowe had deciphered Knell's papers.

Phelippes, who always enjoyed explaining things, assumed a schoolmasterly air. 'Under the terms of King Henry's will, he has a place in the succession by way of his mother, Lady Margaret Clifford. Her maternal grandparents were the Duke of Suffolk and Mary Tudor, King Henry's youngest sister. So naturally, when we saw his name in the paper that you and Marlowe so cleverly deciphered, our interest was pricked.'

'With respect, Thomas, that seems to be a somewhat distant thread.'

'Yet so depleted is the Tudor bloodline that this young man, or perhaps his father the present Earl of Derby, is the only English candidate whose claim could be supported,' Beale said. 'There is, of course, the Scottish King James, who has never foresworn his mother's supposed right to the English throne. He might have some support in England.' He stopped and a look of irritation crossed his face, as though his inner mind were considering the idiocy of those who might support such a course. 'But I digress. Our concern today is with Lord Strange. Even though the loyalty of the present generation of the family has never been questioned, the Stanleys showed on Bosworth Field that they are capable of switching sides when it seems to their benefit. And they are from the north, where Catholic sympathies are still strong.'

'And let us not forget Deventer,' Phelippes put in. In January, Sir William Stanley, a cousin of some sort of the present Early of Derby, had shocked the country when he'd surrendered the fortress town of Deventer, in the Low Countries, taking six hundred of his men across to the Spanish side.

Will thought about all that. Though it seemed fantastical, he could see that a confused and divided country, invaded from abroad, the Queen deposed or worse, might accept a minor sprig of the nobility as their new monarch even if he was a puppet dancing to a tune being sounded in far-away Madrid.

'Which brings us to the subject of John Towne,' Beale continued. 'Knell's report said that he was to find a place in Strange's household, and once there, to await further instructions. What role he is to play thereafter we cannot tell. But we did receive intelligence that a Jesuit priest had landed on the south coast in late April. He was spotted coming ashore but slipped away from our agents before they could apprehend him. His description matches that of the man who Towne met in Abingdon.'

That, at least, was some corroboration of Knell's story. But Will was surprised by the next question.

'What is your opinion of the circumstances of Knell's death, Shakespeare?' Beale asked, one quizzical eyebrow raised. 'You were present when he died, I understand.'

Something in the big man's eyes counselled Will's mind to caution. 'It looked like self-defence to me—Knell drew first, attacked with great vehemence, and chased John down the street. It was only when he was trapped that he pulled out his own sword.'

'So you deposed to the coroner,' Beale said. 'Yet I sense some doubt in your mind. Doubts you did not express to the authorities.'

Will held Beale's gaze, acutely aware that if he changed his story, he might be accused of perjury.

'It seems to me that John deliberately set out to provoke Billy,' he said carefully. 'He knew Knell's temper and how to inflame it. And he is a skilled swordsman, unlikely to have struck a mortal blow in error. So yes, it could have been deliberate. But this is mere supposition, upon which no fair-minded jury would be likely to bring a conviction.'

'Well, it seems that the coroner in Thame saw it the same way. A few days ago, John Towne was released from custody after a finding that he killed William Knell in self-defence. I, however, am not so convinced of his innocence. Thomas, does that dago keep any decent wine here? All this talking has left me quite parched.'

Giving his superior an irritated look that was blithely ignored by its target, Phelippes got up and went rummaging in a cabinet for wine and glasses. When they had settled again, Beale seemed content to leave the stage to Phelippes. They are a well-rehearsed pair, like a couple of actors who had shared the stage many times and could anticipate each other with perfect timing. Still, the next question was, once again, seemingly irrelevant.

'Lord Strange has a company of players, Will. Did you know that?'

'Yes, of course, Thomas. Everyone in the theatre knows it, though they are but tumblers and acrobats, not performers of serious plays.'

'True. But he has conceived a desire to transform his company into a proper acting troupe, and he is recruiting actors for the purpose. There are not so many such in London who are not contracted to one or another of the other companies, so it is certain that Towne will sooner or later be approached to join them, or vice-versa. Which brings me to your role in all this. We want you to join the company as well.'

'And what am I to do? Keep an eye on John Towne? Become a spy once again?' Will found it impossible to keep his disgust with the whole notion out of his voice.

'Yes, in a word. And while you are at it, we want to know if Lord Strange can be trusted, too.' Beale's tone brooked no argument. 'Put aside your scruples, Shakespeare. The realm faces great peril in the year ahead, and if there is danger coming from the direction of Lord Strange, we need to know about it. And to be frank, if you discover there is nothing in all this, you will be doing us a service too. So there it is. Will you help your country?'

Will stared at him, then made the inevitable capitulation. 'It seems that I am flanked on all sides. Yes, I will do it, though reluctantly.'

'Good, that is settled.' Beale spoke as if he had never expected any other outcome. 'Well, I must get on. Thomas will explain our requirements in detail. Good luck to you, and you may be assured that your service will be rewarded with the gratitude of the state.'

'Will, I know you are reluctant to become involved in such affairs once more,' Phelippes said as the door clicked shut and they resumed their seats, 'but Robert was speaking the truth—we have few others we can trust to do this task. And you showed us in Italy that you could act with intelligence and discretion.'

'Ah, sweet flattery!' Will said sardonically. 'But I suppose I should not complain. At least I will be paid if I am employed by this lordling in his acting company.' He knew he sounded dour, but in truth, he was flattered by the confidence that was being placed in him by some very powerful people. 'So, Thomas, tell me how you are going to get me into Lord Strange's marvellous new acting troupe.'

Phelippes smiled the wolfish smile he always wore when making a new plot. 'Marlowe is the key to that particular lock. His success with *Tamburlaine* has made him the darling of all those in London who love the theatre, of whom Lord Strange is one. Young Stanley enjoys the company of poets and playwrights, and no doubt will invite Marlowe to his London home. You can accompany him and we will see how things progress from there.'

It seemed a remarkably loose arrangement, but Will recognised that, in truth, it could hardly be anything else. At least Marlowe, with his quick wit and inventive tongue, could be relied upon to prise open even the smallest opportunity. Even so, he had his doubts. How could he, a mere player, ever hope to get close enough to Lord Strange to divine his mind on anything so dangerous as treason? And why would Towne trust him enough to let slip his own part in this supposed conspiracy? Always assuming there *was* a conspiracy, and that the whole thing wasn't a fiction dreamed up in Knell's jealousy-addled brain. But the time was past to make such objections.

'All right. But if I am going to do this, I must ask you for one further favour, Thomas.'

'Name it, and I will do it if it is in my power.'

'Warn the authorities in Stratford off from any further harassment of my father.'

Phelippes frowned. 'Not entirely straightforward. Such an intervention might heighten their suspicions, rather than lower them, and we cannot entirely control what local councillors might do. But I will do what I can.'

With which promise Will knew he had to be content. Their business concluded, he followed his former colleague out through the courtyard and back to Cheapside, where they would part, he to go and meet Ned at Mistress Mary's and Phelippes to return to Seething Lane.

But before they separated, Phelippes grasped his forearm to make one last point. 'It is entirely possible that there is smoke without fire in this case. Be careful in your assumptions and remember that even if you are able to put our minds at rest with respect to Lord Strange's loyalty, you will be doing us as great a service as you would if you were to uncover the conspiracy at which Knell's report seems to hint.'

Will watched Phelippes make his way down the crowded street and now that he was alone, he released the inner tension by muttering a stream of curses under his breath. He had, he knew, little choice but to do as he was told, but that didn't mean he had to like it.

'Are you all right, sir?'

The words came from a street urchin who had sidled up unnoticed, no doubt hoping for an errand that might earn him a penny or two. He was a filthy, tousle-haired lad who could not have been much more than six years old.

'Perfectly all right.' He fished into his doublet pocket for a sixpence, which he tossed at the boy, who caught it with the unconscious agility of the street. 'Go and buy yourself something to eat.'

He watched, smiling, as the lad, wide-eyed at his good fortune, skipped away up the street, dodging between the legs of goodwives and labourers until he disappeared from view. The small, impulsive act of charity restored his good mood and he turned to make his way home.

Chapter 12

'A child *and* a pregnant woman?'

'Yes. It seems that some fool put scraps of metal on top of the wadding in the mistaken belief that it would make for a more spectacular shower of sparks.' Marlowe could barely disguise his contempt for the unknown stagehand who had caused this calamity. 'Instead, the hot metal skewered two spectators, and now the Admiral's Men are banned from performance pending an investigation.'

Will shook his head. The terrible incident with the gun had been the talk of the London theatre world for the last week, and though some had openly laughed at the misfortunes of a rival company, most understood that such an accident could as easily have happened in one of their own performances and were sympathetic towards the luckless members of the Lord Admiral's company of players.

He shivered and pulled his cloak tighter as a flurry of wind brought a blast of cold air sweeping across the misty surface of the river. A small ferry boat came into sight, the ferryman drifting easily on his oars as he took advantage of the making tide. Kit's ear-piercing whistle stimulated a flurry of oars and the boat shifted course towards the wharf.

'How are the actors taking it?'

'Poor Ned Alleyn has gone into a decline and refuses to see anyone. The others—Attewell, Gabriel Spencer, Cowley and the rest—are brazening it out as best they can, telling everyone it was a tragic accident and trying to raise some funds for the victims' families in atonement.'

'And no doubt the Puritans will argue that this is yet another reason to close the theatres,' Will said gloomily.

164

'They can argue it.' Kit jutted his chin out, acquiring a pugnacious expression as though he was himself an advocate before the authorities. 'But Tilney is mindful that the theatres are popular with everyone from the Queen down, so I have no doubt that the Admiral's Men will be back on the stage before long, as soon as an appropriate period of penance has passed.'

By now the ferry boat was bobbing a few feet below them, the ferryman holding tight to keep his minuscule vessel close to the wharf. With the agility that was so useful on the stage, Will leapt neatly down the short drop, landing in time to lend a steadying hand to a less nimble Kit, whose awkward arrival threatened to capsize the boat itself. But in a few moments, they were settled on the stern thwarts and the boatman had shoved them off out into the expanse of the river.

'Where to, sirs?' he asked, taking a quick look over his shoulder to make sure that they could safely clear the wharf-end.

'Derby House. The private steps,' Kit said, adopting a lofty air.

'Right you are, sirs. The tide is a-making, so I reckon on a half-hour journey. Sixpence apiece, shall we say?'

'You're a rogue,' Will said, cutting off Kit, who had been about to agree with a wave of his hand. 'Be content with half that.'

The boatman's gap-toothed grin signified good-natured agreement, and without any further speech, he put his back into the oars. In moments, they were out in the middle of the river and sweeping past the massive, crenelated bulk of Baynard's Castle, London home of the Earl of Pembroke. Once past the outfall of the Fleet Ditch, the making tide eased them past Arundel House, Somerset House, the Savoy Palace, Durham House, Yorke Place, all the great residences of England's preening nobility, their many-windowed facades and reeking chimney-pots visible at a distance behind the gardens that separated them from the river.

'So how did you arrange this?' Will asked as they swept around the great bend that brought the jumbled buildings of Westminster and the grey bulk of the cathedral into view.

'A lucky coincidence. Thomas Kyd was the key. You know he is scrivening for Lord Pembroke?'

Will laughed. 'Of course I do. Greene couldn't decide whether he was outraged or envious when he heard that our Tom, creator of *The Spanish Tragedy*, was earning a steady living clerking for an earl. Though he says that Lord Pembroke seems to regard him as a kind of house-pet to be shown off to curious visitors, along with his collection of Indian beads and head-dresses that Raleigh brought back from the New World, and the simpering antics of his wife's pet ape. Of the three, the ape, to hear him tell it, gets the most interest.'

'Poor Tom.' Marlowe didn't sound in the least sympathetic. 'Anyway, it seems that Lord Strange came to Baynard's Castle on some errand or another, and Kyd became friendly with the Stanley household steward, who was bemoaning the fact that Lord Strange had charged him with reorganising his acting troupe, something for which, poor man, he knew he had no skill. Knowing that Tom was a theatre man, he applied to him for help; of course he could not oblige, being indentured to Pembroke for the time being, but he undertook to ask around among the theatre fraternity. It didn't take long before I heard of it and went straight to see him.'

'And offered your services?' Marlowe had been vague that morning, simply telling him that they were going to Derby House, and Will had assumed that he was to accompany his more famous friend in some more humble capacity, an acolyte, as it were.

'No. He wanted me to take it on, but I told him that I am a poet, not a mere mechanical.' Will laughed at the implied insult, which was robbed of any malice by Marlowe's sly grin; he could easily imagine how much fun he'd had teasing poor Kyd. 'And then I suggested you, since you know far more about how to organise a theatre company than I do.'

Marlowe glanced at the sweating boatman, whose face wore the bland look of someone trying to pretend he wasn't listening to every word and lowered his voice to a whisper. 'Besides, it's you that our friends at Seething Lane want inserted into Lord Strange's household, not me.'

Derby House was one of a line of relatively modest residences that stood between the riverbank and the narrow lane of Cannon Row, between the two royal palaces of Westminster and Whitehall. Having paid the ferryman, they made their careful way up the slippery, weedy steps of the private jetty to a wooden door set into a high stone wall. A bell set into a niche beside a massive wooden door summoned a liveried servant who conducted them through a small walled vegetable garden, into the house and down a narrow corridor past a kitchen from which the smell of roasting meat emerged to tantalise Will's empty stomach. Stopping at a door, the footman tapped once and without waiting for a response, swung it open and gestured the two visitors into the room that lay beyond.

'Master Marlowe and Mister Shakespeare,' the flunkey announced solemnly, bobbed his head, and left.

The small, grey-haired man sitting behind the massive desk that took up half the space in the cramped, dimly lit room did not look up at this announcement, continuing to write with one hand while using the other to wave them to a pair of straight-backed chairs. The pen scratched away for a few moments more, the completed document was sanded and placed on a neat pile on one side of the desk, and the quill was returned to its place in its inkpot. Only then were they favoured with the attention of a pair of piercing blue eyes, above which bushy grey eyebrows were arched in interrogation.

'You must be Marlowe,' he said, looking at Will.

'I fear not, Master Barnes. This gentleman is the illustrious creator of *Tamburlaine*. I am merely William Shakespeare, sometime actor, book-holder, general factotum, and occasional patcher of plays, at your service.'

'You are both theatricals.' Lord Strange's household steward shrugged his indifference, not in any way discomfited by his mistake. 'I know nothing of plays, playhouses or players, save that it is all lies: boys walk upon a stage pretending to be women, holding some flowers, from which we are to deduce that they are walking in a garden; a single leafy bough does duty for an entire forest; commoners strut as kings, claiming dominion over the world entire, though they be masters of naught but the clothes in which they stand; a trapdoor opens and by the issue of quantities of smoke we are supposed to believe that therein lie the portals of hell. And the sweating masses believe it all, though why they should do so is a mystery to me.'

'As it is to us poor poets, who must somehow earn our living by guessing what will please them.' Marlowe laughed, not in the least discomfited by this little recitation. 'But I think you do yourself insufficient credit, Master Barnes, for your words suggest that you have in fact grasped the essence of our business, which is to say, illusion. Our words may in the strictest sense be lies, but they craft a vision in the minds of those who hear them, not all of whom are mere common men. Your master, for instance, is known to love plays and players.'

'Aye, so he does. There are days when Derby House resembles a kind of menagerie within whose cages stalk poets, pamphlet-writers, makers of music, scene-painters and the occasional fraudulent actor like you, Mister Shakespeare, strut and seek to impress His Lordship. All hoping that some pennies will drop from his table into their laps.'

'Yet even poor players such as I must put food upon our meagre tables, Master Barnes, and hence we must needs find our income wheresoever we can.' Will was enjoying this sour steward's pithy observations. 'Which might, perhaps, bring us to the point of our journey up the river today?'

Barnes nodded, placed his elbows on the table, and steepled his fingers beneath his chin, a little ritual that Will took to signify that he was ready to talk of business.

'The fourth Earl of Derby kept a company of players for his own entertainment. The present earl, Lord Strange's father, has no interest in such frivolities and disbanded all of the company except the clowns and acrobats. As well as providing amusement to the Stanley household, they have enjoyed some success on the London stage and in the regions. They have even travelled overseas, with my Lord of Leicester's troupe. All this you must already know.' They nodded their confirmation. 'However, Lord Strange, being of a disposition to enjoy the theatre, has decided—with the earl's agreement, of course—that this tumbling company should be reorganised into a proper acting troupe to perform here in London, at the family houses in Lancashire, and elsewhere in the regions, so as to burnish the reputation of the house of Stanley at court and in the country at large.'

Kit and Will maintained their expressions of polite and bland interest. Of course, none of this was news to them.

'His Lordship, having formulated this program, looked to me to take it forward in its particulars.' Barnes sighed a little theatrically. *Every man has something of the actor in him*, Will thought, *even this one, who makes out he has nothing but disdain for the breed.* 'I have served the Stanley family for nigh on twenty years, and I do not believe that I flatter myself when I say that both father and son trust me and rely upon my advice in many matters. But this command found me, as it were, all at sea. And so, seeking to ease my burden, I sought the counsel of Mister Kyd, who, in turn, directed me to you, Shakespeare.'

Will smiled. He could well imagine Barnes and Kyd, men who shared a bleakly dour outlook on life, commiserating with each other over a small beer in some dingy tavern.

'And here I am, as commanded,' he said brightly, 'with Master Marlowe here as reinforcement. How can we help lighten the load on your shoulders, Master Barnes?'

'In a few words—relieve me of it entirely.'

'A few words that carry a heavy freight. Actors must be found, costumes and properties purchased, places to rehearse and perform negotiated, and plays commissioned. It requires a deal of work and an even greater deal of money to create a theatre company.'

Barnes waved that away. 'His Lordship has set aside some funds for these purposes, though I expect you will claim that it is an insufficient sum, like any other chaffering tradesman.'

'Quality costs,' Will said simply. He heard the door click open behind him, saw the look on the steward's face, and smiled. 'But it seems to me that His Lordship would want the company bearing his name to be of the highest quality, employing the best actors who are dressed to look their parts, performing new plays that will astound London audiences.'

'So he does. And let us not have any of your penny-pinching ways applied to this project, Davey Barnes.'

All three stood and turned to bow in the direction of the utterer of these words, a slim young man of medium height sumptuously dressed in a soft yellow padded doublet, immaculately white falling-band shirt collar and a tall wide-brimmed black hat decorated with a single enormous ruby. But the face beneath the hat could best be described as homely. A broad forehead was disfigured by a prominent mole above his left eye, rather unruly brown hair curled about

170

prominent ears and fell to his lace collar, framing a long face that ended in a neatly trimmed and pointed beard. Pale, watery eyes regarded his visitors from pouchy sockets that suggested their owner suffered a deficit of sleep. The gaze they bent upon them was friendly but seemed to Will to be guarded. This was not, he thought, a man who would let you see far into his soul.

'I but seek to ensure that Your Lordship's pennies are spent wisely and well,' Barnes said, unperturbed by the sudden appearance of Lord Strange at his office door, clearly a regular occurrence. The heir to the house of Stanley flopped into a large armchair, allowing the others to return to their seats, albeit now oriented towards the young aristocrat.

'Which of you is Marlowe? You? Welcome to my house, Master Marlowe. Barnes, you should have told me that the creator of *Tamburlaine* was also visiting us. I would have arranged a more apt reception for the writer who has set all London talking. A carpet of roses and a dozen singing maidens, at the very least!'

'I stand corrected, my lord.' Though Barnes' expression was entirely respectful, his tone conveyed an indifference to his master's jocular rebuke that in another might have been construed as insolence. Clearly, their relationship was one of long-standing and could tolerate such deviations from the usual constraints between master and servant.

Marlowe broke the tiny silence. 'It is I who am honoured by your interest in my humble works, my lord, though your enthusiasm and support for the playhouses, and for us poor poets and playwrights, is well known and does credit to your family. Without it, many a fine poem and many a learned tract might never have seen the light of day.'

Will tried but failed to keep a straight face through this piece of flattery from his usually so-cynical friend. Lord Strange must have detected the tiny twitch of his lips, for he turned an enquiring eye towards him, one eyebrow raised ever so slightly. 'And you are Shakespeare. We have a family called Shakeshaft in Lancashire. Are you related?'

'Not that I am aware, my lord. Though perhaps we shared ancestors of a warlike temperament?'

Strange's laugh was a gentle chuckle that warmed his otherwise cold features. 'You look mild enough. Clerk-like, it might be said.'

'Oh, he is of a most mild disposition,' Marlowe said with an impish grin, 'except upon the stage when he can take on the aspect of a tiger should the requirements of the play demand.'

'Yet you will not be upon any stage at present, if rumour be true.' Barnes' words were more question than statement. 'Kyd tells me that the Queen's Men have been disbanded.'

'Swift-winged rumour outruns dull, plodding fact in this case, Master Barnes,' Will said. 'It is true that, with our troubles in Thame and Dick Tarlton's illness, the company's affairs are in some disarray. But no doubt when Dick has recovered and financial matters are resolved, we will be back on the London stage again.'

'I have oft enjoyed Master Tarlton's wit when he appeared at court,' Lord Strange said. 'I hope that his recovery will be swift and that he can soon entertain us again. Meantime, the ill wind that has sunk the Queen's Men has blown you in our direction. Barnes has explained what we want from you?'

'He has, my lord, and I am most happy to serve.' He paused, uncertain as to how far he might press Lord Strange on the many questions that were already teeming in his head. Fortunately Marlowe, more adroit and less intimidated by aristocracy, must have sensed his uncertainty.

172

'Does my lord have any particular ideas as to the direction that the new company should take?' he asked. 'Do you for instance have a preference for comedy over tragedy? Or vice-versa?'

'Oh, I have no preference for one or the other. Both, probably.' He leaned forward in his chair, as if to signify his seriousness. 'But what I do want is a company that will rival the best in the land, even my lord of Leicester's troupe. They played for us this summer past, at Lathom House. *Telamon*, do you know it?'

Will nodded. 'About the father of Ajax, if I remember rightly, my lord. It is a tragedy—Telamon hires two cutthroats to murder the husband of Castibula, with whom he has fallen in love. She swears vengeance but cunningly agrees to marry Telamon. At the marriage feast, they both drink from a poisoned cup that Castibula has prepared. They die, but Castibula has had her revenge.'

'That is the essence of it. It might seem thin stuff, but the players made it into a fine play, full of modern allusions and poetical conceits.' Strange's face became dreamy for a moment, as though he was seeing again in his inner mind that production in the great hall of his family's mansion in far-away Lancashire. 'It was watching that play at Lathom that inspired me into this venture and made me decide to create a new company where the finest actors can perform the best new plays by London's finest poets.'

'A most worthy enterprise, my lord,' Marlowe said eagerly, 'and one that will no doubt bring you and the name of Stanley great glory. And if I might be allowed to make a small contribution to its success, perhaps I might write a new play for a new company?'

No suggestion could have pleased Lord Strange more. He clapped his hands in delight and his face was transformed by a broad smile at the prospect of having his company launched into the world with a play by London's current theatrical darling. 'That is a very merry prospect, Master Marlowe, very merry indeed. We shall be the talk of London, shall we not?' He beamed his happiness at them, like a child who had been told that he can have his heart's desire for Christmas.

Will found himself smiling in response, forgetting for a moment the vast gulf in rank that lay between them. At this moment they were all united by the mysterious bonds of the theatrical world, all equal in its odd fraternity.

A footman appeared at the door and whispered in his master's ear. Strange nodded, shooed the man away with a flick of his long fingers, and stood, forcing everyone else to follow suit.

'I fear, my friends, that I must away. Lady Strange and I are leaving for the north in a few days' time and there is much to be done before then. We will be back in London after the Christmas season, and I shall look forward to hearing what progress you have made. Barnes, when the gentlemen are ready to leave, you may give them use of the barge.'

After His Lordship had gone, the others settled themselves back in their seats.

'Well then, *gentlemen*, shall we resume?' Barnes said, an ironic smile on his lips.

The clock had moved on by a mere quarter-hour before they had finished agreeing on the essentials. Will would be paid a handsome eight shillings a week for his work, and in the matter of funds for the necessary acquisition of props and costumes, Barnes proved sensible, if not exactly open-handed. Though Lord Strange intended that the company should be self-supporting once it was established, with sharers contributing the necessary capital to sustain it, at the start, he would meet the wages of the actors who wore his livery. As for Marlowe's new play, Barnes said that it would be up to His Lordship to determine what payment he was willing to make for it once completed. By the end, Barnes had unbent sufficiently to offer them a parting glass of wine, produced magician-like from some recess in the big desk.

'Let us drink to the success of Lord Strange's Men,' he said, raising his glass. 'You have much relieved my mind, Mister Shakespeare. His Lordship, as you can surely tell, is greatly attached to this project. But since I must answer to his father the earl for his expenditure upon this fancy of his, I find myself in as precarious a position as one of his lordship's acrobats, perched upon the shoulders of others while keeping my various balls in the air and spinning without fault. It is helpful to know that those shoulders are steady and will not give way under pressure.'

***

'What is it about you that fills men like Barnes with such confidence?' Kit asked as they stood shivering on the dock waiting for the arrival of the Stanley family's barge. 'I have noted it before. Every man seems certain that William Shakespeare is dependable and will never let them down.'

'My dowdy patched doublets and baggy hose, perhaps?' Will suggested, laughing. 'Unlike you, I look like a man in need, and a man in need can be trusted to work hard to earn his shillings.'

The barge, its crew all decked out in the Stanley livery, arrived at the foot of the little jetty. They were helped aboard and settled onto the thwarts that ran across the boat's stern, beneath a gold-tasselled red canopy to keep off the sun and rain. With furs bundled across their knees, both men felt like lords as they were conveyed out into the river and downstream.

'Imagine what our friends would say if they could see us now.' Marlowe giggled.

'Greene would be emerald with envy, Tom Watson would be spluttering with indignation, and George Peele would be asking how many plays he had to write to enjoy such favours,' Will said. 'Speaking of which, I thought Henslowe and the Admiral's Men have you hard at work on a second *Tamburlaine*? How are you going to produce a play for Lord Strange at the same time? You are not, it must be said, the quickest of writers.'

'You will help, of course.' Marlowe's grin was mischievous. 'Think of it, Will, we can work together. You come up with the plot, I'll do the poetry, and we'll share the credit.'

Somehow Will doubted that his friend, when it came to it, would relinquish a scintilla of credit. But even so, the prospect was alluring. Marlowe could teach him a great deal, and it would be the first play he had worked on from the very start.

'And the names Shakespeare and Marlowe will sound forever in the annals of poetry!' He laughed, putting his hand out to grasp Kit's in token of his agreement.

'For certes. Though I am sure you meant to say Marlowe and Shakespeare.'

Will laughed again, then shot a cautious look at the barge crew before changing the subject. Fortunately, their faces were blank, engrossed in the task of rowing against the tide. 'What did you make of my lord Strange?' he asked, keeping his voice low.

'Does he have the demeanour of a traitor, do you mean?' Will flinched at Marlowe's casual use of the word. 'No, he does not. But then, few do, save the most inept. For a member of the aristocracy, he seems likeable enough, and it is obvious that his passion is for our rather queer art. Beyond that, I make no judgement.' Marlowe shifted in his seat, turning to face Will. 'I do have some other news that impinges upon the general subject, though. Phelippes wrote me that John Towne has been released.'

'So he is free and clear?'

'Aye. The Queen has issued a pardon, no doubt at the urging of Beale and Walsingham.'

'Then he will likely turn up in London before long. And if what Billy Knell heard was true, he will come knocking at my door, as an easy path into Lord Strange's household.'

'And if he doesn't?'

That possibility hadn't occurred to Will. 'Then I shall have to approach him directly, I suppose. Though I don't want to show my hand by seeming importunate.'

'Why don't you have a word to Tom Kyd and maybe one or two others. Eventually, one or another of them will suggest that Towne come to you.'

Will nodded. 'That will serve. And no matter how dubious his motives, if he does join, I will have one actor recruited, at least. Who else can I talk to?'

'You can try Will Kempe. I hear he is out of sorts with his colleagues among Leicester's Men. Young Ned, of course, and yourself. That's four. What about the other members of the Queen's Men?'

'Those who are sharers will never leave, even temporarily. The Dutton brothers, perhaps.' Will lapsed into silence. For the first time, he realised the enormity of the task he had taken on. He would be a busy man in the weeks and months ahead.

The barge swept in towards the Blackfriars Steps with an ostentatious flurry of oars, and they climbed out and up onto the wharf, attracting the gawping attention of passengers awaiting passage across the river by more humble means of transport. As always, the presence of an audience played to Marlowe's vanity, and he drew himself up and marched haughtily towards the gate, parting a crowd that assumed he must at the very least be an earl. Will followed in his wake, barely able to keep from laughing, and they parted with promises to meet on the morrow.

Chapter 13

'Stop fussing, woman! I am like to live a few more years yet. Has not the Queen's physician said so? Get you gone and bring us some wine and some of those sweetmeats you think I don't know about, hidden away in the back of the cupboard in your parlour.'

Thus chastised, Dick Tarlton's housekeeper, a pinched-looking, nervous woman, scuttled out of the room, closing the door behind her with a little more force than was necessary as a kind of meek protest.

Tarlton, who was sitting up in his big wood-framed bed, his shoulders propped against the pillows, shook his head in annoyance, a gesture that set the tassel hanging from his bright red nightcap swinging. 'I cannot do without her, but she is forever fretting that I am too hot, too cold, that I must have more air or less, that I don't eat enough or that I am becoming gross. In ten years I do not think I have ever heard her pronounce herself content.'

'Is it true, what the Queen's doctor said?' Will asked, laughing. 'That you will be plaguing us all for many a year? You look hale enough, despite being abed long after honest men are about their day's toil.'

As though Will had summoned some demon of illness, Tarlton gave a cough, which then induced another and another, seemingly unstoppable. His face reddened, and he clasped a handkerchief to his mouth in an attempt to stifle the hacking, phlegm-filled convulsions. Eventually, it stopped, and Tarlton flicked the kerchief away under the bedclothes, thinking to hide it before Will could spot the redness of the blood that had stained it, an effort which was not entirely successful.

'Her Majesty's physician,' he said, wiping his eyes with the backs of his hands, 'is a gentleman, very learned, and a man of great good humour. But he knows no more of physick than any of his breed. I have some malady of the lungs which he says will take its course no matter what he prescribes, and therefore I must lie in my bed and rest until such time as it declares its future intent.'

The housekeeper reappeared, a suspicious look on her face—plainly she had heard the coughing downstairs—and deposited wine and a small plate of sweetmeats. She and Tarlton scowled at each other, and he shooed her away once more. It was like a piece of dumbshow in the theatre, which Will had the feeling was enacted daily.

'Doctors are easily deceived,' the comic went on, a mischievous grin appearing on his misshapen face. 'There was one, I remember, near Islington. A gentleman at court asked me whether I knew aught of this man's skill with physick, as he was considering using his services. I undertook to test him by the following means—half filling a urinal with good wine, I took it to the doctor and told him that it was a sick man's water. Could he tell me the patient's condition?

'The fellow inspected the glass with a serious mien, frowned thus'—Tarlton screwed his face up into a comical facsimile of a man concentrating—'and tossed the water up and down. "The patient whose water this is," he finally said, "is full of gross humours. I prescribe purging and the letting of ten ounces of blood." With which I replied, "You are a dunce, Sirrah,", drunk off the wine, and threw the urinal at his head.'

Tarlton beamed with pleasure at Will's laughter. He had probably told this story hundreds of times, but it obviously never failed to amuse the teller as much as the listener.

'I was tempted to try the same trick with the Queen's physician, but I had an attack of good sense and decided to leave the poor man's reputation intact. But enough of my woes. What of you? How does the new company proceed?'

179

'Well enough,' Will said, settling into the chair that the housekeeper had placed beside the bed. 'Lord Strange has been true to his word and has been generous in the matter of expenses, so money is not a problem for once. The seamstresses are hard at work making costumes and I have accumulated a fine collection of props. I have bought enough tables, chairs, candlestick holders, goblets and jugs to furnish a small house, and enough helmets, spears and halberds to arm a household guard. His Lordship has decided that we must stage our first plays at Derby House, and I have carpenters at work building a stage that we can erect when needed, and artisans are painting back-cloths to hang beneath the gallery so that we can have a tiring-room.'

'Good progress in four months. I remember it took us twice that long to set up the Queen's Men.'

'True. But as important as all these things are, a playing company must have players and plays. I am deficient in both.'

'Oh? You surprise me. You've tried the Admiral's Men? Only God—or perhaps Master Tilney, our true deity—knows when the ban will be lifted on them, and they must have some hired players you could poach.'

'They have proven surprisingly loyal. It's said that Tilney will not maintain the injunction beyond Christmas, that being enough time to appease the Puritans. Richard Cowley is interested in joining us, but the others swear they will hang on until their company can go back on stage.'

Tarlton swirled the wine in his glass for a moment, considering. 'Leicester's company is at sixes and sevens. The earl is distracted with military affairs at present, what with all the rumours that the Spanish will attack this summer, and so has not been employing his players as often as he was wont to do. Some of them have been lent out—George Bryan and Will Kempe have both recently returned from Denmark and Saxony, and I hear that Kempe is unhappy that the company is idle.'

Will's ears pricked up at that name, for William Kempe had a great reputation as a comic actor, second only to that of Tarlton himself. If he could secure Kempe's services, it would be a great feather in the new company's cap. 'Would Kempe join a new company like ours, do you think?'

'He might if I suggested it to him.' A gleam of amusement came into the older man's eyes. 'He is a prickly sort of creature, but easily flattered. I will tell him that you asked me who I would judge to be the best clown in England, and that the only name that came to my lips was that of Will Kempe.'

'That will do the trick, I am sure.' Will laughed. 'By the by, have you heard anything of John Towne? I am told that the coroner found him innocent of wrongdoing, but no one seems to have seen or heard of him since his release.'

Tarlton's face creased into a grimace at the name. 'Nay, I have heard naught, and care not if I never heard or saw him again. He might have convinced the coroner in Thame that he is innocent, but I will never forgive him for killing a man who was my friend and one of the finest actors in England.'

'I have no affection for him, either. But I must have players, and he is skilled, whatever his faults as a man.'

Tarlton's shoulders rose in a shrug. 'Since it is for you, if I hear aught, I will pass it on. But be wary of him, Will. There is something unhinged about the man.'

Will could hardly disagree with this assessment given everything else he knew about Towne. But he could not share any of those misgivings with Tarlton. 'Well, at least the verdict will allow the company's affairs to be settled,' he said, changing the subject.

'That it will, which will be a relief after all these months. Billy's will can be probated, we can pay out his widow for his share, and the company can start touring again. And when we do, we will need your services once more, Will.'

181

'You shall have them, and gladly, though I am obligated to Lord Strange, so you will have to allow me to work for both companies for a time at least.'

'Among farming folk, there is a saying that one should make hay when the sun shines. Rake your hay in with my blessing, since there seems to be the prospect of two suns smiling upon your field.'

The distinctive report of a cannon being fired sounded through the open window, followed by the angry cries of startled starlings. Tarlton's house was barely fifty yards down Bishopsgate Street from James Burbage's playhouse, which he had grandly named 'The Theatre', as if to imply that there were none other in London worthy of the name, and the gun signalled that a play was to be performed there that day.

'I must go soon. Pembroke's Men are doing George Peele's *The Battle of Alcazar*, and I promised him I would be sure to see it.'

'All blood and gore and not a decent comic's part in it, or so they say. You helped Peele with something recently, did you not?'

'*Jack Straw*. He plotted, I versified. Sometimes the other way about. The end result was pleasing.'

'Billy always said you had a future as a writer, so I'm glad you have at least made a start. And unlike Peele and Watson and all the rest, you have trod the stage, and know what it is to fling some self-regarding poet's fancy out upon the ears of an audience that is half-educated and half-not.'

Will nodded in the direction of The Theatre, whose banners could be seen above the grove of trees that stood between it and Tarlton's house. 'Burbage and Henslowe say they want plays written by poets so that they can attract the attention of the gentry, and care not that their high metaphors and classical allusions fly above the heads of the poorer sort before ever they reach the ears of those seated in the tuppence and threepence seats.'

'And so we actors must use antic gestures, comic dumb shows and improvised speeches if we are to avoid being pelted by apple cores and nutshells from the groundlings. When you come to write your masterpiece, Will, keep that in mind, and give us parts that we can speak without risking life and limb.'

Will picked up his hat and jammed it on his head. 'I shall. And now I really must away.'

'Go, go. But come back and visit me soon.'

***

The Battle of Alcazar was indeed a bloody spectacle, with dead bodies littering the stage by the end. But the apprentices, labourers and artisans who surrounded Will on the floor of the playhouse took great pleasure in the tale of intrigue and murder among the princes of Morocco, a verdict with which he found himself easily able to agree as the happy, chattering throng made their way out of the playhouse.

The sun was still high in the western sky, and he decided that, rather than joining the crowds heading back to the city along Bishopsgate Street, he would take a walk through Finsbury Fields, the open parkland that lay to the west of where he was now standing.

His path took him along Holywell Lane, a muddy track that passed through open pastureland dotted with sheep before curving slightly southwards, where there stood three windmills, their white canvas sails creaking as they turned slowly in the small breeze. Outside one of them, a two-wheeled dray was being loaded with newly-ground flour, the sweating labourers chattering happily as they heaved the sacks up to join their fellows already deposited in the cart's tray. The dray's donkey, a thin and mangy-looking creature, twitched its ears and startled Will by giving out a long bray for no apparent reason.

Following the road would take him past the old manor house of Finsbury Court and back into the city by way of the Moor Gate, but his attention was instead caught by loud cheers coming from the other side of the fields, where the archery butts had attracted a sizeable crowd that had come to watch young gallants show off their skill with the longbow, England's ancient winner of battles. On an impulse, he abandoned the road back to the city and made his way past a reed-fringed duckpond to join the crowd.

The competitors, separated from the throng by a simple hurdle fence, were a mixed lot. Some were clearly professionals, judging from their over-developed upper bodies, sinewy forearms and their sober workmanlike leather jerkins. Others were most likely the sons of the gentry, strutting about like overdressed peacocks, chatting to each other, making jokes and blowing kisses at the maids in the crowd. The spectators, mostly happily inebriated by this time of the afternoon and consequently in a jolly mood, shouted advice and otherwise did their best to distract the concentration of the bowmen. If any of them loosed too soon or wobbled in their aim, a great shout of laughter went up at the red-faced competitor's discomfiture. It was all part of the fun.

Finding a place where the crowd was not too thick, he watched a short but powerfully built youth step up to the mark. He was clad from head to foot in bright green, and an enormous feather floating from the top of his cap lent him a jaunty, frivolous air.

But he seemed to be a competent enough bowman. He settled into his stance, legs apart and shoulders squared, drew a long breath, raised the six-foot bow, squinted along the length of the arrow drawn back near to his chin, held it for a moment or two, and then loosed. The arrow hummed past the spectators towards the target, some three hundred yards distant. But instead of thumping into the target, it buried itself into the turf twenty yards short, bringing forth a round of jeers from the crowd. Far from being embarrassed, the youngster just shrugged, made an inaudible but laughing remark to the little group of companions who stood behind him, and extracted another arrow for his next shot.

Will had watched many archery competitions in his youth, for they were a staple of country fairs in towns like Stratford, where it was compulsory for the yeomen to keep their skills up against the possibility that they might be mustered for war, though no such array had been required for nigh-on a century. So he knew what to look for in an archer, and watching this young popinjay at work, he sensed that there was something not quite right. He was not using the full power of his physique, as if he was holding back just a fraction of his strength. Sure enough, his next two shots fell well short of the mark, and he stepped back to yield his place to the next competitor for this round.

'What do you think, Cuts? Worth a wager?'

The familiar loud booming voice of Robert Greene came from somewhere in the crowd to his right. The big man was not hard to spot. His height and bulk made him stand out in any crowd, and that day, he wore a high red hat flamboyantly decorated with yellow feathers that made him seem even taller. The smaller man standing next to him was, by contrast, dressed entirely in sober black, though he too wore a hat, black with an enormous brim that kept half his face in shadow and made his eyes invisible.

Threading his way Will through the crowd, Will found a place standing just behind and to one side of them, where he could see the field but at the same time remain unobserved.

'You're a glutton for punishment, man,' Greene's companion exclaimed, with a laugh. 'Wasn't losing nigh-on a full pound to me at the bear-baiting enough for you?'

'That was yesterday. Today I am lucky.'

'Well, then. What do you think of yon coxcomb?'

185

Greene peered across at the green-clad youth, who stood trading jokes with several equally flamboyantly dressed young companions while he waited for his next turn. 'He's a popinjay, all show,' was the verdict.

'Then let me give you a fair chance to win back some of what you lost yesterday. A crown says his next shot will hit the target fair and square.'

Greene looked again at the archer, now flexing his shoulders as he moved up to the shooting line. 'Done. Loosen your purse, Cuts. You will owe me a crown momentarily.'

Will, listening unobserved to this exchange, smothered a smile. He had a fair idea of what would happen next.

The bowman settled himself once more, frowned in concentration, drew and loosed. This time his arrow, instead of falling well short, thumped right into the centre of the wooden target. Greene's muttered oath was echoed by quite a few others in the crowd. It was an old trick, one that Will had often seen played at country fairs—the archer always had that final winning shot in him, but feigned incompetence for a few rounds to gull the bettors into complacency. Usually, he had his friends place bets in his favour for the last round, and they would divide the spoils between them. No doubt Greene's companion had deduced that something of the sort was going on that afternoon.

Greene, on this occasion the unknowing cony so often portrayed in his pamphlets, sheepishly fished in his purse for a coin, which he flipped into the air. It was caught and deftly secreted away somewhere in the pockets of the other man's doublet.

'Keep that crown in a safe place, my friend. I will win it back from you ere long.'

'So say all gamblers.' The other man was mild. 'And what of your friend here, who has been listening to us with such interest? Is he a gambling man too?'

Will was startled; he had not had any inkling that he had been noticed.

'Shakespeare?' Greene said. 'What on earth are you doing here? I thought you were busy with this new company of yours.'

'I'm giving myself a half-holiday, Rob. Went to see Peele's latest play at The Theatre and thought I would stop by and watch a few rounds at the butts on my way home.' He turned his attention to the other man. 'And to answer your question, Mister Ball, I am not attracted to games of chance, particularly those where the dice are loaded.'

Greene looked confused. 'I didn't know you were acquainted with Cuts.'

'He is not,' that man said, revealing gapped teeth in a quick smile. 'Your friend has merely deduced who I am from your curtailed use of my nickname. Pleased to make your acquaintance, Mister... Shakespeare, was it? Let me name myself properly. Edward Ball, who the world has seen fit to dub "Cutting" Ball.'

The source of the nickname was Ball's profession. He was a cutpurse, a man skilled at the art of separating gentlemen from their purses, though his reputation was more sinister as the leader of a gang of equally disagreeable thieves, cut-throats and confidence-tricksters whose depredations were feared all over London.

It was well known that Greene had struck up an unlikely friendship with Ball, for the poet had a surprising appetite for the wildness of life among London's disreputable and degraded poor. Ball was, no doubt, the source of the 'cony-catching' tales with which Greene frequently entertained his friends, in which he gleefully recounted what he always said were the crimes of others (though Will suspected that his participation was not always as passive as he made out), wherein petty thieves and con-men bilked their victims of their money and goods by way of all sorts of clever stratagems.

187

'I am thirsty,' Greene announced abruptly. 'And since my crown has made its way into your purse, Cuts, I think you can buy us a round.'

They made their way out of the crowd, whose attention was by now absorbed in the next round of the day's competition, going to a temporary booth that some enterprising tavern-keeper had set up under an old oak tree, from where he was dispensing ale from huge jugs. Having bought three tankards of small beer, they settled themselves on three simple wooden stools that the innkeeper had provided for the use of his patrons.

'Shakespeare is liveried to Lord Strange, for whom he is creating a new acting company,' Greene said for Ball's benefit, though that man seemed little interested, giving no more than a nod before turning his attention to the apple he was peeling with a wicked-looking little knife he had extracted from his boot as they sat down. 'How goes it, Will? Do you have your actors yet? And Marlowe tells me you are writing a play together.'

Will laughed. 'Kit's horse is running ahead of its traces. He has promised me that he will help with a play, but I have scarcely seen him for the last two months. All I can get out of him is that his new *Tamburlaine* is claiming all his attention, but that he will come and help when I can find a suitable subject. In the meantime, I spend my time in the library at Derby House searching through His Lordship's books for a plot.'

'That doesn't sound like hard labour to me.'

'So His Lordship's steward said when he found me reading Suetonius one afternoon, hoping to find a story somewhere among *The Twelve Caesars* that might serve.'

For no logical reason, Barnes had been quite put out by Shakespeare's easy assumption that he could ransack the shelves of the extensive library at Derby House as he pleased, but Lord Strange, returning from the north in February to take up his seat in the new parliament that the Queen had called for 1588, had been insistent that the big room overlooking the river should be at his disposal. So there was little that the steward could do or say other than to poke his head in from time to time in the hope that he might catch Will out in some malfeasance.

'Mighty Caesar himself?' Greene suggested, his mind instantly drawn to the solution of any literary puzzle. 'Surely there must be a story in *that* life?'

'My ambition does not fly so high, though it might not daunt Kit. Besides, there is little chance that the authorities would approve any play that ends in regicide.'

'You could start with the dictator's murder, perhaps. His assassins all came to an unpleasant end, after all.'

Visions crowded into Will's mind of crowded squares filled with toga-clad citizens baying for the blood of Caesar's murderers, stirring speeches condemning—or perhaps even defending?—the actions of the self-declared defenders of the Republic, battles, even a ghost or two. Yes, it could be done. But still, it felt as though doing such a story justice, and in verse, was beyond his skill. After all, he had never done anything more demanding than patch old plays and dabble with a half-finished comedy that might never see the light of day.

'*Arden of Faversham*,' Ball suddenly said, earning a startled look from the other two men. Will had assumed that the cutpurse was more absorbed in his apple than their conversation.

The remark mystified Will, but Greene seemed to instantly understand the reference. 'You constantly surprise me, Cuts. I never know what is floating around in that noggin of yours.'

Ball acknowledged the compliment with a comical imitation of a courtly wave. 'It's a story from the boy king's day involving a wicked wife who plotted with her lover to kill her husband, a man who was made wealthy by the dissolution of the monasteries, so that she could inherit his fortune and marry her paramour, a low-born creature who had once been a tailor.'

'A murder? Hardly the most edifying of subjects for the first play for a new company.'

'What do you want to do, Mister Shakespeare, take the pennies of the ordinary folk who crowd your theatres in the hope of seeing a tale of flesh and blood, or win the approval of your la-de-dah gentles up in the lord's boxes?' Ball said, causing Will to smile at the man's unconscious evocation of the very dilemma that he had been discussing with Richard Tarlton that morning. He really was a surprising fellow.

'Cuts is right, Will. Besides, I do not doubt that you could weave some moralising into the story, enough to satisfy the Master of the Revels. After all, the murderers did end up on the gallows.'

'Nay,' Ball corrected, 'the tailor was hanged at Tyburn, but she was burned.'

'Even so, a mere murder seems to offer little material for a whole drama.'

'There was more to it than that. If I recall it aright, there were several bungled attempts before they finally succeeded, involving various cut-throats and poisoners. You could weave some witchcraft into the tale as well, that always appeals to the goodwives.' Greene's eyes were bright with enthusiasm for the whole project.

'I thought you despised playwrighting, Rob.' Will laughed. 'Perhaps *you* should write it with me instead of Kit. Think of it: *Arden of Faversham, The Lamentable and Tragical Tale of a Most Heinous Murder, set forth by Robert Greene, poet.*'

For a moment, Greene looked as if he might be tempted. Such a play might earn him a share of six or seven pounds; no inconsiderable sum. But then he returned to form and snorted his disdain. 'Nay, I will leave that field for you and Marlowe to plough. But you can be sure I will be there when it is first performed, bragging that it was all my idea and that you two provincial bumpkins could never have written it without my inspiration.'

'And here's me thinking it was my suggestion,' Ball said.

Greene clapped the smaller man on the back, causing him to wince. 'So it was, Cuts, though I doubt Mister Shakespeare will give you any credit on the handbills. Well, I must be away.' With these words, Greene stood and emptied the dregs of his tankard onto the grass. The others followed suit and having returned the drinking vessels to the innkeeper, they went on their way, Greene and Shakespeare heading towards the Moor Gate, Ball saying his farewells and heading westwards along Chiswell Street.

'I'll put the idea of *Arden* to Kit,' Will said as they passed through the gate under the bored eyes of the city's guards. 'He is a most surprising man, your friend Cutting Ball.'

'He is, but don't be fooled, Will, he might seem mild enough, but he can be ruthless when he is crossed. I have seen him slit a man's throat as neat as a butcher bringing down a cow, and with about as much compassion.'

'I am warned.' Another thought came to him. 'Ball must know the city and its inhabitants well.'

'Certainly. He has lived here all his life. And his gang of pimps, thieves and cut-throats have a network of spies and lookouts all over the city that would make Walsingham's watchers and intelligencers look like amateurs.'

'Then perhaps he could help me in another way. I am trying to find an actor by the name of John Towne, who I wish to recruit to the company, but who seems to have gone to ground.'

191

'Towne, you say? The name seems familiar.'

'The man who killed William Knell in a fight while we were on tour in Thame.' Will was a little reluctant to provide that detail, but he had little choice if he was going to recruit his help.

'Oh yes, I remember.' Greene frowned. 'And you want to work with him again? That seems a little… adventurous.'

Will shrugged. 'The coroner found him innocent of any wrongdoing, and he is a fine actor. I am struggling to get good players for one reason or another, so I would like to track him down.'

'Well if anyone can find him, Cuts will. For a price, of course. You go that way?'

'Yes.' The street leading to Will's lodging ran to the right, following the line of the wall, whereas Greene had a longer walk ahead of him to his rooms in Billingsgate, near the bridge. 'Talk to Ball and see what he can find out. Discreetly, mind. I have silver enough to pay him, though I'll not be bilked.'

Greene laughed. 'You really are still a tradesman at heart, William Shakespeare. Fear not, Cuts knows you get milk from a cow if you feed it hay.'

Will wasn't sure whether he was the cow or the farmer in that analogy, but he accepted it as a reassurance of sorts and waved Greene on his way.

Making his way home along the narrow street almost completely in shadow from the bulk of the wall on one side and the three-storey houses on the other, his thoughts turned to the tale of Thomas Arden of Faversham. He would have to do more research and see what Kit thought about it, but the more he contemplated it, the more it seemed a likely prospect as a subject for a play.

It had been, in the end, a surprisingly productive day. He was confident that Dick Tarlton would help him recruit the services of the clown, William Kempe, he might at last have found a subject for a play, and with luck, Cutting Ball and his men would find where John Towne had been hiding all these months. So it was a smiling Will Shakespeare who surprised Ned Bentley at their lodging in Silver Street with the suggestion that they go out and find some ordinary at which to eat rather than putting up with their landlady's plain fare.

Chapter 14

London, March 1588

Marlowe, consulted the next day on the subject of the new play, was instantly enthusiastic.

'Of course I remember the story. I should have thought of it myself. Faversham is in Kent, after all, and it was a notorious case, still talked about in Canterbury to this day. In fact, if I remember rightly, Raphael Holinshed wrote about it in some detail in one of the *Chronicles*, it was so famous.'

They were breaking their fast at Mistress Mary's, a small but cosy cookshop on Throgmorton Street, just opposite the three-towered Drapers' Hall, once the home of old King Henry's infamous chief minister, Thomas Cromwell. At that time of the morning, the little shop was full of customers, mostly weavers and dyers in their drab stained jerkins and patched hose, enjoying the plain but wholesome fare that Mistress Mary served up to her customers—soft fresh bread, cheese, fruit, washed down with small beer. Conspicuous as a treasure galleon among fishing smacks, a couple of well-dressed wool traders sat in a corner, deep in earnest discussion as they picked at their food.

'Is there enough in the tale to make a play, though?' Will said, cutting a pear in two and offering half to Marlowe. 'Greene seemed to think so. I thought for a moment he was going to try his hand at writing it.'

'Ha! Did I not tell you that Rob secretly hankers to hear his words performed from the stage? But his talent is for low comedy and high-flown satire, not tragedy. Though the tale of Thomas Arden's death does have comic elements. His murderers were not all that competent.'

Will raised his eyebrows in a silent invitation for Kit to continue.

'To begin at the beginning, Arden's wife Alice was in love with a former tailor going by the name of Mosby, though whether he first seduced her or she was simply a wanton is not certain. However that may be, they conceived a plan to have Arden killed so that she could inherit the man's very considerable wealth—he had made a fortune buying monastic properties cheap from the Crown and selling them on. After some suitable time had passed, the two conspirators would marry and that would be that.

'But such a plot is more easily conceived than executed. At first, they tried poison, engaging the services of a painter who was known to have skills in such things, but this failed when Arden refused to drink it. Then Alice, by devious paths, found her way to a foul, black-hearted ruffian named Black Will, who undertook to do the deed. He made no less than four attempts to execute his commission, assisted by an accomplice named, if I remember aright, George Shakebag—though that may be a nickname, Shake-bag being a common term for a petty thief—and with some help from one of Arden's servants.'

'Four tries? This Black Will doesn't sound like much of a murderer,' Will said, incredulous. 'And what, four others involved in the conspiracy? It's a wonder that half of London didn't know what was afoot.'

'True enough, but they didn't give up. Mosby tried to pick a fight with Arden at the St Valentine's Day fair, hoping that he might then dispose of him in a swordfight, but Arden refused to be drawn. And then, finally, they succeeded, concealing Black Will in the house and surprising Arden after supper during a game of backgammon. He was killed most foully, first strangled and then stabbed to death.'

It was indeed a horrendous tale, but Will began to see the dramatical possibilities in it. Misguided love, jealousy, incompetent and bungling murderers, all were themes that could work on the stage. 'But how does the story end? Greene said the chief culprits were executed, so I assume they were caught?'

'Aye, and they were as incompetent in the disguising of their crime as they were in its execution. They laid his body out in a field adjacent to the house in Faversham where the deed was committed. It was found soon enough, and the mayor summoned. The murderers were careless, and the investigation soon found enough evidence to arraign both Alice and Mosby. They were condemned and executed in short order.'

'And Black Will, Shakebag and the rest? What happened to them?'

'No one knows what happened to Shakebag. Black Will died on a scaffold in Flushing for some other crime committed after he fled England. There were others, too, who were involved in the conspiracy, but I don't recall their fates.' Marlowe took a draught of beer, wiping his lips with his sleeve. 'There was one curious aftermath—for years afterwards, no grass grew where Arden's body had lain, a minor miracle that attracted the superstitious attention of the simple-minded. And there was a story told of a curse, laid upon Arden by a woman who had been cruelly dispossessed by him of her lease of that very field.'

Will leaned back against the wall of the narrow booth, thinking. He would have to find out much more about the whole story, but with the addition of a more sympathetic character or two, perhaps a comic role (he would need something for Will Kempe), it might serve his purposes.

Marlowe regarded him steadily, a gleam of amusement in his eye. 'You can see it, can't you?'

'Yes, if you will help me. I will work out the plot, you write the verses, as we agreed.'

'That is what I promised, and I shall keep my word.'

'Even if Tamburlaine thunders from the east, commanding your every devotion for the telling of the second part of his story?'

'Even so.' Marlowe's solemnity cracked into a sly smile. 'Tamburlaine's command I could resist. Those of Henslowe and Alleyn, however, may be much more difficult to ignore. They are like to be much more insistent, and besides, their importuning is backed by silver, or the promise thereof, at least.'

'But I'll wager that Lord Strange's gold will exercise a greater pull on your attention since it is more plentiful and more certain.' Will laughed and held up his hands. 'But don't worry, Kit, I'll not try your loyalties too much. It is time I tried my hand at versifying, so I will do what I can if you will be my auditor.'

They shook hands with such gravity that, had the merchants in the room been watching, they might have concluded they were completing a deal of great financial value and consequence.

'How goes the rest of your enterprise?' Marlowe asked, demolishing the last of the cheese. 'Have you found your actors? Or is Lord Strange going to have the first company in London whose playwright performs all the parts of his plays?'

'That would be a novelty. I think I have Cowley, at least while the Admiral's are out of commission. I saw Dick Tarlton yesterday. He is going to talk to Will Kempe, and I have hopes of George Ashford and Tom Blunt, perhaps Augustine Phillips. So if all goes well, with Ned and I, we shall be seven, enough to get started, though I could wish for one or two more.'

Marlowe looked around the room, which had by now almost emptied of customers. Apart from a morose-looking fellow sitting close to the window nursing a half-full tankard, the only other person in the shop was the owner, Mistress Mary herself, who was behind her counter wiping used trenchers clean and polishing the pewter of her goblets.

Even though there was little chance that they could be overheard, tucked away as they were in a little booth at the back of the shop, Marlowe leaned forward a little. 'And John Towne? He has not appeared at your door?' he asked, keeping his voice low and almost comically conspiratorial. 'Beale has been harassing me on this matter, and the other. He says Walsingham is impatient to hear of your progress.'

'I cannot conjure the man from nowhere,' Will said, exasperated. 'In truth, I am surprised that he has not turned up. But I have engaged Rob Greene to help me find him.'

'Greene?' Marlowe was puzzled. 'How can he help?'

'Not he himself, but his associates. Cutting Ball and his gang.'

'Ah! Well, I might not tell Seething Lane about that little detail. Resorting to the employment of criminals is apt to make Master Beale queasy. And Lord Strange? What have you learned about him?'

'I have barely seen him. He came back from Lancashire in February and has been attending the parliament almost continuously since. Walsingham will likely have seen more of him than I have. We have spoken once or twice at Derby House, and that is all.'

Marlowe stared at him, a chilly calculating look in his eyes that made Will shiver inside. He had always thought of Kit as a friend and this glimpse of him as a cold-blooded spymaster was disconcerting. But as the sun dissolves the mysterious mists, so Kit's inner imp banished solemnity with his familiar droll grin.

'I see I shall have to employ my, ah, *creative* talent when I write my report.' Then he turned serious again. 'They are worried, Walsingham and Beale and Phelippes. Reports are coming in every day about the Spanish invasion fleet, and they are more certain than ever that we will be attacked this summer. So they want to make certain that they have put a stopper on all and any plots and stratagems aimed at unseating the kingdom, however remote the threat, before the enemy appears in the Channel.'

Will nodded. The nervousness of the Queen's ministers was natural enough. Every day a new rumour seemed to be whispered in the streets: that the Duke of Parma was building a huge fleet of barges with which to cross with his army from the Low Countries; that a secret expedition had landed in Wales—though the next day it was said to be in Cornwall; and that one of the chain of beacons set up along the coast to warn of the approach of any enemy had been lit up. It turned out that this last had been a plot with a more prosaic aim, the beacon having been fired by a gang of thieves intending to take advantage of the ensuing confusion to engage in a campaign of petty theft among the houses of the gentry while the latter was called out to do their patriotic duty.

'I will do what I can. His Lordship has given me free run of his library, and now that we have a subject for our play, I have a good reason to spend more time at Derby House.' Though he kept it from his voice, Will felt the familiar tide of disgust at being forced to do this unsavoury work of spying upon his fellow men, however noble its ultimate aim might be.

Kit brushed crumbs from his doublet and took his cape from where it had lain draped across the partition that separated their booth from its neighbour. 'I must go and take up my pen once more in Tamburlaine's cause. When shall we meet again?'

'Next week? That will be enough time for me to have read Holinshed's account of the Arden story, and with luck, Greene will have heard something from Cutting Ball and his mates. Can you come to Derby House? It will increase my credit with His Lordship if he knows you are helping me.'

'Of course.' He frowned and made a show of patting his pockets. 'I seem to lack coin. Can you…?'

'Jesu, I have seen better acting by marionettes at the fairground.' Will chuckled, reaching for his purse to settle the reckoning with an equally amused Mistress Mary.

199

Out in the street, they watched the comings and goings of the cloth merchants across the road at the Drapers' Hall.

'You told me, did you not, that John Towne was once in love with Knell's wife?' Marlowe asked.

'Yes. He may still be in love with her, for all I know.'

'And she with him?'

'Perhaps. It was hard to tell when I met her. Why do you ask?'

'It is curious, is it not, that we should be writing a story about a woman who conspired with her lover to kill her husband...' Kit let the sentence trail off.

'What are you suggesting? That Rebecca had some part in Billy Knell's death? That she and Towne are conspirators?' The idea seemed outlandish.

'Is it so impossible?' Kit shrugged. 'But perhaps I have spent too much time among people of base motive who are capable of any crime. It leads me to see the darker hue of men's characters more often than their sunnier side. Forget I said anything.'

But watching his friend make his confident way down the street, Will experienced a kind of shiver of premonition. The idea that there was some kind of connection between the old tale of Thomas Arden and the present-day events surrounding the death of William Knell seemed ridiculous. Yet the thought seemed to snag itself onto some peg in his mind, and he knew it would stay there until he had proof that dislodged it.

***

The library at Derby House was a fine wide room on the river side of the building, illuminated by three tall windows that overlooked the small garden below and the busy Thames beyond. They had been thrown open to admit the morning sun that streamed in from the east, along with the merest zephyr of a breeze that still managed to rustle the papers on the big table that dominated the centre of the room.

Sitting in a high-backed chair behind the table, Will flipped through the pages of a copy of Raphael Holinshed's *Chronicles of England, Scotland and Ireland* that was propped on a small reading-lectern in front of him, searching for the chronicler's entry on the murder of Thomas Arden. It began prosaically enough.

> *About this time there was at Faversham in Kent a gentleman named Arden, 1551 Anno, most cruelly murdered and slain by the procurement of his own wife. The which murder, for the horribleness thereof, although otherwise, it may seem to be but a private matter and therefore as it were impertinent to this history, I have thought good to set it forth somewhat at large, having the instructions delivered to me by them that have used some diligence to gather the true understanding of the circumstances.*

The writer seemed almost apologetic for including the entirety of the tale since most of his book was concerned with the lives of the country's great and powerful, with wars and pestilence, royal marriages and popular uprisings, not the murder of mere merchants. The fact that he had diverted his attention from the grand themes of his chronicle said much about the horror this particular plot must have induced in his mind, as it no doubt had among his fellow Englishmen.

From the start, it seemed that it was a story of strange and tangled relationships. Arden himself, Holinshed averred, was a 'man of tall and comely personage', while his young wife Alice was 'well-favoured of shape and countenance'. The third point upon which the dramatic triangle balanced was the former tailor Mosby, a 'dark, swarthy man' who had risen in the world to become a servant of Lord North. Alice, it seems, had fallen under this man's amorous spell, and she contrived for him to live at the Ardens' house in Faversham, where they carried on an adulterous affair under the very nose of the master of the house. Holinshed asserted that Arden knew of their scandalous liaison but chose to ignore it rather than offend his wife, since there were benefits that he hoped to gain at the hands of some of her friends.

Thus matters might have stood, in an uneasy and awkward stasis, but Alice conceived a desire to be rid of her husband so she could marry Mosby. In Faversham, there was a painter who, it was said, had some skill with poisons. Applied to, he undertook to make a swift-acting potion that she could place in the bottom of a bowl and cover with some palatable liquid, such as milk. But Alice was somewhat light of head, and she'd forgotten the necessary order—poison before milk—and instead added the poison *to* the milk, which did not mix properly and turned the milk an odd colour. Arden, noticing this and disliking the taste, refused to drink all of it and put it aside. Even so, it must have been a strong concoction, since even though he had swallowed no more than a few drops, he was forced later that day to dismount from his horse while journeying to Canterbury, and 'purge himself upwards and downwards', as Holinshed none too delicately put it.

How to achieve a murder and yet escape the consequences? It was not a subject to which Will had ever given a moment's thought. Why would he? Yet as he turned the page, the question began to intrigue him. Had Alice succeeded on that first attempt, it might have been assumed that poor Thomas Arden had been afflicted with one of those many mysterious illnesses that so often appeared and struck down their victims without rhyme or reason. Presumably, the painter would have an inkling of Alice's crime, but gold might be sufficient to ensure his silence, and Alice would have had plenty of that commodity as inheritrix of so rich a man as Arden.

At some point Alice must have realised that she, a woman, could not achieve her design without help, and on the next page Holinshed told how she engaged the services of a man named Dick Greene (Will smiled at the appearance of that name, anticipating the present-day poet's amusement when it appeared as a character in the as-yet unwritten play). He had a grudge against Arden, owing to a dispute over some land attached to the recently dissolved Abbey of Faversham, a dispute so bitter that they had come to blows. Knowing this, she offered him ten pounds if he could find someone who would do the deed.

The story was not yet a play, but Will's mind began to grapple with how it might be turned into one. He stopped reading for a moment, leaving one inky finger resting on the book to keep his place while he thought about how this scene might work. How would Alice have convinced this man Greene to do what she wanted? She would not have come right out with it. Perhaps Thomas Arden had ill-used his wife, and she might have used that fact to enlist Greene's sympathy. But that would not be enough, for no man would become a party to murder merely in order to avenge a woman abused by her husband. Neither would the old land dispute, long resolved, seem sufficient motivation for Greene to renew his quest for revenge, so perhaps he would have to invent some more current cause for disagreement that would drive his interests to join with Alice in her plot. All that would require some further thought.

He returned his attention to the text, which now turned to the recruitment of Black Will to the enterprise. Greene, accompanied by another man, a goldsmith named Bradshaw, contrived to go up to London, joining a small party of serving men travelling in the same direction. Near the village of Rainham they encountered Black Will and his companion, the oddly-named George Shakebag. Bradshaw had, it seemed, once served with Black Will as a soldier in Boulogne; he was, he told Greene, 'as murdering a knave as any in England'.

Greene's ears must have pricked up like a dog finding its scent when the serving-men with whom they were travelling invited the newcomers to join them for the journey onwards to Gravesend. Poor Bradshaw! Will could well imagine his reluctance to be caught up with a man who had appeared from his past, all unbidden, an uncouth villain, given to punctuating every sentence with a curse. But he was perfect for Greene's purposes, and so he proceeded to engage the ruffian's services to kill Thomas Arden.

The scene now shifted to London, where Black Will, not unreasonably, wanted to know how he could identify his victim. So Greene took him to St Paul's churchyard, where Arden was known to walk abroad to get the news of the city, accompanied by one of his servants, a man named Michael. Black Will instantly determined that he would kill both men that very afternoon in some deserted corner of the churchyard, to the alarm of Greene who had to explain that the servant was also in on the plot, and so must be spared.

Shakespeare stopped and counted on his fingers. By his reckoning, there were now six people who were involved in this murderous plan. Will was no maker of conspiracies, but even to him, it seemed obvious that this was already too many to keep the plot secret for very long. To make matters worse, though Black Will and his companion Shakebag might have been tough and frightening villains, they were also almost comically inept. In succeeding pages, Holinshed told how attempt after attempt failed. First the servant Michael, evidently a timid soul, became frightened that he would become a victim of the murderers, and deliberately foiled their first attempt by locking a door that should have been unlocked. Then a projected attack on the open downs failed when Arden unexpectedly fell in with acquaintances instead of riding alone. Fog intervened to foil another attempt, causing Shakebag to fall into a ditch.

At this point, Will was laughing out loud at the sheer incompetence of the two ruffians, so much so that he hardly heard the door to the library creak open to admit a young maid, festooned with all the accoutrements of her profession— cleaning cloths and duster jammed into her girdle, broom clutched in one hand, a bucket and mop in the other—such that she seemed for all the world like some domestic soldier, armed to do combat against squalor, the eternal foe of all maids. 'I am sorry, sir,' she said, evidently confused by his presence. 'Master Barnes said that the library would be empty at this hour and that I was to clean straight away.'

Will laughed. Barnes was playing a little joke, for he knew full well that Shakespeare was working in the library that morning, having admitted him there himself, with an admonishment 'not to be too long, since His Lordship is expected today.' Exactly which lordship—Lord Strange, or his father the earl—the steward had not said. Perhaps this interruption was his way of signalling that Will's time was up.

'I am sorry—Mary, isn't it?—but I am not finished yet.' He fished in his purse for a coin. 'Here's sixpence if you'll give me another hour.'

The girl looked doubtful. 'It won't be worth my place if Master Barnes finds out I haven't done my duty.'

'Don't worry. I will make sure all is right with Master Barnes.'

This reassurance seemed sufficient, and the girl took the coin, slipping it into some secret place in her bodice.

Left alone once more, Will returned to his Holinshed. It was now, the writer said, time for the Saint Valentine's Day Fair, a big event in Faversham that Alice and Mosby had decided should be the theatre for their next attempt. There, Mosby revealed an interesting new complexity to his character, a strand of honour that had hitherto been hidden. He could not, so he said, murder his rival in cold blood. Rather, he would pick some quarrel at the fairground and thereby provoke Arden into a fight. But Arden was impervious to Mosby's insults, having by now endured them for some years, and he refused to be provoked. What a strange creature this Thomas Arden must have been, to have put up with his wife and her lover carrying on their affair more or less openly, yet never taking a single step to put an end to it.

Alice, despite all these failed attempts, was in no way discouraged. Mosby, on the other hand, seemed at this point to have sickened of the whole thing. The two quarrelled and he fled from the Arden mansion. Alice sent a messenger after him, imploring him to return. When he did so, she beseeched him to go through with the matter. As though to dispel his last doubts, she pointed to Arden's evident unpopularity, saying that 'there was not any that would care for Arden's death, nor make any great inquiry for them that should dispatch him.'

So Mosby acquiesced in the final murder attempt. Sending away all the household servants except for the servant Michael, who seemed to have recovered his courage, and one or two others who had been made privy to the plot (was no one loyal to poor Arden?), arrangements were made for Black Will to be hidden in a closet. Arden, away at a neighbour's house, arrived home sometime between six and seven in the evening, there to finally meet his fate.

Mosby engaged the victim in a game of cards, positioning him at the table so that he would not see Black Will hidden in his closet. Then, at an agreed signal, they struck. Black Will burst forth from his cupboard, and started strangling Arden, while Mosby seized a pressing iron—'of fourteen pounds weight', according to the chronicler—and delivered a crushing blow to Arden's head. That should have been the end of him, but as the murderers were about to lay his body out in the counting-house, he regained consciousness with a great groan. Black Will promptly stabbed him in the face, thus putting the matter beyond doubt, and coolly removed the dead man's rings and emptied his purse.

Will shuddered reading these details, which must have come from the evidence given later at the trial of the murderers. Thomas Arden had not been a very admirable man, that much was clear from the chronicle, but surely he had not deserved such a cruel death. Had he realised at the last, as Mosby and his wife looked on, that they were the true agents of his demise? Had he seen a momentary look of triumph in Alice's eyes? If so, he must have felt the terrible despair of betrayal.

Black Will having disappeared into the night, Alice coolly set about removing all signs of everything that had transpired in the parlour, cleaning away her husband's blood and tidying up the rushes that had been displaced by his death throes. To make it seem that Arden had been killed in a frenzied attack, she took a knife and pierced his breast 'seven or eight times'. Then, this grisly work being done, she calmly sent out to invite two of her neighbours to supper, making some pretence that Arden was late coming home, and proposing that they should in the meantime make merry, playing cards and dancing to music played upon the virginals by Alice's daughter.

Eventually, the neighbours left, no doubt mystified by the continued absence of the master of the house, and the conspirators set about removing Arden's body from the counting house and out into the snowy fields. By then it was very late, and those of the household servants who had been sent away began to return. Alice, making out that she was now worried about the whereabouts of her husband, sent them back out in search of him, all the while making great fearful lamentations. Such was the commotion that the Mayor of Faversham was eventually summoned, and he organised a search which in due course found Arden's corpse, half-covered in snow.

This mayor was a determined and astute man, and Alice had not been entirely thorough in her efforts to disguise the evidence of the crime. In short order, the searchers found bloody footsteps leading from the house to the dead body and in a tub in the washroom, they discovered the knife with which she had stabbed her husband and the bloody cloth she had used to clean away the blood. Frightened servants were questioned and soon confessed their parts in the plot. Eventually, Alice too confessed, implicating Mosby, who had fled to the house of Adam Foule, where he was soon apprehended.

Trial and condemnation followed. Mosby and his sister were hanged at Smithfield, while Alice Arden was burned at the stake in Canterbury. Of the other plotters, the unfortunate servant Michael was apprehended, as was Bradshaw who, though entirely innocent, was nevertheless implicated on the evidence of Alice Arden. Both men ended on the gallows. Greene escaped for a while but was eventually caught and condemned. As for Black Will, the chronicler reported that he had been executed at Flushing, in Zetland, though for which of his many crimes it was not clear. Shakebag was never heard from again.

Will sat back in his chair and stared out, unseeing, at the river, busy with its daily burden of traffic. The tale of the brutal murder of Thomas Arden was every bit as dramatic as Greene and Marlowe had suggested. Could it be made into a proper play? If he knew London audiences, they would love the darkness and the bloodletting. And the ineptitude of Black Will and Shakebag could be turned into some fine comedy to lighten the blackness, while Mosby's bouts of indecision seemed to hint at a character of some complexity. Arden, the victim, would have to be made out to be more admirable than he was in life, and the play might need one or two other characters to balance it out. But yes, he could see the outline of a good play in this story.

Pushing the big book aside, he dipped a quill in its ink and began to write.

Chapter 15

The library door behind him creaked open once more, and Will, intent on capturing his ideas on paper before they fled his mind entirely, lifted one hand in an absent-minded gesture of permission for the maid to enter. 'Don't mind me, Mary, I will be finished soon. You can work around me meantime.'

A low masculine chuckle alerted him to his mistake, and he twisted in his chair, expecting to behold David Barnes. Instead, he was confronted with the sight of Lord Strange, who stood with hands on hips grinning in the doorway. Will dropped his pen and scrambled to his feet. 'My lord! A thousand apologies. I was told that you would be returning, but I had not expected you so soon.'

'Speak me no apologies, Mister Shakespeare. I told you that you could have the run of my library, and it would be churlish in me to deny you its use when you are plainly working upon my behalf.' He came into the room and gesturing for Will to resume his seat, took another at the end of the table to Will's left. 'Though Barnes does seem to have some notion that you have been malingering, idly passing your time reading the Greeks and Romans.'

'The poet's path to his ultimate creation rarely follows a straight line, my lord. Like a man sifting for gold in the stream, we must search through many tons of dross before we can find our specks of gold.'

Again the low chuckle. 'I said as much to Barnes, but without your colourful image. Fortunately, I do not need to employ poetry to make my views clear to Davey. But tell me, have your prospecting efforts yet yielded any bullion for us to inspect?'

'They have, my lord, and I found it in our own homely Holinshed rather than in the more exotic climes of Suetonius and Plutarch.'

'Oh? Some story from ancient antiquity, like Leir? Or are you proposing to venture into the weeds and marshes of our more recent history? That might take some care.'

'It is indeed a tale from our near-past, though one involving lowlier folk than monarchs and lords. Does Your Lordship know the story of the murder of the Kentishman Thomas Arden?'

Strange frowned. 'From Kent, you say? No, I cannot say I do.'

'Neither had I until Robert Greene directed me to it.' Will was certainly not going to mention Ball's part in his inspiration. 'I think it has possibilities, but Marlowe and I will have to do much work to realise it for the stage. Shall I tell you something of the story?'

As he talked his patron through a summarised version of the tale, he watched the young man's face become ever more animated—the tired look disappeared from his eyes, his gloved fingers tapped the table at each twist and turn, and he laughed out loud at Will's commentary on the foolishness of the conspirators. It was as though all the weight that seemed to bear upon his shoulders had been lifted for those few moments of shared enthusiasm for a literary project.

Yet at the end, his first reaction was dubious. 'It seems a gruesome subject for a play, does it not? And none of the characters in your story seems to have any moral worth whatever, which might trouble the Master of the Revels.'

'That was my first thought also, but I think we can improve upon history a little, by adding one or two characters and perhaps finding some good in others that is not so apparent in the chronicle. We can find through fiction the grace that was not there in life.'

This seemed to satisfy Strange. 'Then I doubt not that it will be a fine play, Shakespeare. And Marlowe will be helping you, you say?'

'I will prepare the plot, he will do the verses, or so he has promised.'

'Then let us have it ready for summer. A private performance, here or at Lathom, to introduce the world to our new company.' The lordly head tilted to one side. 'There is no doubt that we will *have* a new company by then, is there?'

'Of course, my lord,' Will replied blandly. 'Why would you think otherwise? I have reported daily to Master Barnes, and I assumed that he has passed on news of our progress to you.'

'He has many duties that keep him busy, and of course must satisfy my father's demands as well as mine.' The sleepy blue eyes hardened a little, conveying without words mild resentment that he must rely upon a servant not completely beholden to him, no matter how trusted by the Stanley family. 'He said merely that you were having some trouble acquiring the services of the necessary number of actors.'

'Including myself, we have at this moment eight players who have agreed to perform under Your Lordship's livery, sufficient to undertake a play such as *Arden*, though I would welcome one or two more if we can find them. And I still have hopes that Will Kempe, my lord of Leicester's jesting player, will also join us.'

'I would like to see Robin Dudley's face should you achieve that feat.' For a moment the serious visage had the look of a mischievous boy. 'And you have everything else you need? Davey has made no difficulty with money?'

Will smiled. 'Master Barnes is a commendably diligent steward of the Stanley family's treasury, my lord, and is determined to ensure that every penny and groat is well spent, as is proper, but otherwise, he has been entirely open-handed.'

'An answer that would do a lawyer proud. Or a parliamentarian.'

'Fortunately, I have no ambitions to be either, my lord.'

'Which might be a loss for the kingdom. You may be an actor and a poet, but you talk a good deal more practical sense than most of the geese I meet in Whitehall.'

'You do not find life at court to your taste, my lord?' Will feared that he might be presuming too much on their as-yet young relationship with this question, but the hoot of laughter from Strange reassured him.

'It is at times a comedy, at others a tragedy. But most often it is pure boredom, the endless twittering of empty-headed birds repeating over and over the gossip heard in corridors or from behind the arras. The great lords spend all their time waiting for the Queen to emerge and then they trail around after her like fishing smacks following a stately galleon.'

'Or perhaps they are like the planets, endlessly circling the sun, as Master Copernicus contends?'

'That is a handsome image, but I prefer mine, for while the planets can never close with the object of their attraction, these lords swoop close to the royal person as soon as she appears from her apartments, hoping to catch her eye or have a moment to whisper in her privy ear.'

'What is she like, the Queen?' It was a naïve question, the sort of thing that a serving girl might ask her mistress, and Will felt something of a fool for asking it. But he had never even seen Queen Elizabeth, though she often had herself carried through the streets of London so her loyal subjects could offer up their adulation.

It seemed to genuinely stump Strange. 'What is she like? I am not sure that anyone at court can really answer that question, except perhaps the members of the Privy Council—Leicester, Walsingham, Burghley—who spend the most time with her.' He frowned. 'She is no longer young, of course, and it shows even through the layers of paint with which her ladies attempt to disguise the fact. Yet you can still sense the high-spirited girl she once was, particularly when she laughs—it has a silvery quality to it, shimmering, like the leaves of a birch tree in the breeze.'

'You are most poetical, my lord. Perhaps you should be doing the versifying for our play instead of Marlowe.'

Strange flapped a gloved hand to wave that away. 'You flatter me, of course, as I must flatter the Queen and those close to her. It is the way the world works— lesser men seek ever to compliment the greater, upwards and upwards until we reach the monarch, who must indeed be drowning in false sentiment.'

Will laughed. He liked this young aristocrat, just a few years older than himself and heir to the great Stanley fortune and the Derby earldom, who disguised in a kind of feigned world-weariness an unsentimental, clear-eyed view of the world's machinations. 'I wonder that Her Majesty can ever tell false from true if every word uttered in her ear is laden with self-interest.'

'Ah, but that is her secret, Shakespeare. She listens to everyone, sifts everything, but gives no man her counsel unless she must. Thus the flattered queen flatters in her turn, leaving every man the impression he has left his imprint upon the royal brain. It is a womanly knack that she uses to great purpose.' A sardonic little smile curled his lips. 'You should see the looks on their faces, these eminent counsellors, when they realise that they, with all their knowledge and skills and experience, have been managed by a mere woman.'

It was Will's turn to smile. 'Perhaps if these great men bethought themselves of their own mothers, wives, their daughters even, they might be less easily gulled.'

'That would require a humility that few of them possess. No, I think Her Majesty will continue to have them all dance to her merry jigs until her last breath.' He stopped and his face straightened, as though he sensed he was being too frivolous. 'You must not think her unserious, Shakespeare, merely playing feminine games for her amusement. They are powerful and strong-minded men, these lords of her Privy Council, and she has their respect, even if it is at times grudging. And none question where the realm's power lies.'

That much Will knew well enough from his own time working for Sir Francis Walsingham, who never looked more harried than when he returned to Seething Lane from a particularly testy encounter with the Queen. But Lord Strange knew nothing of Will's connection with the secretary, and if he was to keep it that way he would have to be careful what he said.

'I hope you will forgive my impertinence, my lord, in asking you about Her Majesty. I am but curious about the way in which this government of ours actually works. Power, after all, can be the stuff of great drama, as Marlowe showed us with *Tamburlaine*.'

'Do you harbour ambitions to write plays upon the subject, Shakespeare? Like your friend Marlowe? That might be a perilous path to tread.'

'What path is not perilous for a serious writer? But I take your point, my lord, and shall be cautious,' Will said.

'Yes, I think you will.' There was a little mockery in that. 'But after you have given us our country murder and a harmless comedy or two, perhaps we shall produce a history that is also a commentary upon power and its uses.' The sardonic expression returned. 'My family has, after all, some experience with the subject.'

Will nodded dutifully, though he feared that any story that featured the Stanley family's history of treacherous twists and turns might not find favour with the authorities. Still, that was a problem for another day.

'Meanwhile, I have a country murder, as you call it, to write and get on the stage. Where does Your Lordship wish to stage it? Here, or at Lathom?'

'Oh, here, if we can. But it depends somewhat upon my father. He holds the Lords Lieutenancies of Lancashire and Cheshire, and his duties this summer may take him north, and the household with him.'

'We can easily enough perform it in either place. As long as there are no complicated stage effects, none of your thunder and lighting or battles and the like, we can do it with just a few players and some properties.'

'Good.' That single word might have signalled the terminus of their conversation, but instead of rising, Lord Strange again gave a little drum roll with his fingers on the table, and frowned a tiny frown, as though uncomfortable with whatever he wanted to say next.

'Is there anything else you wish to know, my lord?' Will asked gently.

'No, no. I am perfectly satisfied with your progress and look forward to seeing the results of labours with Master Marlowe.' Another pause. 'But there is another matter upon which I would like your help.'

'You have but to ask, my lord.'

'It is a matter of poetry, see you. My lady's birthday is approaching, and I have it in mind to give her a gift of a poem, in my own hand. A sonnet in the Italian style. But I cannot make it scan.'

Strange slid a hand inside his doublet and extracted a paper which, when unfolded and placed on the table, Will saw was covered in lines of poetry, roughly scrawled in an untidy hand that seemed remarkably at odds with the neat, even fastidious character of its owner. He read it through twice, and then returned his attention to the face of his patron, now set in that look of anxiety common to any poet submitting his creation to the audit of another.

'I see the problem. It starts in the third line, you see? It is too short and needs a syllable or two…'

For the next half hour the social gap between the two men dissolved and they became equals, artists struggling with the demands of their art. They scribbled new lines, crossed words out, underlined infelicitous expressions, and produced, eventually, a poem that, while far from perfect, represented a considerable improvement upon the clumsiness of the original.

'I shall never be a poet, I fear.' Strange sighed when they had finished.

'If you will permit me an observation, it is the quality of the sentiment that the poem conveys which is important, not its mere form, which can in any case be learned with practice. And for that, you need a poetical soul, which my lord assuredly possesses.'

A flush of pleasure coloured the homely face. 'You flatter me, I think.'

'I would flatter the devil himself if I thought it would get a play from the page to the stage, and I would pour a stream of adulation into the ear of that oaf Henslowe to make him part with a few shillings to buy costumes, but I would never lie to any writer about the quality of their work. That is much too serious a thing about which to speak with false tongue.' As Will had intended, by the end of this little speech Lord Strange was laughing out loud.

'Heavens, Ferdinando, I swear I have not heard you laugh so happily this many a month. Spending time with Mister Shakespeare must be doing you good.'

Will had not heard the door open to admit Alice Stanley—Lady Strange, a raven-haired beauty who Will had encountered only once before on his visits to Derby House. On that occasion, she had been imperious and distant, quite unlike her demeanour now. Both men scrambled to their feet, and Will bent into a small bow over the proffered hand.

'And what, pray, are you doing that causes such merriment?' she asked, peering curiously at the scattered drafts littering the table. 'Do not tell me that you are trying your hand at playwriting, Ferdinando, like wretched Oxford.'

Laughing, Lord Strange slipped a hand under his wife's arm and half-turned her away from the table, allowing Will to gather together the pages and slip them into his satchel. 'Will and I were merely looking through some drafts of his new play, and the occasion of our laughter was an absurdity in the plot.'

Lady Strange looked dubiously from one to the other. 'What is it about, this new play of yours Mister Shakespeare?'

'A murder, my lady, that took place in Kent during King Edward's time.'

'I find it hard to believe that there might be much occasion for mirth in such a subject. But you are the poet, and doubtless know your craft.'

'Come, my dearest,' Lord Strange said, grasping her elbow a little more firmly. 'Let us away and leave Will to his labours. He has much to do if he is to get our play ready before the summer.'

'*Our* play, is it now, Ferdinando?' Lady Strange could not suppress a smile. 'The Earl of Oxford has a competitor, I swear.'

'Fear not, madam. Mister Shakespeare has convinced me that my talents lie elsewhere. Come, we must away. Will, I look forward to the next draft of our play.' With that, the pair swept out of the room, leaving Will to replace the draft poem in a casket that stood in the middle of the table, among various other papers where Lord Strange would have no difficulty finding it. He hoped that no one else would do so before His Lordship had a chance to return and retrieve his sonnet.

He had what he needed from Raphael Holinshed, so he closed the big volume, leaving it on the lectern where it had been propped. Taking one more look around, he picked up his cloak from the chair across which it had been draped, and made his way out of the house, into the shadowed silence of Cannon Row, and from there to King Street and the long walk home.

Chapter 16

'Well? What do you think?'

Marlowe held up a hand to stem Will's impatience, his eyes never leaving the four pages of close-written words that lay on the table between them. His lips moved as he read, silently mouthing the words as they formed in his mind, and his brow furrowed in concentration. Then, having finally reached the last line, he nodded once, twice, and looked up at his friend.

'Who is this man Franklin to whom you have given such a big part? I don't remember any such name from Holinshed.'

'He is a conscience of sorts. The play needed someone, apart from poor innocent Bradshaw, who has some honour.'

Marlowe nodded, considering. 'I see what you mean. The rest of them are a rather villainous lot. Perhaps we can also use Franklin as a kind of chorus? Or at least as a mirror through which to see the reflection of Arden's character.'

'My thought also. Speaking of Arden, it seems to me that we should soften him a little, make him more a-weary of the world and long-suffering, rather than the arrogant and grasping speculator that he seems to have been in life. That will make the horror of Alice's crime seem all the greater.'

'Hmm. Yes. But let us not make him too nice. This is a story about the black hearts of pitiless, grasping people, of bloody revenge, not a morality tale.' The glitter in Marlowe's eyes told Will that his friend was looking forward to expressing all this savagery in words.

'You know best, Kit. But you think this plot will work upon the stage?'

'Oh yes, my friend. Though we will have a deal of work to put some poetry around the scaffolding of your plot.'

'We? I thought you were going to do the versifying yourself.'

'Of course. But the work will go faster if we do it together, will it not?' Marlowe looked around the room, Shakespeare's lodging in Silver Street, surveying the domestic squalor of unmade bed, strewn clothes and, perched on the end of the little table at which they sat, a platter containing yesterday's half-consumed supper of cheese and hard bread. 'Though perhaps we should repair to some place more fitting to the work of poets.'

Will laughed. 'A tavern, you mean? Honestly, Kit, I swear you could drink an ocean of ale dry.'

Half an hour later they were comfortably installed in their familiar booth at the back of Mistress Mary's, with two tankards filled to the brim with her ale, and half a capon sitting in its grease on a trencher. The tools of their trade lay on the table between them: a newly purchased bottle of ink, three freshly sharpened quills, and a pile of paper.

Marlowe took a deep draught of ale and wiped his lips with his sleeve. 'Now, how shall we begin?'

'Arden and Franklin? Alone on the stage, talking about Alice's infidelity with Mosby?'

'That gets straight to the point.' Marlowe unstoppered the ink bottle, picked up a quill, held it in the air for a moment and then began writing, saying the words out loud as they were formed on the page.

>   *'Arden, cheer up thy spirits and droop no more!*

The Duke of Somerset—the Lord Protector during King
Edward's minority, you'll remember—*has freely given to*
you and your heirs
By letters patent from His Majesty
All the lands of the Abbey of Faversham.
Read them and leave this melancholy mood.'

Will blinked in surprise. In five lines, ejected straight from his brain without a moment's pause for reflection, Marlowe had established the source of Arden's wealth and that he was in a melancholy mood. Could he match Marlowe's practised skill?

'So, Arden is melancholy. Let us explain why.' Will took up his pen, dipped it into the ink, and wrote at the top of another sheet of paper the single word *Arden*.

'Franklin, your love prolongs my weary life,
And but for you how odious were this life,
That shows me nothing but torments my soul,
And those foul objects that offend my eyes!'

'Foul objects?'

Will waggled fingers to silence Marlowe, and continued:

'Love-letters pass between Mosby and my wife,
And they have privy meetings in the town:
Nay, on his finger, did I spy the ring
Which at our marriage-day the priest put on.
Can any grief be great as this?'

Marlowe clapped his hands. 'Yes, that is excellent. Mosby wearing Arden's own wedding ring. Now Franklin might say to his friend that he should expect nothing better from women, who are ever false and wavering.'

'Aye, but even so it is monstrous, intolerable. And particularly with such a one as Mosby.'

'What is he, this Mosby?' Marlowe was now inhabiting the character of Franklin.

'A mere tailor, who by servile flattery and fawning has crept into the service of Lord Clifford and is now steward of his house.'

'What? Would a nobleman countenance such a peasant?'

'Lord Clifford would.' Will frowned. 'Hmm. Let us say that Clifford and Arden are not friends; the first hint that this man has many enemies.'

'Good. And then Arden swears vengeance on his wife's seducer. Let me see...'

Marlowe began again to write, this time in silence, and when he was finished, slid the completed words across the table for Will to read aloud.

> *'That injurious ribald, that attempts*
> *To violate my dear wife's chastity*
> *Shall on the bed which he thinks to defile*
> *See his dissevered joints and sinews torn,*
> *Whilst on the planchers pants his weary body,*
> *Smeared in channels of his lustful blood.'*

'That sounds more like your bloodthirsty Tamburlaine than my humble land-speculator.' Will laughed. 'But it makes the point. He should say somewhere how much he loves his wife...here, perhaps?'

Marlowe squinted at the place in the newly created text where Will's finger lay and made a little mark on the paper. 'I'll add something later. And Franklin? What says he to his friend's intemperance?'

'He tries to calm Arden's temper, and counsels him to charm her back to his side—*intreat her fair: sweet words are fittest engines to race the flint walls of a woman's heart.*'

Marlowe snorted. 'He would be better off giving her a good thrashing! Your Franklin sounds like a giver of pointless advice.'

'Aye, perhaps he is. I think of him as Arden's conscience, oft ignored but prescient.'

In this fashion they worked through the rest of the morning, oblivious to the rise and fall of conversation in the little cookshop as the daily tide of apprentices and cloth merchants came and went, scribbling a dozen lines of poetry, stopping to read them out loud and debate the merit and meaning of their newborn creations, scratching lines out and adding addenda to be worked on later, pausing every now and then to sharpen blunted quills and quaff a mouthful of ale.

By late afternoon, when Mistress Mary was ready to close her shop for the day, they had finished in rough draft most of the play's first scene. The play's main protagonists had been introduced, and the murderous couple's first attempt to poison Arden had failed. To be sure, there were gaps where they had done no more than sketch the action, which Marlowe would fill with lines of verse, and much of what they had written would need to be scanned and, no doubt, rewritten with more felicitous poetry. And they had had some disagreements along the way—Marlowe had wanted to introduce an element of magic by way of a painting that could kill those who looked upon it, a notion that Shakespeare thought daft. In the end, they decided to keep it as a device but have Alice reject it as too chancy. But overall both men were satisfied with what they had achieved for the

222

day as Will securely stoppered the ink bottle and slid it, along with the precious completed sheets, into his satchel. Their play was, he thought, well-launched.

'I fear that I will have to leave you to work alone for a while,' Marlowe said as they went out into the warm early evening. 'Henslowe and Alleyn are demanding more pages of *Tamburlaine* than I have yet written, so that task will have to occupy me until Thursday at least.'

Will was not entirely surprised. He had anticipated that his friend would find himself torn between his competing projects. 'Then I will take myself down to Derby House and install myself in the library for a few days, which will greatly annoy Barnes, I make no doubt.'

'I think you enjoy teasing Barnes, Will. And how does His Lordship? Is he in residence still?'

'Yes, he is required at court, though it is a place that he seems to detest.'

'Oh?' The casual query was accompanied by a sharp look. Will had come to think of it as Marlowe's intelligencer expression.

'You may sheath the sword of your suspicions, Kit. He detests the shallow fawning of the courtiers, but he respects the Queen and her chief ministers. If Lord Strange harbours any disloyalty, he hides it exceedingly well.'

'Which might mean nothing more than that he is a skilled dissembler.' Marlowe sniffed.

Will threw his hands in the air. 'You are impossible! But in truth, I like the man. An aristocrat he may be, but he has been generous in his support for the new company, and I swear his mind is more excited by the prospect of a new poem than by any matter of politics.'

Marlowe's shrug signified acceptance, if not defeat. 'Well, we shall see. You may be right, but I know that Phelippes and the rest would counsel constant vigilance. Let us meet again on, say Friday? At your lodgings?'

'Done. And I will have by then at least the next scene ready for your magic touch.'

Chapter 17

The two-horse dray, laden with its cargo of tanned cowhides, made its way along busy Cheapside, horses' hooves clip-clopping wearily on the rough cobblestones, urged along by an occasional half-hearted flick of the whip by their driver, a phlegmatic countryman who made this journey once a month.

Coming to the inevitable constriction where the traffic had to squeeze past the Cheapside Cross, he hauled on the reins to bring the dray to a halt. Half a dozen carts and a fine carriage were lined up ahead of them, slowed almost to a halt as they worked their way through the narrow pedestrian-choked gaps between the monument and the houses on each side.

'I reckon it were best for you to jump off here, sir. It will take me a good quarter-hour to get past this lot.'

'Good advice, and I'll take it,' Will shouted back from his perch atop the mound of hides, which had made an admirable bed upon which to spend the last half hour having a pleasant nap while the cart made its way up from Westminster, where he had begged a ride to bring him back to the city from Derby House.

Having clambered down and given the carter a final farewell wave, he threaded his way through the crowd with the long-practised skill of a Londoner, turned into Wood Street and in a few minutes was at the door of his lodging in Silver Street. There, he found an anxious Ned Bentley waiting for him in the hallway. 'Ned? What is the matter?'

'A man is waiting to talk to you, up in our room. A poxy-looking, villainous man. I didn't like the look of him, so I came down here to warn you.'

'Does the fellow perchance to own a big black hat?'

'Enormous; I have never seen the like. How did you know?'

Will smiled and patted the boy on the shoulder. 'Fear not, Ned, we are in no danger. He is one of Rob Greene's less savoury acquaintances. We set him to the task of finding out where John Towne might be, so perhaps he is here with news.'

Will led the way up the stairs, taking them two at a time. At the top, the door to his room was warped and required a solid shove to get it open. The noise gave Ball sufficient warning for him to turn from the paper-strewn table at which he was standing and greet the room's owner with a leering, gap-toothed grin. 'Mister Shakespeare. You are returned, I see.'

'That fact is plain as a pikestaff. But what are you doing here, Ball? I thought we agreed that you would send word when you wanted to meet and that we would choose some more discreet place to do so.'

Ball shrugged. 'I must have forgotten.' He glanced at Ned. 'Is this your boy? Does he have your ear in the matters that concern us?'

'I am no one's boy!' Ned was indignant but held his tongue when Will placed a restraining hand on his arm.

'He may look like a mere stripling to you, Ball, but Mister Bentley is a fine actor and a member of my company, so I will ask to you stay civil when you address him. And yes, he has my trust. Now, again, what brings you here? News of John Towne, I hope.'

Ball's eyebrows rose a fraction, and then he shrugged his insolent shrug again, clearly dismissing Ned as a creature of no account. 'Your friend Towne has indeed appeared, as sudden as a jack-in-the-box.' His hands mimed the action of the children's toy. 'And he is lodging at the Dolphin, in Bishopsgate.'

Will tried to place the establishment. 'Just without the gate, opposite St Botolph's Church?'

'The very one. The landlord told me that your Mister Towne had taken several rooms and plans to stay there for some months.'

'That will cost a penny or two.'

'A shilling a week, I am told. Paid in advance.'

Will smiled at Ned's inadvertent whistle. 'That is a lot of money. I had not thought Towne was so rich.'

'He isn't. He told the landlord he could only pay for a week, but that his credit can be relied upon, as he expects to come into money within the month.'

'Which he believed?'

'That he did, though he grumbled about it. He said that this man Towne is an odd fellow, surly, and keeps to his room most of the day except for when he comes down to the tap room for dinner, taking some ale and the cheapest ordinary fare. He has not had any visitors since he arrived, but all the while when he is eating his dinner, he is looking around, furtive-like, as if he is looking out for someone.'

'An observant man, this landlord of yours. And talkative, it would seem.'

'I have a hold over him,' Ball said with a shrug. 'He squeaks whenever I squeeze his pips.'

Poor man, to have his pips in the unscrupulous hands of Cutting Ball. 'And did he tell you anything else, this squeaker of yours?'

'Only one thing—Towne asked the ostlers to look out for a certain Frenchman. They were to advise him privily when he arrived.'

'Every second foreigner arriving in London is a Frenchman. How are they to recognise him? Does he have a name?'

'He is called Foy. A tall man, with a hooked nose, the boys were told.'

227

Something tugged at Will's memory. *A tall man with a hooked nose.* Did that not match the description that Billy Knell had left of the man Towne had met with in secret in Abingdon?

'Well, Mister Shakespeare, have I met the terms of your commission?'

Will held the cutpurse's gaze for a while before nodding his assent. He got up and went to the foot of the bed, where a big chest stood. Opening it, he rummaged inside for a small bag of coins, extracted two, and sent them flying, one at a time, across the room. Ball plucked each from the air, the leer never leaving his face. After a quick inspection to satisfy himself that they were genuine, he slipped the coins into a secret pocket sewn into his greasy leather jerkin. Picking up the long black cloak he had left draped on the back of a chair, he settled it on his shoulders with a theatrical swirl that set Will's papers a-flutter. 'Well, I am away. I like your play, by the way.'

'You astonish me, Ball. I had no notion that you could read.'

The habitual leer became a grin. 'Judge not a book by its cover alone, Mister Shakespeare. I am a man of many parts.'

'As are we all. Now, let us go downstairs, and get you out of the door before my landlady appears. She is of a nervous disposition and I would not like to have her affrighted.'

'I did not like that man,' Ned said after Ball had left.

'I don't like him much either. But Greene told me that if anyone could find John Towne, it would be Cutting Ball, and he was right.'

Ned's handsome face creased into a questioning frown. 'I know we need actors, Will, but why are you so determined to recruit Mister Towne? I do not recollect his company with any pleasure.'

'Yet he is, you will concede, a capable enough actor. Marlowe and I have him in mind for our Mosby.'

'I suppose so, though Dick Cowley could do it just as well. But it is your play, Will, so I suppose you know best.'

'I do,' Will said complacently. 'But I need you to help me. John most likely knows nothing as yet of Lord Strange's company, and even if he did, he is a prideful fellow and might not wish to come a-begging for a position. So I need a go-between.'

'Me? But he doesn't like me. In fact, I don't like him very much either.'

'I thought you were an actor. Surely you can dissemble just a little.' Will thought for a moment. 'Let us think on it as if you were enacting a role upon the stage. Why are you at the Dolphin in the first place?'

'That's easy—I will wait until the northern coach has left, the one that goes in the afternoon, and pretend that I have been farewelling someone. A friend or a relative.'

'Good. Then you go into the taproom and wait until he appears for supper. Seem surprised to see him, get talking, and tell him about the company. But do not say we are short of players.'

That puzzled Ned. 'Are we not?'

'Of course we are. In truth, I need two or three John Townes.'

Enlightenment began to dawn. 'You want to flatter him?'

'Exactly. John must believe that he is doing me a favour by joining the company. So you should say that I have approached several actors—mention some names, such as James Tunstall or Will Sly—but that I think they are but middling players. Hint that I need someone of the first rank. After that, you must proceed according to your judgement. Find out what his plans are. If he shows interest in the company, tell him that you will suggest his name to me.'

'And then *you* ask *him*, ever so humbly, if he will deign to grace our stage. I had no idea you possessed such guile, Will.'

Will laughed and patted Ned on the shoulder. 'It is a thing that comes with age, my friend. And as the Latin has it, *mater artium necessitas*—the mother of invention is necessity!'

Of course, as Will knew but Ned did not, John Towne was under instructions to join Lord Strange's household in some capacity, so it was always likely that he would have found his way to Shakespeare's door. But this little piece of subterfuge would make sure he did so sooner rather than later.

In the end, it was hardly necessary. Ned, reporting back after encountering Towne at supper the next day, said that the actor had taken the bait swiftly and easily. The youth had, it seemed, elaborated upon his role quite considerably, exaggerating the difficulties Will was supposed to be having and flattering Towne's ego by saying that the company would be greatly enriched by his talents. The older actor, far from being reluctant, had quickly agreed and himself proposed that he should meet with Will as soon as may be.

So it was that Will came face to face with the man he had last seen in Thame a year ago, in the custody of the local coroner and facing an uncertain future. They met at the Dolphin, where Towne had secured a cosy and relatively quiet corner table in the inner recesses of the large and noisy taproom, ideally placed, Will noticed, to observe the comings and goings of this busy coaching inn. Apart from having a good view of the room itself, the activity in the yard was clearly visible through big bay windows that also bathed their table in warm morning sunlight.

Towne was finishing his breakfast—a sweet omelette made with currants, accompanied by bread, butter and the inevitable tankard of ale—as Will arrived and slid onto the bench opposite him. Pushing the plate aside, Towne dabbed at his lips with a napkin, poured himself another draught of the thin brew, and gestured to Will to help himself to a spare tankard.

In appearance, he had changed little. The same thinning black hair, exaggerated moustaches and slight chin-beard, the same dark, unsmiling eyes that managed to convey disdain for the rest of mankind no matter what the rest of his face might be doing, the same wiry, muscular body held square-shouldered and erect as though on parade, and the same long unadorned fingers that tapped the table in a kind of involuntary nervous twitch. But he did seem a little older and more care-worn than when Will had last seen him—there were flecks of grey in his hair and two narrow creases between the brows, seemingly etched there by worry.

'Well, Shakespeare, you seem to have fallen on your feet.'

Towne's manner was as brusquely superior as ever, the sneering tone calculated to offend, but Will, having anticipated this, kept his face cheerful and his smile bland. 'Not luck entirely, John. I was helped along by some friends. But tell me, how do you fare? Being imprisoned must have been difficult.'

Towne raised his shoulders in a shrug. 'The gaol at Thame is hardly the Clink. I was allowed the liberty of the town three days a week, and the gaoler was not ungenerous in the matter of victuals.'

'Still, I have been imprisoned, and I know what it is like to be uncertain of the future.' Thus summoned, the memory of that dank prison cell in Verona was as vivid as ever, and Will shuddered at the recollection. 'But in any case, I am glad that you were finally acquitted.'

'Are you? The damned coroner took his time to decide to hear the matter and then fumbled his way through the law as if he had never before seen such a case. It might have gone more quickly if you and the others had been there to testify in person.'

'We had no choice, John, you know that,' Will said patiently. 'The company could never have simply waited around in Thame until the coroner was ready to hear the case.'

'Aye, I know well enough that no-one and nothing will get between Dick Tarlton and a day's takings,' Towne said sourly. He seemed to realise that his interests were not going to be served by any further airing his grievances, and he attempted a smile. 'But it ended well enough. The coroner could find no case against me, and the royal pardon was absolute. And your written deposition was helpful, Shakespeare, for which you have my thanks.'

This last was a little grudging, but Will accepted it with a nod, all the while curious about Towne's description of the coroner's findings, which seemed somehow ambivalent. It was as if Towne did not himself believe in his own innocence. Will certainly did not, despite his deposition.

'Anyway, all that is in the past. Let us talk of more pleasant things. You know from Ned about the new company, Lord Strange's Men? Then let me be plain— I need players, good players, and should you wish to join our ranks, you would be most welcome.'

Towne's fingers drummed on the table twice. 'Who else do you have? I'll not join a company of second-rated actors.'

'Dick Cowley, George Bryan, George Ashford and Tom Blunt have all signed on. And I have high hopes of Leicester's man, Kempe, though I confess he is proving elusive. Tom Pope and Augustine Phillips are interested but not yet committed.'

'Bentley mentioned two others, Sly and Tunstall?'

'They would fill gaps, certainly. But neither is as fine a player as you, John.'

Towne accepted that small flattery as nothing less than his due. 'And the matter of money? How is the company to be financed?'

'Lord Strange will pay the players for a year until a proper company can be formed. Six shillings a week whenever the company is performing.'

'And plays? Has His Lordship also provided funds to buy playscripts? Or are *you* going to write them?'

Will ignored the sarcasm, keeping the amiable smile on his face. 'Not me. As much as I would like to claim the title of company playwright and the money that goes with it, His Lordship has instead engaged the services of another to write plays for us—Christopher Marlowe.'

That name called forth a snort. 'You fly high. Since I got back to London, that name has been on the lips of every actor and theatre-goer I have encountered. It is said that he is a sodomite, and an atheist to boot.'

Was it? Will was vaguely disturbed that Kit's reputation for unorthodox behaviour was being bruited abroad so openly. 'That's as may be, but he can write a play, and we are lucky to have his services.'

'And what is he writing for us, this new genius?'

'A curious subject, even for Marlowe. He calls it a revenge play, and it is about an infamous murder that took place in Kent. Marlowe is from that county; did you know that? The story concerns one Thomas Arden, who was murdered by the connivance of his wife and his wife's lover. I am helping Kit with the plot, while he does the verses. He is a genius! It is all written in blank verse, like *Tamburlaine*, and in pentameters that trip off the tongue so easily that even a bawling town-crier could mouth the words and sound true. An actor such as yourself will weave miracles with his words.'

His enthusiasm was unfeigned, even though in truth the play was far from complete after three months of intermittent work on the text. Marlowe, distracted by the demands of Henslowe and Alleyn, had struggled to find the time to devote to this other project, much to Will's frustration. But what he had done so far was brilliant, and Will had no doubt that it would be a fine and popular work for the stage. But more to the immediate point, he hoped that the prospect of speaking lines written by London's most popular writer of plays would be the last morsel of bait to hook John Towne, his theatrical fish.

Instead, Towne scowled and shook his head. 'He may be great as Aeschylus himself, but I mislike the subject of this play.'

'Why so? It is a story of great passion, which is the very stuff of drama, And the guilty, murderers and conspirators alike, get their just rewards at the end, so it is moral enough.'

'Yet still it is… tawdry. I can think of no other word.'

Will laughed. 'If tawdriness was to be the prime cause of disqualification, half the plays in London would have been banned ere now. Believe me, John, Marlowe is making us a great play with this tawdry subject, one that audiences will come back for time and again.'

Towne leaned back against the wall behind him and grasping the tankard with both hands, he swirled it and stared for a few moments at the foaming liquid inside, as if it were an oracle that held the answer to the questions in his mind. 'Well, if you and my lord Strange are set upon it, I suppose that I must accede. But cast me not in the role of the murderer, I pray you.'

'That I will not,' Will said, relieved. 'So you will join us?'

For answer, Towne extended his hand across the table. The fish was hooked.

***

'For a while, I really thought he was going to say no,' Will told Kit the following day when they met at Mistress Mary's. 'He is a very hard man to pierce, closed as the shutters on a winter's day.'

Marlowe's attention was focused on their bottle of ink, which he was attempting to thin with the addition of vinegar begged from Mistress Mary. 'Remind me never to buy ink from George Sutton again, no matter how cheap he offers it.' He finished the delicate task of pouring the vinegar, stoppered the bottle and gave it a good shake.

That done, he gave Will his full attention. 'If what Knell said was true, he was always going to take the opportunity to join Lord Strange's household in some capacity. But no doubt he did not wish to seem anxious to do so, lest he raise suspicions, as any spy would.'

'You do seem convinced that he is a traitor, whatever the evidence.'

'He *may* be innocent, that I grant. But can we afford to act as if it were so? I think not. So, once you had agreed, what else did our Mister Towne say?'

'Not much. We talked a little more of the company, the merits of our actors, where we would be performing, that kind of thing. He was curious about our patron, naturally enough.'

Marlowe's attention seemed to sharpen a notch. 'What did he want to know about Lord Strange?'

'Oh, nothing really odd. What he is like, his interests, how often he was at court. Questions that a market gossip might ask.' Will frowned. 'Though now I think on it, he did seem particularly interested in Lord Strange's travelling habits, how often he was at Lathom and how often in London, whether he had any regular visitors. He was not insistent, you understand, just slipped questions in here and there, seeming innocent.'

'Seeming innocent, but perhaps not. Admit it—your nose is twitching like a mouse scenting cheese.'

'Not an elegant image. Still, I am not yet convinced that John is anything other than what he says he is.'

'Good. You keep believing that, and I will play the cynic. Between us, we will ferret out the truth about this man. Now, shall we get to work?'

For the rest of the morning, they laboured happily on *Arden*, working in a rhythm they had developed over half a dozen such sessions. Usually, Will arrived with a plot for the next section of the play, scratched out on wax tablets, and they talked for a while about the scene upon which they were about to work. Then Marlowe began to compose the lines of verse, working with a facility and speed that Will still found astonishing. Not that his collaborator's work was perfect in every line, and they frequently engaged in friendly little battles about some word that seemed wrong or a line whose rhythm was uneven. It was an amiable partnership that cast Will as the eager apprentice to Marlowe's poetic mastery.

By this time, they were well launched on the telling of their story. The first and second acts were complete, dealing with Alice's aborted attempt to poison her husband, the recruitment of Black Will, and the first attempt by him and his companion Shakebag to execute his commission by attacking Arden in the churchyard of St Paul's. Holinshed's text had simply said that the villains had 'missed their purpose', but Shakespeare had come up with an amusingly comic way of foiling the plot, involving an apprentice at a bookseller's who knocks Black Will on the head as he closes the shutters of his stall (he had seen something similar happen once in St Paul's churchyard). Marlowe, for whom comedy was a foreign country, at first thought the whole conceit low, though in the end conceded that the play might benefit from this gentle bit of levity.

Their work that day was to be the third act, in which the servant Michael thwarted the killers by failing to leave the doors of Arden's house unlocked. Marlowe had described the attempt itself in an economical eighty or so lines of clear, straightforward dialogue, but Will was not satisfied that he had cleared the ground sufficiently to make the story believable.

'Think on this, Kit—why is Michael moved to his double treachery, first planning to betray his master, and then changing his mind to prevent Black Will and Shakebag from getting into the house to execute their fell design?'

'He is afeard that they, bloody ruffians that they are, will kill him also. He is, after all, the only possible witness to their crime. Is that not enough?'

'Perhaps. But there was something else. Let me see...' He riffled through some pages, his close-written notes taken from Lord Strange's copy of Holinshed's *Chronicle*. 'Yes, here it is—*The cause that this Michael conspired with the rest against his master, was that it was determined that he should marry a kinswoman of Mosby's*. But which kinswoman?'

'Sister? It would have to be someone close enough to be bound by Mosby's word, not some distant cousin.'

'And what if we make Mistress Alice offer the promise of this sister's hand without telling Mosby? She is our principal villain, after all, bent solely upon the destruction of her husband. Mosby, on the other hand, waxes and wanes, manipulated by Alice.'

Marlowe frowned, his mind evidently turning to the practical problem of writing lines to give this idea effect. 'Yes, I see. It can be done, I suppose. We will have to add something near the beginning to say that this little plot has been concluded, but that offers no difficulty.'

Several more ideas presented themselves in Will's mind, tumbling forth so quickly that he was tripping over his words. 'The third act. Michael's resolution stumbles. He is caught between his promise to Alice to connive at the death of his master, who he knows has never done him any wrong, and his fear of being murdered in his turn by Black Will and Shakebag. This so disorders his mind that he cries out aloud with the agony of it, waking his master.'

'Who, disturbed by this commotion, is moved to see for himself whether the doors are locked and rates his servant when he discovers that they are not.' Marlowe finished the scene with a smile. 'You are a little soft on this Michael, I think. But it will serve.'

'I have another idea. Thomas Arden was to all accounts an unpleasant, grasping man. But we must make him the wronged party to this quarrel. So I want to open this scene with him and Franklin arguing about Alice, the one saying that she is beyond redemption and the other counselling patience.'

'What, in the face of a wife who parades her infidelity so brazenly? He seems to be a feeble fellow, this Franklin, to counsel forbearance in such a case.'

'Aye, but bear in mind this is a device to paint Alice's wickedness and Arden's blamelessness.'

Marlowe pulled some blank sheets of paper from his satchel. 'Well then, why don't you write that part of the scene and I'll do the other half, then let us see how well they marry.'

'What, now?' Will was surprised. He was used to working in the quiet solitude of his lodgings in Silver Street, not amid the noise and clatter of Mistress Mary's.

Marlowe glanced around the room as if noticing the clamour for the first time. 'Why not? A poet should be able to write anywhere. Besides, with what I have already inscribed, we can get the whole scene finished today if we write it now.'

So they set to, each labouring over their own pages, ignoring the comings and goings of apprentices and cloth merchants, the orders bawled to the kitchen, whose steam and smoke-filled interior could just be glimpsed through the curtains behind Mistress Mary's counter, and the bustle as trenchers laden with meat and bread and jugs of beer were delivered to the long communal tables. To his surprise, as his mind was drawn into the task of finding the right words to express his ideas in poetic dialogue, the cacophony seemed to recede and become no more than a kind of low hum, a background noise no more consequential than that of the city heard from Finsbury Fields.

When at length he was satisfied with his efforts and laid down his pen, the sounds of the room came rushing back with the force of a tidal race, and he found himself marvelling that he could think at all in such a din. Looking up, he realised that Marlowe must have finished his section of the scene some time ago, for he was regarding Shakespeare with a kind of benign but superior amusement.

'You are done?' Will said. 'Then let us each the be other's auditor.'

Marlowe's work was, as usual, near faultless, needing but a jot here and a scribbled correction there. That done, he awaited Marlowe's verdict on his own work.

'Nothing? No changes?' Will's original paper was unmarked.

'What need to change that which is perfect?' He picked the page up again and peered at it.' I particularly liked "good counsel is to her as rain to weeds, and reprehension makes her vice to grow as Hydra's head was plenished by decay". Excellent neat images, both.'

Will felt a flush of pleasure at Marlowe's approval, which he disguised by busying himself with gathering the pages of the play together and put them back into his satchel. 'What is the time?'

'An hour after noon, or near enough,' Will guessed.

'Then I must away. Henslowe and Alleyn are panting for my presence this afternoon to begin rehearsing part two of *Tamburlaine*.'

'I had not realised you were so far along. Is the play then complete?'

'It wants a few more pages but is otherwise ready to be fair copied for performance. Though Henslowe will want changes.'

'How so? Has he now acquired that which he never before had, to wit, taste?'

'I see your dislike of our impresario friend has not abated.' Marlowe laughed. 'No. Both he and Alleyn are afraid that I have made *Tamburlaine* too bloody so that the master will not let it pass.'

Will snorted his contempt for that idea. 'If Master Tilney could approve *The Spanish Tragedy*, with its tearing out of tongues and dashing out of brains, it seems to me that there is little in the way of bloodiness to which he would not give his assent.'

'I am sure you are right, but Henslowe was ever timid, and he influences Alleyn. But I shall resist, and we shall see. And yourself, where do you go this afternoon?'

'To speak with lawyers.' The mere prospect made Will feel gloomy. 'There are contracts to be writ and sundry other legal pieces of paper that must be drafted to comply with the statutes that govern our craft. It is tedious beyond belief. If by some miracle I was to be translated to great temporal authority, my first act would be to condemn all lawyers.'

'You are full of spleen today, my friend. First poor Henslowe and now the hapless practisers of the law. I must be gone. Shall we meet again in, say, three days? I fear that *Tamburlaine* will engage me for that long.'

'Aye. Come down to Derby House if you can. His Lordship is in residence and he would be happy to see you.'

'I shall. Until then, farewell.' Marlowe made his way to the door, weaving his way through the throng, leaving Shakespeare standing, bemused, as he realised that once again his friend had left him to pay the bill.

Chapter 18

London, early July 1588

'I said I would not play the murderer!' John Towne hissed, half under his breath.

'Nor is Mosby any such thing.' Will took the other man by the arm and steered him away from the stares of the other actors. 'He and Alice are plotters and schemers, that is true. But it is Black Will and Shakebag who are the murderers.'

Towne snorted his indifference to that argument. 'A distinction that tells no difference. He is a black-hearted villain, and I'll not play him.'

'He is also at the very centre of the play. Look you, Kit and I have written him as a man who has doubts about the course of action that is forced upon him by his love for Alice. It is she who is the real villain, not Mosby.' Will sensed that Towne's truculence was beginning to subside. 'He is no simple character, this man, and we need a good actor to make him live on the stage.'

A long stare preceded the little shrug of the shoulders that Will knew from past experience with Towne signified imminent surrender. This time his wheedling was even rewarded with a small, tight smile. 'Well then, let us get on with it. Who is to be Alice? Bentley, I suppose?'

'Of course. It is a big piece, but I think Ned is capable of it. Cowley will do Arden and I will play Franklin.'

'Are we going to get started, Will?' Richard Cowley called from the other side of the room. 'Time is a-wasting.'

'What, do you have some other engagement, Dick?' Ned laughed. 'Some other play to con and rehearse?'

'You saucy wench!' Cowley responded with an answering chuckle. 'I'll paddle your behind if you respect me not.'

Ned stuck his tongue out. 'You'll have to catch me first, old man.'

'Enough, children,' Will said, joining in the general laughter. 'Come, John, let us go to.'

Towne's touchy ego smoothed and peace restored, they got to work on the new play. Their purpose that day was not to rehearse it in its entirety—an impossibility in any case until the actors had an opportunity to memorise their lines—but to acquaint each of them with their roles and to agree how the play was to be performed.

On their arrival that morning at the upstairs room at the Mermaid, the use of which had been secured with much cajoling and wheedling of a doubtful innkeeper, each player had been given a long roll upon which had been inscribed their particular part, carefully copied from the master playscript.

Preparing the actor's scrolls had been a long and arduous task, particularly since the play itself was far from complete and contained many gaps in which the actors would, for now at least, be required to extemporise. This was work that would normally be done by a scrivener employed for the purpose, but Will felt a particular sense of ownership of this playscript. Unlike *Jack Straw*, this was his own conception, even if most of the words were Marlowe's, and he had decided to undertake the job himself. It had proven much more arduous than he had expected. Conscious of the need for the actors to be able to understand every word, he had to write in a careful, scholarly hand quite different from his usual rapid scrawl. By the end, his wrist was sore with the effort.

The assembled players—Towne, Cowley, Ned Bentley, George Bryan and Thomas Blunt—took to their task enthusiastically, even Towne quickly overcoming his initial distaste with the role he had been assigned as Will told them the play's story and how he and Kit had conceived the various parts. By the time an hour had passed, every member of the assembled company was satisfied that they had fully grasped the essence of the drama they were to present, and it was agreed that they would spend the next few days learning their parts, ready for the first rehearsal in a week's time.

'We should work in pairs,' Richard Cowley suggested. 'You and I, Will, since Arden and Franklin are such friends; Ned as Alice and John as Mosby; George as Black Will and Tom as Shakebag.'

'That's well thought on,' George Bryan said. 'Who is to play the other roles— Greene and Bradshaw? And the painter, Clarke?'

'And don't forget Michael, Arden's servant,' Towne put in.

'I hope for Anthony Ashford and Tom Pope for the first two when they join us next week. As to Clarke and Michael, I am not sure. It may be that someone must double.'

'Well, yes, that would work. Clarke is only in the first scene,' Cowley mused. 'But we still need at least one more principal actor and some minor players.'

'I know, I know,' Will said. 'Our company is not yet complete. But I have hopes that Augustine Phillips may join us, and also Will Kempe.'

The latter name called forth a whistle from George Bryan. 'Kempe! That would set the tongues a-wagging in Southwark. Would he leave Leicester's Men, do you think?'

'He says that he will, but only when the time is right. I am trying to persuade him with the help of Lord Strange's money that the time is now.'

243

'I wish you luck.' Cowley chuckled. 'I worked with Kempe once. He is as skittish as a virgin on her wedding night.'

'Aye. But I have another weapon in my armoury that I can bring to bear— Dick Tarlton has spoken with him and added his voice in our favour.'

'How is the old man?' Towne asked. 'I had heard that he was ill.'

'Your news is stale, for that was months ago. Last I saw of him, two days ago, he was fit as a fiddle, ready to get up on stage and dance a jig.'

Towne accepted this news with a nod, which coincided with the arrival of a spotted youth bearing a tray filled with food, a jug of ale balanced precariously in its middle, and half a dozen small tankards tied to a rope that looped across his skinny shoulders. With a nonchalant skill that would have won the admiration of a fairground juggler, the boy deposited food, ale and tankards on the table and, having received a few coins by way of a tip from Will, skipped off through the door and back downstairs.

Food and drink worked their usual alchemy and before long, the little group of actors were deep in convivial conversation. At first, there was the usual theatrical gossip. There was a rumour that the ban on the Admiral's Men might be lifted within the month and the Earl of Sussex's players were recruiting actors for a new country tour. Leicester's Men had also performed at court, delivering George Peele's *David and Bathsheba*. The Queen was, it was said, delighted with the play, though some at court were scandalised by what they saw as a veiled allegory of the supposed romantic entanglement between the Queen and the company's patron, the Earl of Leicester.

Then their talk turned to the question that was on every Londoner's tongue— when would the Spanish invasion fleet appear? Throughout spring and into these early weeks of summer, the rumours of invasion had migrated from whispers muttered behind the hands of knowing courtiers out onto the cacophonous streets of London, where rumour chased rumour and mere pebbles of hard fact were transformed into fantastical speculations in the blink of an eye. Purported spies were seen everywhere, any strange ship seen off Land's End was believed to be the harbinger of the Spanish king's great fleet (until it revealed its true identity as a mere merchantman plodding its way up the Channel), and it was said that rebellions were being plotted in the north, in Norfolk, in Kent, and even, absurdly, in London itself.

The latter notion had been fuelled by the extraordinary events in Paris two months before when the mostly Catholic population of that city had risen up and chased their Protestant King Henri III out of his capital. Could the same thing happen in London? Will doubted it. The Queen was popular with Londoners and regularly progressed through the city's streets, where she was received with adulation by an admiring populace. But that didn't stop the rumours from circulating.

'I was at the Royal Exchange the other day exchanging some bills,' Richard Cowley said, 'and I overheard a gentleman saying that since the rebellion at Paris the Privy Council has become most uneasy, and they are afraid that we will have our own Day of the Barricades when the king of Spain's fleet appears.'

'No doubt this "gentleman" is an intimate of Lord Burghley,' Tom Blunt jeered, 'and knows all his secrets.'

'I know not who he was,' Cowley replied hotly, 'but he spoke with authority.'

'Everyone who speaks at the Royal Exchange pretends to authority. It is how they gull each other into parting with their money to invest in dubious ventures in the Indies or expeditions to America.'

This was an argument that might easily get out of hand, so Will intervened. 'The Parisian mob had many other reasons to detest their king. Methinks the council is jumping at shadows, for our queen is at one with the city's population.'

245

'True enough.' George Bryan nodded his agreement. 'But she is not so well-beloved everywhere in the country. The north, for instance. Yorkshire and Northumberland have ever been pains in the Tudor backside.'

'Not entirely without just cause, if you ask me.' John Towne had said virtually nothing since the end of their rehearsal, and his tart pronouncement took Will by surprise. 'What says our patron on such matters, Shakespeare? You have spent time with him, have you not? And his father is lord lieutenant for Lancashire.'

The question would have seemed innocent had it not been accompanied by a tiny twist of the lips that verged on being a knowing smirk. What was Towne fishing for?

'Lord Strange and I discuss poetry and plays, not politics, so I cannot tell you what he thinks.' Will did his best to disguise his irritation.

Cowley, no fool, had also picked up on Towne's expression. 'What are you implying, John? That our patron might not be entirely loyal?'

'Did I ever suggest any such thing?' Towne was bland, the smirk replaced by a grin that seemed intended to disarm. 'But as I said, his father is the lord lieutenant for Lancashire, and I merely wondered whether Shakespeare might have caught some crumbs of opinion from His Lordship as to the temper of the north. After all, if he is distracted by the need to look after the crown's interests in the north, he will have scant interest in our company.'

'And if there *is* an invasion, the playhouses will be closed down for certes.' Thomas Blunt's round face crumpled in dismay at the thought; he was known to be impecunious and could not afford to lose even a day's income.

Will held up a hand, anxious to divert the current of this conversation. 'All of this is but speculation. The Spanish may be beaten at sea before ever they land, and if they are, Parma's army will never be able to cross from the Low Countries.' He sighed. 'As for the theatres, we must hope that the Privy Council will see the

246

benefit in keeping them open for the distraction of the populace through troubled times. But Richard is right. We are actors, not politicians, and there is little we can do to change the course of the world's affairs. We can but hope for the best.'

That sounded feeble, but it was the truth, and it seemed to be sufficient to calm everyone. The food and drink having been consumed, they made a collective move toward the door and the stairs leading down to the tavern's taproom below, with an agreement that they would meet again in a week to commence rehearsing the play.

John Towne hung back as the others left and plucked at Will's sleeve. 'A word with you, Will,' he said, startling Shakespeare with the unaccustomed use of his first name. 'Since Tarlton is back on his feet, will the Queen's Men be touring again soon, do you think?'

'Dick seemed to think so, though he did not speak to me of any confirmed dates.'

'And the company's financial affairs? They have been reconstructed?' The question was posed with a certain delicacy, as if Towne was reluctant to speak openly of the cause of the company's financial disarray—his own killing, accidental or otherwise, of one of the company's principals.

'Tarlton said nothing of it. But he did say that the company's remaining sharers met last week and authorised the payment of Knell's share to his widow.'

'Ah. Then Rebecca Knell will be a wealthy woman after that transaction.'

'She is richer by some eighty pounds, I should think, though I have no certain knowledge of the sums involved.' Will smiled. 'It seems I cannot satisfy any of your questions this day, John.'

Towne shook his head and pulled his cape over his shoulders. 'As well, then, that none of them were of any great importance, mere matters of idle curiosity. I must be going. You have given me a long scroll to learn, and I had best be getting on with it.'

Will watched the back of the other man as he disappeared down the stairs. There was something unconvincing about that last protestation. Were Towne's questions about Lord Strange more urgent than might be explained by a natural wish for reassurance in these restless times? It was hard to tell. And then there was his casual mention of Rebecca Knell. Towne had said nothing less than the truth when he said she was likely a wealthy woman. With the share of the Queen's Men and the other property that Knell had bequeathed her, she was a wealthy widow indeed, and just eighteen years old! No doubt she would be besieged by suitors once that word got around. Would Towne be one of them? The tone of his words had been curiously impersonal, as though he barely knew the woman, which seemed strange given the intensity of their past together.

Slinging his satchel over his shoulder, he closed the door behind him and made his way downstairs and out into the street, where a grinning Ned was waiting to accompany him back to Silver Street, chattering and laughing with excitement all the way. It was impossible to feel gloomy in Ned's company, and by the time they got home, Will had all but forgotten his worries about finding players, finishing *Arden*, and managing the expectations of his little troupe.

Over the next few weeks, those worries dissolved one by one. Anthony Ashford, Thomas Pope and Augustine Phillips all succumbed to his repeated entreaties, though Will Kempe remained disappointingly elusive. Nevertheless, a week after their first meeting, the company's personnel was to all intents and purposes complete. As for the play with which he hoped to introduce the new company to the world, it seemed that the players themselves had done much to finish it without his help. Cowley's idea of rehearsing in pairs had worked brilliantly. The players had learned their parts much more quickly, and when they'd encountered those gaps in the written text where Marlowe's invention had run dry, they'd been inventive in filling them with words of their own.

248

Even John Towne seemed to be getting into the spirit of things, judging by Ned's eager reports at the end of each day. His professional instincts, once aroused, had banished whatever reservations he may have had about the part he was to play, and within a day or two, he and Ned had mastered their scripts and were busily inventing improvements to their characters. The others, too, had ideas that they wanted incorporated into the playscript, communicated by way of brief notes on scraps of paper sent by messenger to Silver Street, or in conversation over beer or wine when they gathered in twos and threes at their favoured taverns. Will listened to them all, his quick brain cutting and sewing the copy of the script that he carried in his head, but saying nothing, merely nodding and agreeing that all these ideas should be given consideration when next he met with their poet.

Effecting such a meeting, though, seemed to be ever more difficult.

'Ned Alleyn is convinced that the Admiral's Men will be back on the stage very soon,' Marlowe had told him at their last encounter, a week ago. 'He and Henslowe are at me day and night to finish part two of *Tamburlaine*.'

Will was sceptical. 'Ned's optimism is like one of those illusions seen across the sands of Arabia that seem solid and real until they are approached, but which then magically dissolve into thin air. The Puritans on the city council will not relent of their ban until they must. The accident was too great a gift for their cause.'

'That may be so, but they are insistent.' Marlowe at least had the grace to look sheepish. 'I fear that you will have to do more work on Arden than we agreed. I will help as much as I can, but...'

So when Lord Strange's new company reconvened after two weeks of working apart, it was for the most part Will's words, not Marlowe's, that were newly interpolated into the play. Not that any of the players seemed to care who had written the words that gave effect to their various dramatical ideas as they prepared to get to work on their first full rehearsal in the main hall of Derby

House. For everyone except Will, it was the first time they had been to their patron's family residence, where they had been admitted after the half-hour walk down from St Paul's by a surprisingly cheerful David Barnes, who stood beside Will and waited while the actors peered curiously around the room in which they would eventually stage their play.

It was an opulent space, with four big windows overlooking the Thames to admit light, wood-panelled walls hung with tapestries on the other three sides, and a fine parquetry floor littered with fresh rushes. At one end, there was a low dais with a long table and a dozen chairs set behind it, and a broad gallery running the width of the room above. Otherwise, the hall was devoid of furniture.

'So where are we to perform, Will?' Richard Cowley asked, hand on hips, as he surveyed the room.

'The carpenters have made a temporary stage that can be placed in front of the dais there. But we will do without for this rehearsal.'

'And where shall we store costumes and props, and prepare for entrances and exits? It is called a tiring-room.' This last was directed at Barnes. For some reason, Cowley thought he had to explain the term to the steward.

'I am aware of the concept,' Barnes said, with a wisp of a smile. 'Mister Shakespeare has spent a good deal of time inducting me into the finer aspects of your art.'

'When we perform, curtains will be hung there and there,' Will gestured at the spaces underneath the gallery on each side of the dais, 'through which we can make entrances and exits. Behind, there is a wide corridor which will serve as our tiring-house.'

Cowley, who seemed to have appointed himself as the spokesperson, if not leader of the troupe, nodded his approval. 'It will serve well enough for our purposes, I think. Shall we get to work?'

While the actors rustled in their pockets and satchels for their parts, Barnes took Will by the arm and took him aside. 'His Lordship bade me tell you that you have but to ask if you need anything. Also that, though he is detained this morning, he will come and see how things progress if time and chance allow.'

'Thank you for the forewarning, Master Barnes. Let us hope that His Lordship is pleased with what he sees.'

Barnes nodded and slipped out of the door, leaving Will to join his companions in the middle of the room. 'Now, where shall we start? At the beginning? That means you and I, Dick, and Ned. Clear a space, and the rest of you can sit on the dais like lords.'

An hour later, they had successfully traversed the first three acts of the play, which brought the action to the failure of the third attempt to kill Arden, in the fog upon Rainham Down. The players had attacked the play with gusto, revelling in Marlowe's poetry and pausing only to discuss the particularities of performance—how, for instance, to stage Black Will's being knocked out by a shopfront shutter (a device that the actors thought hilarious, much to Shakespeare's satisfaction)—and had halted for a short break to fuel their energies for the rest of the play with a refreshment of pottage, mutton pies and ale that Barnes had thoughtfully sent in.

'Let us pass over the next scene since it is not yet writ,' Will said, summoning the group from the refreshment table.

'What is in it?' Augustine Phillips asked through a mouthful of bread.

'Nothing much. Arden announces that he is going to go to the Isle of Sheppey, there to dine with Lord Cheney, the warden of the Cinque Ports. Some of that is written, but Marlowe wanted to add a scene in which Michael and Clarke argue over Mosby's sister, Susan. It is that which he has not yet penned.'

'My confusion is complete. Has not Michael been promised Susan's hand as the price for his part in the conspiracy? How then does the painter enter into it?'

'Keep up with us, Gus!' George Bryan called from across the room. 'Remember? Back in act one, Alice promised her hand to Clarke as a bribe to get him to help with poisoning her husband.'

'Is it my fault that Shakespeare recruited me to this enterprise so late?' Phillips said grumpily. 'I have not had the same opportunity to take in all the finer points of the play that you have withal.'

Cowley, ever the peacemaker, gave him a cheerful if perhaps too forceful thump on the shoulder. 'Ignore George, Gus. Late or no, an actor of your standing is a welcome adornment to our company.'

Phillips, who was somewhat older than the rest of the company and could be as touchy as John Towne when he thought his dignity was being assailed, accepted this little piece of hyperbole with a nod. 'Since they are amazingly free with this poor girl's marital prospects, I suppose it is inevitable that Clarke and Michael must come to blows at some point. When will Marlowe have the scene for us?'

Will waved a hand. 'A day or two. Or perhaps three. Kit was less than certain. But anyway, it matters not. In the meantime, we can get on with the next scene.'

'Which is what? The next attempt on my life?' Cowley asked.

'Well, upon Arden's life. I think yours is safe enough.'

'I don't know, have you *seen* him act, Will?' said George Bryan, with a cheeky grin. 'The groundlings might contravene you.'

Will couldn't help laughing. These two were always bantering with each other and meant nothing by it. 'Be that as it may, Dick gets a rest for the moment. The first line is yours, Tom.' This was directed at chubby, round-faced Thomas Blunt, who was playing the villain Shakebag. 'You come in from one door and George from the other. The scene is somewhere on the coast of Kent and we are shrouded in dense fog.'

The two players retreated to their respective 'doors'—at present just the corners of the dais where, come performance night, curtains would be hung from the gallery above—and then came back into the room, using dumb-show to indicate that they could barely see anything.

'Oh, Will, where are you?'

'Here, Shakebag, almost in hell's mouth, where I cannot see my way for smoke.' Bryan, who had his arms out before him as if feeling his way through an invisible mist, turned away from his colleague on the opposite side of the stage.

'I pray you speak still, that we may meet by the sound,' Blunt said, 'for I shall fall into some ditch or another unless my feet see better than my eyes.'

'Did you ever see better weather to run away with another man's wife, or play with a wench at pot-finger?'

Ned giggled at this piece of lewdness, earning a reproving look from Will.

'Nay,' Blunt replied from the other side of the room, 'This were a fine world for chandlers if this weather would last, for then a man should neither dine nor sup without candlelight.' He stopped and cupped a hand behind his ear. 'But, sirrah Will, what horses are those that passed?'

'Clop, clop, clop' Phillips said loudly, and the rest of the company gave a collective giggle.

Bryan was undeterred by the interruption. 'Why, did you hear any?'

'Aye, that I did.'

'My life for yours that it was Arden and his companions, and all our labour's lost.'

'Nay, say not so, for if it be they, they may as easily lose their way as we have done, and then we may chance meet with them.'

'Come, let us go on like a couple of blinded pilgrims. And here I fall into a ditch.' His voice took on a hysterical quaver. 'Help, Will, help, I am almost drowned!'

'So where is our ditch?' Cowley asked through the general laughter at George Bryan's mimicry of a drowning man. 'Does the stage have a trap?'

'Not at present.' Will frowned. 'Though I could ask the carpenters to make one. The problem will then be getting poor George out from underneath since it is only a few feet high. Perhaps he can simply fall off the edge?'

'It might serve if done right.'

'Let me think on it. Now, Anthony, you are on next, as the ferryman.'

They ran quickly through the last part of the scene, in which the ferryman confirms that Arden has indeed got clean away, much to the chagrin of Mosby and Alice, who have come out onto the moor to check on progress. John Towne and Ned Bentley had the last lines of the scene.

'These knaves will never do it. Let us give it over.' Towne was a picture of gloomy despondency.

'First, tell me how you like my new device.' Ned's flirtatious batting of eyelids at Towne verged on the edge of comedy.

> *'Soon, when my husband is returning back,*
> *You and I both marching arm in arm*
> *Like loving friends, we'll meet him on the way.*

And boldly beard and brave him to his teeth.
When words grow hot and blows begin to rise,
I'll call those cutters forth,
Who in taking up the fray,
Shall wound my husband to the death.'

Towne gave a great flourishing bow in exaggerated approval of this new plan. 'A fine device,' he said. 'Why, this deserves a kiss!' With which, he seized Ned around the waist and suited the action to the word by planting a smacking, loud kiss on the boy's lips, to general laughter and, from the far corner of the room, a loud and enthusiastic clapping of hands. Turning, Will beheld the elegant form of Lord Strange, who had entered the room unnoticed, accompanied only by Barnes. The actors, recovering from their surprise, ducked their heads in collective obeisance, though Ned Bentley required a poke in the ribs from Towne to abandon his open-mouthed look of surprise and make his bow.

'Forgive my intrusion, Mister Shakespeare,' Lord Strange said with a smile, 'but when I arrived and Barnes told me that you were here and rehearsing, I decided I must come and observe your machinations.'

'You are most welcome, my lord. Allow me to introduce the members of your company. Though you know some of them, I think?'

'Indeed. That is Mister Cowley, is it not? And Mister Phillips? We have met at court, I think.' Both men nodded and made another genuflection, more formal this time, as befitted men who had performed at court. 'And I have had the pleasure of seeing Mister Pope and Mister Bryan upon the stage, though we have not otherwise met. Welcome to my house and our new company. The others I do not know.'

Will gestured Ned forward. 'Allow me to name the youngest member of or company, Ned Bentley.'

Ned's obeisance wobbled a little and his stammered greeting to Lord Strange was almost inaudible, prompting their patron to smile. 'I trust that your voice will carry a little further when you declaim upon the stage, Mister Bentley.'

'Fear not, my lord. Ned can roar like a lion when needs must. Now, let me name Thomas Blunt, Anthony Ashford and John Towne.'

Towne was clearly irritated that he had been left until last, since he believed he was more senior than the others, and his foot tapped impatiently on the parquetry floor as he waited for Blunt and Ashford to mutter their way through their introductions. Will, while keeping his own face as immobile as possible, looked on intently as the other man finally came forward and, placing one foot in front of the other, went down in a graceful bow. 'I am honoured, my lord, to serve so great an English family.'

'Do I hear the strains of a northern tongue, Mister Towne?'

'Your ear is most acute, my lord. I was born in Mawdesley.'

'Then I know it well; it is but five miles from our house at Lathom.' His smile broadened and he extended a hand. 'It will be a fine thing to have a northerner in the ranks of our fine new company. But I have detained you all long enough so I shall leave you to your evolutions. Mister Shakespeare, a privy word, if I may.'

The other actors, recognising a cue when they heard one, retreated to the dais, leaving Will alone with Lord Strange. Barnes, similarly discreet, waited by the door.

'How goes the play, Will? I would that I could stay and watch your rehearsal, but I must be away within the hour.'

'The play progresses as happily as I could wish, my lord. I am confident in the first half, and tomorrow we will tackle the last. One or two rehearsals after that, with perhaps some writing and botching on Marlowe's part to polish the playscript, and we will be ready to perform.'

'So you could with confidence perform in a fortnight or so?'

'Yes, my lord.' He smiled. 'In truth, a fortnight is a rare luxury. In the Queen's Men, we would regularly rehearse a new play but a day before putting it on in front of an audience.'

'Then let us make it so. I have in mind a private performance, here at Derby House, before my father and his lady wife, and some others of their friends.'

Will nodded his agreement, and then was startled as his patron took him by the arm and led him into the centre of the room, gesturing for Barnes to wait by the door. There was, he thought, some kind of tension in his patron's features, a wariness about the eyes and the shadow of a frown across his brow. 'I am leaving this afternoon for the north. My father and I have been charged with arousing the militia in Lancashire for the defence of the county against this Spanish invasion plan.'

'There is news, then? The Armada has sailed?'

'No, not yet. Or not that we know of. But Burghley and the rest of the council want the country in a state of preparedness, and so we are dispatched north.' The frown lines deepened. 'But there is another matter about which I wish to speak with you. Though we have known each other but a short time, you have shown me that you can be relied upon to do that which you are commissioned to do, and by that means you have earned my trust, something I do not give lightly.'

'My lord, I—'

'Save your protests, Will. You are no mincing maiden, to blush at a compliment that is well-earned.' That was accompanied by one of his rare genial smiles. 'But to return to the point. It is simply this—I have set in train, through

257

the office of the chamberlain, an invitation for Her Majesty to attend your performance in a fortnight.'

'A great honour, my lord,' was all that Will could think of to say, as his mind raced, considering the implications.

'She has not yet received the invitation, let alone accepted it. But I wanted you to know that it is a possibility.'

'Can I tell the rest of the company?'

'What do you advise? We may not know whether she will attend until a few days before.'

Will considered. 'Discretion might be the best course. Cowley and Phillips have both played before the Queen on other occasions, but the others have never appeared at court, and it might unsettle them if they know that Her Majesty might be in the audience.'

'Not just the Queen. If she comes, she will be accompanied by Leicester, for certain, and maybe other great lords. But I agree, let us keep this between us. And Barnes, of course.'

'We shall do our best to make sure that it is a great occasion, my lord, and bring honour to the house of Stanley.'

'The honour of the house of Stanley needs no further burnishing.' That was tart. 'Rather it is the Clifford name that causes me greater pause. You know of my mother, Lady Margaret?'

Will nodded, remembering his briefing from Thomas Phelippes. Margaret Clifford, estranged from her husband the Earl of Derby, had been banished from court for the last nine years after offending the Queen, though very likely there was politics behind that offence since she—and of course her son Ferdinando— stood in the line of succession under the terms of King Henry's will.

'Her Majesty loves me well, notwithstanding her antipathy towards my lady mother,' Strange went on, seeing that Will had grasped the essential point, 'but there are those at court who see in me a threat because of my lineage. Perhaps even the Queen herself, though she shows no sign of it.'

'And so you hope to shore up your favour with Her Majesty by means of this entertainment.'

'It is only one piece in the puzzle, but yes, you are correct in the essence. So you see why it is important to me that all should go well.'

'For that, we shall have to pray to the deities of the theatre, whose caprices have wrecked many a play and made fools of many a player,' Will said with a smile. 'But I shall do everything I can to ensure that it is an event that all will remember.'

Lord Strange nodded and gave Will's arm a friendly squeeze. 'That is all that I can ask. Now, I see that Barnes is looking as though he will burst with impatience, which means that I must be away.'

***

'So we are to perform *Arden* in two weeks,' Will told Kit Marlowe when they met the following day. 'And like as not, before the Queen herself!'

'With John Towne on the stage?'

'Of course. He will be playing Mosby.' Suddenly the implications of that crashed into Will's brain. 'Jesu! You don't think he might be an assassin?'

'If he is, our lives will be worth no more than a piece of chaff thrown upon the wind.' Marlowe was grim. 'But before we panic, let us consider. He has not, so you say, behaved in any way that seems outwardly suspicious?'

'No. As I said, he has been his usual self, which is to say touchy and prideful, but professional.'

'And when he met Lord Strange? Did they seem to know each other?'

Will thought back to the rehearsal the day before. 'Lord Strange identified his northern accent—they have ears like bats, these northerners, for their accents—and it seems Towne's place of birth is not far from Lathom House. But otherwise, no. They were strangers to each other, that I would swear.'

'Has Greene's man reported anything?'

'Cutting Ball, you mean?' Will had asked, through Greene, that Ball use his associates to continue keeping a watch on the Dolphin. 'No, nothing. If Towne has received instructions from anywhere or has met with this mysterious messenger, it hasn't happened at the Dolphin.'

Marlowe stroked his chin, considering. 'In short, there is no evidence at all to suggest that John Towne is anything other than what he says he is—a mere player. Perhaps you are right and there is nothing to worry about, but I still feel, somewhere in my bones, that there is something not right here, and we should be cautious.'

With which sentiment Will could do nothing other than agree.

Chapter 19

'What do you think?' Ned asked, hands on hips.

The object of the question was a fine white linen shirt that he had just slipped over his head, selected from an untidy pile of its fellows that lay on the shopkeeper's counter. The shopman himself, a short, fat man whose dark complexion, black hair and soft brown eyes suggested origins somewhere in the Mediterranean, stood by and looked hopefully from Ned to Will and back again, uncertain as to who was the buyer.

'It looks very well on you, young man,' he finally ventured. 'You will not find a better quality lawn shirt anywhere in Cheapside, that I will warrant.'

'No doubt,' Will said. 'And if he were an earl or a duke, my friend here would buy it without quibble. But alas, neither of our purses will stretch to a full crown for a shirt.'

That was the signal for the inevitable round of chaffering to begin, and ten minutes later, they stepped out of the dim confines of the shop, the new shirt rolled up, tied with string and tucked under Ned's arm, into the noise and chaos of Cheapside at noon.

'Hungry?' Will asked, knowing that for Ned there was only ever one answer to that question. Following their noses, they found a nearby pie-seller and soon were busy chomping their way through the heavy crust and trying to avoid dripping gravy onto their clothes as they stood beneath the shop's tattered awning.

'Isn't that John?' Ned said through a mouth full of pie. 'Across the road there, with that beautiful girl.'

Will peered across the street, frowning. Ned was quite right—the urbane, well-dressed figure on the opposite side of the road was indeed John Towne. And the beauty with whom he seemed to be carrying on a low-voiced altercation was Rebecca Knell, Billy Knell's by now comfortably well-off widow. Since meeting her for the first time almost nine months ago, Will had called on her once or twice when he'd found the time, out of an obscure sense of duty to his dead friend. She had received him politely, but with a mild curiosity as to his interest in her. She was, it seemed, enjoying her new-found independence, and after a couple of encounters, Will had decided that his obligations, such as they were, had been completely discharged.

But that obscure urge to chivalry was again animated by the scene unfolding across the street. Even at this distance, with the busy stream of pedestrian and wheeled traffic interrupting his view, it was obvious to Will that Rebecca was fending the man off, not physically but with gestures and words. Then, as though she'd had enough of whatever the argument was about, she turned and walked off, leaving a confused-looking Towne standing. After a few moments, he started walking, following her along the street, just a few yards behind.

'What do you think is going on?' Ned had lost interest in his food and was following the pair with his eyes. 'And who is that girl?'

'I don't know the answer to the first question. As for the second, she is Rebecca Knell, Billy's widow. Come on, let's follow and see what we can find out.'

Ditching what was left of their pies, they threaded their way across the street, narrowly avoiding being run down by a cart laden with beer barrels, whose driver shouted curses at them as they ducked in front of his horses and caused them to shy. By the time they reached the other side, their quarry had disappeared into the crowd. Turning eastward, they hurried along the street, dodging in and out of the knots of people gathered in front of the barrows and kiosks that sold everything from fresh meat to buttons and ribbons. Their progress thus slowed, Will began to fear that he had lost them entirely.

Then, emerging from a little crowd of women collecting water at the Great Conduit, he spotted Towne's back just as he disappeared into a tiny alleyway between two houses. Slowing to an unhurried walk so that he could plausibly pretend innocence should Towne unexpectedly re-emerge, Will gestured for Ned to follow him into the deep, dark shadows of the alleyway. It was deserted, as far as he could make out in the gloom, and they made their way cautiously through until it opened into a wider street beyond, lined on one side with three-storey houses that faced a high brick wall on the other.

A few paces down the wall, the wooden doors through an arched gateway were open, giving a glimpse of the expansive garden beyond, from which the voices of John Towne and Rebecca Knell could be heard in loud argument, no doubt believing that they were private. Putting one finger to his lips, Will pressed up against the wall and listened.

'How many times must I tell you, John? No!' Rebecca's voice was steely, determined.

'After what I have done for you? For our love?'

'For our love? Is it love to murder another's love?'

'What do you mean by that? You cannot say that Knell loved you, nor you him.'

'Whatever my feelings for him, I know that William cared for me.'

'And so, now that he is dead, you suffer pangs of regret? Is that it?' Towne's voice was bitter. 'So now I see it plain—you would let me swing for liberating you from your husband's tyranny.'

There was a silence, and then an audible sigh from Rebecca. 'As God is my witness, William was not the man he wished the world to see, and I had good cause to wish for his demise. Yes, I admit it, I wanted him dead, and gave you the means for it. But I have regretted it ever since, and I swear—and you know—that I never gave you any encouragement after that day to do what you have done.'

'What? You told me, over and over, that when Knell was dead, we could marry. Or are you changed?'

'Aye, I am changed. Do you not see, John? If I were to marry you now, the world knowing what it does, the harvest of our union would yield but loathsome weeds. That you have compassed William's death changes everything. To marry the man known to the world as his killer would give me the name of an odious strumpet, and that I could never bear.'

'The coroner—'

'I know, the coroner found no reason to charge you with murder. But you know, and I know, that murder it most certainly was, if murder be the deliberate and intentional killing of another.'

'Well then, have it your way. He was a fool, your husband, easily provoked into a fight that he could not win. And yes, I did it with a purpose, so you can call it murder if you wish.' Towne was contemptuous, but his next words took on a pleading tone. 'I did it for love of you! To release you from this marriage and to offer you true happiness in matrimony with a man you said you loved. Or was that false, too?'

'Nay, John, I did love you, for a time at least.' That sounded weary. 'Say rather that it was a sickness, not a reflection of my true self. Often at night, I wonder if you did use some magic arts to bewitch me.'

'I? So I am to blame entirely? Lady, I did not bewitch you, rather it was I myself who must have been enchanted, to believe your protestations of affection.'

264

'They were not false. But surely you must see, John, that marriage is impossible now. Had you found some more discreet way to achieve your aim—poison, say, or an accident—it might have been possible. But any marriage now would be forever tainted. The world would detest me for marrying my husband's killer.'

'And so, to preserve your reputation, I am to get nothing? Neither marriage nor money.' Towne's voice took on an edge of menace. 'I must have been mad to have ever thought you fair, Rebecca. But now I see you for what you are—not a dove, but a raven; not kind but foul, as foul as any witch. I now see the beauty that bewitched me for what it is—mere gilding that betrays the base copper underneath. I'll be done with you.'

'Done with me? Am I to share my husband's fate, then? Murdered in my bed for revenge?' Towne must have had nothing to say to that, for Rebecca's voice hurried on after the smallest of pauses. 'Aye, I see you could compass it. I know you, too, for what you are, John Towne—a mere seeker after gold. It is my money and William's that you are after. Well, you'll not get it. I'll marry where I please, but I will not marry you!'

There was silence. Will imagined them glaring at each other, like protagonists in a play who have run out of lines. Then Ned sneezed. Will grabbed him by the arm, and steered them back towards the alleyway's entrance, talking at the top of his voice in a broad country accent.

'I'll tell thee, Goodman Watt, this year's harvest was the worst I have ever seen, the ears blasted and withered as if the devil himself had taken a hand. Bellies will be cleaving to ribs before next winter is out, I'll be bound.'

'Er... aye, Master, er, Brown, I know. My own wife is complaining that the price of bread is already going up. Fourpence, it cost her just yesterday for a loaf from Davey the baker.'

Chattering loudly in this vein, they quickened their steps until they were well inside the dark tunnel of the alleyway. Will decided to risk a quick look behind him and was relieved to see no one.

'Is that true, about the harvest?' Ned asked as they emerged back into the sunshine on Cheapside.

'I have no idea. It was the first thing that came into my head.'

'Let's hope that Mister Towne is equally ignorant about all such country matters. So are you going to tell me what is going on?'

Will looked sideways at his young friend. 'I am not sure I know myself. But we can't linger here to talk about it. They might come out of that alleyway at any time.'

'Come on, then,' Ned said, starting down the street. 'I know just the place.'

Bemused, Will followed. They turned right into Ironmonger Lane, lined with open shopfronts and stalls where an astonishing variety of iron goods—pots, pans, griddles, hatstands, pokers, buttons, knives, spoons, buttons, pins—were laid out for sale. A blast of heat assaulted them as they passed one of the smithies where all these objects were made. Inside, Will caught a glimpse of smoke-wreathed flames illuminating the sweating muscles of a young blacksmith hammering away at a piece of half-molten ore, his face a picture of concentration.

At the end of the lane, they turned left into Cateaton Street, another narrow thoroughfare barely wide enough for a carriage to pass, and then Ned ushered him into the entrance of a small tavern called the King's Arms (though to which king the name referred was impossible to make out from the faded sign that swung above the door).

Inside, it was dark and cool, and completely deserted. Ned went up to the little counter that ran along one side of the room, and rapped confidently on the wood, summoning a small, wizened man with an extraordinarily wild-looking grey beard.

'Well if it isn't young Ned, back so soon.' He peered around Ned's shoulder at Will. 'Who is your friend? Is Master Marlowe not gracing us with his presence today?'

Ned laughed, a trifle nervously. 'Master Marlowe is, so far as I know, across the river at The Rose, working on rehearsing his new play. This is my good friend Mister Shakespeare. Also a playwright.'

'Then welcome, Mister Shakespeare. What will it be? I have new-tapped a barrel of my best ale at your disposal.'

Settled at a table near the back of the room with a couple of tankards of ale between them, Will contemplated Ned with new curiosity. 'You've been coming here with Kit?'

He didn't intend for it to sound like an accusation, but the question brought a flush to Ned's cheeks. 'Once or twice; it is one of his favoured haunts. You know what he is like—can't write a word unless he has an ale in front of him.'

'And you've been helping him to write?'

'Not exactly. Just keeping him company. What was going on in that garden? Unless my ears are deceiving me, John all but admitted that he murdered poor Master Knell.'

Will took a sip of the ale. Surprisingly, it was very good. But then, Kit always knew where the best ale could be found in London. Between him and Rob Greene, a man needed no other victualling guide to the city.

'That was the nub of it,' he said cautiously, 'though you'll notice he didn't use those exact words.'

'You don't seem surprised.'

'The truth is, I've wondered about that day. I've replayed the scene over and again in my head, like some kind of accursed rehearsal that never ends. And what I remember most, in every repetition, is the look in John's eyes as he delivered the killing blow. There was something, I don't know, *cold* about it, as if he was simply dispatching an animal, not a man.'

Ned gave him a look of puzzlement. 'You didn't say that in your deposition?'

'How could I? It could have been a fancy on my part, the product of an over-wrought imagination. But now we have John's own words to confirm that he killed Billy intentionally.'

'In order to get rid of him so he could marry his wife. It sounds like our play.'

'That was what Kit thought when we first decided to try our hand with *Arden*. At the time, I thought the idea that Rebecca might have had a hand in her husband's death was ridiculous, and I told him so. But it seems he was right.'

Ned frowned. 'But she doesn't sound like our awful Alice, though, does she? I mean, if I remember Widow Knell's words aright, she says she did no more than acquiesce to John's plan.'

'We don't know that our Alice *was* awful,' Will pointed out. 'Raphael Holinshed says nothing about her motive for wanting her husband dead, other than her infatuation with Mosby. In fact, he makes Arden out to be a figure of virtue, patiently putting up with his wife's immoral doings. But for all we know, he might have beaten her black and blue every night he was in Faversham.'

'As would be his right,' Ned said complacently. 'No matter how badly he might have treated her, conspiring to kill her lawful lord was a grievous sin.'

'For which she paid the price. She was burnt at the stake, remember? And Rebecca would suffer the same fate if all this came to light.'

268

Ned looked stricken, as if this thought had never occurred to him. 'And John would be hanged, I suppose.'

'At best.' In fact, the traitor's death had been known to be meted out in such cases, so abhorrent was the idea of husband-murder.

'So what do we do? Go to the sheriffs?'

Will gave him a long look. Given what Ned had already heard, he realised that he had no choice but to tell him everything else. 'There's something else you don't know. John is suspected of being a papist spy. Knell found the evidence and was planning to report it to the authorities, but he died before he could do so. I found a draft of his report among his papers and sent them to Sir Francis Walsingham.'

Ned's mouth was agape. 'Sir Francis…'

'Walsingham, yes. The Queen's private secretary. Kit and I have had some dealings with him in the past.'

'Kit? Don't tell me you are both bloody informers!'

'Intelligencers is the term we use,' Will said, dryly. 'Kit is the serious agent, I have merely been… coerced into helping him and Sir Francis.'

With all the resilience of the young, Ned was already past the shock of discovering that both his friends were in fact spies, and he was exploring the possibilities for adventure that might flow from that fact. Will almost laughed at the transparency of the expressions that chased each other across his young friend's face.

'So John is a papist spy. What is he supposed to be doing here, then? In our company?'

'I didn't say he *is* a spy, merely that he is suspected. We think he has been ordered to enter the service of Lord Strange, though for exactly what reason we do not know.'

'So that's why you were so anxious that he should join us. And now you can't turn him in because you want to find out what he is up to.' The handsome face split into a big, crooked smile. 'It's going to make our next rehearsal interesting.'

That was an understatement. Now that Ned knew what was going on, was it even possible that they could carry on with the rehearsal for a play that was a mirror of John Towne's apparent crimes? How long could they keep going without Ned or himself giving the game away by letting something slip? Matters would have to be brought to a head soon, one way or another.

'When is Dick back from the country?' Cowley had, for reasons best known only to him, decided to slip away and visit his family in Kent, thus bringing proceedings with the play to a halt.

'The day after tomorrow, I think he said.'

'We have two days, then. A lot can happen in two days.' He drained the last of his ale and stood up, an action that summoned the landlord from some hidden corner of his domain with the speed of a rat sensing cheese, ready to receive the handful of coins that Will dropped into his upturned hand before scuttling away again, back into his lair. 'Right now, though, I need to talk to Kit.'

'And what about Mistress Knell?'

What about her, indeed? Will couldn't imagine that she was involved in the conspiracy, whatever it was. And her words in the garden—'*I have regretted it ever since*'—suggested that her part in her husband's death was at best reluctant. The chill thought came to him that she might herself be in danger from Towne, particularly if he thought she might be motivated to take that damning admission of his to the authorities.

'I don't know. I really don't.' Picking up his hat, Will eyed the staircase in the corner of the room that led to a gallery up above. 'I suppose yonder hairy dwarf rents rooms out, up there?'

'He does.'

Ned held Will's gaze, all innocence, until Will could contain himself no longer, and allowed his face to reshape itself around an amiable grin. 'Well, I suppose it was inevitable.'

'You aren't angry?'

'Why would I be angry? I don't own you.' He slapped the boy on the back and gave him a gentle shove out into the street. 'Now, you go home, and I'll join you later. Speaking of Kit, do you know where he will be this afternoon?'

Ned shrugged. 'At home, I think, working on *Tamburlaine*.'

Thank goodness he wasn't across the river at The Rose, which would have been a much more considerable journey than the walk out to Bishopsgate, where Marlowe kept a couple of rooms above a tailor's shop. Making his way through the Moor Gate, he walked out onto the grassy expanse of the fields that lapped up against the city's northern wall—until recently a marshy swamp, much improved by a great drainage project back in the seventies, though it was still treacherously muddy and crossed by unexpected little rivulets that could make crossing it a hazard—towards the row of buildings that lined Bishopsgate Street.

As he picked his way along the rough track, his mind dwelt on the subject of Ned Bentley. In truth, Will was a little relieved that the youth was transferring his amorous affections in Kit's direction. It had been a pleasant affair while it had lasted—their nightly tumble among the bedclothes a kind of guilty but somehow still innocent form of recreation, a relief from the stresses of the day in uncomplicated and affectionate sex. Over recent weeks their encounters had become less frequent, and there had been nights when Ned had not come home at

271

all, reappearing bleary-eyed in the morning with mumbled explanations that Will allowed to pass without comment. The reason for these absences was now obvious.

Will was not distressed. He had a wife and three young children, and had no need, he realised, for any other domestic entanglements, notwithstanding that the said family was three days' travel away and living in a country town whose environs could not be more different than this other world of his, in London. Ned on the other hand was, he suspected, like Kit—his nature permanently bent towards his fellow man. As far as Will could tell, he had never shown the slightest interest, beyond the purely aesthetic, in anything to do with women. That he was happy thus and not at all abashed by the evident disapproval of the Church and society as a whole, seemed all of a piece with his happy, carefree nature. He and Kit would be a good pair.

He had expected to find Marlowe deep in his work, probably reluctant to be interrupted even by his friend William Shakespeare, but as he approached the house with its faded tailor's sign of a thimble swinging above the downstairs door, the noise coming from an upper window warned him that the playwright had company, and boisterous company at that. With a sigh, he made his way past Simon the tailor, who was doing his best to ignore the noise coming from the upper rooms of his house while he worked on the sleeve of some customer's doublet, and made his way up the creaking stairs.

Sure enough, a party of sorts was in progress, led inevitably by Robert Greene, his face nearly as red as his hair as he sang at the top of his voice a crude drinking ballad telling in some detail of the downfall of an unfortunate milkmaid seduced by a scoundrel from the city. The others in the room were barely more sober: ebullient Tom Watson, Will's erstwhile collaborator George Peele, elegant Thomas Nashe, and his old friend Dick Burbage, saturnine and handsome as ever.

Of their host, there was no evidence save for a paper-filled desk that stood beneath the window of the parlour. Kit had the luxury of two whole rooms to himself, and before the others realised he was there, Will slipped through the connecting door into the other, a spacious bedchamber complete with a four-poster bed and an array of chests, stools and settles that would have made one of the Queen's courtiers proud. There he found Kit standing in his shirtsleeves, his back to Will as he noisily emptied his bladder into a chamber pot. Will waited until the tinkle of water had ceased before announcing his presence with a small cough.

'God's breath, can a man not even take a piss in his own house without being interrupted?' Kit turned, still fiddling with the buttons of his breeches, to find out who had committed this heinous breach of protocol. 'Oh, it's you, Will. Where did you pop up from?'

'The usual place—the street.' Will was sardonic. 'I thought you were working this afternoon?'

'So did I, but then Greene and the rest turned up from some cards party or another, flush with their winnings and bearing bottles of wine.' Kit looked haggard, his eyes puffy and his pale skin blotchy.

'Can we get rid of them? I have news that cannot be shared.'

It took them nearly half an hour to persuade the drunken revellers to go and find some other place to disturb with their shouted witticisms and bawdy songs, though to his credit, Greene took the hint quickly enough when Will, adopting the air of an aggrieved impresario who had arrived to find his poet carousing when he should have been working on his play, suggested that the writer be left in peace. It was Watson and, surprisingly, Burbage who proved most stubborn, the latter cup-shotten, a state in which he was rarely ever seen. But at last, they all left, making their way merrily and noisily down Bishopsgate Street back towards the city.

Surveying the wreckage of the room, Will pulled up a couple of stools next to the big table in the middle of the parlour and poured them both some wine.

'Thank God for that. You know that I love my friends, but sometimes they can be a trial.'

Will, whose own nature was rather more solitary than Kit's outgoing sociability, could not agree more, and said so, raising his wine glass, filled with a rather pleasant French claret, better than anything Will could afford, to emphasise the fact.

'Now, what is your news that brought you here so fortuitously for my peace of mind?'

Wasting no words, Will filled him in on the events of the day. Towne's pseudo-confession, when he heard it, acted like a tonic on Kit, who suddenly looked as alert as a lymer hound on the scent of its quarry. He let out a long, low whistle, a little smile of vindication on his lips. But the smile faded when he realised that Ned Bentley was now aware of everything that had been going on. 'Was that wise, do you think? Ned is but a boy.'

My boy, who you are now bedding, he thought but did not say, keeping his face inscrutable. That was a subject for another day. 'What choice did I have? He heard everything, or enough that his curiosity would not be easily satisfied with a few glib words from me. Besides, he is hardly a boy. He'll be turning twenty this summer.'

'Is he? He looks much younger than that. And he *is* still playing women's parts.'

'Aye, and with his looks, he will probably be able to do so for a year or two yet, though his voice will betray him eventually.' Such was the ruthless logic of the theatre. 'Anyway, my point is that he is old enough to know what he is doing. And I think we could use his help.'

274

'You are right, of course. You usually are.' The sun was beginning its westwards decline, throwing the east-facing window into shadow and sending a chill through the room. Kit stood up and found a blanket to wrap around his shoulders. 'But must confess that I am puzzled as to how to proceed from here.'

He sat, and started talking again, ticking each point off with his fingers as he went. 'Item—you now have Towne's confession to murder, but you cannot really use it, since you heard it from the other side of a garden wall. You might have misheard, and no jury would convict on that evidence.

'Item—there is no sign of this mysterious contact that Towne was supposed to be making. I take it that Ball has reported nothing new?' Will shook his head. 'Then I doubt that Walsingham would want us to do anything that might lead to Towne's arrest before we know what else he is up to, which means we must keep him under surveillance until some kind of contact is made.

'Item—you are proposing to put this murderer on the stage in front of the Queen in less than two weeks' time. That is a risk we cannot take, so this must all be resolved one way or another before then.

'Item—we are no wiser about Lord Strange's role in all this. He may be wholly innocent—or as innocent as any man might be in these benighted times—or he may be deeply involved in a plot to topple the Queen and her government. We simply do not know.'

As Kit made each point, Will became a degree gloomier. 'I suppose you will have to make a report of some kind to Seething Lane, which will do nothing to ease their anxieties.'

'Phelippes is already hounding me day and night for news, so yes, I will have to tell him something. In the meantime, there is little we can do except keep a close watch on John Towne and hope that something develops.' Kit gathered up the playing cards that were scattered on the table, shuffling them idly as he spoke.

'And then there is the matter of the widow Knell. She risks being burnt at the stake if a court believes that she conspired in her husband's murder. Did she, do you think?'

That question had been turning over in Will's mind for the last hour. 'Her own words seem to damn her. She is a strong-willed, spirited young woman, married to a jealous man who beat her. I do not doubt that there were moments when she would have wished for his death. But somehow, I think her part in this conspiracy was fleeting, a moment of rage that trapped her into condoning Towne's plan.'

'You will have to go and see her.' Marlowe was firm, issuing orders rather than making suggestions. 'She could be part of this wider conspiracy, if it exists, in which case we must smoke her out. And if she is not, she may possess the levers we need to prise open the secrets of your Mister Towne.'

That will be an interview that requires careful preparation, Will thought as they parted, leaving Marlowe to return to his interrupted work on the second part of *Tamburlaine*.

Chapter 20

The sudden tolling of the midday bell from the church startled Will out of his contemplation of the Knell house on Broad Street, quickly joined by the rolling cacophony of the rest of the city's churches as one by one they added their voices to the daily chorus by which Londoners told the time.

That the house should be unchanged seemed odd, considering what he now knew about its occupant, and he had spent the last few minutes, cloak pulled tight around his body to protect against the light rain drizzling down from an unseasonably grey sky, simply standing in the middle of the nearly deserted street, reluctant to take the final few steps to the door. A passing pedestrian threw him a curious look and muttered under his breath, and Will realised that there was no point in putting things off any longer. He finally got into motion, splashing his way across the street and up to the door of the house.

A sharp rap produced nothing but silence for a space, and he was about to knock again when a small, shuttered window set into the door slid open to reveal the homely visage of the serving-woman who Will remembered from his last visit.

'Shakespeare, is it?' she asked, without any preamble.

'Aye, it is, Emily. And a fine good morrow to you, too.' Will said, unable to keep the irritation from his voice. 'Is your mistress within? I sent a message this morning.'

Without any further words, the woman slid her little window closed and, after some jangling of keys and withdrawing of bolts, opened the door and stepped back with what little grace she possessed to allow him entry. 'The mistress said ye would be coming by, and to take ye through into the parlour. This way.'

Having divested himself of his wet cloak, which Emily reluctantly took to hang somewhere to dry, he settled himself into a chair in the room where he had first met Rebecca Knell, almost nine months ago. Barely had he done so when the mistress of the house arrived, followed by Emily bearing, with ill grace, the obligatory tray laden with wine glasses and trifles of food—marchpane, gingerbreads, and some little fruit pies. Rebecca, he remembered, had a surprisingly sweet tooth.

'Mister Shakespeare, you are most welcome.' The voice was as beguiling as ever, though her face seemed wan and pale, with a melancholy cast that the bright smile could not quite disguise. 'Though I was somewhat surprised to receive your note this morning since I did not know that we had any business together.'

She gestured at him to return to his seat, taking her own chair, an ornately carved, high-backed, throne-like affair by the window. The maid placed the tray carefully on a small table and, at a gesture from her mistress, withdrew to leave them alone.

Will picked up one of the wine glasses and sipped. It was a Cretan malmsey, of good quality but somewhat sweet for his taste. To buy a little more time, he swirled it around in the glass for a moment and then raised his eyes to meet the innocent-seeming blue orbs of the woman opposite. At that moment, Will found it hard to credit that she was guilty of the crime to which she had all unwittingly confessed the day before.

'I am not here on business exactly. The matter is somewhat... delicate.'

She waited, her expression politely enquiring.

'And it has to do with John Towne.'

A blink, nothing more, at the name. 'Oh? Is he back in London? You told me when you were here last that the coroner in Thame had acquitted him, but that he had disappeared.'

'Yes, he is. In fact, he has joined us at Lord Strange's acting company.'

'Indeed? Then I am pleased for him, that he has some employment.'

Her expression remained bland. An invisible stranger, had he been present, would have concluded that the subject was of no more than passing interest to her. Irrelevantly, Will wondered whether Rebecca played at cards. If so, she would be impossible to beat. 'He is a fine actor, and we are lucky to have him. But I am surprised that he has not been here to see you.'

'Me? Why would he come and see me? We have no reason for congress, in public or in private.'

'Yet you were intimate once, were you not? I merely wondered whether he might have attempted to renew his connection with you. With an eye to matrimony, perhaps?'

'I think, Mister Shakespeare, that you are beginning to try my patience.' The haughty look would have done a duchess proud. 'Whatever my affections once were for John Towne, they have been extinguished by events, and are as dead as the ashes in that fireplace.'

'Forgive me, Rebecca, for my impertinence.' Will was all contrition. 'I am just trying to solve a puzzle. You see, we have been rehearsing our first play, and John has been, shall we say, disturbed of late. Unable to remember his lines, becoming agitated over trifles, that kind of thing. So I have been casting around seeking some kind of explanation.' All of this was nonsense concocted by Will and Ned the night before. In reality, John Towne had shown not the slightest sign of distress when faced with the part.

'And you think *I* might be the cause of his agitation?'

'The thought had occurred to me.'

'Then you are misled by your imagination, I fear. Perhaps it is the nature of the play itself that he finds difficult. I know little of your craft, but William used occasionally to be troubled when he found the matter of the play not to his taste.'

'Perhaps so. This play concerns a murder, in Kent, during the old king's time.'

'An unchancy subject for a play, if you ask me. But I daresay that you and your colleagues know what will entertain in the playhouse.'

'It is a heinous story. The wife of a man of business conspires with her lover to have him murdered. We—Marlowe and I—think it will be a great success when we have got it onto the stage. John is to play the woman's lover and co-conspirator. It is central to the plot, yet he seems unable to come at it.'

'I can see that must be infuriating. But as I say, I have not laid eyes on John Towne since before you all left to go on tour, a year and a half ago.' She took a sip of wine, picked out a marchpane confection from the array of dainties on the tray, and held it in her fingers as if considering its fate, which was to disappear into her mouth.

The girl's eyes didn't waver as the silence lengthened, regarding him with a faint amusement, almost as if she was daring him in some way. This was getting him nowhere, he realised, with a touch of irritation. Time, perhaps, to show the dagger.

'Rebecca, why are you lying to me?' The baldness of the accusation caused her to blink. 'I know that you met with John yesterday, and perhaps several times before that.'

'You have been following me!' The attempt at outrage didn't quite work, undermined by the glimmer of fear in her eyes.

'A chance encounter on the street, nothing more. But telling enough.' Will closed his own eyes and recited from memory. '*I wanted him dead, and gave you the means for it.*'

This time he broke through her defences. She gave a tiny cry, and her hand flew to her mouth, bunched into a fist as if she would stop it up and prevent any further speech. 'You were there!' she whispered. 'It was you, wasn't it, on the other side of the wall, with someone else? John swore there was no one there.'

'We heard it all. Or enough, at least, to have you both condemned out of hand.'

He had expected tears, but there were none. She was visibly struggling to control her emotions, but her eyes were entirely dry. She was not going to deploy that most feminine of weapons in her defence, out of a pride that Will, in spite of himself, found appealing. It was the kind of straight-backed self-respect that he saw and admired in his own wife when she was pushed into a corner. Lesser women might feign weakness and try for the sympathy of their male oppressors, but neither Anne Shakespeare nor Rebecca Knell would ever do so. Still, the stakes were too high to loosen the screws.

'You know what they do to husband-murderers?' he said, keeping his voice as cold and menacing as possible. 'It is usual to be burned alive, at the stake. A terrible way to die.'

Her face paled further, though she remained defiant. 'If you heard our conversation, then you also know that I repudiated John, regretted ever agreeing to his plots.'

'That might be so, and you will have your chance to say so in open court, I make no doubt. But you *did* conspire with him to kill Billy, did you not? That fact cannot be denied.'

Now at last the tears did come, though not in a flood, just tiny involuntary drops that leaked unbidden from the corners of her eyes and ran down the ridges

281

on each side of her nose. 'He said that he would provoke William into a fight, and asked me for a token with which to taunt him. That was the extent of my involvement. I regretted it the instant he had gone, and never thought that he would actually go through with it.'

Enlightenment dawned in Will's mind. '*You* gave him the handkerchief.'

'Yes. It was one of Heminges', left here by chance on a wholly innocent visit.' Will offered her his own kerchief, which she took and used to dab at her eyes. 'When Tarlton told me that John had killed William, I knew what must have happened, and I was appalled. But what could I do? If I said anything, I would implicate myself.'

'And then John turned up, and demanded that you keep to your half of the bargain, and marry him?'

'Yesterday was the third time he'd asked me. Each time before, I put him off with excuses. But yesterday was too much, and I repudiated him forever. And then I realised what he had always been after. Not love, but money, William's money.'

'Why do you say that?'

'When I rejected his suit—not yesterday, but the first time he asked me, three days ago—he grew angry, called me a wanton gigolo, and said that I had bewitched him, that he had perforce abandoned marriage to another, a maid whose dowry would, he said, have outweighed all the wealth that I could bring him. That was when I realised that he has no affection for me at all, it is all feigned. He only wants to marry me for my money.'

'Yet, why does he need so much money? Is he in debt?'

'He could be. But I think it is simply that he has been poor all his life and he cannot stand it. He thinks of himself as a great actor, as great as William or Dick

Tarlton, who have made fortunes for themselves on the stage. But he isn't, is he? Despite your protestations otherwise.'

'No, he is not. John is a journeyman actor, at best. Billy knew it, and so does Dick.'

'There, you see? John wants to be rich, but he cannot find a way to get there except by marriage to this other poor maid, or to me. To him, it matters not.'

'And he was prepared to kill to get his way. With your connivance.'

'No! It was a moment of weakness, despair even. You are a man. What can you know of a woman's suffering? How can you know what it is like to know that you must simply endure your husband's beatings and foul language when he is drunk?' The flash of furious defiance slowly subsided before Will's eyes. 'I thought that perhaps John's wild plan would give me a way out, and so I gave him the handkerchief and allowed him to think that we might marry after. But I swear upon all that is holy, that I regretted it the instant he left and never, ever thought that he would go through with his plan. You must believe me, Mister Shakespeare, you must.'

The trouble was, Will didn't entirely believe her. It was not her husband's death that made it impossible for her to marry Towne, but the manner of it. She was right in that—marrying the man who had killed her first husband in so public a fashion would be seen as indecent. But she had hinted, had she not, that if Towne had achieved his purpose more discreetly, by poison, say, then she might well have married him?

On the other hand, it was undeniable that it was Towne who had driven this plot, unlike in the play they were rehearsing, where he and Marlowe had made Alice the true engine of the murder. A jury would have no sympathy for Rebecca, would believe a man over any woman, but in Will Shakespeare's judgement she did not deserve to be condemned, and he made up his mind at that moment that he would do what he could to protect her.

But he wasn't ready to release her just yet. There was more information that he needed. 'I asked you once whether you thought John might have papist leanings, do you remember?'

The question seemed to confuse her. She frowned. 'I thought it an odd thing to ask at the time. And said that I had seen no such evidence.'

Will allowed himself a small smile. 'Aye, and you turned the whole question neatly back at me by saying that I was as likely to be a papist as John. But in your encounters with him since then, have you seen or heard anything that might be thought odd? Think carefully. Your answers might be your salvation.'

If that remark mystified her, she showed no sign, merely furrowing her brow in thought. 'I can think of two things. He said once that, because of me, he had neglected matters of great import, matters that would raise him far above his present state. I don't know what he meant by that. He did not seem to be talking of money.'

'And the other?'

'I told you, I think, that John never talked of his time on the continent. But once, just once, he let slip that he had studied at a place in France called Rems, or something like that. I fear I have no French. Does that mean anything to you?'

Will shrugged. 'No, nothing. But it may mean something to others.' He rose to his feet and picked up his cloak.

'You are going, Mister Shakespeare? With matters so... unresolved?' Dismay showed in her face and the waver in her voice. 'What then is to become of me? Am I to expect the next caller to be the recorder's pursuivants, coming to haul me off to gaol?'

'By rights that is what ought to happen.' Will did his best to sound stern, though in truth he was both sympathetic and moved by her plight. 'But I believe you. John is the true guilty party here, and it is he who must be brought to justice.'

Her relief was short-lived, as her mind processed the implications of Will's reprieve. 'Yet, surely, if he comes to trial, my part in the affair must come out? And then I shall be condemned.'

She was right. And that meant that he had to find some way of catching Towne, extracting a confession from him, and at the same time protecting Rebecca. The glimmer of an idea as to how he might achieve that began to form in his brain, but he decided to keep it to himself.

'I know it is asking a lot, but for now, you must trust me when I say that I will do what I can to keep your part in this affair a secret. I will be honest, I may not succeed, but it is your best chance.'

'I don't have much choice, do I? Yet something tells me that you are a man of your word.' She tilted her head to one side, eyebrows raised in a query. 'You are one of Walsingham's men, aren't you? A spy of sorts.'

It was Will's turn to be startled and on the defensive. 'Why would you say that? I am what I seem—an actor and aspiring poet, nothing more.'

'Oh, I think you are much more than that. William told me that you came to the Queen's Men at the insistence of Sir Francis. He was annoyed at the time, said that it was wrong that the Queen's secretary should foist upon the company such an unwanted duckling, an untried actor of dubious worth. But now I see it. You are still in the secretary's employ.'

'Perhaps I am, but not in the way you think. I have done his bidding from time to time, but I am not, I promise you, on his payroll.'

'But you have some influence with him? Is that how you think you can keep me safe?'

'If it comes to it, I flatter myself that I have been of sufficient use to Sir Francis that he will listen to me. But there is another way to achieve that end which will not require such a direct appeal.'

'Which you are not going to explain to me.'

'Which I am not going to explain to you. You will just have to trust me, as I said.'

She nodded and picked up a bell to summon the maid, Emily, who appeared with suspicious promptness, ready to conduct him to the front door.

'Thank you for calling on me, Mister Shakespeare. You have set my mind much at rest. Please feel free to visit again should you have any further news for me.'

Making his way back to Silver Street, Will thought about the ploy that had come into his mind during that confrontation with Rebecca. It could work, provided that John Towne still had a shred or two of conscience. But it would need a huge amount of work on his part before their final rehearsal of *Arden* in two days' time.

Chapter 21

Will felt as if he had only just fallen asleep when he was woken by the crash of the door to his chamber being flung open. He jerked himself upright and, shrugging off sheets and blankets, reached instinctively for the dagger that he kept beside the bed.

Dimly, he made out a figure in the gloom. 'Who's there?'

'Don't worry, Will, ish jush me,' came the reply in the slurred voice of Ned Bentley.

'Christ and all his Saints! I thought you must be some murderer.' Putting the knife down, he fumbled for a tinderbox and struck a spark to a taper, with which he lit a candle. The acrid smell of cheap tallow generated a wavering light, by which he beheld an apparition. For though the voice belonged to a youth named Ned Bentley, the body from which it had emanated seemed to be that of an old, decrepit man, complete with a long straggling grey beard and equally long grey hair beneath a vast black hat with a battered, drooping brim that looked suspiciously like the one which usually graced the head of Cutting Ball. His clothes were villainous, the worsted doublet patched, the long cloak stained with something unspeakable, the hose drooping and the shoes muddy.

In short, he looked like the kind of vagrant who the Watch would happily lock up in the Clink without giving it a second thought. But the blue eyes were, unmistakeably, those of his young friend Ned, though admittedly they were somewhat bloodshot and bleary.

'For God's sake, where is the bloody chamber-pot? If I don't piss soon my bladder will burst.'

'By the fireplace where it always is, you idiot.'

Ned stumbled across the room and occupied himself for the next few moments with the task of unbuttoning himself and releasing a stream of urine into the pot, letting out a slow sigh of relief as he did so.

'Empty it, will you? Else the place will stink all night.'

Ned grunted and took the full pot over to the window where, unsteadily, he pushed open the shutters and unceremoniously poured the contents down into the street below, muttering the traditional warning, 'gardy-loo!' at a volume so low as to be useless should anyone have had the misfortune to be passing below at that moment. Luckily, it was still the middle of the night, and the street was deserted.

Will got out of bed, pulled his doublet over his shoulders, and lit another candle or two. 'So are you going to tell me where you have been, dressed in that extraordinary costume?'

Ned sat on a chest, flung the hat into a corner, and divested himself of wig and false beard, thus transforming himself into at least a resemblance to his ordinary self.

'I've been at the Dolphin all evening,' he said, running a hand through the blond hair that had been confined beneath the wig. 'Keeping an eye on Mister Towne.'

'Jesu! What possessed you to do that? What if he had recognised you?'

Ned grinned his lopsided grin. 'Got a penny for an old codger, my master? So as I can get meself a mug of ale?'

The voice was a surprisingly good imitation of an old drunk, and Will had to laugh. 'I can see that when you are done playing women's parts, we will have a place for you as a comic.'

'Don't you want to know what I learned?' Clearly, Ned was bursting to reveal the fruits of his night's work. 'You are going to be amazed.'

'Amaze away. Tell me where you came up with this hare-brained idea.'

'It was Mister Ball's notion, actually. Indirectly.'

'Cutting Ball? Greene's friend?'

'Do you know another?' Ned was droll. 'He came looking for you this morning, while you were out. Said to tell you that he had nothing to report and that he was pulling his men off the job anyway, seeing as how there was no more money to pay them.'

Will frowned. That was true. His resources could only go so far, and unless he applied to Seething Lane for more funds, he could not keep paying Ball to maintain their watch on Towne.

'Anyway,' Ned went on, 'I told him I would pass the message on. But I got thinking that perhaps I could fill the breach by keeping a watch on Mister Towne myself.'

'And hence the old man's disguise. Where did you get the wig and the beard? From our costume chest, I suppose?'

'Don't worry, they will go back in the chest in as perfect a state as they left it. I know they are expensive. I'm more worried about the hat. It belongs to Mister Ball and he said there would be hell to pay if I lost it.'

That made Will laugh again at the idea of Ball giving up his precious hat to anyone. 'Never mind. None of the various parts of your disguise seem to have come to any harm, so you are quite safe. You went to the Dolphin, I take it?'

'Yes. Ball told me to tell the landlord that I was one of his men, and that he was to give me credit. When I got there, the poor man was amazingly obliging.

Just about fell over himself to give me a corner booth where I could watch everything, and then kept sending jugs of ale over. I'm afraid I got a little drunk.'

Whatever hold Cutting Ball had over the landlord of the Dolphin, it was clearly powerful if he was prepared to abandon the instinctive dislike of extending credit that was common to most of his breed.

'Anyway, after about a half hour, Mister Towne turns up, has a look around the room, and settles himself into the booth next to mine.'

Will gaped. 'And he didn't recognise you?'

'He didn't,' Ned said, complacently. 'Why would he? What he saw when he looked in my direction was a drunk, half-asleep old man. In fact, I might have closed my eyes and let out a bit of a snore to encourage him in that notion.' He stretched his arms. 'Speaking of drink…'

'There is some sack somewhere in that cupboard. Help yourself.'

Ned hauled himself to his feet and busied himself finding the wine bottle, taking out the stopper, and pouring himself a goblet full of the amber liquid. 'Want some? No?' Refreshed, he resumed his seat on the clothes chest. 'So for a little while, nothing seemed to happen. I nursed my ale and mumbled a few words, keeping up the pretence that I was on the edge of passing out. And then a man appeared on the other side of the room, at the door into the coaching yard, looked around, and made a line directly towards Mister Towne.'

'What did he look like, this man?'

'It was hard to tell—I had my eyes half-closed, you see—but he was very tall, dressed all in black with a high black hat that made him seem even taller. I couldn't see much of his face under the brim, but he had a big, long nose. Kind of hooked at the bridge. Next thing I knew, he had slipped into the seat opposite

290

Mister Towne, and they started talking. Fairly quiet, but I could hear them clearly. Some quirk of the way sound travels in that room I suppose.'

'What was the stranger's voice like? Foreign? A working man?'

'A gentleman, I would have said, with a cultured sort of voice.'

A tall fellow with a hawk nose who by his voice seemed gentle-born. The words floated across Will's mind from Knell's secret report to Walsingham. This was clearly the man that Knell had seen meeting with Towne in Abingdon. 'Go on. What did they talk about?'

Now Ned looked a little shamefaced. 'I have no idea. They were talking in Latin.'

'They…Latin?'

'Of which language I have none,' Ned pointed out, redundantly.

'Neither would most of the customers in the Dolphin's taproom, I would expect. They could have stood on tables and shouted for all anyone there might have understood what they were saying.' Will couldn't help laughing.

'All I can tell you is that they were talking very urgently together. I thought the tall man was giving Mister Towne some instructions. He certainly seemed to be the master of the situation, and John was very deferential.' The look on Ned's face told Will that there was more to tell and that his young friend was still pleased with himself, despite his inability to understand what his quarry had been talking about. 'I realised I was getting nowhere, so I knocked my tankard onto the floor.'

'You did what?'

'Knocked my tankard onto the floor. Made a great clatter and beer went everywhere. I made sure it rolled past their booth so I could make a show of getting up and stumbling around on my hands and knees to retrieve it.'

For once, all words deserted Will. He just stared at Ned, imagining the scene—the startled conspirators, Ned in his old man disguise mumbling away among the rushes on hands and knees trying to pick up his beer tankard.

'I farted, too.'

'You…' Will's laughter was a great bellow of sound in the little room which once started couldn't be stopped. It took a full minute before he was finally able to recover his composure, holding his sides as the belly laughs subsided into a series of giggles.

'I'm sorry, good sirs,' Ned said, in his old man's voice, blinking and slobbering. 'Did I get any ale on ye? No? Thash good then. P'raps ye can spare a few pennies for a poor old fool to buy hisself another bottle o' mad-dog?'

'Stop, or I will split my sides! And John *still* didn't recognise you?'

'No. But here is the interesting thing. As I straightened up, Mister Towne slipped a packet of papers into his doublet, very furtive-like, as if he didn't want anyone to see them, even an old drunk like me.'

That made Will sit up. 'Well, well. What kind of papers? Could you see what was written on them?'

'Not really. There was something written on the cover, but the packet was sealed with wax. By then I thought I might have pressed my luck a little far, and I decided to get out of the taproom before Mister Towne guessed my identity.'

'That was wise. You came straight here?'

'Yes. Didn't even stop for a piss!'

'Well done, Ned, well done indeed.' He stood up. 'Get yourself to bed. you've earned a good sleep for the rest of the night.'

Ned stood, stretched, yawned hugely, and, discarding doublet and cloak, sat on the bed to pull off his boots. Down to hose and shirt, he dropped onto the bed and a few minutes later was snoring softly.

Will sat and thought for a moment, and then picked up the candle and, shielding it with his hand against the slight breeze from the window that threatened to put it out, settled himself at his desk. Pulling a few sheets of clean paper from the pile stacked in one corner, he sharpened his quill, dipped it in ink, and began to write.

***

'It's a daft idea.'

'Why so? Do you have a better way to get at the truth?'

Marlowe scowled at Will. 'Arrest both of them and hand them over to the authorities to question.'

'On what charge? We have no proof that they are engaged in any kind of conspiracy, let alone one that is treasonous. Even Sir Francis can't arrest people without a warrant, and he'll not get one based on what little we can tell him. This way, there is a good chance that Towne at least will confess.'

'That, as the gamblers say, is a long bow. Show me the pages again.'

The sheaf of papers in question was the product of his night's work, a new scene of some half dozen pages that he had created in a kind of creative trance as he worked through the darkness by the light of a single candle, his pen flying across the paper with barely a pause to consider a phrase or substitute a word that might seem more apt. By the time he had finished and laid down his pen, flexing cramped fingers and yawning hugely, dawn's weak light was creeping across the city. He had sat for a few moments contemplating his work, wondering at this unexpected fluency, so different from his usual struggle to extract words from a brain that seemed to be swimming in them.

Leaving a still-sleeping Ned, he had pulled on doublet and cloak against the cold and hurried across town to Kit's lodgings on Bishopsgate Street, where he had roused his friend from slumber with a few pebbles sent up to rattle against his window. A bleary-eyed Kit had reluctantly come down to open the door and conduct him back up the stairs to his rooms, while Will chattered wildly about the plan he had conceived the day before that would, he hoped, flush John Towne out of the shadows.

Marlowe, eyes narrowed in concentration, read the close-written pages through, for what was now the third time. 'Well, at least it's good poetry. When do you rehearse?'

'Cowley came back from the country today, so we are having a final rehearsal tomorrow. Dick Burbage used his father's influence with the Carpenters' Guild to allow us the use of their hall, near the Moor-Gate.'

'Convenient. And what about Ned? Are you confident he can play his part in this?'

'He's a good actor, and resourceful. But I don't propose to tell him in advance what is going on.'

'That seems risky.'

'It is. But if this is to work, John must have no inkling as to what is coming, and the best way to achieve that is if Ned knows nothing either. I can rely, I think, on his instincts when the moment comes.'

'It is dangerous, though.' Marlowe sat back and crossed his arms on his chest. 'Consider, this is a man who has shown he is willing to kill without hesitation. He is a master swordsman, and if you trap him, he will surely resort to violence.'

That was true, and it was a spectre that had hovered in Will's mind even as he had conceived his plan. But it was a risk he would have to take. 'I learned to handle weapons in Italy, and I can match John with sword and dagger, if it comes to it. But this is a rehearsal. There is no reason for any of the actors to be armed.'

Marlowe nodded. 'Well, I don't suppose I can stop you anyway, and it is a bold plan. I just fear for your and Ned's safety.'

Will shrugged. There was nothing else he could say to relieve his friend's anxiety on that point.

'And the play is to be performed before the Queen the day after, you say?'

'Yes, though no one other than you and I know that. As far as the rest of the company is concerned, we are performing for Lord Strange, his father the earl, and their guests.'

'God. It's a risk, Will, don't you think?'

'It is. But do you see any other alternative? I do not.'

Silence, and then Marlowe shook his head and smiled. 'No, neither do I. Well, *iacta alea esto*, eh?'

Will smiled back. *Let the die be cast*, Caesar's words on crossing the Rubicon, seemed entirely apt.

Chapter 22

London, July 1588

The Carpenter's Hall was a modest building crouching among the houses that lined the street running beneath London's northern wall. The hall itself was deserted for the day, save for the grizzled old doorman, it being a half-holiday for the apprentices and members of the guild, who ostentatiously picked out a huge iron key from the half dozen of its brothers that hung on a ring at his belt, and opened the big, elaborately carved wooden doors. With an obsequious little bow, he ushered Will and Ned inside, where the main hall of the building was in darkness until the shutters were thrown open to admit light from four tall windows. Through the diamond-shaped glass panes they could see the vegetable plots and a small orchard that lay immediately to the south, and beyond that a hedged pleasure garden, neatly laid out in the French fashion.

The hall itself was wood panelled between the windows and boasted a parquetry floor, devoid for the present of any rushes. There was a row of carven seats built into each of the long sides, like the choir stalls of a church, but otherwise, the room was devoid of furniture. At one end stood a low platform, with a few chairs stacked on one side, that would be their stage.

'This will do well, I think,' Will said, dumping his satchel and cloak on one of the carved chairs. 'The stage is perhaps a little small, but it will serve. Now all we need are the others.'

As if his words had been an incantation, the members of the new company of Lord Strange's Men began to appear at the door, starting with Richard Crowley and Gus Phillips, who arrived still chewing on bread and cheese they had evidently snatched from some streetside stall to make their breakfast, and giggling at some joke that they had shared in the street.

'Ho, Shakespeare! You look like death itself. Have you not been sleeping?'

Will was startled by Cowley's jibe. Of course, it was true—he had barely snatched more than a few hours' sleep in the last two days, but when he had inspected himself in the mirror that morning, he had not thought he looked particularly tired. 'Oh, you know,' he said vaguely, 'the city. It's not as restful as the country...'

'Restful? It depends on what you have been doing in the country.' Phillips laughed, pulling the stopper out of a bottle of beer, which gave a satisfactory hiss. 'Did you not note Dick's bandy-legged walk? All the way here he's been bragging that he spent all his time in the country in bed, with his wife on her back. I am amazed he can walk at all.'

Before Cowley could think of a retort, George Bryan, Tom Blunt and Anthony Ashford arrived in a chattering gaggle, and the next few minutes were spent in noisy greetings and friendly banter. Thomas Pope straggled in, looking tousled and sleepy, and was subjected to volleyed shouts of 'slugabed' and 'lazybones' from the others, all of which he took in sheepish good part.

'At least you aren't the last to arrive,' Cowley said, with a frown. 'As usual, we must await the arrival of his high-and-bloody-mightiness Mister John Towne.'

Will wondered what Towne had done to annoy the usually good-humoured Richard Cowley. 'Has anyone seen him this morning?'

No one had, though that was hardly surprising since his lodgings at the Dolphin were outside the walls, whereas the rest of them lived within the city proper. It was a little perplexing. Had something happened to Towne? Had he somehow worked out that he had been discovered, and decided to run? Perhaps, after all, he *had* recognised Ned's old man disguise.

'Do you want me to go and find him?' Ned asked, his face managing to convey to Will that he shared his concern, though his voice was bright and cheerful. 'The Dolphin isn't so far away.'

Will made a show of giving it some thought. 'No, let's get started. Most of the first half of act one is you, me and Dick, anyway. Hopefully, he'll turn up in time for his appearance.'

So they started. Though they clutched them in their hands as a kind of security, neither Shakespeare nor Cowley really needed the folded rolls of paper upon which Will had inscribed their parts. Marlowe's lines, tripping along in their regular pentameter, had proven easy to memorise, and so they could focus on getting their delivery just right. Cowley's Arden was a man much put-upon, alternating between self-pity and furious rage directed at his tormentor, Mosby, and Will was almost playing himself as the voice of sweet reason, trying to keep his friend calm.

Ned, when he appeared as Alice, affected a pleasantly feminine voice, a little low perhaps, but still believable enough to attract a smattering of applause from the other actors who stood around the stage watching their colleagues, appraising and critical. Though dressed in his usual woollen doublet and patched hose, he somehow managed to move and look like a young woman. It was a remarkable skill, to create such an illusion with nothing more than his voice and some tricks in the way he walked and held himself. Not for the first time, Will realised that this pleasant and amusing young man was also a very fine actor.

Their parts in the scene done, Shakespeare and Cowley left the stage, to be replaced by Anthony Ashford, playing the innkeeper Adam—a kind of go-between connecting Alice with Mosby—and Augustine Phillips, in the more substantial role of Michael, Arden's treacherous servant. Will watched with only half his attention, looking over his shoulder every few minutes to see whether their missing actor had finally arrived. But in the end, it was Ned who spotted him first.

'Mosby, my love!' Ned delivered the line looking across the heads of the other actors, who found themselves being roughly shouldered aside by John Towne pushing his way towards the stage.

Divesting himself of his hat, which he sent spinning away into a corner of the room, he jumped up onto the platform. 'Away, I say, and talk not to me now...'

Ned, with nothing but a blink of the eyes to show his surprise, smoothly launched into his next line, and they played through the rest of the scene. At the end, they paused and bowed to the rest of the company. Towne had never been popular with the other actors, who found it difficult to penetrate his chilly reserve, but at this moment they appreciated the sheer confidence of that entrance, the act of a skilled performer, and they signified their approval with laughing applause and jokes.

Will smiled with the rest. This accomplished actor was also a heartless murderer, a fact that only he and Ned knew, but the successful execution of Will's plan depended on neither of them showing their true feelings until the right moment. And so he applauded, nodded, smiled, and then clapped his hands to bring their attention back to him. 'Well done, John. Now, shall we proceed with the next scene?'

Over the course of the next two hours, they worked their way steadily through the play, stopping from time to time to engage in technical wrangles over details of staging—how to signify changes of location whenever it wasn't made clear in the text, where to enter and exit the stage, what props they would need—in the heated but friendly way of professionals everywhere. But at the end, they were collectively satisfied that they could confidently present *Arden of Faversham* to their patron and his guests the following day.

For Will, it had been the most taxing two hours of his acting life. Of course, as joint parent of the play, he was anxious to ensure that their staging of it would do justice to Marlowe's (and his, he reminded himself) creation. He had his own part as Franklin to perfect, he had to keep track of the various decisions that they had made along the way about timing and staging, and there were sections of the play where he had had to conjure new text on the spot, to cover gaps that Marlowe had left or where his words seemed, in the light of rehearsal, not to work. All this would have been stressful enough, though by now well within his ability as an actor and company book-holder, but he also had the added worry of John Towne.

Throughout the morning, he had kept a surreptitious eye on his fellow actor, trying to divine his mood and mind. If Towne was aware of the scrutiny, he did nothing to show it. The man's demeanour was coolly professional, and he stepped through his lines without hesitation. Will had wondered whether he would stumble over the scene in which Arden was finally killed, involving strangulation and multiple stabbings, but he performed his part with barely a skipped beat. His early protestations that he would not play the murderer seemed to have been forgotten as he stabbed Cowley in the back with a wooden prop-knife whose blade retracted into the haft.

In fact, by the time they had finished, Will was beginning to doubt himself. If he had not heard with his own ears that confession from the other side of the garden wall, nor heard Rebecca's confirmation of the plot to kill William Knell, he would never have believed that John Towne had anything on his conscience at all. Marlowe had thought the plan he was about to put into motion was dead daft, and perhaps the poet was right. But given that they were to perform *Arden* in front of the Queen the very next day, he could not take the risk of leaving matters as they stood. So, as the company collected together their various possessions and readied themselves to go out and find a tavern in which to slake their thirst and find something to eat, he plucked the fine velvet sleeve of Towne's doublet. 'John, can I have a word?'

300

Towne's black eyebrows went up in surprise, but he allowed himself to be drawn aside from the rest of the group.

'Marlowe thought that the play needed an extra scene in the third act, between scenes three and four, in which Mosby and Alice quarrel about the consequences of their plot.'

'Why?'

'What do you mean, why?'

'I mean, why do we need them to quarrel? At this particular point in the play.'

'Well, er... we think we need to show both characters as having some doubts as to their course. After all, by this stage, they have tried three times to kill Arden, first by poison, and twice by the incompetent hands of Black Will and Shakebag. It would be natural for their resolution to be shaken by this point, and for that to cause tension between them.'

Towne considered that and, to Will's relief, seemed to accept his logic, though reluctantly. 'It seems a little late in the day to be adding new scenes,' he grumbled. 'He *has* written the verses?'

Will laughed. 'You know Kit. He had the idea, but alas had no time to write the words. So I did it last night.' He pulled a sheaf of papers from his bag and waved them vaguely in the air. 'I thought we might run through the scene now, just with you and Ned, since there are no other characters involved. Then, if it feels right, we will put it into the performance.'

'Just me and Bentley?' There was a new edge of suspicion to Towne's voice. 'Won't Cowley and the others want to know what we are doing?'

'Oh, I'll talk to them later, when we catch up with them at the tavern,' Will said airily. 'After all, we might not use the new scene if, between us, we decide that it is not right.'

When Towne finally nodded his agreement, Will looked around for Ned. *Clever boy.* The young actor had managed to detach himself from the others, who were already outside and making their noisy way down the street.

'Where are they going?' Will asked him.

'The Mermaid, I think, though Gus seemed to think it was too far to walk.'

'He always was a lazybones. Well, we'll join them there later. Now, here are your parts. Shall we begin? John, you have the first speech. Mosby is disturbed, troubled that he cannot sleep for worrying. He reflects that life was simpler when he was a poor man...'

Towne took his position to one side of the stage, quickly scanned the words of the speech to get the sense of it, and then, holding the playscript before him, began to declaim to an invisible audience:

'Disturbed thoughts drive me from company,
And dries my marrow with their watchfulness.
Continual trouble of my moody brain
Enfeebles my body by excess of drink,
And nips me as the bitter north-east wind
Doth check the tender blossoms in the spring.
My golden time was when I had no gold:
Though then I wanted, yet I slept secure.
My daily toil begat me night's repose,
My night's repose made daylight fresh to me.
But since I climbed the top-bough of the tree
And sought to build my nest among the clouds,
Each gentle stirring gale doth shake my bed,
And makes me dread my downfall to the earth...'

Towne stopped, and read through the next few lines, his lips moving soundlessly. 'Ah, I see. He is worried that there are too many who know about the conspiracy—Greene, Clarke the painter, and Arden's servant Michael.'

'Yes. But he thinks he can deal with them by setting them against each other. It's all in that one line: *I can cast a bone to make these curs pluck out each other's throat.* Not a great deal to work with, I grant you, so you will need to use some gesture to make it obvious. Shall we move on? From *How now, Alice.* Ned, you'll enter from behind the curtains, there.'

Ned walked across the stage, managing to make his face a picture of misery. Towne grasped him by the elbows and looked intently into the boy's face.

'How now Alice? What, are you sad? Then make me partaker of your pensiveness—for fire divided burns with lesser force.'

Ned responded in his curiously seductive low woman's voice. 'I will dam that fire in my breast, till by the force thereof my part consume.'

'Ungentle Alice, your sorrow is my sore. You know it well, and 'tis your policy to forge distressful looks to wound a breast where lies a heart that dies when you are sad.' Towne cupped Ned's chin in his hand, leaning in so that their faces were just inches apart. 'It is not love that loves to anger love.'

Ned twisted away from the other's grip, and with a venom that caught the other off-guard, positively hissed his next line, 'It is not love that loves to murder love.'

'How mean you that?' Towne/Mosby sounded puzzled, and Will knew that the actor had heard the deliberate echo in the play's words.

'You know how dearly Arden loved me.'

'And then?'

'And then conceal the rest, lest that my words be carried with the wind, and be published in the world to both our shames.' Ned glanced up from the script and sent Will a swift glance. 'I pray you, Mosby, let our springtime wither. Our harvest else will yield but loathsome weeds. Forget, I pray you, what has passed between us, for how I blush and tremble at the thought!'

Towne frowned, hesitated as if he had for the moment lost the thread of the play, then he looked down at the script, and picked up his part once more. 'What? Are you changed?'

'Aye, to my former happy life again,' Ned replied, reading from his script. 'From title of an odious strumpet's name to honest Arden's wife, not Arden's honest wife. Ha, Mosby! It is you that has made me slanderous to all my kin. I think I was bewitched. Woe the hapless hour and all the causes that enchanted me!'

Towne's mouth opened to speak his next line, but no words emerged, and the frown was back, deeper and more perplexed this time.

'Are you all right, John?' Will said softly. 'The next speech is a long one, and important. Do you want a moment to con it?'

'What? Er, yes.'

Will risked a quick look in Ned's direction while Towne's attention was focused on reading through the twenty-odd lines of the speech; the younger man's eyes were sparkling with mischief. Clearly, he too had recognised those phrases, modified into poetry, that they had heard from the other side of the garden wall just a few days ago.

Towne looked up from the pages of the playscript. 'You wrote these verses, did you, Shakespeare?'

'Of course. Did I not say so? Is there something wrong? Perhaps you do not like the way they are writ.'

'Can we get on with it?' Ned said, all youthful impatience. 'I don't know about you two, but I am in need of food.'

'You're always in need of food,' Will said, with a laugh that sounded in his ears more like a nervous giggle. 'But he is right, John. Unless you have some objection?'

A flash of fury crossed Towne's face, and for a moment, Will thought he was going to throw the script down onto the floor and march out. But instead, he seemed to gather himself, visibly bringing his emotions under control, and resume his actor's stance. 'What was your last line, Bentley?'

'Ah...' Ned pretended to think. 'Woe the hapless hour and all the causes that enchanted me.'

Taking a deep breath, Towne resumed, saying his next lines quickly, almost tripping over them. 'Nay, if you ban, let me breathe curses forth. I have neglected matters of import that would have placed me above your state, forwent advantages, and spurned time. Aye Mosby has forsaken Fortune's right hand, to take a wanton gigolo by the left, for I left the marriage of an honest maid, whose dowry would have weighed down all your wealth, and whose beauty and demeanour far exceeded yours.'

He stopped and, wrenching his gaze away from Ned's imperturbable blue eyes, stared hard at Will for a moment or two. Then, swallowing hard, he started again, but now in a low voice that barely carried across the stage, as if he could not bear to say the words.

'I was bewitched. And you all unhallowed have enchanted me. But I will break your spells and exorcisms and put another sight upon these eyes that showed my heart a raven for a dove. Until now I knew you not. You are not kind,

305

but foul, like any witch. And now the rain has beaten off your gilt, and your worthless copper shows you counterfeit. Go, get you gone. I am too good to be your favourite.'

The last sentence came out almost as a croak, and Towne looked stricken. But Ned was not about to give him any respite. 'Aye, now I see,' he barked, the softly feminine tones entirely abandoned, 'and too soon find it true, which often has been told me by my friends, that Mosby loves me but for my wealth, which too incredulous I never believed.'

'Stop! Enough!' Towne looked, bewildered, from Will to Ned and back again. 'Rebecca...'

'Rebecca?'

'Come, Shakespeare, do not play the simpleton with me.' For a moment he seemed to rally, with a touch of the old supercilious anger. 'These slanders did not come from thin air.'

'Slanders? How are they slanders? They are but words in a play.'

'Which you have stolen from life! Or which have been dripped into your ear by that hell-bitch Rebecca Knell!'

'With whom you plotted to kill her husband,' Will said, now dropping all pretences and adopting the mien of an inquisitor.

'Not so!'

'Save your protests, John, they are hollow. I heard your quarrel in the garden behind Cheapside and got the rest from Rebecca's mouth. She has confessed all, that she conspired with you to murder Billy Knell so that you could marry.'

'There was no murder. The coroner exonerated me.'

'Aye, but the case can be reopened. With Rebecca's confession, you will soon enough feel the hangman's rope around your neck.'

'She will not do it. Too much else will come out.'

Now it was Will's turn to be confused. 'Such as?'

Towne's look was pitying. 'You think you know her, don't you, Shakespeare? Well, you don't. She lies as often as she opens her mouth. I will lay odds that she did not tell you that she had already made several attempts to rid herself of her husband before she asked me to do it for her, dangling the prospect of her hand and his money as bait.'

'I don't believe you.'

'Aye, she has you bewitched, too. But I do not lie. She tried poisoning him, at least twice to my knowledge. Knell, the fool, suspected nothing. He made a great joke of it, saying that his wife's cooking made him so ill that they had to engage a cook.'

That at least was true. Will remembered Knell making the same jokes.

Towne, reading some hesitation in Will's face, pressed home his counterattack. 'She will have told you, I make no doubt, that Knell abused her and beat her. That is not true. He doted on her. It was she who would flay him with her tongue, and he put up with it, the senile old dolt.'

Senile was not a word that Will would have used to describe Billy Knell, but he let it pass. 'Even if everything you say is true, the fact remains that you confessed, in the garden, to murdering Billy.'

'So says you.'

'And I,' Ned said, the knowing smile on his face stopping Towne in his tracks.

307

'You?' His face wrinkled in thought. 'You were the other so-called "farmer", nattering about the bloody harvest.'

'So you see, John, you are skewered. Two witnesses and Rebecca's testimony, however tainted, will be enough to convict you.'

Towne's defences collapsed as suddenly as a castle wall undermined by sappers. He buried his face in his hands, and for a moment Will thought he was going to weep. But when the familiar dark countenance emerged from its temporary shield, there were no tears of either grief or fury. Instead, Towne looked defeated, resigned to whatever fate would now befall him.

'I see I have no choice but to confess a second time. Yes, I intended to kill Knell. It was not self-defence, though I tried to make it look that way. But whatever she says now, I was going to marry her after a suitable time had passed. That was agreed between us, and until a few days ago I believed that nothing had changed.'

Perhaps that was true. 'She changed her mind, didn't she, because you had been so clumsy as to do your killing in a public place and public way so that the stain of it can never be washed off. But of course what she didn't know is that you had no choice in the matter.'

That puzzled Towne. 'I don't know what you mean.'

'What I mean is that once Billy had discovered your other secrets, it became much more urgent to kill him. You couldn't afford to try more subtle methods that might not work—arranging an accident, say, or another attempt at poison— because you knew that he had information that could condemn you to a traitor's death.'

'I still don't know what you are talking about.'

Will sighed theatrically. 'Must I spell it out? Billy witnessed your meeting in Abingdon with a Catholic priest when you were instructed to find a place in Lord Strange's household.' He held up a hand to forestall Towne's indignant refutation. 'Hear me out. You must have realised that Knell had overheard you, and you decided that he must die sooner rather than later, lest he betray you. It was a risk, provoking him to draw on you, and I doubt you expected to be locked up in Thame for as long as you were, but it worked in the end. The authorities were convinced that you had acted in self-defence, and you were free, ready to marry Rebecca and follow your instructions by joining our acting troupe.'

'You are chasing phantoms, Shakespeare. I never met anyone in Abingdon, let alone a Catholic priest.'

'No? A tall man, with a hook nose? The same man you met at the Dolphin two days ago?'

Before Towne could deny it, Ned decided to intervene again, this time in the voice of an old drunk. 'Remember me, master? Got a penny or two for an old man wot needs a drink?'

'I...' Whatever Towne had intended to say was swallowed up in a strangled, wordless cry. His face crumpled and his body swayed as though he were about to collapse. At a gesture from Will, Ned went and picked up one of the chairs from the corner of the stage, into which Towne slumped, seemingly defeated.

'I had no choice. None.' He looked up, and Will saw a flash of the same fury he had seen in Thame. 'Oh, Knell was marked out for death, all right. But I wasn't planning to do it like that. I'm not a fool. I knew he had to die in a way that left no clue that I might be responsible. I hadn't decided, thought there was plenty of time. Then he said something that made me realise he knew more about me than he should. I think he wanted me to know that he was watching me, the fool. So I decided then and there that he had to die sooner rather than later.

'But I needed to know what he actually had on me. I searched his room and found there a bundle of papers. One was partly in code, which I had no means of deciphering, but that which was written clear said that Knell was some kind of intelligencer, employed no doubt by Walsingham. I had to assume that the coded paper reported on my meeting with… with the priest. I could have just destroyed it, but that would have achieved nothing. It was the author of the report who had to be silenced. I left the papers where they were so that Knell would suspect nothing, intending to collect them after I had disposed of their author.

'The rest was easy. I still had the handkerchief that Rebecca had given me, with which I knew I could provoke the old idiot into drawing against me, and I knew exactly where I would make him chase me so that I could finish him and make it look like self-defence. What I hadn't expected was that the authorities in Thame would be quite so zealous as to lock me up and keep me in gaol. I thought they would allow me out on bail, and then I could retrieve the papers and destroy them.' He stopped and looked up at Will. 'You have read that report, haven't you? How else would you know what I was instructed to do? Which means you are one of Walsingham's gang of spies, too.'

'Not quite. But I am known to the secretary, and I have done work for him, in Italy. So I recognised the code and I arranged for it to be deciphered.'

It took a moment for Towne to absorb the implications of that. 'Then I am doomed if the government knows everything.'

'Perhaps.' Will took a deep breath, for he was about to go a long way out on a limb, far exceeding any authority that Walsingham or Phelippes might have given him. 'But it is possible that the secretary might find a way to look past your treachery if any evil that might come from it is averted.'

'By which you mean…?'

'The government does not know everything. For instance, who is the priest? I assume you knew him at Rheims?'

'How do you know I was at Rheims?'

'Something you said to Rebecca Knell, though she could not pronounce the name properly, and had no idea of its significance.'

'So the bitch betrays me again,' Towne muttered. 'All right, confessional time. But you must promise me you will intercede with Walsingham on my behalf.'

Will nodded. 'Of course, though I cannot guarantee what he will do.'

'Your guess is right. I belong to the True Faith, to which England will one day return. You southerners don't know how deep the faith abides in the north. King Henry might have stamped out the monasteries and King Edward could burn our priests at the stake, but many refused to let go of the old ways. My father is such a one.'

A note of bitterness edged his words. 'We were a wealthy family once, but he refused to go to the heretic church and refused to pay his recusancy fines. Then one day a man arrived, an agent of the Earl of Derby, who offered to pay his fines if he would sell his land to the earl—at a hugely discounted price, of course. He had no choice but to accept. It was made clear to him that he would be prosecuted with all the force of the law if he did not agree to this devil's bargain. So we were reduced to penury.'

'Derby, you say? Lord Strange's father?' Ned asked, surprised.

'What, do you think that a belted earl would be above such knavish tricks? You are naïve, boy.' Towne returned his gaze to Will. 'With no prospects at home, I ran away. To London at first, and then to France, where I met a man, an Englishman, in a tavern in Paris. He was, he said, a fellow-Catholic, exiled from his own country for his faith. But, he said, the true religion would be restored in England before long, and that there was a place for people like me to help achieve it.'

'The seminary at Rheims.'

'It was a place, this man said, where the future Catholic clergy of England were being trained. Brave priests were already being sent into England to prepare the way, to keep the faith alive and encourage the population to prepare to rise up when the time came. I had never contemplated becoming a priest, but he persuaded me that I should at least go there and decide for myself. He furnished me with the necessary introductions, and off I went.

'When I got there, I was soon accepted there and began studying to become a priest. But my instincts were right—the priesthood was not for me, and after a year I told the master of the college I wanted to leave. He made no difficulty about it, knowing that he had no hold over me, but he made me swear that if ever one of the brethren from Rheims wanted my help, I should offer it. I gave my promise and thought no more of it.'

'Until Abingdon.'

'Yes. The priest—for that is what he is, as Knell guessed—left a note for me with one of the grooms at the Crossed Keys, asking me to meet him at a certain house in the town. It was carefully worded to seem innocent, but there were certain references that made it obvious to me that the sender had also been a student at Rheims. So I met him, late at night, thinking I was unobserved.'

'What is his name, this priest?'

'He goes by the name of Gilbert Foy, though I doubt that is the name his mother gave him. I myself had never met him before; he must have studied at the college after my time.'

'And it was he who instructed you to find a place in the household of Lord Strange.'

Towne's eyes narrowed. 'So Knell heard that much. And that's why you were so obligingly determined that I should join this damned acting company.' He sighed and lifted his shoulders in the tiniest of shrugs. 'It seemed an odd thing to ask, and he would not tell me why he wanted me in Lord Strange's household, other than to say that I should expect further instructions. How I was to achieve this aim was up to me, though I had no idea how to do it. In fact, the whole notion was abhorrent to me. After all, it was this man's father who had ruined my family and stolen our land. But Foy was adamant. Lord Strange is, he said, a friend to the cause.'

Will said nothing and kept his face still, though he could sense out of the corner of his eye Ned's surprised look at this last revelation. 'And then you killed Billy Knell and found yourself in gaol.'

Towne's scowl was eloquent. 'Obviously, that was no part of my plan. How could I have known that Knell was an informer? Anyway, I was sure that the coroner would eventually acquit me, and then I planned to find a place with Lord Strange, as a clerk, perhaps, though it wasn't a prospect I relished. Then when you asked me to join you, it seemed like a gift from God. Little did I know that I was walking into an elaborate trap.'

Will nodded, ignoring Towne's self-pity. 'And so this priest, Foy, appeared two nights ago with your instructions. What were they?'

'Simple enough. I was to deliver a letter into Lord Strange's hands.'

'That is all?' Will was genuinely surprised. 'All that planning and plotting, just to deliver a letter?'

Towne shrugged. 'Well, Foy could hardly deliver the letter himself, could he? He is an outlaw in this country, and risks death if he is exposed.'

313

'And do you know what the letter says?'

'No. It was sealed, and it remains so. But Foy was most insistent that I hand it to Lord Strange personally, closely observe his countenance while he read it, and act accordingly. If he was angry or even puzzled, I was to say that I was a mere courier and knew nothing more. If he seemed pleased by what he read, I was to tell him of Foy's presence in London and offer to convey any return message to him.'

A wavering voice came from behind Will and Ned, over by the main door. 'Will you gentlemen be much longer? Only I has to close up the main door soon, see?'

Without thinking, Will turned towards the old doorkeeper. A loud yelp of pain from Ned was his only warning before Towne's shoulder crashed into him with surprising force, throwing him off the little stage and onto the floor. By the time he had struggled to his feet, Towne was through the door and out into the street, leaving behind a dazed doorman whose attempt to stop the fugitive had earned him a solid buffet that left him staggering. Glancing back, Will was horrified to see Ned sitting on the edge of the stage clutching his stomach trying to staunch the blood that was oozing out between his fingers.

'You, doorman!' His shout got the man's groggy attention. 'Go and find a barber-surgeon, or better yet a doctor. Now!'

Ned's young face was contorted with pain. 'Bastard must have had a knife hidden somewhere. Christ, it hurts!'

'Let me see.'

Will gently pulled the boy's hands away from the wound and opened his doublet. The shirt beneath was soaked with blood, and when he lifted it away to reveal the skin beneath, it started oozing again from the wound. But the knife that Towne had used must have been a small one, an eating knife perhaps, because the

314

incision was narrow and did not appear to be deep. He helped Ned take the shirt off entirely, and then tore a strip of linen from the bottom, where no blood had yet penetrated, and then folded it into a wad which he told Ned to press against the wound.

'It's not as bad as it looks. I think you'll live. Can you hold on until the doctor gets here?'

'Not much bloody choice, do I?' Ned croaked, with a crooked little smile, and then shivered. Will slipped the boy's discarded doublet over his shoulders and patted him on the shoulder. 'Good lad. When he's patched you up, go home and I'll meet you there.'

'Where are you going?'

'To find that bastard and make sure he is brought to justice!'

Chapter 23

Will realised the moment he emerged from the ornately carved door of the Carpenter's Hall that finding John Towne was not going to be easy. It was late morning, and the narrow street jammed between the high grey-stoned city wall and the buildings that lined its southern side was busy with pedestrians and drays and carts making their way into the city from the various northern gates. Needless to say, there was no sign of Towne, who must have long disappeared into the crowd.

The obvious thing for Towne to do was to go straight to the Dolphin, where he could retrieve his possessions and, presumably, the incriminating letter, before making a more permanent escape. If he hurried, he might just intercept him in time. He turned right and set off at a run down the street, past All Hallows Church and through the dark arch of the Bishop's Gate, causing heads to turn as he wove his way in and out of the traffic.

He slowed and caught his breath as he approached the long, low structure that was the Dolphin Inn, and ducked his head walking through the low doorway into the big taproom. It was almost deserted, except for a small bony-faced man who stood behind his counter listlessly cleaning a pewter ale tankard. 'Can I help you, sir?'

'You're the innkeeper here?' Will dredged a name up from his memory. 'Mister Soames?'

'Aye, that's me. Who wants to know?'

'My name is Shakespeare. I am looking for a man who is lodging here—a dark fellow with black hair that is starting to thin on top, name of John Towne.'

'Aye, we have a guest who might fit that description. But his name isn't Towne.' The man's eyes narrowed in suspicion. 'What business might you have with him?'

'Private business,' Will said, curtly. 'Business involving Edward Ball.'

Producing a royal warrant signed by the Queen herself would not have been as effective as his use of Cutting Ball's name, at which the man flinched a little and then turned nauseatingly obsequious. 'I am sorry sir, I meant no offence. Any friend of Mister Ball is most welcome at my establishment, and if I can be of any assistance…'

'You could start by answering my question. Have you seen Mister Towne?'

'Yes. Well. He calls himself John Winter, and he came in not half an hour ago, all in a lather, and went up to his room. Came back down ten minutes later with a bag slung over his shoulder, settled up his tally with good coin, and left.'

'How long ago was this?'

'Not fifteen minutes, sir.'

Damn. It looked as though his quarry had slipped the net. He could be anywhere in London or he might even have acquired a horse and headed away from the city. 'Did he take a horse?'

'Don't think so, sir. He went out the front, the way you came in. If he was after a horse, he would have gone out the back and into the yard, where the post horses and rented nags are kept.'

'That is unfortunate, most unfortunate.' Will shook his head. 'Take me up to his room.'

The barkeeper's face adopted a sly look. 'That would be most irregular, sir, even if ye were a servant of Her Majesty. We're a coaching house, and all sorts of people stay here, couriers and the like, and they rely upon our discretion.'

Will knew what the man was after. Opening the small purse hanging at his belt, he extracted sixpence and slid it across the counter. The man contemplated the coin for a second, allowed his brows to rise in a mockery of offended conscience, and then slid his grubby hand across the table to scoop it up and put it in his pocket. 'This way, sir, if you please.'

They climbed a flight of stairs to a broad balcony that overlooked the taproom and gave access to the rooms on the floor above. Three rooms along, the barkeeper pushed open the door and stood aside to let him in. It was a small space jammed beneath the sloping thatched roof of the inn, with one window that looked out onto the street below. Will was not at all surprised that the room was neat and tidy, the bed made, no clothes lying around, and the little writing table under the window bare of papers. Such tidiness seemed entirely in keeping with John Towne's fastidious character. The only evidence of disorder was an open clothes chest, from which Towne seemed to have extracted various items in considerable haste, leaving the remaining clothes in a crumpled pile at the bottom.

Will scratched his head in puzzlement. He had to assume that Towne had taken with him the letter that was originally intended for Lord Strange. He remembered something else that Ball had told him. 'Was there one of the ostlers with whom Towne was particularly friendly?'

Soames scratched his head, frowning in concentration. 'I don't rightly know, sir. There are three of 'em, and all three are rascals. But if I remember rightly, it was Wilfred who looked after his horse when he first arrived. He's down in the yard now, sir, if you want to speak with him.'

'Lead on, Mister Soames, lead on.'

Back down the stairs they went, and out into the yard, which was quiet at that time of day. At the back of the long, narrow space was a substantial-looking stables, in front of which three boys were lackadaisically playing at dice. When Soames and Shakespeare appeared, all three scrambled to their feet, looking guilty.

'Don't any of you lazybones have work to do?' Soames shouted his outrage. 'Get you back to it, or you'll feel the leather of my belt on your backsides. Not you, Wilfred. This gent wants to ask you some questions.'

Wilfred, a tall, gangling, spotty boy, slouched over as the other two retreated into the stable.

'Hello Wilfred,' Will said, keeping his voice friendly. 'I just want to ask you a few questions about a friend of mine, Mister, er, Winter. You know who I mean?'

'Aye. Weasel of a man, with fading hair on top.'

Will could not help smiling at the brevity of that description. 'That's the fellow. Now, when he first came here, a month or so ago, he asked you to keep an eye out for someone, didn't he?'

Wilfred looked at Soames, who nodded his permission. 'So he did, sir. Gave me sixpence for doing him the service, like.'

'And did this man turn up?'

'Yes. Never seen a man like him. A real longshanks, taller than me even, with a great beak of a nose. Talked like a foreigner. Frenchie, maybe?'

'Uh-huh. And when is the last time you saw Mister Winter?'

The boy's face became shifty. 'Maybe half an hour ago, sir.'

'Did he ask you to do anything for him? Leave you with a letter, perhaps?'

319

'No, he didn't.'

Will glanced at Soames, whose face was blank, and then turned a considering gaze back to the youth. He let the silence grow for a while, and sure enough, Wilfred began to fidget. 'You are lying to me, youngster. This is the Queen's business, and I don't need to tell you, do I, what the consequences will be for lying to one of her officers?' Will sensed the shock at that statement as it hit the innkeeper standing beside him, but he didn't move his eyes from the young ostler.

'He told me that it were a secret, that I wasn't to tell nobody about it,' Wilfred finally said, almost whining. 'I was to keep it safe and give it only to the foreigner when he came again.'

'And where is this letter now?'

The boy looked again at Soames, seeking his approval, which was given with a quick nod. He turned and went towards the stable door, the older men following behind. Inside, the other two youths, thoroughly chastened, were hard at work shovelling hay. Wilfred led them to one of the horse-stalls which was currently unoccupied, and then went to the back wall. There, hunching his body so that neither Will nor Soames could see, he fiddled with a brick, which came loose in a puff of dust. Setting the brick aside, he reached into the cavity behind and extracted a packet, which he handed to Will.

While the boy made a great show of putting the brick back in place (no doubt he kept a small hoard of boyish treasures there), Will inspected the thin leather wrapping that had been fashioned into a kind of wallet, closed with string. 'Did Mister Winter give you any message for the foreigner when he comes?'

'Only to say that the letter could not be delivered.'

'That's all?'

'Aye. Nothing else.'

Will fished in his wallet and found a shilling, which he flicked in the boy's direction. 'Thank you, Wilfred, you have been very helpful. I think I am done here, Mister Soames. The boy can go back to his duties.'

Back inside, Will watched the innkeeper's face as an internal war was being waged between curiosity, fear, and greed. 'I hope I have been of service, sir. And that you will, er, remind Mister Ball of my good offices?'

'That I will, Mister Soames. And you have done your country a great service this day.'

Will almost spoiled the effect of this lofty sentiment with a giggle as he walked purposefully towards the door, leaving poor Soames to fume at receiving no monetary reward for his cooperation, but no doubt also hoping that a good word in the unforgiving ear of Cutting Ball might make his burdens in the way of whatever blackmail he was paying a little lighter.

When he arrived back at Silver Street, Ned was sitting up in the bed, naked from the waist up, with a fine new linen bandage around his middle. Goodwife Higgins, his landlady, fussed around the boy as if he was royalty, plumping up pillows and insisting that he drink the warm milk she had placed on a little table next to the bed. Ned himself, looking a little pale, gave Will a sheepish grin as he entered; the landlady had been, from the day he arrived, yet another victim of Ned's youthful charm.

'Tut, goodwife, it's but a shallow cut,' Will said, winking at Ned. 'He'll live.'

'Shallow cuts have been known to fester, Master Shakespeare,' she replied severely, all matronly authority. 'Now don't you get him all excited. The doctor said he must have rest if the wound is to heal proper.'

'Don't worry, I'll not excite him in the least. Now, if you please…'

Taking the hint, she bustled her way to the door and left them alone.

'What happened?' Ned asked the instant the door clicked shut. 'Did you catch him?'

'I'm not supposed to excite you,' Will teased. Ned threw a pillow at him. 'All right, all right. No, he got clean away. He could be anywhere by now, though I will hazard that he has a bolthole somewhere in London. But I did manage to find this.'

When the string that closed the little leather wallet was untied, its contents proved to be just two pieces of paper. The first, a hasty scrawl in Towne's hand, simply read *I have been exposed and cannot deliver the letter. You are in great danger if you stay in London.* The other was a more substantial document, folded and sealed with a blob of red wax. There was no imprint of a signet or other identifying device, and the only superscription, in an unknown hand, addressed it to the attention of 'My Lord Strange'.

'Should we open it, do you think?' Ned asked.

That was the question Will had asked himself all the way home from the Dolphin. Of course, he was as curious as Ned to discover the contents of this mysterious missive. But there were other considerations. Will's distaste for this whole intrigue had never left him, and he was tempted to simply go to Seething Lane and drop the whole problem back into the capable hands of Thomas Phelippes. After all, he had done everything asked of him so far. On the other hand, Lord Strange had been kind to him, and as the patron of his acting company, was in any case his nominal master. Somehow, he felt a sense of duty towards this somewhat ambivalent young lord.

Which left the question of whether or not to open the letter. At Seething Lane he had learned enough of the art of prising open sealed letters and re-sealing them that he was sure he could do so without leaving a trace. And opening it would tell him what he had to deal with. But ignorance could also be useful.

'No,' he finally said, making his mind up. 'We will leave it sealed. What is the hour?'

'About two,' Ned guessed, puzzled at the question.

Will got to his feet. 'I am going to Derby House. His Lordship should have returned from the north by now.'

'Then I'm coming with you.' Throwing the coverlet back, Ned swung his legs onto the floor and was rewarded with a wave of dizziness. 'Well, perhaps not...'

Will grinned at him. 'You are an idiot. Stay here and rest, like the doctor and Goodwife Higgins told you to. I will be back before it is dark.'

'And if you're not?'

That made Will pause. If Lord Strange really was a traitor, as Phelippes and Beale believed, and if the letter contained information that could betray him, then he might be inclined to do something violent. Some instinct told him that was unlikely, but perhaps taking some precautions was in order. He crossed to the desk, rummaged around for a clean piece of paper, and rapidly scribbled a note.

'If I am not back by the morning, go to Seething Lane—you know where Walsingham's house is?—and give this to a man named Thomas Phelippes. Tell him everything you know. He will know what to do.'

He picked up his hat and swung a cloak over his shoulders and left, leaving an uncertain Ned behind him.

Twenty minutes later, he stood on the familiar damp steps of Paul's Wharf and hailed a boat to take him upriver to Whitehall. Fortunately, boats were plentiful and the competition for custom fierce, so he was able to secure a passage with only a few moments of desultory dickering over the price. The tide was making, and it was a fast trip upriver. In less than half an hour he was disembarking and, having paid the ferryman, he rang the little bell to seek admittance.

The doorman who appeared after a short wait knew him well enough to admit him without fuss.

'Is His Lordship here, Dawkins?'

'He is, Mister Shakespeare, arrived this morning. Shall I tell him you are here?'

'Please. And can you also say that I must speak with him privily on a matter of some urgency?'

That caused an eyebrow to be raised, but like all the servants at Derby House, he was well-trained and discreet. Leaving Will in the library, he went off to find Lord Strange and deliver the message. Ordinarily, Will would have delighted in being left alone among this treasure-trove of books, but he was too tense to read, and instead just stood at the windows, moodily watching the river traffic making its way up and down the Thames.

Sitting in the stern of the little boat, trying to keep himself dry, half a dozen times he had considered turning round and abandoning this foolish undertaking. He was, he knew, taking a considerable risk. Ned was right—it was entirely possible that Strange was deeply involved in some conspiracy against the realm, in which case giving him the letter, without knowing its contents, could provoke all sorts of unexpected reactions. But he was gambling that the reverse was true, that Lord Strange was as loyal as he was himself. He could not work out what proofs had led him to that belief. If anything, it was the lack of evidence to the contrary that was convincing.

Somewhere a bell began tolling, dragging Will from his thoughts, profitless as they were. He frowned. It was late afternoon, far too early for any of the regular church services. Then it was joined by another, and another, a monotonous slow bong-bong-bong, unlike the usual cheerful peal. Odd. Something momentous must have happened, and his mind began wandering off into the realms of speculation—could the Queen have died? No, there had been no reports that she was in anything other than good health.

The door clicked open behind him, banishing all such thought, and he turned to see Lord Strange enter, the man Dawkins behind him. 'Shakespeare? This is unexpected. I had not thought to see you until the morrow.'

'Aye, my lord, and I shall be here again in the morning with the rest of the company, ready to prepare the Great Hall for our performance. But there was another matter upon which I need to get Your Lordship's advice, a privy question.'

Strange's left eyebrow went up to meet the mole on his forehead. 'Really? A matter that could not have waited until the morning?'

'Yes, my lord. A private matter.' He glanced at Dawkins, hovering in the doorway.

'Thank you, Dawkins. That will be all. I will call if I need you. And no loitering outside the door, d'ye hear?'

With a bow and a look of pained forbearance, the footman left, closing the door behind him.

Lord Strange's smile was confiding. 'I always have to give them a warning. They can't help themselves. Now, what is so damned urgent?'

Having got to this point, Will didn't quite know how to proceed. Then, after a moment's hesitation, he extracted the letter from his doublet and simply handed it to his patron.

'What is this?' Lord Strange turned the packet over and over, inspected the superscript and seal, and looked up at Will. 'A letter, obviously. But who is it from? And why are you delivering it?'

'I found it, my lord, among the possessions of one of our actors, a man named John Towne.'

'Towne? Ah, yes, the fellow from Mawdesley.'

'The very one. What you may not know is that a year ago John Towne killed one of the leading players in the Queen's company, William Knell, in the town of Thame, where we were performing at the time. The coroner eventually acquitted him with a finding of self-defence, but I recently came across evidence that the killing was in fact a deliberate act of murder. Confronted with this information, Towne fled. Searching his lodgings, I found this packet addressed to Your Lordship, and I thought it best to bring it to you immediately.'

'This could have waited until the morning, surely?'

'Perhaps it could have, my lord,' Will acknowledged. 'But something, some instinct, made me think that you should see it right away.'

'Hmmm.' He inspected the seal again. 'And you do not know what it contains?'

'No, my lord,' Will said, glad to be telling nothing less than the truth. 'I have delivered the packet into your hands as I found it.'

With a nod, Lord Strange picked up a knife from the table and slid it under the wax. Unfolding the paper he began to read, his lips moving silently as he did so, a frown of concentration on his face. Reaching the end of the first page, he muttered, 'Tut! All this nonsense again,' dropped it disdainfully onto the table, and began reading the second page. After a muttered sentence or two all the colour seemed to drain from his face, and he looked up at Will, who tried to read the expressions that chased one another across his visage. Fear, certainly, but rapidly superseded by anger. Shaking his head, he finished reading and then glanced at the third page, which seemed to contain nothing but a list of half a dozen words.

Strange tossed both onto the table with a gesture of disgust. 'Damn them. Damn them to hell. Will they never stop trying to drag me into their plots?'

'My lord?'

For answer, Lord Strange gestured at the table. 'Read it for yourself. It is treason, and it could send me to the scaffold. But I want you to be my witness that I will have nothing to do with it.'

Will picked up the papers and peered at the neat, closely written lines of script.

> *My Lord,*
>
> *You do know, as all men do who can remember or know by report the history of the last fifty years, the state of this realm of England, in which our Church is overthrown, our country at extreme risk of perishing, and our souls in daily dread of damnation. This state has proceeded not from the disorder of the kingdom's subjects, but began wholly in effect by your ancestor, King Henry Eight, and afterwards has been pursued by our princes' pretend laws, to which our nobility, priests and people have been drawn by force and fear rather than by their own consent. Though the case has long seemed desperate and with no hope of repair, God himself, apprehending our miseries, has so moved His Holiness Pope Sixtus V, his chiefest magistrate on earth, to give us at this time both better means, more hope and readier help than we could ever have deserved or desired.*

For he has inducted the most zealous and mightiest princes in Christendom to help take the whole care of our case into their hands and especially has entrusted Phillip, the high and mighty Catholic king of Spain, to take upon him this sacred and glorious enterprise. For which cause his majesty has commanded sufficient royal forces by both land and sea to be gathered and conducted to our country.

His Holiness having renewed and revived the sentence of Pius V against the pretender-queen Elizabeth, has discharged all men from all other obedience and fidelity towards her, and commands that at the arrival of His Catholic Majesty's forces, be ready to join the said army with all the powers and aid they can make, and to help towards restoring the Catholic faith and deposing the usurper.

That was the end of the first page, and it was dangerous enough. Only a few months ago, the Privy Council had proclaimed that the circulation or publishing of sentiments like this call to overthrow the Queen in concert with the expected landing of the Spanish armies on English soil to be treason. Conscious of the gaze of his patron's pale blue eyes in their pouchy sockets, eyes that he had always thought of as being those of a dreamer, but which now seemed menacing and hard, he picked up the second page.

My good lord, you must know that when the usurper is defeated and chased from the throne of this kingdom, that the realm shall yet be in want of a king. You yourself do descend from the blood of King Henry VII, and by the terms of the Act of Succession, you have a right to succeed as our lawful monarch.

328

Know you that when the blessed day of our liberation from tyranny should come, we whose signs are appended will stand by you with all our powers to enforce your right, and by our might place you upon the throne of England. Everything is in readiness. Powder, shot, halberds and bucklers have been gathered, and armies can shortly be mustered upon the instant of the arrival of the forces at the command of the king of Spain and his generals. All that is lacking is your consent to our plea that you should take your place in leading the realm to its emancipation from the rule of the Jezebel-queen.

Our servant who has been entrusted with ensuring that this our entreaty is delivered safely into your hands can be relied upon to furnish further explanation of our identities, motives, words and deeds, and to convey to us your reply, which we daily pray will be favourable to the cause.

The third and last page was odd, for it contained nothing except a dozen names, which an ever-thrifty corner of Will's mind saw as a shocking waste of expensive paper. But they were not ordinary English names. Rather, they were names that came from Homer: Aeneas, Orontes, Achilles, Priam, and so on. He supposed that they were code names.

'What trouble have you brought into my house, Shakespeare?' The anger in Lord Strange's voice was palpable.

'I swear to you, my lord, that I knew nothing of the contents of this letter before you opened it,' Will said earnestly. 'As I said, I found it among Towne's possessions, and thought it best to bring it to you immediately.'

Strange considered him, one hand going to the small, pointed beard that decorated his chin. 'And this fellow, Towne. What else do you know of him?'

'Not a great deal. He is a close-mouthed man, prickly and difficult to get to know at the best of times. But he is a good actor and I was happy to have him in the company until I found out the truth about Thame.'

'Which is that he is a murderer, you say?'

'Yes, my lord. It was a swordfight, in which he managed to feign self-defence. The coroner let him off, but I found proof that he had committed the deed with purpose. It was a quarrel over a woman, apparently.' No need to be more specific; Lord Strange did not seem to be particularly interested in the sordid details anyway, dismissing them with a wave.

'It seems he was rather more than a mere murderer. You have brought a spy and a traitor into my household.'

There was nothing Will could say to that. All he could so was endure Lord Strange's hard, accusing stare for a few seconds that seemed to last for an eternity before he finally detected a softening in the man's eyes. 'Aye, well. I don't suppose you did it with intent.' The sigh that followed contained elements of both frustration and anger. 'As for this plot—for that is what it is—I know not what to think.'

'Who do you think is behind it, my lord?'

Lord Strange blinked at him. 'That I do not know. But I do know to whom these code names refer. They are all friends of mine, gentlemen in Lancashire and elsewhere. The names are codes that we use privately when we want to communicate without identifying ourselves to those prying hands that open letters and re-seal them while they are making their way to their destination.'

'So these are northern lords? And Catholics, presumably.'

'Some are of the old faith, some not. But look you, there is something odd—the list of names is separate from the letter, and it is written in a different hand.'

Will picked up the list and looked again. Lord Strange was right, the list was in a scrawled, looping script, quite different from the neat secretary hand of the other. 'So it could have been appended separately? Is that what you are thinking, my lord?'

'It is possible. But it could also be a trap. Burghley or Walsingham, even Leicester. Any of them could have intercepted the letter and added the names to see if they could be flushed out, presumably after I have been arrested and sent to the Tower. It is even possible that the whole thing is a fake, concocted to create an excuse to act against them.'

Will opened his mouth and then closed it again, frowning. Of course that was exactly the kind of ploy that Walsingham would have dreamed up. Or Phelippes, or Beale. Though why they should have wanted to do so was a mystery. And surely they would have let him in on such a plan, if it really existed.

Lord Strange watched the expression on his face, which he misinterpreted. 'You are surprised that Her Majesty's counsellors would contemplate such a low trick?'

'Sadly, my lord, I am less and less surprised at anything I hear about the court and its machinations,' he replied, trying to disguise his real thoughts. 'But putting that possibility to one side, what do you think these northern gentlemen hoped to achieve by drawing you into their plot? They must know that you would never give it countenance.'

'Perhaps they do not. What do you know about Lancashire, Shakespeare?'

'Not a great deal, my lord, I must confess.'

'The old faith has never really surrendered there—and elsewhere in the north, for that matter; the further you go from London, the less secure the reformed church seems—and to rule effectively in the county it has always been politic to, shall we say, *seem* to be tolerant of the Catholics who still practice their religion behind the walls of their houses and manors.'

A tolerance not extended where there is the possibility of profit, Will thought but did not say, thinking of John Towne's tale of family woe. Instead, he just nodded to signify that he was following Lord Strange's train of thought.

'My father is laxer than I would be, had I the power in these matters, but out of filial duty, I must seem to go along with him. And so it may be that these gentlemen believe that I, too, incline to the old faith, though I have given them no overt sign to that effect.'

'Might this then be an attempt to draw you out? To discover the cast of your mind?'

'Perhaps.' He slammed a fist down onto then table in a sudden burst of fury. 'God, how I curse the trickle of royal blood that flows through my veins, that convinces every man that I must be mad with ambition to sit upon the throne. In truth, I have no interest in politics, none.' He shook his head in frustration. 'Were I not heir to Derby, I would cheerfully spend my days in happier pursuits—reading, writing poetry, fostering singers and musicians and painters. But like it or not I am heir to one of the greatest powers in the kingdom, and so must be seen at court, and do my duty to the earldom and the Queen.'

'Which duty must surely compel you to take these papers to Her Majesty and lay the conspiracy before her so that she and her ministers can take action.' Will knew he was being presumptuous in offering such blunt advice, and he awaited an explosive response. Instead, he got another of those slightly cynical, lopsided smiles.

'The very ministers who may well be trying to trap me? No.' His eyes went back to the list and ran down the code names. 'If these men are real rebels, they are fools to think that all they have to do is raise the flag of rebellion and the sweaty masses will rally to them. In truth, they are all lesser men, knights and squires, who do not have enough of a following to do any real damage, though it is true that the addition of the Stanley name might change that equation.' Another shake of the head, and a small sigh. 'Misguided idiots. But they are also my friends, and I'll not betray them.'

It was Will's turn to feel frustrated. Did he not realise that it was this very ambivalence, even though it was motivated by considerations of personal honour, that made him untrustworthy in the eyes of the Walsinghams and Burghleys of this world? At the same time, he felt a little sorry for the man. Had he been born to some other mother he would simply have been Ferdinando Stanley, heir to the important but otherwise unthreatening Earldom of Derby. But that drop of royal blood made him a target for other men's ambitions and meant that he must always be wary of every shadow, sifting every nuance of meaning in the words spoken at court, and living in cautious fear of unseen manipulators who might destroy him at any moment. It could not be a comfortable life, despite its luxuries and riches.

In the few seconds that Will's mind had been thus detained the subject of his contemplation had picked up the letter again and scanned it through once more. Then, to Will's gasping surprise, he methodically tore each page into small squares and placed them on a silver platter. Picking up a tinder-box, he struck a spark and in a few seconds, the whole lot was consumed and reduced to ashes.

'There might be copies, my lord,' Will protested weakly.

'So there might. I will take that risk. And you will say nothing of this, you understand?'

'Of course not, my lord.' Will said, though in his sinking heart he knew he would shortly be breaking that promise. 'But I am not the only one who knows that these papers exist... existed. John Towne...'

'He fled when confronted with this other matter of murder, you said?'

Will nodded. 'He stabbed one of the other actors—Ned Bentley, you will recall him as our boy player, though he is hardly a boy any longer—and got away while I was tending his wound. I do not know where he is now; hiding out somewhere in London, I should think. He wasn't at his lodgings when I went looking for him there.'

'Then he must be found.' The statement was flat, and Lord Strange was looking at him with the clear implication that doing so was Will's responsibility.

'I might be able to arrange that,' he said, cautiously. 'There are certain people that I have come to know who are well skilled in searching London's darker streets and alleys.'

'And when they find him?'

Will drew his finger across his throat, surprising himself with a gesture that seemed at once absurdly melodramatic and at the same time blood-curdling. Lord Strange, not in any way discomfited, signified his agreement with a curt nod. 'If these... contacts... of yours require compensation, you may apply to me. Discreetly, mind. What *is* that infernal noise?'

The tolling of bells that he had heard earlier had been steadily increasing in volume while he and Lord Strange were talking, though neither had noticed, so intent were they on the subject at hand. On cue, there came a hasty and loud knocking at the door, and without a pause to wait for permission it swung open to admit a breathless David Barnes. 'Forgive my intrusion, my lord, but I have portentous news. The Spanish fleet is in the Channel! More than a hundred ships, they say, sighted off the Lizard yesterday!'

A muscle twitched in Lord Strange's cheek, but otherwise, he showed not the slightest hint of any other emotion, absently picking up the hat which he had discarded earlier and jamming it on his head. 'Calm yourself, Davey. I can hear the bells for myself, but where did you get this report from?'

'It is being cried up and down King Street, my lord. The Privy Council has ordered out the militia, though none seems to know where and how they are to be mustered.'

'And where is the Queen at present?'

'I believe she is at Richmond, my lord.'

'Then I shall go there immediately. Get Tempest saddled, and I'll take Oakes and Moreland with me. They are both on duty today, so they shouldn't be too hard to find. Probably in the kitchens, scrounging food.'

Barnes bowed once more and made his departure.

'God, it seems, is a better dramatist than you or Marlowe,' Lord Strange said, with a smile of genuine humour. 'Perfect timing, wouldn't you say?'

'Indeed, my lord. Exquisite.'

'I expect that I will be busy over the next few days since in my father's absence I will likely have to go north to muster the Lancashire levies. So I shall leave you to deal with this matter of Towne. Oh, and it goes without saying that the performance of your play tomorrow is cancelled.'

'Of course, my lord. I had assumed as much.'

With a final nod, Lord Strange went out through the still-open door, leaving a bemused Will Shakespeare scratching his chin and with much to ponder.

Chapter 24

'That's all the names?' Thomas Phelippes stood behind Will, peering over his shoulder through the thick eyeglasses he used whenever he had to read.

'Of course.' Will allowed himself a smug smirk that he thought was entirely justified. He had, after all, just reproduced both letter and list from memory, and with barely a moment's hesitation.

Taking his seat on the other side of the small desk in the cramped room at Seething Lane that Sir Francis allowed for his chief cryptographer's sole use, Phelippes read the two papers through once more, one finger reflexively tapping the table in concentration.

'What do you think, Tom?' Marlowe, turning away from the small window that admitted a little light and air, along with the noise of the street below, was as impatient as ever. 'Is it a real conspiracy, do you think?'

That was the question that Will and Kit had turned over half a dozen times that morning after Will had dragged his friend out of bed at first light to tell him the story. A sleep-dazed Marlowe had been grumpy at first, but once he had grasped the import of Will's tale, his mind had instantly engaged with the problem. Ever the suspicious conspirator, Marlowe argued that Lord Strange could have been lying and that the list of plotters was, far from being minor gentry, a list of important northern lords who really could raise the country.

'And if that is so,' he had said, excited at the implications of his theory, 'he must be stopped from going back to Lancashire where he can lead them into rebellion!'

Will, on the other hand, was not so sure. The man's anger when he had first read the letter had not seemed to be counterfeit, and he could understand his desire

336

to protect his foolish friends if they were, as he averred, minor lordlings of no real consequence. And there was the matter of the letter and list being in two separate hands, which left open the possibility that it was some kind of trap, maybe even one set by Walsingham or Burghley.

They had argued the point half a dozen times over breakfast, and in the end, Kit had thrown his hands in the air and insisted that they go to Seething Lane and lay the whole story before Walsingham, Phelippes or Beale, whoever happened to be there. Unsurprisingly, the secretary was at Richmond with the rest of the Privy Council, anxiously awaiting further news of the great Spanish Armada, and the whereabouts of Beale was unknown.

But Tom Phelippes had been there. If he had been surprised at the unexpected appearance of his two part-time intelligencers at the door, he did not show it, hustling them upstairs to his little room without any further fuss. There, having heard out Will's story, he had asked him if he could reproduce the letters and the list of names. With more than a twinge of guilt at so promptly betraying the confidence of his patron, Will had called on his powerful memory and quickly written out every word.

'Without knowing the identities that lie behind these code names, it is impossible to know for certain,' Phelippes said, his native caution asserting itself. 'It might be a real plot to strike at the right moment, or on the other hand, it could as easily be a trap, as you suggested, Will.'

'Lord Strange feared as much. He even thought that the plot might have originated from here.'

Phelippes grunted his dismissal of that idea. 'Do you really think we would have laid out such an elaborate plan without telling you? That would have been a recipe for disaster.'

337

'Lord Burghley, then? Or Leicester?' Both were known to run spy networks of their own, though neither was as well-organised as the operation run from Seething Lane.

'It could be so, but I doubt it.' Phelippes shrugged. 'But since this man Foy is a Jesuit priest, it is possible that it is a plot engineered by the Spanish.'

Will shook his head. He had given that question quite a lot of thought. 'No. The timing argues against that. If this is an attempt to find out whether Lord Strange is willing to lead a rebellion in concert with an invasion, why leave it until the very moment that the Armada has sailed? Surely the Spanish would have wanted to know where he stood long before this?'

'True enough. Which brings us back to the only other possibility, which is that this is a real plot to incite a rebellion in the north, clumsily conceived to be sure, and launched by a person or persons who are not in the confidence of the king of Spain, and therefore unaware of his precise invasion plans.'

'Rheims, perhaps?' Marlowe put in. 'A plot from the brain of their new-appointed cardinal?'

'William Allen, the head of the English College at Rheims, where they have been training priests for years to come into England and incite the local Catholics to mischief,' Phelippes said, for Will's benefit. 'Pope Sixtus elevated him to the College of Cardinals last year.'

'Rheims is where John Towne studied for a while,' Will said thoughtfully. 'And it is where he met Foy for the first time.'

'Did he indeed? Then I think it likely that this plot was conceived in the mind of Cardinal Allen and designed to be executed in broad conjunction with the Spanish invasion, but without the specific knowledge of the Spanish themselves.'

Marlowe was agitated. 'That may be so, Tom, but since we don't know the identity of the plotters, surely we must assume that it is a real threat and that Lord Strange is involved? And—'

He was stopped by Phelippes' raised hand. 'Be still, Kit, lest you burst a blood vessel. You are right, of course, but I see no way of finding out who they are, short of interrogating Lord Strange himself.'

'Or we could try and catch the man Foy?' Will said tentatively. 'Towne left a verbal message at the Dolphin to warn him off before he disappeared, but a few coins will stop that caper. The owner of the tavern could be induced to alert us if he turns up.'

'And then we arrest him and try to find out what he knows. Though if he's a Jesuit, breaking him will be difficult. But it is worth a try.' Phelippes rapped his knuckles on the table and got to his feet, all decision. 'At the very least, it would seem prudent to prevent Lord Strange from leaving the capital to go north, something that only Sir Francis can effect. I shall go to Richmond now and try to get some private time so that I can lay all before him.' He clapped a hand on Will's shoulder. 'You've done well, my friend, even if we have not yet unravelled all of the skeins of this little plot.'

***

Over the next few days, the atmosphere in London resembled that of a man in the grip of fever, restlessly tossing and turning between bouts of delirium brought on by every piece of news that came in from the south coast or arrived aboard the skiffs and wherries coming upriver from where an army was slowly being concentrated at Tilbury.

The Spanish fleet, now said to be more than a hundred and fifty ships, had been engaged off Plymouth, and one of their number had been blown up. The next day, both fleets were becalmed in Lyme Bay. The day after that, it was said that the Spanish were planning to land at the Isle of Wight, a possibility that was scotched by fickle winds that blew the invaders past the entrance to the Solent and across to the far side of the Channel. Finally, a week after it had first been sighted off the Lizard, the news came that the Armada had dropped anchor off Calais Roads, at a kind of maritime stalemate with the English tormentors who had harried them all the way.

These bare facts, carried through the city by all the mysterious ways that news makes its way into the ears of the population, came accompanied by more lurid rumours. The Spanish were, it was said, bringing a shipload of halters with which they intended to hang all Protestant Englishmen, and another with scourges that would be used to flog their wives and daughters. Children were to be branded on the forehead so that they would always be known as the offspring of heretics. Another rumour said simply that the Spanish king had ordered his armies to slaughter every man, woman and child in the country over seven years of age.

Most of these stories were probably nonsense, or so Will thought, but they served to keep the people of London in a state of perpetual ferment, suspicious of all foreigners (who had to be forbidden the streets for their safety), by turns fearful and defiant.

In such an atmosphere, trying to track down the whereabouts of John Towne proved difficult. Ball had accepted the commission to try and find him with his usual disturbing smile, palm out in expectation of payment, though that was overtaken by a look of genuine astonishment when Will dropped a surprisingly weighty purse into his hand.

'Well, then. Someone badly wants to find this man Towne,' he said, 'and unless your fortunes have changed, Mister Shakespeare, I'd be guessing it is not you.'

'Never mind who is paying. Can you do it?'

'I can try, but I have never seen London so disturbed, and that will make it more difficult.'

'How so?' Will was genuinely puzzled.

'Well, see, the problem will be one of too many leads, not too few. Every foreigner, every man and woman not known to their neighbours, all of them are suspected of ill-doing at a time like this. So I make no doubt that there will be many sightings of your man John Towne, but few of them will be true. No amount of money will shorten the time to sort truth from malicious fiction.'

Will shrugged. 'Your problem, not mine. There is something else I want you to do. There is a particular foreigner, a tall man with a hooked nose, who I want you to intercept and apprehend if he arrives at the Dolphin looking for Towne. You can rough him up if you have to, but we need him alive and able to talk.'

'A foreigner? If he talks foreign, I would be surprised if he isn't picked up by the town watch and slung into the nearest gaol long before he gets anywhere near the Dolphin. But I'll do as you ask.'

That conversation had taken place on Monday, the day after he and Kit had met with Phelippes, but a week later even Ball's many and diverse seekers and searchers of information had been unable to find any trace of John Towne, and Will thought he had probably eluded their grasp. Likewise, there had been no word from the Dolphin reporting the appearance of the foreigner, Foy. From Seething Lane, too, there had been silence, which offended Kit's sense of self-importance, but which Will took phlegmatically.

'No doubt Secretary Walsingham is spending every minute of his time at Richmond with the rest of the Privy Council and has little to spare to keep a couple of lowly intelligencers informed of his every action,' he counselled after watching Kit march back and forth a dozen times across the width of his little chamber. 'And if you don't stop that pacing, you'll wear a hole through the floor

341

and find yourself sitting in Simon the Tailor's lap, with his pins sticking in your arse.'

That image at least had brought a smile back to Kit's cheeks. 'Oh, to hell with it. Let's go and find a drink.'

Which they did, at the Mermaid Tavern. There, the fraternity of actors, writers and poets, just like the rest of London's population, found some solace from uncertainty in customary habits and familiar places. The inn was packed, and they made slow progress through the crush towards the corner where the stentorian roar of Rob Greene's voice carried above the general hubbub, stopping along the way to give and receive shouted greetings with friends and acquaintances.

'Rob is putting on a one-man play for us,' Dick Burbage said when they finally emerged from the crush to the circle standing in thrall to the big man, who stood on a table declaiming for all he was worth. 'He's being the king of Spain at the moment, I think.'

Greene's act consisted of a series of impersonations of various great personages, and he was indeed pretending to be the Spanish monarch, issuing orders to his admiral in a loudly effeminate, outrageously lisping voice. 'Good my Admiral, I wish you to thail with my great fleet, and thmite thothe Englith dogth. What'th that? You thuffer from the thea thickneth? Why did you not thay tho before? I shall thend you ten more priesth, to pray for your good health.'

'Apparently, the Spanish Admiral, a fellow named Medina-Sidonia or some such, has a horror of the sea and suffers badly from sea sickness, and the king of Spain has a most atrocious lisp,' Burbage said through the side of his mouth, barely audible against the sound of laughter and applause. 'Though where Rob got that information from, I have no idea. He is rather entertaining, though, don't you think?'

So he was, in a crude kind of way, and Will joined in the general merriment as Greene worked his way through a mincing Medina-Sidonia, a pompous Francis Drake, a dithering Admiral Lord Howard, and a panicked Lord Burghley running round in circles, squawking orders at an imaginary Privy Council. This last impersonation skated on thin ice, something that Greene himself seemed to apprehend as he abruptly brought the show to an end, accepting more applause with a sweeping, theatrical bow, leaping to the floor and demanding more ale— of which it was evident he had already had a surfeit—as his reward. Will obliged by plucking Greene's sleeve and gesturing him towards an unoccupied standing table in the corner of the room, from which refuge he shouted an order for a jug of ale and three tankards.

'You will talk your head into a noose one day, Rob.' Kit giggled.

'Nay, I am too nimble for your master's plodding watchers,' Greene replied, his feet doing a little jig in demonstration of his supposed agility. 'Most haven't the wit to hear what I say aright. And *you* aren't going to turn me in, are you?'

'God, no, not with the company you keep. I'd be dead in a week, probably, if Cutting Ball thought he was going to lose his chief source of gambling winnings.'

Greene made a face. 'True enough. Do you think he cheats?' The question was asked entirely in jest.

'As often as the sun rises in the east, Rob,' Will said. 'Speaking of Ball, have you seen or heard aught of him lately?'

'This very morning.' Greene's expression became impish. 'He bade me give you a message, should I see you today. Something about your fowl being nicely trussed up in the basement.'

The look exchanged between Kit and Will gave Greene cause to hoot. 'I knew it! You are up to something with Cuts, aren't you? Are you going to let your old friend Robert Greene into the secret?'

'Would it then be a secret? Nay, Rob, do not take me amiss, but this mystery must remain close-kept.'

'Walsingham's business, then.' Greene tapped his nose. 'I shall ask no more, having no desire to find myself on the wrong end of that gentleman's ungentlemanly questioning.'

'I thought you would see things my way.' Kit was wry. 'But your message means we must away, and soon, for I see Watson and Peele have spotted you, and once they start talking there will be no escape for hours.'

Sure enough, the pair of poets had just appeared at the door and peered around, surveying for friends, Peele looking as tousle-haired and scruffy as ever in stained woollen doublet and patched hose, while Watson, as if to provide a visual contrast, was neat and fashionably dressed in a blue suit, the breeches slashed to reveal the black satin beneath, and a flat hat sporting a spectacularly long white feather.

Detaching themselves from Greene, they made their way across the room, trying to avoid being detained by any more of their acquaintances. In this they were not entirely successful—Gus Phillips grabbed Will's arm and dragged him into a morose circle of drinkers, the actors of the seemingly stillborn company of Lord Strange.

'Have you heard, Will? All of the theatres, the bull court, the bear-baiting, and the gambling houses have all been ordered to close until such time as the Queen's Majesty should decide otherwise.'

Will hadn't heard that piece of news, though it explained why the Mermaid was so busy. 'Nay, but we can hardly be surprised. With the country seeming likely to be invaded at any moment, the last thing the Privy Council would want is any public gatherings where apprentices and the like might get out of control and riot.'

'What about private performances, like our *Arden*?' Dick Cowley asked after everyone had finished muttering their outrage at this state of affairs. 'Are they banned too? Have you had any word from Lord Strange?'

Will was getting irritated. 'No, I have not. I should imagine His Lordship is busy for the moment. Too busy to be concerned with mere players, don't you think?' He sighed. 'Look, I promise that the instant I know anything from His Lordship, I shall come, hot-foot and sweaty, to tell you. Now, I fear that we must leave you.'

He was still shaking his head when they got out into the street. 'Have they noticed, do you think, that England is at war?'

'Don't be too hard on them.' Kit was serene. 'They are only paid when they are performing, so it is only natural for them to be concerned about where their next shilling is coming from.'

'Aye, well I know it, for I am in the same barge as they. But there is little any of us can do about it except hope that our sailors defeat this armada and stop Parma from crossing the channel.' He shrugged, dismissing the subject. 'Shall we go? We will be at the door of the Dolphin within a quarter-hour if we hurry.'

To his surprise, Kit shook his head. 'Think, Will. If Ball's men have this man Foy under lock and key, there is no hurry. And neither you nor I have any authority to arrest the man, let alone interrogate him.'

Will hadn't thought of that. 'What do you suggest we do, then?'

'Go to Seething Lane and get Phelippes to send some pursuivants to collect him?'

So they set off eastwards across the city, along Budge Row, past the drapers' shops and candle-makers booths that lined Candlewick Street, through Eastcheap with its rows of animal carcasses hanging from the hooks outside the butchers' shops, along Tower Street past the spire of St Dunstan's, to arrive at last at Seething Lane, almost in the shadow of the Tower itself. Sir Francis Walsingham's town house and headquarters were about halfway up, a fine two-storey brick residence in no way distinguishable from its prosperous and well-maintained neighbours in this quiet street.

Sir Francis himself was, naturally enough, not at home. Neither were Beale or Phelippes. The only officer of the secretary's household of any standing was Walter Williams, who greeted them with his usual pomposity in the big first-floor workroom. 'Thomas will be here within the hour,' he said. 'But if the matter is urgent, as your agitation seems to say that it is, no doubt I can do whatever is required.'

'Can you order out the pursuivants, Walter? No, I thought not.' Kit was dismissive. 'We will wait for Tom, I think.'

Ignoring Williams' discontent, they settled down to wait with as much composure as they could muster. Will fretted at every wasted minute, fearing that their prey might escape at the last moment. Kit, usually the more excitable of the two, was a picture of resigned calm.

'No help for it, Will.' From somewhere in his doublet he extracted a pack of playing cards. 'Let me show you some tricks with the cards. It will help pass the time. Come on, Walter, you too.'

By the time Phelippes arrived, more than an hour later, all three of them were still absorbed in Kit's demonstrations of the many and nefarious ways in which the cardsharps bilked their coneys. Where he had learned these practices, Will had no idea. Clearly, Robert Greene was not the only poet in London who spent time among the city's criminal underworld.

So fascinated were they that none of them realised Phelippes was there until he coughed to get their attention. Once they had laid out their story, Phelippes wasted no time. Scribbling a note of instruction, he sent a disgruntled Williams, who clearly wanted to be more than a mere messenger boy, off to deliver it to a couple of the pursuivants, the officers of the College of Heralds who were usually employed to find and arrest recusants and illegal Catholic priests.

'Where will they take him?' Will asked. 'To the Tower?'

Phelippes laughed. 'Your sense of drama is getting the better of you, Shakespeare. No, he won't be lodged anywhere so grand. We have a number of houses that we use to examine such people discreetly.'

Will didn't want to think too closely about what methods such an 'examination' might entail.

'Well, sirs, I think your part in this stratagem can now be concluded.' Phelippes was uncharacteristically formal. 'You have done well, and I shall of course commend you to Sir Francis.'

'That's it?' Kit gaped. 'We are dismissed?'

Phelippes looked at him coldly. 'Yes, Master Marlowe, you are, for now at least. No doubt if we need your services again, we will ask.' Then his features relaxed a little, losing their severity. 'Come on, Kit, you know how these things work. You have both done your part, but this is now a matter for the state to deal with. I am sure you would like to know what will happen next, but I cannot tell you.'

'That's all very well, Thomas,' Will said pugnaciously, 'but we are talking of the fate of my patron, and that of the company of players I have assembled.'

One blond eyebrow climbed up in the direction of the equally blond hair. 'And you think the fate of a company of players should weigh in the deliberations of the government of a country that is at war? Whose very existence is threatened?'

347

Will flushed at the rebuke, recognising that it was deserved. But it had the effect of causing Phelippes to relent a little. 'Obviously, Lord Strange's fate will depend somewhat upon what our mysterious Jesuit has to tell us. But Her Majesty has been advised that Lord Strange shouldn't return to Lancashire at this time, particularly since the Earl of Derby is like to be returning from Flanders with the other peace commissioners within days and can therefore take personal command of the Lancashire levies.'

Neither Will nor Kit had known that Lord Strange's father had been a member of the embassy that had been trying to negotiate peace with Parma, an embassy that had no doubt been terminated the moment the Armada's sails had appeared off the Lizard. 'He does not know he is under suspicion, of course, and I rely on you, Shakespeare, to keep it that way. If matters progress poorly for him, I am afraid he will find himself in the Tower, and you will be without a patron. But as I say, all depends upon this priest you have helped us catch.'

And with that Will had to be content as Phelippes ushered them out of the door and down into the street.

***

Three days later news came that caused the city to erupt into celebration. On Sunday, 7th August, the day after their meeting with Phelippes, the English sent fire-ships into the mass of Spanish ships lying hove-to in Calais Roads, causing mayhem, setting several of the enemy ships on fire, and causing the rest to cut their cables and flee before the wind. Then, the very next day, the pursuing English fought a series of running battles off the town of Gravelines that had done further damage to the great Armada and sent it scurrying before the wind into the North Sea, heading, so it was believed, towards Scotland.

'Does that mean it is all over?' Ned asked Will, as they made their way along a Cheapside that seemed to have turned itself into one long, heaving party. It was close to dusk, and the bonfires that the city authorities had ordered to be built at intervals along the street (and all over London) were about to be lit.

'Clearly, the Londoners think so,' Will replied, with a wave at the crowd gathered around the nearest bonfire. 'It depends, I suppose, on what the Duke of Parma does.'

Ned looked puzzled. 'Parma? But how can he cross if the Spanish fleet has gone north?'

Will thought about his only experience of naval warfare, that long-ago encounter with Barbary Pirates in the Mediterranean, when a shift of the wind had saved them from defeat. 'I am no mariner, but I do know that winds can change, and to all accounts, the Armada is still formidable, despite the damage it has sustained. And then Parma has ships of his own. If he is adroit enough, he might slip across the Channel while the bulk of our fleet is still in the North Sea, chasing after Medina-Sidonia.'

As he was talking, several pitch-soaked torches were hurled into the piled-up timber, where they lodged, smoking and spluttering for a few moments. Then licks of yellow flame probed and snaked until at last the wood caught and the fire spread, slowly at first, and then with a roar. An effigy of the king of Spain had been perched precariously on top, complete with exaggerated ruff, painted-on beard and leering mouth, and topped with a conical hat in the Spanish style. It caught alight to cheers and catcalls from the crowd and was rapidly consumed, disappearing into the darkening sky in the form of sparks and smoke.

Will glanced sideways at Ned and watched the boyish face, illuminated by the flames from the bonfire. With all the insouciant resilience of youth, he had got up off his sickbed within a few days, and he seemed entirely recovered from what could easily have been a devastating injury. There had been no sign of the wound turning putrid, thank God, and though he was still a little pale, he seemed none the worse for wear.

349

Ned, sensing Will's attention, returned his gaze. 'Kit has asked me to move in with him.'

'I'm surprised he took this long.' Will laughed. 'He's been besotted with you since he first met you.'

'Has he?' Ned seemed genuinely surprised. 'I had not noticed.'

'Oh, Kit can dissemble when he wants to, believe me. But I could tell.'

'You don't mind?'

'I told you once before that I don't own you, and I don't. Go with my blessing, if ever you needed it.' He frowned. 'But one word of advice—though Kit is my best friend, I have no illusions about him. There is a wildness, a refusal to follow convention, and a carelessness of others that makes him unpredictable and dangerous. Take care, Ned, that he does not do you injury along the way.'

Ned seemed to think about replying, and then just nodded, turning his attention instead to a passing street vendor, from whom he bought a bag of hazelnuts and a bottle of beer. The beer bottle emitted a low hiss when he pulled the stopper, and they companionably shared its contents while chewing on the nuts and watching capering children running around and around the bonfire under the eyes of their half-drunk parents.

After a while, they grew bored and decided to make their way back home. Though night had fallen, and it was well after the usual curfew hour, London's streets were still busy, and it took some time to navigate their way through the gangs of rowdy apprentices, always on the lookout for some jape at the expense of passers-by, revellers in various states of inebriation, and the occasional painted whore emboldened by the general air of dissolution out from their usual lairs in darkened laneways into the broad main thoroughfares. But at last, they arrived back in Silver Street, having avoided any mishaps.

'I take it, since you have said nothing, that there has been no sign of Mister Towne?' Ned asked as he pulled off his boots.

'No, nothing. I suspect he has escaped London by now.' Will's silence about developments after Ned had been stabbed had been deliberate, given the need for secrecy, but the necessity had pained him.

'Hmm.' Ned seemed to brood for a moment, and then his face brightened. 'A pity. I owe him at the very least a punch on the nose in return for the puncture he gave me.'

Will laughed at the pugnacious, fighting-cock look on the boy's face. 'I'd pay to see it, but I fear it is not to be.'

'More to the point, we will have to find a new Mosby when we get back to work.'

'You are a true man of the theatre, Ned, I can see that. The world might be burning, but your first concern is casting for a play.' He frowned. 'Cowley can probably do it, and I'll play Arden. Then all we need to do is find someone to be Franklin.'

'Me? I am well past the time to be starting to play men's roles, don't you think?'

'Alice is a big part, and you have mastered it,' Will said, thoughtfully. 'But let us make this your last woman, eh?'

351

Chapter 25

This time, the summons came in the form of a handwritten note, delivered by a servant in royal livery rather than verbally by the mouth of a surly lackey. But it was no less peremptory for all that.

> *You are requested and required to come to me at the Palace*
> *of Whitehall at your earliest convenience upon receipt of*
> *this communication, which will also serve as your entry*
> *pass through the palace gates.*

Both handwriting and the signature were familiar—Sir Francis Walsingham, master secretary to Her Majesty Queen Elizabeth. A note in Walsingham's own hand was not to be taken lightly, and its urgency was reinforced by the liveried youth, who made it clear he was going to wait on the doorstep until Will was ready, and that he would escort him to the palace.

The palace. That meant the royal court. Which meant he should take a little more care with his dress than usual. Poking around in his clothes chest, he extracted his best doublet—a plain burgundy affair with brass buttons that needed a bit of a polish, but which would do in a pinch. He possessed no ruff, settling instead for a translucent linen falling-band collar that sat neatly over the doublet. Pulling on his boots, he picked up his best hat—a slightly old-fashioned flat affair with a simple band devoid of jewels or decoration—jammed it on his head, and made his way back downstairs, bidding the boy lead on with an exaggeratedly courtly wave of his hand. To his surprise, he was conducted to Paul's Wharf, where a small barge was waiting. Neither boat nor the four oarsmen were decorated with any kind of livery, an indicator that discretion was required, though his escort's red tunic emblazoned with its Tudor double rose gave the game away to the half-dozen curious onlookers on the wharf.

Settling onto the padded bench beneath the little canopy at the barge's stern, Will was thoughtful as they pushed off and joined the passing stream of wherries, smacks, tiny rowing boats, heavily laden lighters and scuffed barges, and all the other polyglot fleet of vessels for whom the Thames was a highway.

In the ten days that had passed since that evening when the city had celebrated the success of the English fleet at Gravelines, news big and small had swirled like the eddies on this very river. The Armada had made it as far north as the Firth of Forth, dogged all the way by the English fleet, which had only turned back because victuals were running out, and Lord Howard was afraid to leave the Channel unguarded. It had taken him a week to beat his way back south against the prevailing winds, in atrocious weather, to arrive in Harwich on the 18th of August.

That same day, Will and Ned had watched with many others as the Queen's barge, escorted by its own fleet of protective vessels, made its stately way down the river towards Tilbury, where the English army had finally been amassed under the command of the Earl of Leicester. She returned two days later, and though no one knew whether the danger had finally passed, there was a sense of relief among the London crowds and the gossips in the nave of St Paul's, a feeling that even if Parma and his armies should manage to cross the Channel, the English were ready for them.

The next day, Ned had shifted his few possessions to Kit's more spacious rooms over in Bishopsgate Street, and though Will had been cheerful enough about it, he had to confess that he now felt a little lonely without the younger man's presence of an evening, even as he stretched in enjoyment of that rare luxury, sole possession of a bed. In the week since, he had seen them together, just once, across the crowded taproom of the Mermaid when he had poked his head in one afternoon. Kit had been holding court, as usual, his head wreathed in smoke from his pipe, and telling some story that provoked a gale of laughter from everyone around him, including Ned, who had been regarding Marlowe with a kind of adoration on his face that Will had never seen before. The punch of jealousy that felt in his gut was unexpected, and he had turned away and slipped back out into the street before either of them spotted him.

The recollection of that moment came to him as the barge slipped around the great bend in the river and the jumble of roofs that was his destination came into view. The bargemen skilfully manoeuvred their vessel towards the shore, and with a bump they arrived at the Whitehall Stairs. Conducted ashore by the liveried servant who had said not a word all the way downriver, he walked up the long shallow flight of steps to a gateway, where a guard looked briefly at Walsingham's note (could the man even read? Will doubted it, but the signature was enough) before waving them through.

Following his escort, he walked along a shadowed path between a series of substantial buildings, which the youth, now proudly in his element, identified as the Royal Chapel and the Great Hall. Beyond lay a broad courtyard with a range of low red brick buildings around three sides and a magnificent three-story white building enclosing the fourth, a building so splendid that it stopped Will in his tracks.

'The Banqueting Hall,' the young man said smugly, allowing Will a moment or two to gape before gesturing him onwards, across the courtyard and into the row of buildings that enclosed its western end. Once inside, Will lost any sense of direction as they climbed stairs, walked along corridors, passed through deserted antechambers, and finally arrived at a door, no different from its neighbours, upon which his guide gave two raps, listened for a moment, and then opened, gesturing Will inside.

His mind flashed back to that day, more than three years ago, when he had first encountered Sir Francis Walsingham. But this room was deserted, though the desk over next to the window was piled with papers patiently awaiting the return of the room's master.

'Master Secretary is on his way back from Tilbury, where he has been attending the Queen's Majesty,' the young servant said. 'He is expected within the half-hour.'

With that, the door clicked shut and he was left alone with his irritation. If Walsingham had known that he was not going to be at Whitehall before noon, why make his summons seem so urgent and immediate? Just one of the many ways in which powerful men played games with their underlings, he supposed. Still, it was a mark of trust that he had been left alone in what was obviously Sir Francis' workroom.

He wandered over to the window, which he was astonished to realise overlooked the river—he would have sworn they were on the other side of the palace—and resisted the impulse to look at the papers on the desk. They interested him very little anyway, for he had none of Marlowe's fascination for matters of state, or for that matter, for secrets.

Instead, his thoughts went back to Stratford, and his family. He had not been home in more than a year and he felt a sudden yearning to be free of this place, this great teeming antheap of humanity with its smoke and stink, its raucous noise and its perpetual sense that chaos was never far away. A vision came of Warwickshire in the summer, warm and green and smelling of freshly gathered hay, and he saw himself riding across the Clopton Bridge, as uneasy and uncomfortable as ever on horseback, the swirling Avon below, eager to greet his family at the house in Henley Street.

That they were all well he knew from Anne's barely literate letters. Little Hamnet, his three-year-old son and heir, was a talker, she said, taking after his father no doubt, never stopping all day long, unlike his twin sister Judith, who said so little that her mother was a little worried about her. Susannah, now five years old, was already helping her mother around the house and was the apple of her eye. That was a comfort, but he longed to be back in their arms, playing games and talking with his sensible, solid wife about the events of the day in Stratford, and listening to his father's gripes about the gloving trade and what it was doing to the joints of his fingers.

Sighing, he decided to sit in one of the two chairs placed next to the fireplace, where, after a few minutes, he fell into a light dozing sleep. When he was aroused by the click of the door opening, nearly a full hour had gone by, as a fleeting glance at the clock told him as he scrambled to his feet. He had got himself suitably erect just in time for Walsingham's appearance at the door.

He could barely disguise his shock at the old man's appearance. The hair and beard were shot with grey, his skin was sallow, lines of worry were etched into his brow, and the pouches beneath his eyes were evidence of a tiredness that went to the bone. But the eyes themselves had changed not one whit—dark blue, they spoke to a penetrating intelligence and fierce determination that no affliction of the body would ever subdue, and at this moment they were suffused with a kind of brightness that, had they been in any place other than the prosaic confines of a palace, Will would have interpreted as ecstasy.

'Shakespeare! It does my heart good to see you here, young man.'

This surprisingly effusive greeting took Will aback. The Walsingham he knew was dour, precise, though often kindly and occasionally given to a kind of wry humour. This ebullience was entirely out of character. 'Master Secretary,' he said, making his bow, 'I too am glad to see you well.'

That got a bark of a laugh. 'You flatter like a courtier, my friend. I am afraid I am old and broken down, and probably not long for this world. But there are a few sparks left in me yet. Sit.' He gestured at the two chairs. Will resumed the one he had just vacated, and Walsingham took the other.

'Edwards, bring some wine, will you?' That was directed at a hovering servant, who departed on his errand, closing the door behind him. 'I could do with warming up, I've been up since dawn and I find that the mists from the river play havoc with my joints.'

'Your servant said you have been at Tilbury?' Will could not suppress his curiosity. 'With the army?'

'With the army and the Queen. By the Almighty, she is a magnificent woman.' He seemed to barely notice Will's look of surprise at this uncharacteristic enthusiasm and went burbling on like a gossip in the market. 'You should have seen her, Shakespeare, reviewing the soldiery two days ago. Riding a fine white horse, wearing a gilded breastplate, though we had the devil of a job getting her to put it on—she kept saying she needed no protection when among her loyal troops—she was the very image of a general.'

'I heard that she made a great speech before the assembled army.'

'That she did. A fine speech. Let me see.' He closed his eyes, as if calling back to his mind that vision of the Queen in front of her troops, and then began quoting. *'I know I have the body of a weak and feeble woman, but I have the heart and stomach of a king, and of a king of England too, and think foul scorn that Parma or Spain, or any prince of Europe, should dare to invade the borders of my realm.'*

His eyes opened, recalling himself back to this little room in the Palace of Whitehall, and Will offered a little patter of applause that brought a smile to Walsingham's bearded lips.

'Her Majesty has a way with words that outshines any of us mere poets,' Will said. 'And though I may for politics' sake be an occasional flatterer, in this I say

357

nothing but the truth. Even Marlowe, the greatest of us, could not have produced better.'

The more familiar sardonic expression was back on Walsingham's face. 'The Queen would, I am sure, be gratified to hear such sentiments, though I suspect she would think you were doing no more than confirm her own opinion of her worth.'

Will's answering laugh coincided with the return of Edwards, bearing wine on a silver tray, which he proceeded to place on a small table between them and pour before retiring once again.

'Now then, let us to business.' Walsingham was brisk, all trace of the misty-eyed courtier banished. 'You have done well, Shakespeare, even if your methods were a touch unorthodox. It is unfortunate that the man Towne got away, but it does seem that he was a minor cog in the wheels of this plot.'

'Was it indeed, a real plot, sir? Marlowe and I had our doubts.'

'Yes, it was. The priest took some persuading, but eventually, he yielded enough information for us to identify most of the names on the list. As Lord Strange claimed, most were small fry, insignificant in themselves though powerful enough to be a nuisance. But one or two command significant followings, and when taken all together they could be a serious threat if led by a senior member of the aristocracy.'

'Someone like Lord Strange. Yet I must say I believed him when he claimed that he had no interest in politics, let alone usurping the crown.'

'It is what men do that you must watch, William, not what they say. The fact remains that, instead of bringing the evidence of this conspiracy to the Queen, as was his duty, he chose to destroy it.' He waved a hand to still the incipient protest on Will's lips. 'Oh, I know, he said he has a sense of honour towards these men, who he says are his friends, despite their foolishness. I do not believe him. The

358

plot was foolish, and ill-timed, that I grant you—though let us not forget that Parma and his army are still there, just across the Channel, and it would take little for the fleet to be blown away so that they can cross—but I think that Lord Strange might have been at least a little tempted.'

'Which is why you persuaded the Queen to keep him in London instead of allowing him to go north?' This fact Will had heard from a puzzled David Barnes one afternoon at the Royal Exchange, where he had come to hand over a small purse accompanied by the briefest of notes instructing him to use the funds 'in pursuit of the ends whereof we have discussed'; if Barnes was curious about the purpose of that payment, he did not show it, contenting himself with a brief exchange of news before hurrying back to Derby House.

'Quite so. Her Majesty has, you understand, no knowledge of any of this. Though she is most perceptive and can dissemble when it suits her, she has something of a soft spot for young Ferdinando Stanley, and I fear that she would be unable to hide her distaste for him if she suspected the truth.'

Will thought about that and came to the obvious conclusion. 'You mean to keep him under observation in the hope that he will trap himself.'

'That is Tom Phelippes' training showing through, I think. But yes, you are right. This plot may have been nothing, but there will be others, and we need to be sure of Lord Strange's loyalties.'

Another depressing thought came into Will's mind. 'You are going to ask me to continue to spy on him, aren't you, Sir Francis?'

Walsingham seemed to detect the antipathy in Will's words, and he took a moment or two to reply. 'Will, I appreciate that you have no taste for this work that we do,' he said, leaning forward in his chair. 'It is ugly work, I grant you, but it is necessary. I can pay informers, of course—we have thousands of them at our call—but no amount of money will buy the kind of loyal, thoughtful intelligence that you bring to the task. But if you don't want to do it, I will not press you.'

Will didn't want to do it. But he also had to think about his future and the family who had been so much in his mind when he had arrived at the palace earlier. He had put such effort into creating a new theatre company for Lord Strange and he could reasonably claim authorship, or at least co-authorship, of a fine new play that deserved to see the light of day. If he didn't continue serving Lord Strange, his only alternative was to go back to Dick Tarlton and beg for a place with the Queen's Men. Dick might well be willing, but whether there was a place available was another question. Besides, it would be a good deal more precarious an existence than continuing with Strange's company.

And the price? To keep an eye on this enigmatic man, Ferdinando Stanley, a man who, despite the difference in their rank, he rather liked. Could he be a traitor or at the very least be susceptible to the temptations dangled by others who were? Perhaps, but Will's instincts were still in his favour. And perhaps he could keep his patron safe by a kind of double act, looking out for dangerous conspiracies before they flowered into temptation.

'No man can be comfortable serving two masters, Sir Francis, as I am sure you know. But life rarely offers any of us comfort without exacting a price, and I accept that this must be mine. I will do what you ask, though with reluctance.'

Walsingham nodded, then waited a little before his next words. 'There will of course be some financial recompense for your services, though I cannot promise much, the royal finances being what they are. Nor will we burden you with onerous demands. Just keep your eyes and ears open, use your judgement, and make sure you tell us what we need to know.' Accepting Will's tiny nod as agreement, Walsingham settled back into his chair, seemingly more relaxed now that the serious business of their meeting was concluded. 'Marlowe tells me you have the makings of a very fine writer of plays. He was greatly impressed by your work on, what was it, *Arden of Faversham*? An odd subject for a play, I must say, but then I rarely go to the theatre, and I have little idea what might please the masses.'

'We have turned it into something of a morality tale, which should please the censors when it is eventually performed for the public. Though I know not when that will be.'

'I can at least answer that point. The Master of the Revels has authorised the reopening of the theatres from next week, although we have had much loud opposition from the city councillors.'

'That is good news for me and my fellows, Sir Francis. Thank you for telling me.'

Walsingham rose to his feet, signifying that the interview was over. 'Perhaps one day I will come and see one of your plays, Shakespeare, though given my Puritan faith, I may have to do so in disguise, lest I be pilloried up and down London as a backslider!'

It was as close as Will had ever heard Sir Francis Walsingham come to making a joke, and it caused a smile to appear on his face that must have mystified the smart young servant who conducted him back to the steps and the boat that was to take him home.

***

The play was almost done. Thomas Arden had been cruelly done to death, strangled and then stabbed with great effusion of pig's blood that produced satisfactory gasps from the audience. Alice and the other conspirators demonstrated their further incompetence by leaving the body where it could easily be found, and then forgetting to dispose of the evidence—a bloodied towel and stained knife—which a sharp-eyed Mayor of Faversham soon used to wring confessions from all. The professional scoundrels Shakebag and Black Will made their escape. The mayor, having condemned all the other conspirators, all that remained was for Will, in his character as Franklin, to deliver the play's final words.

Coming from behind the tiring-room curtains, he was alone on the temporary stage that stood in the middle of the great hall of Derby House. Though it was late afternoon, clouded skies rendered the light from the tall windows that lined one side of the room weak and watery, so additional light had been provided by candles and torches arrayed around the stage and in sconces along the walls. But even these additional measures were not enough to fully illuminate the space beyond the stage, and Will could barely see the faces of the audience of fifty or so who had been enjoying their afternoon's entertainment, the most important lolling in comfortable chairs at the front, and the lesser folk on benches behind.

As he had throughout the performance, he tried hard to ignore the most illustrious member of that audience, who was seated in a large, carved chair in the middle of the front row, and took his stance, hands on hips and legs firmly planted apart. With a single deep breath, he began the speech.

> *'Thus have you seen the truth of Arden's death.*
> *As for the ruffians, Shakebag and Black Will,*
> *The one took sanctuary and, being sent out,*
> *Was murdered in Southwark as he passed*
> *To Greenwich, where the Lord Protector lay.*
> *Black Will was burned in Flushing on a stage;*
> *Greene was hanged at Osbridge in Kent;*
> *The painter fled and how he died we know not.'*

Having thus catalogued the fates of the various plotters, he moved a little closer to the front of the stage, and adopted a more confiding tone, as one about to tell something curious.

'But this above the rest is to be noted:
Arden lay murdered in that plot of ground
Which he by force and violence held.
And in the grass his body's print was seen
Two years and more after the deed was done.'

Another breath, and his arms spread in a kind of supplication for the last words.

'Majesty and gentlemen, we hope you'll pardon this naked tragedy,
Wherein no filed points are foisted in
To make it gracious to the ear or eye.
For simple truth is gracious enough,
And needs no other points of glossing stuff.'

Will went down in his deepest and most elegant bow, and waited there, head down, until the applause started. There was silence, and for a moment he feared that, rather than approval, their play was going to be subjected instead to catcalls. Then a single pair of hands slapped together, there was a kind of collective sighing out of breath, and the applause rippled out across the rest of the audience. Will straightened, smiling, and allowed his gaze for the first time that day to rest fully upon Her Majesty, Queen Elizabeth of England.

But her face at that moment was turned aside, saying something to the Earl of Derby that was not audible to Will over the sound of clapping. On the Queen's other side, though, Lord Strange smiled and nodded his appreciation for the play, as did Lady Alice, seated at his side. Will went down in another short bow, and as he rose, he waved his arms to signal that the other members of the company should emerge and take their share of the audience's approval.

That final burst of applause was stilled as the Queen rose to her feet, forcing everyone else to do the same in a shuffling wave. 'You have given us a fine play, my lord,' she said in a high, musical voice that carried more than a hint of humour, 'with enough morality about it to satisfy even the most puritanical of our subjects. Who is the poet who penned it?'

'Mister William Shakespeare, Majesty, who you see before you.' Lord Strange gestured broadly in Will's direction, a crooked finger gesturing him to take a step forward from his place among the gathered actors. He bowed once again.

'The words were not mine alone, Your Majesty, for I had help from…' A tiny shake of his patron's head made him change course mid-sentence. '…several other hands. But I am honoured and humbled that Your Majesty should have found them pleasing.'

The Queen's dark eyes flashed at that, and there was the hint of a sardonic smile on her lips. No fool, she had caught Lord Strange's gesture from the corner of her eye. 'Be that as it may, Mister Shakespeare, it is clear that the realm has a new poet, and we shall look forward to hearing more of your words from this new company of Lord Strange's.' She turned and tapped the Earl of Derby on his padded sleeve with her fan. 'Your son does you great credit, Henry, and is an ornament to our court. Now, I am famished, so let us away to supper.'

There was a swirl of confusion as those who were to accompany the Queen back to the palace of Whitehall arranged themselves around the royal person according to rank, the chamberlain, Lord Hunsdon, taking precedence at the monarch's right-hand, and Lord Derby at her left. Slowly, the crowd sorted itself out and followed the Queen through the big doors at the far end of the room, while those left behind bowed them out in a continual rustle of silks.

To Will's surprise, Lord and Lady Strange did not accompany the sovereign. While his wife chatted to various of the household retainers, Strange made his way to the stage, where the actors were still assembled, a broad smile on his face.

'Gentlemen, if I may so honour you all, well done, well done indeed! I think we may say that our company is well and truly launched.' A small but weighty purse appeared from somewhere in his doublet. 'And I hope you will allow me to offer this small financial token of my appreciation, and that of Her Majesty.'

As Will took the purse, which was heavy indeed, the company applauded their patron enthusiastically, and he went along to shake the hands of each of them, a gesture that was perhaps more touching than the financial reward. That done, he came back to Will and, taking him by the arm, steered him apart from the others. 'Very quick of you, Will, to take my hint about Marlowe. The Queen recognises his genius, of course, but cannot approve of his rather, um, unorthodox views.'

Kit's views about religion, which had always tended dangerously towards atheism, were hardly unknown among his intimates but had found increasingly frequent expression whenever he gathered with his friends to their amusement, puzzlement or dismay, according to their own sensibilities. Will (and for that matter Marlowe himself) should hardly have been surprised that his words were reported, but it was a little startling to know that they had reached the ears of the Queen.

'Then perhaps it might be politic for neither he nor I to take credit for this play, at least for now,' Will said. 'Not that it matters a great deal, for the public generally cares not a fig to know who wrote a play, merely who performs in it.'

'Yet it has value, does it not? Financially, I mean.'

'Yes, of course. Your Lordship's players will of course have first call to perform *Arden*, but in due time we can sell the playscript to other companies and split the proceeds.' It was a comforting thought, that they might get seven or eight pounds between them when they felt that the time was right to sell the script.

Lord Strange nodded at this insight into the arcane workings of the theatrical world, then leaned his head in and dropped his voice to a confidential semi-whisper. 'You have heard no more of this fellow Towne?'

'No, my lord, I am afraid not. I have had people searching London from one end to the other, but there is no sign of him. I suspect he has eluded us, and like friend Black Will, has taken ship for foreign parts.'

'Then we must hope that he, too, comes to his just end at the end of a rope.' Will, who hoped for no such thing, increasingly convinced as he was that John Towne was little more than a courier, just nodded at this. 'I am indebted to you, Shakespeare, for your discretion in this matter, which could easily have undermined Her Majesty's faith in me had it come to light. But as you see, her esteem for me seems undimmed.'

Again Will nodded, as being the safest way of expressing himself. The Queen's trust in Lord Strange continued, as he well knew, because Walsingham had chosen not to inform her of what he now knew of the conspiracy. But he would be watched from here on, and Will himself would be one of the watchers, a thought that gave him no pleasure at all.

'And what are you two conspirators muttering about?' Lady Strange's hand on his arm startled him out of his thoughts.

'Tush, Alice, we were but gossiping about the theatre, and making plans for our fine new troupe,' Lord Strange replied before Will could think of a reply.

'Hmm. Whenever I see you two together you always have the look of naughty schoolboys caught in the act of some piece of mischief. But I liked your play, Mister Shakespeare. Most edifying.'

'Thank you, my lady. I hope it will be the first of many to be performed by Lord Strange's players.'

'Indeed. But perhaps your next effort should be something a little lighter in style?'

'I do have one idea,' Will said, looking tentatively at Lord Strange, whose eyebrows went up in encouragement. 'It is set in Italy, in Verona, a fair city that I have had occasion to visit. Two friends travel from that city to Milan, which is an important dukedom in that country, where they meet and fall in love with the same girl, though one is already betrothed to a Veronese lass.'

Lady Alice's silvery laugh cut Will off mid-sentence. 'Say no more, Mister Shakespeare. I can already see in your premise that this will end in farce.'

'I do intend it as something of a comedy, my lady. But with perhaps some meditations upon the nature of friendship also.'

'Excellent! I shall look forward to seeing it upon this very stage.' Commandingly, she took her husband's arm. 'Now, Ferdinando, we must make shift to the palace, must we not? Lest the Queen forget your face.'

With a helpless glance at Shakespeare, Lord Strange allowed himself to be propelled by his wife across the room and out. He turned back towards the other actors, who were chattering among themselves by the stage.

'Well, my friends, we have earned ourselves a drink, don't you think? Let us repair to the nearest tavern.'

THE END

Historical Note

The story of William Shakespeare's so-called 'lost years' is the perfect territory for a writer of historical fiction, occupying as it does a kind of tantalising no man's land between a scanty set of known facts and the possibilities of speculative imagination. Little is known about his entire life, but this particular period, from 1585 to about 1592, is a particularly blank canvas. All that we know for sure is that Shakespeare in 1585 was most likely in Stratford, doing nothing much and married with three children, and that nearly seven years later he was sufficiently well established on the London theatre scene to have come to the apparently jealous notice of Robert Greene. In between those two markers we have no idea what he was doing.

As I chronicled in the first novel in this series, *What News on the Rialto?*, one possibility is that he travelled—in my imagination, to Italy. But by the end of that book he was back in England, presumably ready to get on with the career that was to define his life. So when I sat down to start thinking about this sequel, the real question was how and when might he have done so. The animating idea that runs through *The Queen's Player*, that he might have started as a company book-holder and general factotum, was sparked by a particularly vivid description of what such a person actually did in Katherine Duncan-Jones' biography *Shakespeare: An Ungentle Life*. It seemed to me that this was a very plausible way into the theatre for a young man with no previous acting experience (young actors were usually apprenticed as youths, an opportunity that would have been impossible for the 24-year-old Shakespeare), but a good education—particularly if he came with the powerful recommendation of Sir Francis Walsingham.

The rest of the plot is hung on a trio of factual pegs. One is the death of William Knell in the small market town of Thame, on June 13th, 1587. He died pretty much as I related in the novel, as a result of a swordfight with fellow actor John Towne. History does not record what led to the quarrel that had such a deadly outcome, but it is true that he was, after an interval, cleared of any wrongdoing and formally pardoned. In making Towne the villain of my piece I have no doubt traduced his character, since for all I know he led a blameless and otherwise unremarkable life. The same is even more true of Rebecca Knell, who married John Heminges in March 1588, a fact that I have omitted to mention in my narrative, since it was rather inconvenient for my timeline. Heminges was, of course, one of Shakespeare's later colleagues and the co-editor of the First Folio, which preserved the great bulk of Shakespeare's work for posterity. He and Rebecca had at least thirteen children, so one assumes the marriage must have been a reasonably happy one.

The second factual peg for my story is the person and character of Ferdinando Stanley, Lord Strange. He might indeed have been a contender for the throne of England after Elizabeth died, were it not for the fact that he himself died in sensational circumstances in April 1594 (the queen was to live for almost another decade), almost certainly as a result of poison, though exactly who administered the fatal dose and, more importantly, who might have been behind it, remains a subject of speculation to this day. But more immediately for my purposes, he was the patron of one of the companies with which Shakespeare's name has long been associated. It is true that he appeared to be politically ambivalent, and thus was the object of some suspicion among Elizabeth's counsellors, though it is most likely that he was in fact completely loyal to the Tudor regime. The plot that I have suggested in these pages prefigures a later, and much more serious, attempt to suborn him in the months before he died, the so-called Hesketh Plot.

And finally there is the play, *Arden of Faversham*. Not all that often performed these days, it was in its time a popular offering. The play's authorship is unknown, but most scholars agree that Shakespeare had a hand in it, and attribute the 'quarrel scene' between Alice and Mosby to his hand. His collaborators have at various times been thought to be Robert Greene and Christopher Marlowe, and more recently Thomas Watson. For obvious reasons I plumped for Marlowe. It is actually quite a remarkable work, with finely drawn characters and some very funny low comedy.

Of course even a work of fiction requires research, and I had a great time exploring the world of Elizabethan theatre, which worked very differently from the modern experience. I was lucky enough to have the chance to see one of Will's later plays performed at the Globe Theatre in London, and can attest to just how much more raucous and 'alive' his theatrical experience must have been, with actors seeming to engage much more directly with the audience members standing around the stage. But I also read widely on the theatrical practices of the time; while I don't want to bore you with an exhaustive list of all the books I consulted, anyone who is interested in learning more about the subject should read Andrew Gurr's *The Shakespearean Stage*. And for those whose interest might be piqued enough to find out more about what scholars have speculated about Will's start, Stephen Greenblatt's *Will in the World: How Shakespeare became Shakespeare* is an excellent starting point.

Finally, if you are sufficiently nerdy to want to get your head around the geography of Elizabethan London, there is a great tool called the Agas Map of Early Modern London, a quite remarkable digitised map that allows the user to explore the streets and alleys of the city pretty much as they existed in Shakespeare's time, which is quite handy since the traumas of the Great Fire and the Blitz and the subsequent reconstructions have almost completely obliterated the old city, most of whose landmarks now exist only in the form of street names.

About the Author

Born in Hertfordshire, England, Anthony Wildman migrated to Australia with his family in 1967. He grew up and was educated in South Australia, where he acquired a degree in history and politics from the University of Adelaide, which was the start of a lifelong fascination with both subjects.

After a career in business that saw him working in the oil industry, banking and finance, and finally management consulting, Anthony has embarked on a new phase of his life as a writer and novelist.

Though his long-term home is in Melbourne, Australia, where he lives with his partner Robert, he has journeyed extensively throughout Europe, Asia and America, satisfying his love of travel and new experiences.

He has published four books to date, and he is at present working on the final volume of his *Lost Years* trilogy.

Printed in Great Britain
by Amazon

34740842R00212